Cloud Cover

By Mary Letts

First published by Lulu.com., 2011

Copywright© Mary Letts 2011

ISBN 978-0-9556929-2-5

For my father, who loved climbing.

With many thanks to Omar for his patient editing and advice, and to Jo, Emma and Linda for their helpful feedback, and to Omar Jr. for his cover design.

1

Did she regret not having left with the others? Whenever she subjected herself to a bout of self-examination, this was the one question she always tried to avoid. Because yes, maybe she had made a fatally wrong decision - and it was far too late to correct it now.

The trouble with solitary thinking…well, understanding anything properly was impossible when you had only yourself to talk to! Whilst her mother was still alive, someone to consult, be criticised by or disagree with, life had been much more bearable. Whereas now, left to her own devices with no-one to modify her ideas…of course it struck her, sometimes, that the unadulterated loneliness might have progressively driven her mad.

Still, if the others left merely in response to a communal, instinctive, migratory urge, then why had she not felt it too and gone with them? Obstinacy? Fear of change? At last, she could now honestly admit she had acted on the purely whimsical notion (it was definitely neither logical nor considered) that here, on this desolate mountain island, was the best of all possible places to be, whereas those others had merely set off on a fools' paradise errand to their inevitable deaths.

They had felled the last remaining tree trunks, still standing but no longer alive, to construct their sailing raft; then sewn together all their collected clothing pelts to make a sail - thus pinning faith on the unlikely existence of wind, whilst ignoring the obvious dangers connected to bare skin and toxic air. And the fact they had not returned proved nothing. They might have found an idyllic, fertile island and be busy mating and breeding a happy new race of humans by now, in which case why would they bother to return to boast of their successes to her? Of course they wouldn't!

But in her bones, which were infinitely smarter than her head, she sensed they had not, that they were now indisputably all dead.

She had watched them, already a little forlornly, whilst they shrank to a dark speck on the pearl grey horizon then vanished completely, swallowed by the grim monotone of grey cloud and grey sea. There was no knowing how long ago that moment was, however, without a reliable way to measure time. Her mother used to gauge it by the lifespan of an ibex, but they were now dying well before their prime, and precious few cow ibex gave birth to anything apart from a still-born calf because they had failed to adapt to mountains with no snow.

The eagle population was dwindling too. Once there were dozens wheeling above the high peaks, plunging with wild screams to impale a careless marmot or baby ibex on razor sharp talons. Now though, to see more than a lone eagle was rare - so it took little intelligence to realise all forms of life were on the wane. How much longer would she scrounge sustenance from this barren peak? The juniper berries were ever sourer and more juiceless, the gentian roots had to be fiercely rationed, the scrub berries had shrunk to the size of wizened old marmot droppings, and the marmots were now her sole living companions so she would never dream of eating them. In fact she was totally indebted to them for her survival. So to kill a single one would be an unforgiveable act of ingratitude. Almost of cannibalism.

There were days she honestly felt more marmot than human. Whenever she heard their shrill alarm call or sensed the vibration of an approaching eagle's wings she could freeze as solidly as they did. An eagle's eyes are attuned to pick out movement, so this ability had saved her life countless times when still a child. Admittedly she was a slower digger than most marmots, but speed aside she was just as deft and methodical: she could weave around plant roots without disturbing their tiny, hairlike filaments; could detect animal movement from minute vibrations conducted through soil and rock; and accurately pinpoint the distant sources of subterranean water via an acute sense of smell. Also, she ate a similar diet of earthy roots and bulbs, and could whistle just as ear-piercingly as any marmot scout.

During the time of intense heat living underground had been the only solution for survival, and whatever intelligence was not handed down to her by her mother was undoubtedly picked up from marmots.

Right now, she regretted with dreary disappointment that she had failed to live up to her mother's expectations.

"You *must* breed," her mother had exhorted her, a constant, nagging refrain. "It's not beyond the realms of possibility that very few humans still exist, you know. It's up to us survivors to keep the numbers going."

And her mother indisputably lived according to her own advice, mating with whatever size or shape of human male forged a pathway through the unstable shale which once underlay magnificent glaciers of ice, then panted and puffed his way up to their high mountain refuge. But few of her babies survived birth. And only one besides herself grew to maturity. And he, her only half-brother, had left with the boat crew, why, she was not sure, since they had sailed in from some unknown distant island that recently collapsed, speaking a language neither of them properly understood.

Probably he only left to avoid the utter desolation she was suffering now. She could have mated with him, of course, although her mother repeatedly warned them against the degenerative effects of inbreeding, plus he left before she reached full breeding age. Apparently this 'bleeding' cycle was once a reliable way to measure time, when, long ago, it happened with a regularity linked to the phases of the moon.

But of course the moon might simply be the stuff of fairytale. For neither sun nor moon nor stars had been glimpsed at all since this impenetrable cloud cover hung over them with its brooding, baleful darkness.

Sometimes she even wondered if her father might not have been a marmot but her mother too ashamed to admit it. Not that her mother was prone to sentiments such as shame; it was more that marmots possessed horrifically sharp claws, and vicious, knifelike front teeth, so no thin-skinned person would appreciate close contact with them. On the balance of probability, therefore, her father was a human.

But a stupid one, no doubt, since her mother was never in any position to be choosy; added to the fact he had apparently (actually impossibly!) died falling down a crevasse long after the last glacier had melted. She therefore suspected darkly that his demise was her mother's doing, the necessities of survival having driven her to destroy her mates once their seed was successfully implanted. If you give birth to a child, her mother always said, seek another mate for your next impregnation - that way the breeding possibilities properly multiply, laterally and vertically. But now her own so-carefully nurtured half-brother had left her in the lurch.

Whenever she fretted she might never bear a child, she consoled herself it might honestly be better if the human race were to be eliminated. The petty squabbling amongst the boat crew, the way they desecrated the scrub bushes, plundered the slopes of gentians, and slaughtered whatever marmots they could hit with a catapult (mercifully merely the old dodderers already semi-blind, stone-deaf and oblivious to the danger) had demonstrated only too clearly that they could not co-operate in the calm manner of other herd animals.

Her mother's folkloric stories were indeed replete with self-inflicted deaths: invasions, fighting, rampaging, torture, genocide, plus ravaging diseases that killed whole swarms of populations back then in olden times, when the earth's surface had been so infinitely larger and the world population truly immense.

Of course there was no proving any of those grisly tales of the past were true. Especially since her mother's account of her own life was deeply suspect; in particular the mathematically inverted pinnacle of such conveniently neat numbers: a hundred men, thirty miscarriages, fifteen births, but just the two babies surviving to adulthood. For if, supposedly, conditions were so much harsher in her mother's time, how come a hundred men had roamed these peaks then, yet none appeared now?

Whenever total darkness enveloped the mountains she crawled down the earth tunnel to her sleeping space, where she would curl contentedly into the sleep position. Full darkness was ultimate bliss. Once you closed your eyes miracle colours of a mythical world spiraled and danced against your eyelids. And when you looked again with open, seeing eyes, strange shadowy forms would emerge hesitantly from the deep purple gloom. Sometimes flecks and veins of something beautifully luminous winked and glittered from the curved walls of earth rock. But she never knew whether her eyes invented them, or they had their own existence.

In the night, her mother used to say, you journey back to the beginnings of time to renew your strength. Then, each morning, you return, re-empowered to face the future.

But one night her mother must have lost her way. She found her lying on her side, stiff, crumpled, and so cold she had turned blue - the colour the sky supposedly used to be, and she was no longer breathing. It coincided with the time she herself first began to bleed, so perhaps the gift of fertility had simply passed from one to the other, signifying her mother's time was over.

Normally so deft at digging, she struggled to quarry out the exact right place to bury her mother's shrunken body, making false start after false start - to her half-brother's increasing annoyance. It might, perhaps, have been this helpless indecision that sealed the fate of their separation - along with his obsequious desire to curry favour with the boat crowd.

Darkness sharpens one's hearing. The moment she now awoke she sensed a faint tremor, the minutest vibration carried subterraneously from somewhere down the mountain. The sounds came in irregular flurries, as if from the scuffling, scraping, jostling scenario of two ibex fighting - and yet it was not the rutting season…

Instantly she hurried up her tunnel, armed with a sharp stone. A dead ibex promised plenty of new, strong hide; a wealth of meat, providing she could dry and preserve it properly; and two magnificently curved horns - if they were not already ruined from too much clashing and quarrelling. Inevitably she would meet competition from a ravenous eagle. Well, it was welcome to the head and entrails, eyeballs, jellied hooves and bone marrow, but she was determined to secure the best cuts of meat, the hide and both horns.

She slithered down the loose shale, steadying herself only when she reached the danger ledge where one false move meant a vertical fall to certain death.

The body of the dying ibex lay wedged between jagged rocks, half-upright, as if kneeling in prayer to some aggrieved Mountain God. Its left hind leg was broken so presumably it had fallen - a sure sign of old age because only the snow leopard (if such a creature ever truthfully existed) was more sure-footed on mountain precipices.

One blow from her club put it out of its lingering misery. Her sharp stone then located the incision points from where she could strip off the skin in two mirror-image lengths of hide. The tendons of the broken leg were exposed so she snapped them free with her slate blade - they made the perfect catapult. Meanwhile the lone eagle veered upwards in disappointment, acknowledging defeat. His mate had recently succumbed to her deadly aim with just such a catapult.

It was only when she had almost finished dismembering the carcass; had neatly coated the chunks of meat in a fine dusting of powdered rock and wrapped them in strips of hide, setting aside those bones that were suitable as tools; that she looked up and noticed with alarm that the ibex was not the only body sprawled on the rocks. Two legs protruded from a boulder barely twelve strides away. Although she had grown unfamiliar with their distinctive lack of fur, she immediately recognised them as human.

Their utter stillness suggested death. So, despite a feverish curiosity, she obeyed the pressing instinct for survival by first securing her future meat and leather needs, before creeping down to investigate. Very cautiously she scaled the boulder to gain height advantage over this mysterious intruder, in case it were hostile and cunningly feigning injury.

It, too, must have fallen - perhaps from rashly wrestling with the ibex. Its legs were unscathed but one shoulder was hideously distorted and it had a deep gash on its head, visible despite its thick, matted mane of hair. It wore an unusual skin, palely silver unlike any animal from this region, and the flatness of its chest suggested it was male.

Quelle malchance, she murmured regretfully. Wait an absolute age for a man to visit, then the only one to manage it is virtually dead on arrival!

After closer examination, however, a faltering pulse still throbbed in the pad of his forefinger. There was apparently a method of extracting the precious sperm without actually mating, but her mother had warned "c'ést beaucoup moins agréable." And then flatly refused to explain the technique until Motte was older.

She should carefully weigh her priorities. Put food first, leaving the man meanwhile to the mercy of the returning eagle? Or place her life's purpose to breed ahead of meat, gifting that eagle a golden opportunity to steal it?

She knew what her mother would have done - gone for the man. Should he die, there was still some decent meat on him; less than on an ibex of course, but enough to justify the gamble. She shuddered at the prospect of carving up a creature so very similar to her half-brother, but nevertheless decided to salvage man ahead of meat.

She heaved his body, undernourished so worryingly light, onto the newly salvaged pelt, carefully cushioning his lolling head and strapping it down with her future catapult. Then she dragged him on this sledge, selecting a route where flatter stones would neither rip the hide nor jolt its valuable burden. And luck was on her side. When she returned the ibex meat was still there, untouched by any marauding eagle.

But inside the confines of her sculpted burrow the man smelt vile. His diet must have been exclusively meaty, foolishly lacking any roots and bulbs essential to digest it properly. Wrinkling her nostrils at these hostile odours she gently swabbed his head wound clean, deftly avoiding the fractured skull-bone. Then she manipulated his shoulder as nearly back into its socket as it would go. At which point he moaned faintly and his eyelids briefly flickered open. He seemed to whisper something, possibly in the English language because she halfway understood it.

"If you're…(this part was indecipherable)… to eat me, let's get…"

She intitially assumed it nonsense-talk, the delirious ramblings of concussion. But when she inspected herself closely, absorbing through the unfamiliar lens of a stranger's eyes the stains of blood and ugly signs of slaughter all over the front of her marmot pelts, and saw that earth and blood had smeared her hands, spattered her face and seeped beneath her long, curved nails, she acknowledged he might have genuinely mistaken her for an animal predator.

So, whilst he slept under the soporific effects of her mother's edelweiss brew, she made a strenuous effort to clean up. After all, saving his life would prove a wasted gesture if his healthy animal urges - specifically those all-important mating instincts, could not be fully aroused.

Her appearance had never preoccupied her before. The air was harmful to bare skin in any case, so she invariably wore animal furs, and only briefly noticed her real, natural skin when she changed the pelts, (which, to be honest, was rarely!). She retained a vague impression of the contours of her body, and an even vaguer idea of her face, from long ago when she saw it reflected in a shiny slate slab at the foot of the vanished glacier. But she was only a young child then.

Animals attract mates through the lure of smell. Thus, to her mind, the chief setback (apart from his chronically weak condition) was her aversion to *him*. He must have impatiently gobbled his meat raw; on top of which the foul, rank smelling fur he wore was badly cured and probably played host to armies of lice, fleas and maggots.

Abruptly she prised it off and flung it aside. Then gingerly, painstakingly, massaged a thick globular paste of moistened earth blended with the glutinous pulp of asphodel into his skin. Her mother always swore that along with moss it was the finest antidote to infection. As she did so, she was gratified to note that his male organs were still intact, but disappointingly limp and small and not remotely ready for action. If he died she must extract the sperm immediately, even though she had no idea how. Once his body cooled and stiffened the chance would be gone - and he might be the only male visitor she would ever, ever have.

2

The more time passed, the less hopeful she became of him recovering. And the more she ceased to consider him viably alive, the more she knew it was effectively a waste of time and resources trying to coax him back to health and consciousness, when the obvious signs of irreversible brain injury were there to mock her efforts. For one fleeting, despairing moment, she actually cradled a heavy stone in her hand, mentally lining it up with his temple to deliver a fatal blow…

Fortunately *something* stopped her. Not guilt, nor pity, an indefinable feeling. Perhaps he was company in an oblique way. A rag doll to a lonely child. Also, having been so close to death when she found him, it went against her concept of logical behaviour to nurture something for ages that you arguably should have killed immediately.

Of course, she could always let him die rather than actively kill him. Take a passive route - withhold treatment, food and water. Her mother would have experienced no qualms, but her mother would have extracted the precious breeding seeds first, done so in the beginning before he went into deep sleep and lost the link between brain and body, while those seeds were still potent.

Indecision again. Her familiar failing. Or perhaps not hers alone, but a typical human failing. It might be exactly that which caused the former world to self-destruct and drown beneath the surging waters of converging seas. Those olden day folks maybe set off on a particular course, and although they foresaw the disasters ahead they dithered at the crucial moment and failed to steer clear of them. Or the other problem, obstinacy: choosing your direction and determinedly sticking to it, refusing to admit to an error.

Cautiously, she crawled out of the tunnel entrance into the sultry grey gloom of what might be early morning. Her mother had often derided the failure of language to advance and reflect a proper understanding of the natural world. Why persist using *sunrise* and *sunset*, she used to scoff, long after they knew perfectly well it wasn't the sun either rising or setting - but the earth rotating and revolving?

Well, her mother had been guilty of the exact same linguistic obsolescence, clinging to the old habit-names: *morning, afternoon* etc. long after those day-divisions were obsolete. Because, without a visible sun performing a visible arc, you had no notion when 'noon' occurred. Still, if words and thoughts were confined to the current state of planet earth and her limited understanding of it (all handed down by unreliable word of mouth, and one big mouth in particular) she would have to revert to caveman grunts. Her brain would shrink so drastically she would have no wisdom to pass on to her children! *If* she had any…

She was on a climbing mission for alpine moss. How it succeeded in growing and retaining moisture after such an endless spell without rain was a miracle. Hang it up, moisture dripped from it; apply it to injuries, they healed faster; plus it was dense, soft and comforting to chew. It grew in the fissures of the towering rock pinnacles at the head of the former glacier, and the ibex also coveted it. Had she not cosseted the man with such quantities she would have no need to renew her stocks now, so soon after her last climb. She tried not to resent him in case he might father her child, but she in no way relished the final ascent, which was sheer and devoid of footholds - meaning you literally took your life in your hands.

Long ago, so her mother said, mountaineers had tackled these pinnacles with specialised equipment; metal gadgets called 'pitons', with itchy material known as 'corde' attached to the overhangs. When there used to be snow this whole area was a buzzing winter playground. People came in hordes to slide down the snow slopes with strips of wood strapped to their feet, or to bounce on boards wearing woollen hats, or skid across frozen lakes on sharp blades of metal. They would climb to the high plateaux in circular bubble boxes attached to wires, sometimes even swooping through the air suspended from false wings like gross, oversized eagles. What a mad, mad world it must have been! *If* her mother was right, of course.

As she skilfully descended the perilous rock 'chimney' using footholds the size of a toenail, she imagined negotiating this route when pregnant. How would her inflated, egg-shaped bulge fit into the narrow shaft? It wouldn't! But perhaps the man would act nobly, stay until the birth, help her out during the final stages of pregnancy…

Her mind continued to be absorbed in these whirling thoughts, even when safely back inside her burrow. Foolishly, she now took his inert state almost for granted, letting her hands tend to his injuries on auto-pilot. A hidden sense alerted her to a change, however; a hair-raising, creepy feeling, as if of a ghostly presence. Possibly she also detected a faint glimmer of eye-white in the darkness…his eyes had fully opened!

She was desperately eager to talk, but dithered over what language. French would be her personal preference, but her mother had complained, loudly, repeatedly, that unfortunately English was by far the most widespread world language. And this was precisely why she continually forced herself to practice it internally, in her thinking.

> "Who are you?" she asked inanely, for want of anything more suitably intelligent to launch their very first conversation. Then, hedging her bets, "Qui êtes vous?"

He swallowed, as if testing the flexibility of his tongue, or tasting the words before releasing them.

> "Is there just the one…?" his hesitant speech was poised between a whisper and a swallow. "Or are there two…of you?"

She had anticipated some reaction, showing perhaps that he could hear, even possibly understand and process - but actually speak was beyond her wildest expectations. His tongue punctuated sounds differently to hers, while a strange vibration fluttered against the roof of his mouth. Or had she simply forgotten the unique qualities of a human voice, having for so long mouthed the words of her private thoughts silently in her head?

She noted, also, that he had not bothered to answer her question, instead substituting one of his own.

> "Eh bien, you've got double vision. There's only one of me."

> Again he swallowed. "How…long have I been…?" It was struggling with the letter 'l' that entangled his tongue.

> "Long. Though I don't know *how* long - I never count the days," and because she herself had not spoken aloud ever since her half-brother left, her voice resounded strangely inside her head.

> "Am I…paralysed?"

> "I hope not - that it's not permanent, I mean." It was a little premature to broach the burning issue of mating. "You've fractured the skull. It'll take time to recover, bien sûr."

> He breathed noisily through his nose, like a snorting ibex ready to tangle with a rival. "So, why didn't you kill me?"

> "Mais tu es vraiment fou! *I* didn't cause your injuries, imbécil - you were dying when I found you. I *saved* you."

14

He frowned, but the movement evidently pained him so he closed his eyes. "Weird," he muttered, "I've such a clear image of your hand, or paw - whatever, holding a huge stone ready to dash my brains out." He sighed weakly, "Perhaps I'm off my rocker."

She turned away lest her face betray the undeniable truth of his description. Visual memories left an indelible mark, she knew that from the futile efforts she had made to obliterate the image of a tiny speck of vanishing raft on the indistinct horizon, her very last sight of her half-brother.

And she had a distinctly uneasy feeling that this man was going to be trouble.

She chewed earth to steady herself and provide a pretext to tend to his wounds. This time she would approach from the side where his dislocated arm had never properly returned to its socket and he had no strength to repel her, just in case his 'paralysis' was mere pretence. She massaged the earth very delicately into his distorted shoulder, and felt him trembling.

"You've nursed me well...," his tone sounded mocking, although she had zero experience of the subtle nuances of speech and might be mistaken. "I've been semi-conscious for a while now, so I know. But your concern seems, well...I guess I was wrong about that stone and could be about everything...prompted by a strong dose of ulterior motive."

It was not the ideal moment to divulge her true intentions, but this dystopian world provided nothing remotely ideal. Every survivor these days, surely, must recognise their only imperative, that of procreation... Her mother had had no truck with finer sentiments. Neither should she.

"Well...," she still dithered. His head being hideously swollen and his body without sensation, mating might not be the first thing that sprang to his mind... Still, she must seize the moment: "You being a man and me a woman, we *must* of course make a baby. And you've got to be stronger for doing that."

He stared in total disbelief, *gobsmacked,* she seemed to remember, was the English word for such an open-gaping mouth. "You *say*," he was evidently struggling for politeness, "you're a woman, but... hmm, you do look partially marmot to me. A man must physically *want* to mate, and if he doesn't, then it might help him overcome his...urhh, initial reluctance, if he actively *wants* to father a child. I don't." The effort of speaking had apparently drained him. His voice faded until only occasional scatterings of whispered words were audible, "Selfish... irresponsible...child....dying world."

His pessimistic outlook stemmed from his physical condition, she reckoned. He had spent too long in the open or the minimal protection of caves not to have suffered from radiation - which had probably left him sterile anyway. On top of that, he had half-starved, wolfed his meat raw (if not actually rotting), had a serious accident - falling, dislocating a shoulder, breaking ribs and fracturing a skull, then spent weeks or even months in a coma. He was very unlikely to feel frisky straight away.

Even she, despite sporadic and wildly optimistic dreams, did sometimes fear for her child being the last lonely survivor on an arid mountain amongst a bunch of marmots and a herd of ibex heading for extinction. The odds were unpalatably strong that history would simply repeat itself.

"It's not just the pelts that give an impression of marmot. It's your movements too - and most of all those knife-blade claws." He was trying to be reasonable now, perhaps suddenly remembering that his life was still in her hands. "If you pared down the claws, separated your fingers like so-o-o, then tried walking upright with your arms swinging at your sides, humanstyle, it'd… make a lot of difference."

"Merci bien," her smile was acid, "because that way I'd die for sure. I *have* to scuttle on all my fours seeing as burrows are low roofed - in case you didn't notice - and the only place where one can survive, deep underground being free from radiation, and neither too hot nor too cold. Without these claws how would I dig? I'd have no food, no burrow! How else have I survived when everyone else died? By neatly trimming my p-r-e-t-t-y little nails and giving my soft woman's hands a lovely little weekly manicure?" She snorted, "Pah! If I were to stand up and sashay along like one of your fancy olden day women, I'd bash my head on the burrow roof, and be lying beside you now with my own concussion. Then who'd look after us?"

"OK, OK. You've survived by adapting. You're only somewhat like a marmot, temporarily, because you have to be." But he still sounded patronising not conciliatory, although his sudden diplomacy at least proved he valued his skin.

Later, he claimed to have no memory of the period before his fall. This absolved him from offering any explanation for his arrival on her mountain, or of where he had been beforehand. A million things she wished to ask him, yet he could shroud his entire past in memory loss. It was *very* convenient. And she, who knew nothing of the world except what her mother or her mother's friends had told her, apart from the odd snippet of information gleaned from the people who had seduced her half-brother away and whose theories she did not trust for one millisecond, was intensely curious to know more.

"There's a reason I look like a marmot," she continued (much later on), still brooding over his apparent rejection but simultaneously laying the bait for information. "My mother said to play it safe. There might be hidden enemies out there - watching, waiting. She warned me they had contraptions called *satellites* that could spy on everyone and every millimetre of this earth. She was a bit crazy, I do admit - but some of her stories were true, so I take precautions *just in case.* To keep my existence a secret from these possible unknown, invisible enemies, I'm a marmot whenever I go out. It serves a double purpose anyway, because the pelts protect me from the radiation."

His silence testified that something about these wild ideas had resonated uneasily. Eventually he spoke, more quietly than should have been necessary, considering how deep underground they were.

"It's wise to take precautions. There always have been evil people throughout history, so if other pockets of humanity survived the GD you can bet some are troublemakers. And you can't assume they all live such a primitive lifestyle as you, since some forms of technology might've survived. Protect what you've got is the best strategy, I agree."

"But for what reason - if there's no-one to leave it to when I die?"

"For the freedom to live your own life *until* you die."

The look they exchanged recognised the yawning gulf between them. Maybe some humans never feel duty-bound to breed and are consequently liberated, able to enjoy their own individual destiny, she supposed. Or else our different experiences prior to now have created our contrasting mindsets.

Marmots are so uncomplicated. They breed instinctively. They manage to commune harmoniously (except once a year when the males scratch each others' eyes out, which surely demonstrates the power of the breeding instinct!).

That night she had a bizarre dream. She had morphed into her mother, and all of a sudden gave birth to a million tiny eggs embedded in jellied water that shone like the whites of sober people's eyes. And the calamitous thing was that instead of being elated by her wondrous fertility, she hungrily gobbled up the gleaming pool of eggs before she could stop herself! The shock woke her immediately, and whilst she waited for her racing heartbeats to slacken she could hear from the man's erratic breathing that he was suffering.

"What's the matter?"

"Water," he groaned, his voice weak and agonised.

She crossed the burrow to where he lay, and despite the total darkness she found his parched lips and held the alpine moss against them. She was still shivering from the after-impression of her dream, and from the chill without the covering of her familiar marmot pelts - which she must have shed to give easier birth to the eggs.

"Let me die," he implored. "My head's exploding. I can't stand the constant pain any longer. It's always worst at night, and tonight it's torture."

"You talked too much too soon. You must rest."

"No. Just kill me now, I beg you. The stone's there."

"It only *feels* worse at night. Pain gets concentrated in the dark, that's all."

"I'll never recover, I'll always be paralysed. Kill me, please, show some humanity. You can use my body afterwards - bones, sperm, whatever you want - I won't care by then. But for God's sake put me out of my misery."

"Be patient a *tiny, tout petit peu more*. I know I'm not an expert but I have healed a similar injury - or watched my mother do it. The swelling is going down, I promise you. It may not seem so to you but I monitor it every day, I know it is. I'll put a moss poultice where the pressure's worst, and tomorrow drain off the excess liquid."

"Then stay with me, holding the moss."

What she omitted to say was that the man with the head wound her mother had 'healed' did not survive long. He improved to the point of regaining his mobility and managing to walk. But on the very first attempt to climb up difficult terrain he collapsed with a seizure and died. Her mother maintained it was probably due to the altitude. And then she miscarried his child very soon afterwards...

She sat beside him, perfectly still and silent, until she knew he had at last fallen asleep. In the morning he admitted to feeling less pain.

"That moss is miraculous stuff. Why didn't you use it before?"

"I did, while you were still unconscious. Not lately because it's so scarce and grows only where it's a nightmare to climb, so I was keeping it back for emergencies."

"Aren't *I* an emergency?"

She shook her head and smiled. At least she had extracted permission to use his sperm, although in all honesty she would have taken it anyway, with or without permission. Had she only known how.

3

She lay on her smoothly sculpted earth-bed, wondering, not for the first time, how it was possible to dream in beautiful colours that you had never directly experienced. Her dull, limited spectrum embraced every conceivable tone of grey and several browns, but otherwise minimal shades of green (subdued ones, nothing lively); the dark blue, bordering on purple, of the gentian violet flower; the fresh cream of an edelweiss; and beyond that a motley collection of berries in the blue to red range. All colours were anyway dulled by the leaden cloud overhead.

So how could dreams be invaded by spectacular ice blues, sharp yellows, deep oranges, delicate lilacs, cold, glittering silver and the fiery glow of copper, none of which she had personally set eyes on? It surely suggested dream life could tap into a wider, inherited consciousness that surpassed the limitations of experience. If *only* she could similarly tap into the knowledge and skills of previous times. They were not just passed by word of mouth, like nowadays, but had apparently been assembled in things called books, or virtual books, all in the form of written words that clever people could understand at a mere glance.

She was jerked from her reverie by a dull vibration. It came from the col connecting her high alpine valley to the lower lands.

"Footsteps," she opined, immediately groping for her marmot pelts.

"Can't hear a whispering ghost," he murmured, drowsily roused from sleep.

"Two feet," she was both apprehensive and elated. "*Another* human…"

"Take care then. To see but not be seen."

She opted for the lower tunnel. It emerged into a limestone cave overlooking the course of the defunct stream bed that had once frothed and gushed (long, too long before she was born) through the col. Her marmot pelts were firmly fastened, so to a stranger's eyes the only discernible movement would be that of a large, burly marmot craning its neck over a ledge.

A shrill whistle from the moraine told her other marmots too were monitoring the new arrival. Whoever it was had already headed back via the col, yet evidently planned on returning because their leather knapsack was still propped against a rockslab guarding the cave entrance. Her sharp, far sighted eyes admired its neat gut stitching. A woman's work? Yet why she assumed it a womanly skill she had no idea. Her mother's habitual excuse for the clumsy, bulging seams she struggled to produce was that the bones of high-altitude animals yielded brittle needles useless for intricate stitching, and her own stitchwork was equally crude. She hoped she was wrong. A second solitary woman was not what she craved…

Thankfully the reappearing shape was indisputably male, stereotypically so in fact. Tall and musclebound with long, red-gold hair and broad shoulders - yet he wore the daintiest leather cloak, leather trousers and moccasins. The boat crew resembled oafish cavemen compared to this one's sartorial elegance.

He staggered backwards hauling a decaying tree trunk. Since the old treeline (almost annihilated by the boat crew, long ago now) was on the shoreline a thousand metres below, he must be strong and determined to have dragged it this far. The exact sort of genes anyone would covet for their child. (Though walking backwards showed him an utter chump at self-preservation).

Not content with only one trunk, he repeatedly vanished only to reappear, grunting and heaving in a most satisfactorily virile way, until he had accumulated a sizeable pile.

Her mother had described the clusters of wooden houses called 'chalets' that the winter playgrounders inhabited during the halcyon era of snow and ice, so she suspected he was planning to construct one of these. But apparently not, because after his enthralling demonstration of strength and exemplary determination, he set off to display the equally laudable attributes of skill and patience.

He foraged on the moraine for assorted stones. For cutting, splicing, grinding and smoothing. And far from using any old trial and error method he seemed to know precisely which stone best performed what task. She was both attracted and alarmed by the extent of his knowhow, the boat crew regressing yet further in her eyes - from cavemen into monkeys.

In the blink of an eye he had built shuttering that opened and closed to block off the cave entrance. Without a breather, he then enclosed the area out front by erecting a stockade of sharpened poles fashioned from the former branches, hammering them into the ground with a flat-sided boulder.

Then he lovingly unpacked and drooled over a mysterious wooden implement. An artfully curved branch, both ends connected by a length of animal gut and notched midway to grip a thin, dead-straight tree limb bearing a sharpened stone impaled on its tip. She watched in fascination as he tested this strange contraption, yanking the gut back to maximum tautness so as to launch its dart at lightning speed (her mother's expression, meaningless for her) to knock a tiny pebble off a boulder some distance away.

Her fascination turned to fear, however, when his second shot soared skywards before plummeting back to earth, whistling so dangerously close it virtually grazed her cheek (thankfully protected by marmot skin).

This was a distinctly superior weapon to her catapult. It travelled faster, further, yet with no less deadly an aim.

After this he descended through the col for a considerable time while she busied herself collecting myrtle berries and digging up an aromatic root. She became involved in extracting the root perfectly whole, then dealing with the bonus find of an adjacent ant nest (the little clusters of ant eggs were a rare delicacy), and the presence of this new man all but slipped her mind.

Such lapses of watchfulness were perilous, luckily though she was reminded not by a fatal missile through the heart but the sounds of multiple footsteps.

> "We're real close now, hon. I swear you're gonna love this place. I've made us a nifty stockade to enclose the corral, an' a stretch to one side for growin' crops. There's a mighty fine cave too…"

'Hon's' reply was inaudible, but several shrill, chirpy voices chorused their collective delight. Kids, she surmised - but more, it transpired, than she had bargained for. Six crested the col, and just as she was applauding the fact that he was unquestionably a genuine stud (yet simultaneously worrying he might have already satisfied his lust to breed) she spotted three adults in their wake, one of whom had to be 'Hon'. Ten in total!

A while back she might have celebrated wholeheartedly. After all, ten (eleven including herself) made for a viable community. Sufficient numbers to effectively share the tasks yet without developing destructive rivalries. And, most importantly, a varied pool of genes to avoid excessive inbreeding.

Now, however, since food supplies were further dwindling this size of group worried her. It seemed almost an unsavoury repeat of the boat crew episode. Only this time, instead of a temporary visit there were obvious signs they were putting down roots and planning to stay. She felt a stab of fear they would slaughter the marmots and hunt the ibex to extinction, once they had failed to coax their precious 'crops' from this inhospitable rock-soil.

"So, why not talk to them?" he suggested, after she confessed her anxieties. "That's one way us humans outperform animals. We can talk things through, come to a pack arrangement. But don't get overawed by their superior numbers and more advanced craftsmanship."

"They'll take me for a marmot," she fretted, "and shoot me on sight!"

He shrugged, "Go naked. Play your trump card with your first move. There're two males after all - it's exactly what you want, isn't it?"

He was at last showing genuine signs of recovery. His head had regained an almost regular shape. His eyes were clear and could focus on close range objects without double vision. Lately he could even sit up unaided. But unfortunately he was still paralysed in the all-important area from waist down, while his limbs had chronic muscle wastage from being idle so long - yet she dare not risk forcing premature exercise, not after her mother's all-action regime ended so fatefully for that former patient.

The brain, she now understood, was truly a master-machine. It operated everything, the body and out-of-body too, able through thought-waves to break barriers of time and space and link past, present and future. She assumed it was the brain that created dreams through which (whilst still asleep) you could fly above the cloud barrier and see the universe as it once used to be, when the sun, moon, stars and planets were visible and day and night distinctive, just like man and woman. How she wished she had lived in those earlier times when the world was steeped in beautiful, varied colours and the air less poisonous.

"Let's work on the physical problems first, leaving metaphysics 'till later." (He had this irritating habit of flaunting his knowledge). "Like sewing, - that'd put my fingers to work *and* benefit you. If you'll fetch me some ibex gut, find and cure those wolfskins you so impulsively threw away, I'll make you a fine wolfcoat that'll boost your status and gain their respect. It'll tap into their primitive fears."

23

She frowned in consternation. Partly because she abhorred the remembered smell of his wolf skins, partly because impersonating a predator would represent a cruel betrayal of her marmot affiliations, and partly because she had no idea what *metaphysics* might be.

When she finally tried on the wolfskin, contrary to expectation she experienced a flush of guilty pleasure for it transmitted a beguiling sense of empowerment. She wore it with a crude, jaunty confidence as she emerged onto the mountain slope via the lower exit. Then zig-zagged down to the cave, moving two-legged, human-style, in the upright position. The gait came relatively easily since she had occasionally walked two-legged in the past; now however it was vital to do so - if mistaken for a genuine wolf she would killed in an instant.

> "Hon," she called briskly on reaching the stockade, it being the only name she knew.

> "Who's there and whaddaya'want?" a gruff male voice responded.

> "A friend." There was no time to invent a plausible name.

Her mother had called her variously *Bébé* or *Chou-chou,* subsequently *Motte* - presumably an abbreviation of *Marmotte*. Ultimately she dropped the habit of using names though, they being redundant to a solitary life. She had not even thought to ask the man his; in the limited company of two it is blindingly obvious who is talking to whom, and besides, he would doubtless claim to have forgotten it.

> "Hang about right there," the gruff voice advised, " 'till I go open the gate."

The 'gate' blended seamlessly with the stockade fencing, conveying that these people were more wary and security conscious than their conspicuously raucous arrival suggested. Either they knew those *satellites* had eyes but no ears, or, since the noise was exclusive to red-gold's family, this man and his partner were the cautious ones.

When he opened the gate she realised why. He was in every aspect physically diminutive, even shorter in stature than her. His hair was thin, scaly and lifeless and she immediately smelt the onset of serious ill health.

> "I want to speak to your leader," she announced imperiously.

"Huh, ya' must mean Fin." He smirked, "He's no goddam leader! We practice a totally non-hierarchical system hereabouts. But hang around and I'll go get 'im.'"

She waited fractionally inside their gate while he strode purposefully up the recently lain pebble pathway before vanishing into the cave. Instinctively she drew herself to full height, trying to reabsorb courage from the pores of her wolfskin. It was foolhardy to have entered their corral. Outside was familiar territory where she could escape at any given moment; here she was trapped in their world, outnumbered ten to one.

"Hi there," Fin loped along the pathway grinning broadly, his huge right hand proffered in greeting. "I sure didna' know there was a lady-wolf bang on my doorstep!" He laughed appreciatively.

"I wear this pelt for health reasons," she protested, trying to avoid being magnetized by the yellow glare of bared teeth. "The air up here's highly toxic."

"Oh, we take mighty good precautions 'gainst radiation, don't worry your li'l head." This time the laugh was more subdued. "But I don' guess you came for no idle chit-chat on health issues, so…what's cookin'?"

"I came," she said, homing on the intermittent words she properly understood, "to talk about your living here."

"I take it this here mountain belongs to you then?" He sounded suddenly less enthused.

She nodded. "By inheritance. My family've lived here for many, many generations." It was essentially a load of bluster - but how would he know?

"Good," he said, scanning her pointedly up and down, "you'll know the ropes then. I jus' hope you ain't aimin' to keep it exclusively yours."

"No." She hesitated, aware the tension was growing as tight as a drawn catapult, "But we do need to agree on the boundaries - of territory *and* behaviour."

"Wowee! This is a remote mountain island on post-disaster earth and you want *rules*? You some crazy control freak?"

"Not crazy. Alive, whereas all the others died. Which'll happen to us too if we can't agree rules."

"OK, OK, take it easy! Let's talk turkey then, *if* we must." He gave a shuddering sigh, "I'm all for co-operation, but jeez - rules ain't enforceable without no private mountain police force to back 'em up."

Again he bared his yellow teeth, "Look lady, come inside and meet the fam'ly. I feel kinda nuts negotiatin' with a wolf - and I guess with your health hang-ups you won't be takin' off that lobo-outfit here."

He had seemed such a superb macho specimen from afar, close up though she detected ominous signs of disease. Along with the teeth the so-called 'whites' of his eyes bore an unnatural pollen-hue, while the red-gold of his long locks lacked any semblance of healthy sheen. Perhaps she should not be assessing human health by the animal yardstick of eyes, teeth and hair - yet her sense of smell transmitted the selfsame message. He was healthier than the gate-keeper, but that was no yardstick to crow over.

Her gamble was, if they were to mate, would whatever sickness he was incubating affect her? Worse, would it pass to their offspring? What a bitter, vindictive turn of fate that the grand total of *three* men suddenly materialize, yet precisely *none* classifiable fit and healthy! Still, she was cheerfully oblivious to the condition of her own eyes and teeth. Perhaps hers were as discoloured as theirs...

"Not now," she replied brusquely, "I have to consult with my people first." She surprised herself with this spontaneous lie, but it would be madness to meekly enter their cave alone and unprotected. "I'll be back after one period of darkness. You call it *tomorrow,* I think."

"Hey, d'you happen to be French? You have exactly that typa' accent - but you speak English pretty well considerin'."

"I speak how my mother taught me."

"Jeez', a genuine fruitcake! But I kinda like it!" Something bubbled merrily in his throat.

Not wishing to reveal the whereabouts of her burrow entrances, she headed in the false direction of the former glacier. The majority of marmots were trying to hibernate, but ever since they were deprived of old-style seasons their sleep patterns had gone askew. For the benefit of the scouts awake and on guard she gave the shrill warning whistle. Then, launching into the melodic descent, rested on a note midway down the chromatic scale: this set the danger level at intermediate. (Acute danger was an incessant, high-pitched, ear-splitting whistle.) This briefed them on the human intruders; they were not a deadly threat but neither were they harmless, not armed with that stick-missile contraption.

Marmots were not naturally aggressive. They would bolt for their burrows at the slightest suggestion of danger, normally; but if cornered, threatened or forced to defend their own, they were capable of counter-attacking. They had bone-splinteringly sharp incisors and claws designed to carve a swift route through compacted earth but, equally, tear through flesh - should a situation ever demand it. Thus the reference to 'her people' had not been total fabrication.

The rocks along the rim of the former glacier were fringed with bilious green lichen, scarred here and there by teeth marks where hungry ibex had recently gnawed. Lichen, like alpine moss, had mysterious, parasitic properties that enabled it to suck nutrients out of solid stone, and provide nourishment for any animal that could actually digest it. The current ibex diet was heavily reliant on it.

Ibex had survived in these mountains for more than twenty thousand years (so she had been told), and this region had once been their safe haven. Some of their body parts - primarily the horns - were reputed to have powerful medicinal properties. So, once these newcomers wakened to the fact they were seriously sick, the ibex would most likely be sacrificed.

Except she must prevent that happening.

4

That night the earth rumbled deep in its core. She sat up, instantly awake, while the man slept on unawares.

The marmots were communing conspiratorially amongst themselves, but their generally unflustered reaction proved it was merely one of those routine tremors, not the warning sign of another mega geological catastrophe.

When the sea boiled up, long ago in the cataclysmic flooding, they had apparently whistled with a blood curdling crescendo, then fled their burrows in a panic stampede for higher ground. In this way they warned the inhabitants of the tiny Alpine hamlet where her great great great grandparents were living. Virtually no-one reacted, however. It being bitterly cold and unpalatably early in the morning, a time they preferred to spend lazing beneath their duvets whilst the Friday night excesses of drinking too much 'grolle' wore off. Most, anyway, dismissed it as a moment of marmot madness, an indulgence in the curious lemming-like behaviour that happened every so often, such as when they awoke from hibernation way ahead of schedule.

Fortunately not her great great great grandparents. Driven near demented by the horrendous racket they hurried up the switchback path to the high col, from where they had a panoramic view south and eastwards. Had they not done so they would have drowned along with the whole neighbourhood. And she, of course, would never have been born.

She had often tried to relive that unreal moment through their eyes. To visualise the surge of grey-green water swilling into the valleys, swamping the steep alpine meadows where peaceful cows still grazed, and the odd wisp of smoke curled lazily upwards from occasional chalet chimney, and the postvan set off to deliver letters that would remain forever underwater and unread.

But the old, drowned world was impossible to imagine, even though the dramatic story had been repeatedly retold as it filtered down through five generations before her. Having known no other landscape but this grey world of islands, cloud and water, (except in dreams where for some reason she never seemed to be in a mountainous area) she could not replicate what they had seen. But their horror and terror was deeply ingrained in her psyche.

"When you next meet them," he yawned sleepily, "don't mention me."

"Pourquoi non?"

"Because any man who allows you to go alone, while he stays safely out of sight, must be a coward - or an invalid. Plus, since your motive is to get pregnant, already having a man is bad news."

"I'm more worried I won't understand them. They speak so strangely - have the weirdest accents, use the oddest words."

"Keep it simple then. Just don't sell yourself cheap."

"I'm bargaining. Not selling - quelle bêtise."

Once again she wore the wolfskin, and whistled a tune at their gate. It was opened, as before, by the smaller, sicklier man. Despite his claim that Fin was no leader he seemed to have landed all the dog's-body tasks, and he preceded her up the path with a motion more limp than swagger.

"Hey, it's weirdo-wolf-woman again!" one of the kids taunted from behind a rock, and a stone landed plunk on the pathway, just missing her.

"Cut it out chimp!" he growled, then spun around with an almost benevolent smile, "That's young Zinal, Zin fer short - he's just a kiddo larkin' about, he doesn't mean no harm." But Zin didn't look all that innocent or young to her.

The man had warned her to be wary of close contact in a confined space. She would have no immunity to their diseases, he explained, having led such a solitary, isolated life. She therefore refused to go beyond their cave entrance, so they sat there awkwardly, arranged in a semi-circle facing her.

"Hey sister," Hon was first to offer greetings, parting her own set of yellow teeth in an encouraging smile, "I'm Alphubel, named after that Swiss peak-island, d'you know it? But jus' call me Alpha." She hesitated, "We didn't know anyone could be livin' up here." There was a hint of apology in her tone.

"I'm Vanoise," Motte replied, her wolf mask hiding the vestige of a smile.

Having noticed they valued mountain names in their culture, she had rejected 'Motte' for its proximity to marmotte. Vanoise comfortably suggested itself because the region had been known as 'la Vanoise' in the past. At least for some it had, whereas others insisted 'Il Gran Paradiso' was its original, genuine name. Her mother had loathed this 'Paradiso' tag because of its overtly religious associations, although according to Alessandro, the real reason for her contempt was political not religious - being French she refused to accept the land was truthfully Italian.

The man was suspect on vaguely similar grounds of inconsistency. Ever since his health had improved he spent considerable time and effort painting a vivid picture of what had happened to the earth. She found his stories fascinating, but did not entirely trust them. Because, if he had genuinely forgotten his own past, how could he possibly remember earth's history in such wonderful detail? When she challenged him, his flimsy rationale was that long term memories are more deeply embedded than short term ones. Hmm.

His version went that when the sea rose in its sudden explosive surge, it submerged all land below the altitude of roughly three thousand, eight hundred metres, and that included every single major city in the entire world.

Only scattered groups of mountain people survived, he said, on disparate and isolated islands protruding from the vast, poisonous new oceans of toxic sea water. The salty water struggled vainly to purify the corrosive ingredients released in the catastrophe: the radiation, nuclear poisons, lead, gas, oil, and the billions and billions and billions of dead, bloated, decomposing bodies of humans, animals, fish and birds that lay drowned by the great inundation. Or the GD (Great Disaster) as it had subsequently been named.

He had no fully credible rationale to explain the sudden increase in water this scenario implied, but grand theories, it seemed, were immune to petty objections. He looked so expressively tragic when he described these horrific images, almost as if the unimaginable stench still blasted his nostrils across the immense distance of time and space, that she almost fully believed his account. It was not massively different to the versions she had heard as a child, in any case.

Where we are now, he continued, is a place once called Europe (confusing - her mother had sworn it was France), and this chain of mountainous islands was formally known as the Alps. But, crucially, what he did not know (so he claimed) was if any of the other high mountainous areas of the world and their inhabitants had survived. Or whether the cloud cover overshadowed them too, as it did here.

What was more, the fact that the sea had recently shrunk back slightly, revealing a little more of the lower lands (all decimated and destroyed, of course) had merely worsened the situation - in his opinion - because it meant more radiation and more contagion was now exposed to the already noxious air, and the remaining mountains were even less stable than before.

Although his scenario carried the ring of truth she guessed it vastly exaggerated, because his main motivation was to provide emphatic, irrefutable proof of her stark raving lunacy in wanting a baby.

And, to this end, he warned her it had all happened before. A monstrous flood with a mere handful of survivors; the wrong sort of course, all greedy for possessions and the land of their forefathers, pugilistic and corrupt, pretending they had some hidden entity called God who actively encouraged and sanctioned all their bloodthirsty shenanigans because they were 'chosen' and 'special'. It might even have happened twice for all he knew!

"We should learn from past mistakes," he declared, indolently popping a wizened myrtleberry into his mouth. (It was amazing how much better his breath smelt after however long it was eating a marmot's diet, spiced with slithers of dried ibex flesh). "Humans were a despicable lot, as I've said before, when you add up the sum of misery they created. Goodbye to them. Good riddance too. But if some other idiot, high up in what was once the Andes or Himalayas or Rockies wants to arrogantly assume he's the supreme being, and must reproduce another useless line of descendants who end up ruining the Earth yet again, I'm in no position to stop him."

All these ideas swirled dizzily through her brain as her eyes panned suspiciously over the grouping of Fin, Alpha, Holgathon (the gate keeper), Bernina (his slightly built lady friend who had yet to say a word) and sundry kids of sundry sizes, including, of course, Zin the stonethrower. She *must* concentrate…

Did Fin, deep down, consider himself a supreme being? And was he an idiot? And if so, was he from the Alps, Andes, Himalayas or Rockies?

She was definitely none too keen on the strident yellowness of his teeth or the loudness of his laugh, but it was apparently in his favour that he was called Fin, not Noah, or maybe worse still, Adam or Abraham. She was determined to remain very much on her guard *not* to repeat history.

"My great great great grandpappy got sent away to Geneva, Switzerland, just before the GD. Lucky for him he was way up near the summit of Mont Blanc when it happened, and he later shacked up with a Swiss bird, but for some reason I've still ended up none too Swiss, that's fer sure. Still, I'm glad I got called after that Finsteraarhorn, 'cos I wouldna wanta be 'Monty' nor 'Blanky' like ol' granpa! But hey

31

Vanoise," he paused to clear his throat, "now that we've landed up on your mountain, howz' it to be?"

"Well, I hope we can co-operate. I'm prepared to share my mountain - so long as you give it respect. Meaning the marmots are not to be killed, and the ibex only when old or injured - and I decide which and when. Oh, and we ration water, and vegetation…"

"No probs. We'll be plantin' our own seeds and gettin' self-sufficient. Bernina's got all kinda beans and *such* green fingers…"

"We keep to our areas. The mountain's mine, you can have the cave and moraine. We help each other in emergencies and," she paused, suddenly diffident, "we cross breed, like herd animals, to strengthen the stock."

"Ha! Y'mean you wanna ball with me or Holg?! No need to be so goddam coy. If you're stuck here alone without a guy it's natural. Sure. Any time. Just come on down."

"I want to get pregnant, that's all," she added hastily.

"Well then, I'm your better bet than Holg," he chuckled frothily, nudging Bernina in the ribs. Then he stood up and seemed to weigh his words with sudden caution, "Howz about mineral rights though? How do we split *them*?"

For the second time in their brief acquaintance tension stiffened the atmosphere. She had no inkling what mineral rights might be, let alone how they could be fairly divided, and while she struggled to find a suitably noncommittal response she noticed Holg looking sharply at Alpha.

"Let's leave mineral rights for later," she declared offhandedly. "I've got to go."

"Hey, hey! Not so goddam fast! We should at least seal our deal of today. Hey there hon, go get the Génépi and we'll have us a toke."

Alpha returned with a knobbly goblet bearing a disturbing resemblance to the severed tip of an ibex horn, this was promptly circulated so that everyone could take a noisy - and none too eager - gulp. Its origin might not even be ibex, Motte realised, but something more sinister. Because her mother (completely contrary to her habitual irreligious stance) once told her that the devil himself was a cloven-hoofed creature with corkscrewing horns; and her brother then confided (a very rare moment of communication) that over-sexed crossbreeds called satyrs formerly roamed the earth. They were half-human, half-goat, who grew horns, enormous organs and rutted all night long!

Immediately she smelt the rankness of rotting horn overriding what should be the delicate aroma of finest herb liqueur, she instinctively backed away.

"I...I can't," she stammered, reeling in revulsion.

"Don't tell me you're a fuckin' teetotaller! Leastways, I guess you can't, as yet, be...a fuckin' one!!" Fin snorted.

"I don't want to share a cup - in case of disease."

"Gee, thanks a bunch. Say, if you're that paranoid about poolin' our juices, I mean like, how the hell are you gonna get pregnant?" and he spun around expectantly to face his audience, as if awaiting thunderous applause.

Again she left by a circuitous route. And throughout her climb she could sense Zin's eyes locked firmly onto her retreating back. Not only did he covet her wolfskin, she sensed, he also harboured conflicting feelings towards her. Reluctant attraction combined with violent hatred. A dangerous combination.

The sight of a frail, milky edelweiss flower in the process of emerging tentatively from a cleft in the rocks momentarily banished her feelings of disappointment and apprehension, but they seeped back during the brief time she waited in the burrow tunnel to allow her eyes to readjust to darkness.

"You're right," she admitted, fretfully slinging aside the wolfskin before slipping into her old, comfortable marmot pelts, "humans are *merde*."

To his credit, he did not crow. "Tell me."

"Well, they're happy enough to laugh at me even though they have problems themselves. Plus most of their words have double meanings, half of which I don't get." She sighed, "I *did* think it'd be simpler."

"It *is* simple: stay away."

"Easy for you to say."

He turned abruptly away, offended and angered by her thoughtless comment.

"Your only limitation is not getting pregnant within the timescale you want. Suppose you couldn't walk, had no feeling in your lower body. D'you think I *enjoy* being trapped here, a useless appendage to you?"

She hung her head. "Je veux que tu me pardonneras. I spoke without sensibilité - I'm sorry, very sorry. And...and you will improve, you have some chance to walk again. These mountains are ...like a medicine; everything growing is curative or edible - you have the best possible chance..."

It was as much to reassure herself as him.

Despite having refused the potion in the horn, she was certainly infected. Not by disease but by negative thoughts. They surfaced in the sudden creeping fear that it was all too late, she was past her childbearing years, already a sterile old maid. This idea was further fuelled by a sickening ache in the pit of her stomach, a reminder that it was ages since she had last bled. Owing to stupidly losing track of time, perhaps as many as twenty, even thirty years had drifted by since her brother decamped, not the mere ten she fondly imagined!

And now she no longer knew if the need to breed, which her mother had fostered in her with such continuous fervour, was simply a selfish desire, as the man seemed to suggest. Up until now she had never doubted it the perfect epitome of ultruism, an act of self-sacrifice even, to seek to propagate an endangered species facing ultimate extinction. Today her old, familiar world was under relentless siege. It almost made her wonder whether the former loneliness with its endless, unmitigated sameness was not actually preferable to the unpredictable, threatening situations the presence of others had recently introduced…

But in her heart of hearts she knew it was not. Humans were social animals so isolation surely went against their nature. And whether they managed to cohabit successfully or disastrously was not a question of their nature per se, but simply dependant on the individual urges they called *caractère*. And right now, she and the man were experiencing a clash of it.

"I find it bizarre you ignored the passage of time. Even completely primitive, early man found a way to calculate it - and without the much simpler, arabic system of counting," he sniped.

"Perhaps I didn't want to know how long I was alone. Perhaps I thought it would send me mad."

"That…well, I can appreciate." His voice turned softer despite him knowing she had played her sympathy card intentionally, and his eyes clouded with the haunted look of someone reliving private horrors of their own.

"You should concentrate on healing yourself, not on criticising me. The reason your brain's not connecting with your body is because … il a oublié. We have to clear the blockages and remind it. I'd have massaged you before - if you'd not been so irrationally scared of my claws."

"Stroke away then," he murmured, closing his eyes blissfully.

"Ce n'est pas une plaisanterie! *You* must concentrate. Think of a plant. Your head, the flower, must suck water from the roots - and the roots stretch to the tips of your fingers and toes. As I touch your feet, even if you can't feel anything, *teach* yourself to feel again."

"Anything?" she asked, after a long while.

"Possibly," he sounded supremely doubtful.

"It'll take time," she said, "and meanwhile you can work on your memory. Your short term one."

"I'd sooner forget," he admitted grudgingly.

5

She lay stretched full length on her earth bed, focused on restoring her fertility through the same method she proposed for the man: concentration…

Conjure the warm smoothness of eggs, of pure white, frothing milk and sleepily suckling babies. Daydream of romantic, make-believe lands where long green grasses bend in the wind, apples ripen rosily in the mossy elbows of trees and bees sup nectar from the flowers, and of all those fictional, fruitful things that existed once-upon-a-time in my mother's old-told fairy tales. Do this despite recognising it a foolish, sentimental, over-indulgent part of your feminine caractère…

Visualise the alarming colour red. It presents itself, sometimes, in the tiny veins of flower petals, or threading through the whites of the man's eyes, in the skin of myrtle berries before they fully ripen and the flow of blood from open wounds. The man's tongue has regained a ruddier tone, no longer dominated by the répugnant blend of greyish green, signisfying sickness. Fin's lips are even tinged with it - except one forgets this when he opens his mouth, and there are faint glimmers of rust red in Bernina's hair…

When she emerged from the burrow tunnel, however, she immediately snapped into alertness - there was no lingering dreaminess, no absent minded clouding of her normal watchful state. She was quite sure of that, in retrospect. Despite the comfortable feel of her marmot skins which she had happily reverted to at the man's behest, owing to his new optimism that he might soon be wearing the wolfskin himself, her antennae were as finely attuned to danger as they ever were…

An almost inaudible whoosh of air was the only warning of the incoming missile. It struck her collar bone with crunching force. From the sickening sound and violent, shooting pain that zipped through her she immediately knew the bone had shattered. Staggering backwards behind a boulder, strength draining from her legs like water through splayed fingers, she realised she had lost not only all use of her left arm but was equally powerless in every sinew of her body.

She had seen animals collapse, stunned, seemingly dead - only to leap back to life within seconds. Falling headlong to the ground was sometimes nature's ruse to quickly re-supply the brain with blood and air so it could think its way out of trouble.

The marmot pelts were to blame. Fin and Holg must have flouted her rule of not attacking marmots - or else mistaken her outsized marmot figure for a young, marauding bear. How mortifying to have survived so long only to be caught out so very easily! Had the man connived at it? But in what possible way could injuring her benefit him?

A second missile would prove the killer blow and those curved poles with straight darts had astonishing range and accuracy, she knew from watching Fin. It fleetingly occurred to her to struggle out of her pelts and stand up, stark naked. That way she could *not* be confused with a marmot or bear. But there was no guarantee the marksman was any of the cave dwellers. He might be a complete stranger. Unlikely, but she could not discount it. Not with her life at stake.

The stone tip of the missile lay close. It had snapped from its shaft and - this was what riveted her - was smeared with bright red blood. Her blood!

So, finally, proof that her body had not substituted blood for air, water, or an empty vacuum. She had recently harboured her doubts, but she was a warm-blooded creature after all, who could still bleed - even if not from the all-important birth passage.

Her right hand groped for the source of this blood. It welled steadily through a jagged gash in the marmot pelt, and from colour and consistency looked to be human blood. She of course thought like a human and physically resembled one, but this blood substance was the true essence of any being. And on this account she had sometimes worried that her affinity with marmots came from her father's questionable bloodline. A weak smile played on her lips as she lost consciousness...

The misted grey lid of cloud was discernibly thicker, darker, when she re-opened her eyes, but the mountains were not yet fully shrouded in night. Sluggishly she remembered why she was lying on the mountainside, not in her burrow; and why she could scarcely move. The sound of a heavily shod human marching to and fro, below but closer with every stride, and the sharp, percussive sounds as he beat against rocks with a stout stick - in order to flush out wounded game - instantly reminded her.

She had one crucial advantage - she knew the terrain so intimately she could visualize every rock, stone and bush and thus plan the most viable escape route making use of whatever cover would screen her.

Two factors, though, conspired against her. One, it was impossible to move silently on this shale-covered section of slope - even for someone light and sure-footed. Two, she felt too weak to move at all. Slowly, feebly she heaved herself to a sitting position. Her eyesight blurred and her brain circled, wafting dizzily like the hovering flightpath of an eagle. Gradually it then settled into her skull so she could think more coherently. But by this time the footsteps were dangerously close.

A hunted animal would bolt for it. Not in a straight line so any fool could aim in its unfaltering direction and expect a hit, but weaving and dodging randomly, confusing the hunter into misdirecting his shot. Unfortunately this means of escape depended on fast acceleration, whereas she had virtually no mobility whatsoever.

Her attacker would assume he was homing in on a fatally injured animal. So her wisest course was not to react like an animal; instead of running away she must go towards him. His landmark would be the boulder, her first priority to distance herself from it.

Luckily the failing light would increasingly disorient him (unless it was Fin or Holg and they had memorized the layout of her mountainside), and she felt more optimistic of confusing his aim in the deepening dusk. Gulping a lungful of murky evening air to sharpen her wits, she painfully levered herself into a crouch. Before setting off she launched a small stone uphill as a decoy and, just as she hoped, the hunter fell for it. She heard him blundering clumsily in the wrong direction.

Timing her moves to coincide with his noise, she was almost half-way between the boulder and lower burrow entrance when the crashing sounds of his stick stopped. Now she must freeze in open view where the shale lay thick and the slightest movement made it shift and clatter, and there was no friendly rock to hide behind. She flattened herself and held her breath, grey fur against grey rock. He was doubling back now, approaching the boulder from the far side and still out of sight - yet clearly he had heard her.

She would be plainly visible once he reached the boulder but she clung to a slender hope. If he were a natural born hunter his eyes would first scan the ground for bloodstains, or that telltale outstretched leg marking the spot where his wounded prey lay; he would never expect an intelligent animal to wait in the most exposed spot of all. His panting, rasping gasps were so magnified by her fear that she began to fancy he had already pounced on top of her and was breathing down her neck. But he sounded - if that were possible - more exhausted than her.

She launched herself towards the small cave marking the lower burrow entrance, her injured arm dangling useless and a hindrance the more the slope steepened. She had to force herself to slow down - if her hind legs propelled her too fast she would somersault head over heels. Or overshoot the entrance and have to track back. Meaning she would meet him head-on, unarmed.

She did not hear the whooshing sound of the second missile because the emotion of the life-death drama caused the blood to sing in her ears, drowning other sounds. It flew above her, missing her curved back by a hair's breadth. When it cracked against a rock, its tapered flint tip splintered and a jagged slither ricocheted backwards, piercing her neck. Fortunately the momentum of the rebound was decreasing, so although it tore through the marmot pelt (further slowing it down) it drew only a thin trickle of blood from her real, human skin. But the sensation of a weapon pricking her jugular triggered an irrational, primordial reaction. Skidding to an immediate halt she reared upright like a marmot, then shrilled their persistent, ear-splitting, chilling whistle.

Whether or not it was this unearthly sound that held back her attacker from his final, surely fatal strike, it saved her nonetheless. She was in the midst of crowded marmot territory, and within seconds of her alarm a dozen or more marmots scurried out.

Their reaction was as instinctive and viciously primal as her bloodcurdling whistle - although the smell of her shed blood might have aroused their own, normally dormant bloodlust. The effect was brutal. One moment the man was poised to throw his spear (at close range he perhaps trusted it more, or else had already used his last arrow); the next there was little to show he had ever existed.

A dozen marmots leapt on him, felling him by severing his Achilles tendons. Their needle sharp front teeth and razor claws raked through his flesh. Mere seconds later all that remained were ugly chunks of uneaten flesh, various scattered, bared bones and dark pools of blood draining into the shale slope. And as many marmots as had emerged noiselessly slunk back into their slender burrow entrances. The eagles would clean up later, at first light.

She squatted bolt upright on her haunches for quite a while, half-aware that the darkness had fully smothered the mountains, and that she had thankfully, at last, stopped whistling. Shaking herself free of her trancelike state she limped slowly down into her lower burrow entrance.

She was in such a strange mental state that momentarily it mystified her to discover the man in her sleeping burrow, for she had truthfully forgotten all about him.

6

Fin shook his long lank locks, which had developed a darker, more coppery tone due to the deepening twilight, in utter disbelief. A luminous arc glinted through the gloom showing his mouth was open wide. Either he was smiling or snarling.

"Jeeeeesus! Fuckin' fantasy stuff, man! Who'd've guessed a bunch a' sleepy groundhogs could chew a guy that quick! Man alive, we gotta watch our backs around them. They'd spit you out for breakfast Holg me ol' buddy, before I could do a darned thing to quash 'em."

"An' not just *me*," Holg hurriedly corrected, "I reckon they're none too fussy eaters. The littler kids'd be first choice for tenderness, don't yer reckon? Then *las dos senoritas* for sheer tastiness."

Both smiled again from the exhilarating adrenaline rush, the shared bond of seeing raw nature at its wildest. Suddenly their small rectangular bean patch, which they had been busily planting out and carefully tamping the earth down on so as to create a neat network of irrigation channels, seemed boringly, effeminately tame. Bernina had said it should be done in the evening: *roots in the morning, sprouts in the evening* was her planting mantra, adapted from the olden day distinction of a waxing and waning moon. Fin failed to see how it made any difference, but sometimes you had to humour broads or they could turn real mulish.

"And howz about that super-sized one? Wow! I'd never've believed they could grow to XXXL - must've been their chief, President or whatever, judgin' by the speed they obeyed its crazy whistling. Can't hardly hear prop'ly now. I might've gone permanently deaf."

Holg clamped his hands against his ears and joggled his head from side to side, "Same here. God, sur-REAL…" He experimentally probed for wax, harvesting a dark yellow lump from his right lobe. "They can't be no danger to Wolf-woman though, otherwise she'd 've been chewed up ages back. Strange that, don't ya reckon?"

"Maybe groundhogs are scared of wolves. Could be why she dresses up as one. I get the idea she's not quite the little Miss Inno-cent she makes out."

"Primitive for sure, a virgin - no doubt about it. But secretly craftier 'n hell."

"*My people* - what could the dame be on?! Those Mont Blanc guys swore their edelweiss brew and ibex cornucopiae got'em high as kites. Apparently some potent strains seriously blow your mind so's you never fully recover."

"She seemed stony-cold sober to me," Holg chuckled mirthlessly, "I jus' keep wonderin' if she's got a wolf's pussy…"

Fin glanced at him with a supercilious grin, "I'll let you know bro, soon as I find out. She'll be down again soon, I bet. She's gaggin' for it!"

By the time Motte limped the length of her tunnel the intense darkness of night had come - both to the mountains outside and to the subterranean world of burrowdom. It was too late to stir the man into helping her with her injuries - with his limited mobility and inability to see in the pitch dark he would make a pig's dinner of finding the right medicines, then of putting them on the right places.

She sensed he was half-awake and aware of her return, but had neither strength nor desire to speak to him.

She shivered, envisaging the marmots licking themselves clean of human blood on the other side of the 'wall'. Their tunnelling snaked through the pockets of soil and bedrock mere metres away from where she lay, and, in the utter stillness, they often heard each other burrowing and snuffling. The whole inner mountain was an intricate honeycomb of tunnels, all giving access at some point in their meanderings to the central reservoir of water. She tried to lie still (apart from incessant, involuntary shivering), knowing that broken bones mend faster if immobilised, and, more importantly, the stray splinter chipped from her collar bone must settle back in position, or it might wander through her body until it lodged in her heart and killed her.

Her wounds were the greater risk. The toxicity of the outside air festered infections, and if the stone arrow-tip was tainted she would die. Die childless. Yet her attacker had presumably planned to eat his prey, so to use poison would be suicidal... She would have baited it with a soporific substance, roles reversed.

The night seemed eternal. If sleep truly takes one back to the beginnings of time, a night of insomnia presumably imprisons the mind in the present dimension, where it seethes frustratedly, yearning to escape. By the time the first grey light of morning revealed the mountains to the outer world, so that the faintest reflection of this light stole along the tunnels and feebly illumined the burrow, she had turned as pale as old-time powder snow.

At last she heard him stir.

> "Wehl," he began, trying to imitate Fin's accent based on her attempts to convey it, "How was it fer you ma'am? Did your first sexual communion live up to expectations?"

> "I was…almost killed," she whimpered weakly.

> "Oh, now who's being melodramatic?!" He chuckled, "I did suspect you mightn't find them the most subtle, considerate of lovers. But murder - that's seriously over-egging the 'rough'!"

All the while that he gleefully misinterpreted the situation, sniggering over his mistakenly hilarious take on what had never even begun to happen, she was sinking deeper into unconsciousness.

> In a last gasp effort she whispered, "If you can move, come. I need help."

Finally he understood from her fading voice and whole feeble demeanour that her condition was serious, and at last put energy into crossing the burrow floor. He reversed towards her in a sitting position, his entire weight taken by his hands, his legs dragging uselessly behind him. And he was so frail he had to rest while traversing the puny distance of four metres.

> "Arnica, in alcove. Gentian root and moss. Same place, one handspan to the right." Her voice was barely audible.

When the drubbing, puttering sounds signalled his return, transporting the pouches in his mouth in the style of an olden day retriever dog, her trembling fingers bared her distorted, swollen shoulder with its ugly gash - from which she had already lost an alarming surfeit of blood. Surprisingly, the vampire-style neck wound, which prior to now lay on his blind side, seemed to horrify him far more - in spite of only being a superficial injury.

> "What…on earth?" he gasped.

She shook her head, needing to conserve her draining strength for other things than words. Shakily, she cleaned and cauterized the wounds by probing the damaged areas with alpine moss, wetted by what little saliva her dehydrated state provided. She worked by touch, too exhausted to raise her head to inspect her shoulder, and aware that - apart from the disappearing breed of

Vanoise rock lizard she had not seen since childhood - no creature was flexible enough to view its own neck.

At last she allowed herself to sleep, confident she had cleaned the wounds as best she could.

When she woke again he was sitting alongside, his expression brooding, watchful, her cudgel-like stone gripped in his hand. She felt too weak to care whether he was waiting to bludgeon her, having finally gained the upper hand; or to ward off the enemies he was expecting would invade the tunnel any minute now - so as to properly finish her off.

"W-a-t-e-r," she murmured plaintively.

Seemingly he possessed a vestigial memory of the time when he lay unconscious, because he emulated her method of dripping water onto lips through a carefully contrived, wedge-shaped clump of moss. She might have given him a feeble smile of appreciation, but for the worry her lips were so parched they would simply crack open and bleed.

I brought this on myself, by conjuring those images of blood, of willing it to flow... And how did I contrive that unearthly whistling? It's damaged my voice, strained or snapped some vital part that serves to create the vibration. It was a marmot sound, unsuited to a human larynx. I may never talk with audible volume again - but perhaps that's no bad thing because now I can plague the man with silence the same way he's plagued me.

I've become the helpless one and he the healer; but unless he overcomes his paralysis he'll be a useless provider. How can he climb? Even if he *could* scuttle the full length of the tunnel, what sort of freakish animal could he impersonate, scrambling backwards on hands and rump, dragging his legs behind like a sled? The eagles will simply swoop in delight and peck out his eyes before he plucks his first myrtle berry.

Her dreams turned feverish. Mountains shuddered and rumbled, spurts of red-hot liquid spouted from their summits to pour down slopes, hissing as they ejected billowing clouds of steam where the hot flow met the frozen glacial ice. To escape the unbearable heat she slithered down an open crevasse into an enchanted, smooth blue world of sculpted ice, where sounds were deadened except for the distant echo of someone hammering, a soft *plunk, plunk* sound, like a pulse throbbing in a wrist-vein.

At first the coolness was soothing, but the further she sank into the dark blue depths of the crevasse the achingly cold it became. Then she heard the groaning, grinding sound from the glacier compressing rocks over which it travelled so unbearably slowly, covering no more than a metre per year; and suddenly she was surrounded by hundreds of frozen human bodies suspended in the walls of solid ice, each one perfectly preserved. Was it they who were groaning? Was her father there? (Impossible! protested the rational sector of her brain. He died long after snow and ice had disappeared. But how am I here - I'm dying later than him? But to that there was no logical answer).

"Sssh, lie still," he urged, and his voice seemed to come from inside her ear.

"Ils ont mangé si v-vite," she stammered, "c'était atroce! Then they spat bits out. And yet they're strictly herbivores."

"*Ate?* Who ate? *Fin?*"

"Non, mais non. They ate someone I'd never seen before. Wearing a wolfskin, very similar to yours."

He said nothing, but she could hear him thinking uneasily. "We'll need water soon, the urn's almost empty." But since he assumed she was delirious he was not talking to her, merely voicing his thoughts aloud to steady his nerves.

Ice could arrest decay - another of her mother's hypotheses. Humans used to freeze food to retain its freshness, long ago. But since she could dry ibex meat to keep it wholesome, and shrivel berries to concentrate their flavour, she was not unduly impressed by the preservative qualities of ice.

But she did recall one ice story that had intrigued her; a family memory, handed down from a generation that had lived back in the times of alpine ice and snow. It featured a couple who went climbing on their honeymoon. The handsome young husband slipped and fell into a crevasse, too far down to be rescued, so his distraught young widow went home and spent her solitary life without him. Fifty years later on, however, his body emerged at the foot of the glacier, carried there on the slow current. His widow was traced, and she duly arrived to collect it for a proper, final burial. Those who witnessed the seventy three year old lady with snow-white hair and wrinkled skin embracing a young man of merely twenty five, dead - but still in the perfect bloom of youth, even though they understood the preservative effect of ice, still found themselves believing they were watching a grandmother collecting her dead grandson. The 'credibility gap' was how her mother explained the discrepancy between what they really saw, and what their brain told them they saw.

She opened her eyes in the gloom of near total darkness. Perhaps by next light she would be able to move, hopefully even show her face on the mountainside to pre-empt Fin usurping her terrain. Her declaration 'the mountain's mine' would hold no sway if they thought her dead, and her prolonged absence would surely compel them to investigate, sooner or later - even though her burrow entrance was skilfully hidden, like a trompe d'oeil.

Her fever had abated and her face felt cool, almost cold. The man had covered her with the wolfskin and half-flank of ibex hide, while he himself was only partially covered with the smaller flank of ibex. His legs and feet protruded bare and unprotected, as if their chill didn't matter because he had no sensation of it.

Before he awoke she lolloped along the narrow tunnel, cradling her injured left arm against her chest. It was the gait of a four legged animal forced to operate on three, only more ungainly; the smoother the motion the less her broken bone was jarred but she winced with every awkward twist or turn. She stopped just short of the exit. She could hear the faintest snapping of rocks as they expanded in the morning heat, and the hushed breathing and snuffling of a nearby marmot scout, but apart from that the outer world was silent. Cautiously she inched forwards until she reached the protective shadow of the rock against which the stranger's final arrow had ricocheted, from where she could safely see without being seen.

Fin was a distant figure, planting new poles to plug the hairline gaps in his stockade, whilst Bernina knelt in her alfalfa patch. There was no sign of Holg, Alpha or the kids. Fin's weapon hung from a leather strap, jiggling with every hammer-strike, and the sound of his hammering echoed eerily round the mountains, magnified by the natural amphitheatre of rock. Instinctively she flinched, anticipating that this reckless hammering might attract a bombardment of arrows, but silence and stillness thankfully returned.

Her eyes dissected every detail of the foreground. Absolutely nothing remained from the attack: no blood smears, no remnants of hair, flesh or bone. It was like a murder scene wiped clean of all incriminating evidence. Except…two metres uphill she detected a stone fragment that was fractionally darker grey than the surrounding shale. Was it part of the arrow-tip whose slither had pierced her neck? She bent to collect it as a ghoulish memento, and in doing so spied something much stranger underneath. It was neither stone, bone, plant nor any substance she recognised - not even metal like the rusted pitons. It emitted a weird vibration, and she sensed it possessed an inert power - like a false eye or an artificial hearing aid, which apparently were common enough in olden times. She fingered it suspiciously, sniffed it, squeezed it, but resisted licking it since that would be foolhardy.

She studied the man closely when she showed him her curious find. He stiffened, then sudden beads of sweat sprouted amongst the hairs on his upper lip. He took it and held it hatefully in the palm of his hand. She had the impression he loathed it so intensely he would damn it to extinction if he had that power.

"Where did you find this?" his voice shook, "you must tell me what happened!"

"It's plain as the cloud you know what it is. So you should tell me…and don't plead memory loss because it nearly got me killed."

"I'll tell you what it is if you tell me how you got it. Did Fin give it you?"

"No. I found it. It's the only fragment of the assassin, hunter - whatever he was, that hasn't been, err, entièrement détruit."

He sank back against the burrow wall, if anything more blanched than during his coma. Eventually he drew an unsteady breath and reluctantly began his disclosure.

"It's a silicon chip. Acts as a tracking device so whoever it's implanted in can be monitored, and their movements and whereabouts known."

She looked mystified. "Tell me properly, in words you expect me to understand."

He sighed. "I'll try - but there's no easy way to explain the rudiments of advanced technologies using a Neanderthal vocabulary. In simple terms then, it's a device…OK *thing*...like a tiny pebble that can be inserted into…OK *placed inside*…a person's body. It gives off a signal, like a marmot's squeak if you like, and this tells other people where that person is."

"Don't patronize - you know I can cope with words like 'insert'… So, how comes they hear the squeak, if he wanders far away?"

"They don't. The 'squeak' is metaphorical, not literal. They *watch* or track his movements on a computer screen - but don't ask me to explain computer technology to you in two swift minutes."

"So they know he came here, to this mountain?!"

"If their central computer network's still running properly, and there are no other glitches to the system, yes they do."

She frowned at the re-encroaching jargon, and the danger he implied. "Do they know he's dead? Or that he tried to kill me?"

A flicker of alarm at this new information played across his face, but he steadied himself. "No to both. They only know his location. Or, more specifically, the chip's location."

"So they know where it is now? They've located my burrow?" Her voice trembled with alarm and outrage.

He cleared his throat uncomfortably. "I'd guess not. After all, *I've* been here for weeks if not months by now, yet no-one's traced me here."

She stared at him in undiluted horror. "You've got a chip too? Well, what makes you think they didn't trace you? That man might've tried to kill me thinking I was you! Is that why you suggested I wear the marmot pelts again, a surge of guilt over how much you were risking my life impersonating you in your outfit!"

"I appreciate how it looks to you, but I'm not that evil. If they'd located me they'd have acted immediately, not waited hours, even days, let alone weeks or months. I reckon your burrow's safely deep enough underground for no signal to be transmit…sent out to them. OK?"

"Better - but far from 'OK'. They must have tracked you here, even if you subsequently 'vanished' when I carried you into the burrow. Yet you kept this vital information from me… 'memory loss', huh? Mon cul! Doubtless you came as a spy to steal my ways of survival, or my water supply, and, like a stupid, broody woman who wanted something as innocent as a little baby, I went and nursed you when I knew all along I should have killed you!" She carved a vicious groove in the earthern floor to vent her frustration, then clicked her tongue in fury.

"I promise my motives were never as you paint them now. I came here, yes, but not to spy or harm. I came to escape. I suspected there was water but had no idea anyone lived here, least of all a female and on her own. I genuinely fell from the ridge, am still partly paralysed and absolutely did suffer memory loss. Though I do admit it's returning now, in fits and starts…" He looked at her intently, "For all we know Fin's chipped too. It may be him they traced. Perhaps you should tell me the details of how you were shot."

After she had obliged he studied the fragment of flint in the dim light.

"The bonus is he was only primitively armed. There are far more sophisticated weapons still in circulation - though nothing dangerously hi-tech anymore. Or not as far as I know."

"Oh, you're a weapons expert too?" she gave him a charmingly icy smile. "Let's be clear about this - you have to stay in my burrow for ever, because the minute you poke your nose out they'll trace you again?"

"Sadly, yes."

"Unless we destroy the chip. Where's it 'implanted'? The wolfskin?

"Sadly, no. They put it where you wouldn't want to remove it, otherwise everyone would." He lapsed into brooding silence.

"Well, where…?"

"Isn't it obvious?" He sounded bitter, "What's a vital part of the male anatomy? Where no-one would fancy a deep incision?"

Under the pretext of reorganising her 'larder', Motte assessed the situation methodically and in private. If the chips were being monitored (and surely they must be, for what else was their purpose?) then two had so far arrived on her mountain. Both had then promptly 'disappeared'. Down her burrow, as it happened. But hopefully they didn't know that!

She could possibly dispose of the assassin's so that it reappeared on their 'screen' as far from her burrow as possible, a feat only achievable by climbing La Grande Aiguille Grise. From the summit she could fling it into what used to be Italy. However, this was an impossible task without full use of both arms because, despite the sling the man had made to support her broken collar bone, ascending the north ridge depended on claw-tip handholds, perfect agility and full strength. Added to which there was a glaring weakness: why wouldn't the chip emit signals throughout her climb? Of course it would! That plan was uselessy flawed…

Therefore the man's chip should be dealt with first. But it was embedded plumb in the middle of his breeding seeds! It was a hopeless scenario, exactly like the choice that was no choice at all - between the devil and the deep blue sea. Because leaving it there would condemn him to permanent imprisonment in her burrow (although her mother would definitely have 'released' him - to whatever retribution lay in wait, as soon as his breeding purpose was fulfilled). A further downside to leaving it was that it must be toxic, therefore likely to render him infertile - the more so the longer it remained embedded, so removing it might be the only way he could father a child. Yet (and this was the 'deep blue sea' parallel) the procedure to remove it was as likely, no, *more* likely, to leave him both infertile and impotent. Which he was at the moment anyway, due to partial paralysis…

Motte concluded there was no clear answer to the dilemma. She would leave fate to decide. Her mother might well have been boldly decisive, but this surely meant she was just as often wrong as she was right. Nevertheless, there was valuable insight to be gained from probing the man's defenses:

"Best get your chip out straight away now, whilst you're still paralysed and can't feel the pain."

She studied him, hawklike, searching for the faintest flicker in his eyes that would confirm the genuineness of his paralysis - or prove it fake.

He shrugged, "I'm at your mercy, as you're well aware. But I assure you there's no need. The chip defuncts automatically after a period of desuetude - otherwise they'd be receiving signals from all the dead scouts whose lives they've cheerfully sacrificed, and that'd just overclog the system."

Motte was left no wiser, and immediately after this obscure, high-jargon utterance her acute hearing picked out the now almost familiar sounds of approaching humans. Their labouring footsteps reverberated from the col, along with a strange, rasping, dragging sound. She had no option but to investigate.

But like a vacuous, airheaded woman from the olden days she dithered over what to wear. Her hesitation was not to do with vanity, however; it was simply that she now associated both marmot and wolf pelts with danger. And any newcomers as dangerous too.

"Be an ibex," he suggested, immensely relieved by the welcome reprieve from surgery and seemingly reading her mind. "Stand stock still. The dun grey colour will blend perfectly into the background - sky or rock. That's one advantage to the dearth of blue skies."

7

Fin stood watching warily as five distant adult figures, all total strangers to him, toiled slowly up the path towards the col. He was stranded in an unwisely exposed position out on the dry river bed, hunting for grinding stones. The reason for this being that all Holg's teeth were unaccountably falling out, and he kept moaning his gums were too sore to swallow anything but mash. Holg had suddenly become a liability - little more than a limping, swallowing, whimpering, sometimes literally pooing-in-his-pants, puny baby!

'Course, that did mean he himself had readier access to ol' Bernina, but that apart it left him to do all the heavy work solo, meaning he was anyways too pooped out to have energy for sex. So: plus one, minus one, no goddam advantage whatsoever!

These new guys all looked male, dammit. Broad shoulders, steady strides and not a kiddie in sight were the giveaway. Still, it mightn't be all bad if they settled. It'd bring competition for food and balling, granted, yet extra male reinforcements oughta help him negotiate better terms with wolf-woman. He was beginning to suspect she'd kept all the best terrain inside *her* fiefdom, leaving his lot with the less healthy lower lands and, it looked increasingly likely, a lethally contaminated cave.

Added to that, far from 'gagging for it' her recent high-and-mighty attitude showed she was nothing but a little tease. She'd given him an imperial wave of the hand only that morning, when he'd caught a glimpse of her high up near the Black Spot, as he and Holg called the site of the great groundhog dismemberment. That horror scenario was, in fact, the very last time he and Holg had had a good laugh. It had all been downhill since then, for Holg at any rate.

"It's not virgin territory after all, Samson. I can see this big, brawny fellow scrabbling about in a rocky hollow, just north-north-east of us," Layla commented, handing an ancient pair of binoculars back to Samson, who was leading the group of five, and concentrating fiercely on the smooth, therefore slippery stones of the zig-zag path. "And I'm sorry to say he looks a right geek!"

"Yup," Samson agreed after the merest cursory glance. "Those cowboy types are never solitary though. He'll be a groupie, I bet. Armed?"

"Nope," she replied, adding with a faintly sardonic smile, "apart from a cross pendant hanging round his neck, which those old religionists considered defensive armoury, aren't I right? Why would anyone wear Christian jewellery these days?"

"Same reasons they did in the past. Love sign, identity badge, vampire deterrent etc. They'd argue it was the devil who messed up earth. Then they'd say, if *only* we all believed in their God, he'd restore it to health and normality!"

"But I thought a vast bunch of people worshipped a different God. Yahway - the one fixated on destroying things. Destruction was the only way, apparently, to protect them against their enemies - and absolutely *everyone* not of their tribe and creed was their enemy… - And yet we're supposed to believe homo sapiens possessed a 'higher intelligence'!" She frowned accusingly at the overhead blanket of cloud as if it were God's front doormat. "And why would this God-of-all-things (not theYahway one - the other, Christian one) bother about earth anymore? Surely there are plenty other places in the Universe, many of which've have been flooded, fried or frozen before."

"Well, us humans are supposed to be 'in his likeness' and therefore special."

"Huh! If you believe that crap you'll believe anything!"

"I never said I believed it. We're discussing it, Layla. It's an impersonal, intellectual exercise, not a full-blown war of words."

The three other, older adults followed Layla and Samson in silence, knowing better than to waste precious breath disputing ancient philosophies. They needed to conserve energy because they were carrying the heaviest load: the twelve long poles and the patchwork of hides that comprised the tipi; plus simply breathing had become increasingly difficult the higher they climbed. In truth just two of them were saddled with the weight of the load, because the oldest man, Murchadh, was merely propping himself up instead of supporting it. But that was still preferable to converting the tipi poles into an improvised palankeen to carry him on.

There were reasons both for and against climbing higher. For: a flat area was vital to pitch the tipi, and the mouth of the defunct glacier would provide that, added to which the water source was presumably linked to this glacier. It was in fact the near-certain conviction they would find water that kept them climbing, Murchadh's clairvoyance had as good as confirmed it ... Against: the radiation increased the higher the altitude. Also, Murchadh declared you were a sitting duck if an enemy chose to ambush you on a mountain top because there was no escape, though to compensate you of course had plenty of boulders to roll down and crush them with.

"Well, Parco Nazionale di Gran Paradiso, here we come!" Layla announced, "Let's hope you're more 'paradiso' than wretched 'inferno'."

"Apparently there was a shack or mountain refuge up here somewheres, back in the twenty first century. Think of the luxury lives those jammy people had! Food and water permanently on tap just for the asking, payment possible with measely scraps of paper. Imagine! Plus the bliss of waking up without your first thoughts being: 'Am I gonna die today? What's that new, swollen yellow pustule? That ugly lump suppurating in my groin?'" Samson's hand hurried instinctively to his groin before he could wrench it away. Fate needed no tempting - he had heard you could even catch diseases psychosomatically.

"Bet they moaned all the same. Human nature, innit - never happy with what we've got?" Layla scoffed. "I got told they used to invent dangers and tortures just to stave off boredom. They'd throw themselves off precipices, bungee-this, bungee-that and extreme-everything, purely to get the thrill of cheating death - or to superbly succeed in dying. Daft eh?"

"Yup. And how polar-oppositely-wrong all their future predictions were. Worrying the human race'd soon be in hoc to machines, huh; grow too fat and lazy to move, huh; and, on top of this obesity phobia, live too long - live to be a thousand years old!" Samson stamped his foot in frustration. "Morons!"

The group finally crested the col and fell silent. Even Samson and Layla, habitual blabbermouths, knew all your senses had to be alert and finely tuned to absorb the vibrations of a new environment and successfully read the best place to pitch the tipi. The final, overriding decision was of course Murchadh's.

They were an unlikely bunch of individuals in many respects, but as a team Murchadh was the lynchpin. He was their Chief, the reincarnation of Sitting Bull - and he had the finest feathered headgear to prove it! And there was not one iota of sense modelling themselves on the Native American way of life if they argued against him. Those Native Americans could live off the land and understood the natural world better than anyone, ever, throughout all of history.

Added to which, of course, the precious dynamite happened to be his.

Murchadh was the only one in the group of new arrivals who noticed the capricorn that was really Motte standing, in the familiar pose of its zodiac sign, a hand's breadth below the ridge. From its moderate size and tiny, fledgling horns he assumed it a yearling. These ancient, cloven-footed creatures: capricorns, bouquetins, ibex, bighorn, mountain goats - they were known by a vast array of names (and he naturally favoured 'bighorn' due to its association with Sitting Bull and the famous battle he so gloriously won), were the oldest herd animals in the world, older even than the buffalo, so he was charmed by the vision. It must be a sign, he decided (and he was not thinking zodiacs). An omen, hopefully of a change in fortune at last.

> "Layla and I'll wander around with the divining rod, after we've helped pitch the tipis, that is. The important whereabouts of water is our priority numero uno." Samson obtruded into his reverie.

Motte continued to watch the arrival of this new clan without moving a muscle. Not moving a muscle was her deliberate strategy, in fact, because she had no chance of emulating an ibex deftly clambering over mountain scree when her body supported only the front legs, neck and head (an awkward, forwards craning position, painful too - due to her broken collar bone and deep flesh wound). Her hind quarters were indiscriminately stuffed with whatever the man could scramble together. They looked reasonably convincing when she stood still, but jerked and bobbled like a poorly coordinated circus clown insufficiently rehearsed in its rear-end role if she tried to walk.

By contrast to her static pose and hidden behind her ibex disguise, her natural skin prickled with hostility and her mind whirred suspiciously. These five new intruders might have links to the lone assassin - could have been sent specifically to locate his missing chip. It would be naïve in the extreme to assume their arrival so soon after his disappearance was pure coincidence.

Yet, the longer she watched, the more she felt reassured. Instead of operating as a cohesive, well trained unit they were very obviously a disparate bunch of individuals, markedly different to each other in almost every aspect. The oldest man, who wore animal skin trousers and a thick bunch of eagle feathers perched on his head, was certainly the most eccentric. He alone had sharp eyes open to his surroundings, and his fleeting glance in her direction carried no evil intent, or none that she could detect.

The older woman was the most intriguing. Her skin was dramatically dark, almost as dark as the night sky. Motte had been told by her mother that animal colouration was influenced by habitat (the now extinct alpine hare had been snow-white all winter, yet buff-brown in summer). Humans though, despite travelling widely pre-GD, had persistently failed to echo the colours of their surroundings. Her ancestors had lived in a snowy world for most of the year, for instance, yet only turned white in extreme old age. And her own hair, too - dark chestnut, defying the predominant greyness of the external world.

Curiously, the palms of this dark woman's hands were abruptly, mysteriously pale, as if they had been grafted there but actually belonged to someone else. Or else, were exceedingly fragile. Yet the energy and bustling efficiency with which she single-handedly hoisted the tipi into position, whilst the others bumbled about obstructing her, completely belied this supposition.

Motte was not the only clandestine observer. Zin was also spying. But from much closer quarters, recklessly close considering they had not, as yet, proved themselves a friendly force. He lay flat on his stomach on a massive, three metre high boulder right in the thick of the action. Out of his range of vision a brief, informative plaque was bolted onto one side of this boulder, at head height. It was scratched and dented but still legible - had anyone been able to read. (Only the man, but he was holed up in the burrow). It commemorated the death, on the night of April 17th, 1944, of eight Italian guides and twenty five allied soldiers fleeing Italy, all killed by an avalanche in this approximate spot.

The action Zin was focused on was a strange pantomime performed by the man of huge, gaunt frame and hair plaited in a long pigtail, whom the girl called Samson (amongst various other, more abusive names), and the girl herself, Layla. Samson wandered round and round the boulder in ever diminishing circles, frowning concentratedly, the two ends of a forked branch gripped lightly in either hand. Whenever the tip of this forked branch shivered or dipped he let out a gasp, and Layla sprang forward with alacrity to place a pointed stone over that precise spot.

Zin assumed they were marking out a site for a future building, a religious temple most likely, judging by their solemn mood. But Motte, from her observation post high on the ridge, recognised Samson's gadget as a dousing rod. The boat crew had had one. It was used to find water, or 'divine' it - a religious word implying the process was a special, God-given gift - whereas she knew it could be located simply by using one's nose.

"Looks to be a large deposit, don't you reckon?" Layla's voice rose excitedly.

"*Seems* to be. But it's deep underground and we don't have decent tools for boring. We might have to blast the rock - and that's a scary prospect since we don't know sweet FA about the dynamite. Murchadh said it ought only to be used as an absolute last resort."

"Well, we'll die without water. What's more 'last resort' than that?"

"The cowboy must have found some though - else he wouldn't be alive."

"He's *bright yellow*, Samson! I'd sooner die of dehydration than catch what he's got."

"Maybe the yellow's artificial. Like an alarm signal, keeping enemies at bay. Else it makes him more visible in the grey gloom, so he can be seen by his mates from outer space!"

"Oh, for crying out loud! Don't go there - or I'll shove the dynamite you-know-where!"

"My modus op. is: when you know nothing, be open to everything."

"Not *everything*, Samson - and certainly not effing aliens! I think I'm a trifle less overawed by Murchadh than you are, so maybe I should go get the dynamite."

"Well, listening to him's kept us alive thus far, and we'd be dead as dodos if we hadn't met up with him when we did. Plus, Eartha's far too smart to blindly obey some surrogate old injun' chief who's really a Scot, if he was a *total* fake."

She whistled sarcastically. After which a prolonged silence ensued.

Eventually Zin grew impatient and wormed his way across the rock to peer over. They both seemed to have dozed off, with Layla's head cushioned on Samson's chest. Cautiously he poked out an exploratory foot, feeling for leverage. He could easily jump the three metres, but the jolt of his landing and the stones he would inevitably disturb would wake them immediately. Samson's massive fist was not his only weapon. He had a strip of animal gut wound around it which could garrotte a boy as easily as throttle a marmot, so Zin slithered down diagonally, edging always away from Samson.

When he reached a precarious perch closer to the ground and was poised to jump, confident he could leg it into the ravine before Samson regained his wits and heaved himself upright, Layla suddenly sat up.

He froze, clinging on like a lizard, wishing he could melt into the rock. Any animal would have smelt him immediately but Layla was oblivious to his presence. She scolded Samson for falling asleep on the job and, when nuzzling and nibbling at his ears and mouth did nothing more than faintly change the rhythm of his steady breathing, she sighed, picked herself up - still luckily with her back to Zin - and traipsed off in the direction of the tipi encampment.

He should have seized this perfect opportunity to escape, but a renewed surge of bravado persuaded him to linger. And his awareness that Motte continued to watch him added spice to the dangerous thrill.

Silently, patiently, he eased the divining rod from between Samson's thumb and forefinger, then with deft, sinuous movements unwound the gut string from Samson's wrist. He was tantalizingly close to achieving his goal when, to his horror, Layla reappeared carrying a rucksack made from animal hide, her pockets bulging mysteriously. He shrank behind the boulder, cursing himself for not having run when he had the chance.

To his surprise, she had no more wish to wake Samson than he did. Instead of more nuzzling and slobbering, she sat cross-legged, patiently rubbing two stones rhythmically together. *Rasp, scrape, rasp* was all he could hear for what seemed an age; the sounds so repetitive they lulled him into inaction, because he surely could have used them to drown the sounds of his fleeing footsteps.

He then heard a murmur of pleasure; Layla had clearly got the desired result. Bernina sighed like that when a seed pushed through the soil, and Hon too when Fin pawed her in the right places. Curiosity impelled him to crane his neck around the rock, yet all he saw was her hunched back and straining shoulders. She had emptied the rucksack but its contents were nothing he recognised. Although she was whispering to herself he could not hear the individual words - only sense the fear and excitement transmitted because it paralled his own emotional state.

Glancing up at the ridge, he noticed Motte climbing higher to become an almost indiscernibly dark silhouette against a rapidly darkening sky. Instantly a premonition of acute danger pulsed through him. His false bravado ebbed away and he sped from the boulder in terror, no longer caring if the clattering of stones woke Samson.

Instead of heading for the safety of his cave-home and the manly protection of his father, for some inexplicable reason he bolted across the moraine towards the head of the former glacier...

The ground shook violently even before the sounds of explosions hit his ears - or 'split' his ears more accurately describes it. The rush of air made a mockery of its apparent transparency - it struck with such force that his bones and intestines were crushed as if by an iron fist.

Everything everywhere was exploding. The concussion of sound and air came first, followed by a series of deafening detonations as rocks split and collided, boulders shattered and the air filled with flying stones. Other rocks thundered downwards, disappearing into a new chasm that suddenly opened up where Samson and Layla had been only moments before.

He could make no sense of it. Apparently he had been shot skywards like a pebble from a catapult, because now he was hurtling through the air at frightening speed - along with those thousand million other fragments of rock. Time seemed to both race and stop, so that his numbed brain dared to hope that he had miraculously escaped serious injury and might soon float safely back to earth.

Then, just as abruptly, the dreamlike feeling of suspended time vanished and he was struggling to breathe. The air thickened, a sharp, stinging smell clogged his nostrils, and although the darkness had been developing anyway it was overtaken by a broth of choking smoke-cloud mixed with the fine dust of pulverised rock. He coughed and spluttered, his lungs on fire, until the lack of breathable air together with the acute pain from his stomach and limbs became so unbearable that he lost consciousness.

Motte had retreated beyond the ridge that formed the olden day border between France and Italy. Instinct guided her there, along with a warning whiff of cordite which stung her nostrils seconds prior to the explosion. Her ears were then pummeled by a series of deafening detonations that shuddered through the mountain, and smoke billowed high over the ridge, jettisoning a rain of stones that pattered all around her. Then there was silence, followed by what might have been the cries of a young child, but might equally be the whistling complaints of her nearly burst eardrums.

She had never experienced violence on this scale. It occurred to her that it might be the warning signals of Armageddon, the death throes of planet earth, just like some holy book or other (the Bible, I Ching, Torah, Uppanishad, Koran or Dictionary? She never could remember which of those books of prophecy foretold what) had declared would happen once the forces of good (well, more likely evil) had finally got their way. The man had mentioned it only recently.

Once the explosions seemed over she regained the ridge and peered down through the pall of darkness. Thick smoke continued to obscure the area and visibility was less than twenty metres, partly due to swirling dust, partly to the advent of night. She resigned herself to staying where she was until halflight returned. If anyone were wounded they would have to wait; she could not help what she could not see.

Once the soft grey light of dawn returned she climbed down, wishing she could bound like a marmot rather than having to drag the stuffed ibex hindquarters awkwardly behind her.

The topography of the whole moraine area had been violently rearranged. In place of the boulder where Zin, Samson and Layla had been, a newly formed crater now yawned deep and wide, like a dark mouth from which a wisp of smoke emerged - as if it were surreptitiously puffing a cigarette. She dared not go too close to its rim for fear of sliding in, but she probed near enough to feel a damp chill wafting from it, suggesting the lid had been blown off the minor water deposit. All around there were swathes of destruction: the col had been pinched to a narrower gash, the tipi had vanished, and the entrance to Fin's cave was buried beneath a pile of fallen slabs.

She stared, open mouthed at the brutal displacement of rock on rock. Perhaps they had all died quickly and painlessly - then, uneasily, she recalled hearing the sound of a crying child…but there was no sound or sign of life now.

The silence was eerie; even the marmots were hiding - or fatefully imprisoned in their burrows because of earthfalls blocking the tunnel exits. A wave of panic suddenly swept over her: could she be alone again, the only survivor in an empty world, with this time not even marmots for companionship? Terror constricted her throat…

No, she told herself, no. You're imagining the worst possible scenario, circular tunnels are the strongest structure on earth so it's impossible they've all been destroyed… She picked her way sombrely uphill, scrambling over boulders, dips and ridges that had not previously been there. Where was the triangular rock marking the lower entrance to her burrow? And where the shallow bowl from which the upper entrance sat centrally, like a plug in a circular sink?

Think Motte. Look for the bigger picture. You've emerged from your burrow entrance almost every day of your life, consequently you've a perfect mental image of the mountains and the precise relationships between them. You may know nothing else in this god-forsaken world, but this mountainscape is ineradicably etched onto your brain. All you have to do is line everything up correctly - et voilà!

She had to manoeuvre up, down, left, then fractionally right, until eventually she found the spot from which all the peaks were indisputably accurately aligned. The juniper bush was missing, the grey slab with its cleft had been newly spliced in two, while the entrance - hidden at the best of times - was even more hidden under a generous peppering of stones.

Hooves were fine for pawing the ground but useless at digging. Thus she had to strip off the ibex pelt and ignore the pain from her partially healed shoulder wound in order to locate her burrow entrance. The moment she did so, relief flooded through her and her sense of smell jerked alive. In fact all her senses reawakened once inside the womblike shape of the tunnel, where she could again hear the familiar snufflings and scrapings of marmots scurrying in or out. With marmots for company she would surely regain the will to live!

Then, hard on the heels of relief came suspicion. The man. Was he the catalyst for this disaster? Was the explosion a bomb whose detonation he had ordered via his 'chip', helped perhaps by those satellite-spies that he did not deny existed? It would not surprise her to find him hooked up to his computer (he had admitted to being an expert at that technology) whilst he watched the whole drama of the smoking crater on a glassy screen like he had tried to describe for her.

The tunnel seemed longer than usual because she had to stop occasionally to repair a cave-in, or listen for marmot messaging - in case there were further developments in the outside world that she should know about. The closer she came to the main burrow, the more she trembled with desire to catch him ogling at his screen and plonking on the death buttons of his keyboard. She would not condemn without a fair trial. She was actually curious to hear what reasons he might give to obfuscate his treachery.

"It wasn't my fault, I was programmed to detonate that bomb." This came top of her list of likely excuses.

Then: "*Samson* did you say? Well how about that! Next you'll tell me she was Delilah (Oh, OK, Layla, same thing really - it's the shortened form)… well, of course it was a 'history repeat'. That Samson was always going to pull the mountain down onto himself, tempted of course by the lovely Del…Layla. How long was his hair did you say?"

What she least expected was not to find him at all. Gone, without a trace!

8

The boom of the detonation reverberated around the nearby mountain islands and further afield - in outwardly radiating circles to a distance of fifty or sixty kilometres as an eagle flies. And if audible to the naked ear at that distance, it could surely be detected ten or twenty times that using more sensitive audio equipment.

Had Motte not been deep inside her burrow at the time, she would have been amazed by what next occurred. As silently as an old dirigible, a human shape floated down through the cloud barrier to land feet first at the head of the old glacier. His body was encased in a silver costume made of gossamer-light material, and his face might or might not have been handsome - it was impossible to tell behind his protective mask and artificial breathing apparatus. He folded away his mini-parachute and fished in his top pocket for a small, rectangular gadget.

> "Cormorant to Alpha Ipsilon," he spoke in a hoarse whisper, crouched on one knee as if proposing marriage to an invisible partner, "Can you hear me?"

> Presumably not since he repeated, "Cormorant to Alpha Ipsilon," the whisper a fraction louder this time, "Come on you bloody tossers, listen up. Can't you *hear* me?"

> Evidently this time they could, "Sorry for the abuse mate, owing to stressing over being marooned here incommunicado. Anyways I'll give you the basics…" He consulted something balanced in the palm of his outstretched hand, "Mostly good news. Altitude 3,723 metres, Latitude 45.45, Longitude 6.98 KML, radiation levels 4.3725 PR and 3.2337 OB, humidity disastrously low at barely 22, oxygen ….," (he went on and on in this technical vein) "…and so far no signs of life. Keep you in the picture when I've had a longer recce. Over and out."

No sooner had he pocketed the one gadget, out came another. This he looked through, or if not precisely *through*, certainly he positioned it between his eyes and everything he surveyed, and it emitted a faint hum while amassing its information. Whenever he faced it groundwards it let out a faint *bleep,* perhaps showing it was distressed - or excited - by what it discovered there.

Once he had scanned the area to his satisfaction, the gadgets were swapped over again.

"Cormorant to Alpha Ipsilon, are you there Ipsilon?"

This time they must have been ready and waiting.

"Yeah man. Post glacial terrain with typical corrie and moraine, fold not rift, limestone sub-strata and alluvial deposits further down in the deep valley - ideal for intensive agricultural production after deep cleansing completed. Subterranean water supply def. adequate for primary development stage. So, basically it's OK, our lucky break - it should support a moderate-sized community of say round-about forty head."

"No, no. Not a natural eruption or quake, it was def. a bomb or old-world explosive like TNT or dynamite, but non-nuclear. I rec. it's killed the bastards off, so damn naïve they probably hand-held it! Primitives for sure, living in caves with tools of stone and wood from the traces post-explosion. God knows what the buggers ate 'cos there's no real sign of cultivation and not one single animal worth hunting within sight, though to be fair there's shedloads of marmot shit, but I can't tell if it's fresh or not 'cos I haven't brought that particular filter with me, silly arse that I am. I'm due shut-eye after that exhausting, heart-in-mouth descent - I won't scare you with the details nor bore you with my bravery. Send us a small intrepid commando, five or six, to secure the outpost just in case - there's always an outside poss. there are survivors who need taming. Great to hear your sexy voice. Love you madly of course. Over and out."

Then he blew into a toggle on his padded shoulder so that his silver suit inflated and he could lie down on the stones as comfortably as on an air bed. He had no concerns about security because he was guarded by the humming/bleeping gadget attached, like an old fashioned miner's lamp, to his forehead. It would warn him immediately of approaching danger. Maybe it would kill it on sight, no questions asked.

Motte deduced that since the man had not escaped outside through either tunnel entrance, he could only have left the burrow by penetrating deeper into the mountain. And that way led to the water reservoir, her carefully guarded secret and precious elixir of life. Once he reached that vast cavern of water with its high vaulted arches there were of course plenty of tunnels leading away from it, since every marmot family had their own route to the water - otherwise there would be a continuous daily cavalcade of thirsty marmots traipsing through her burrow! But if he tried those routes he was likely to get lost or stuck, since marmots build their tunnels specifically to suit their size; even she would need to scrape out extra width and height to squirm down them.

His hands, supposedly so good at delicately stroking the mouse pads of computers and at stitching ibex outfits too, would be useless at enlarging tunnels. She therefore felt convinced she would find him either in the section of tunnel between her burrow and the reservoir, or inside the reservoir itself.

She saw him long before he was aware of her. Sitting in one of the circular paddling pools, offshoots of the main body of water, and although the light was dim and the water threw up strange, distorting reflections, she could have sworn he was smiling.

To exult in the likely deaths of fifteen people, including her - since her failure to return last night would surely suggest she had died in the blast - virtually confirmed his enemy status. Yet the smile was neither gloating nor cruel. It was dreamlike, the type of beatific trance-state her mother experienced after a genepi binge or the realisation she was pregnant again. He was sieving the water through splayed fingers, then strenuously patting his thighs and massaging his calves. The multiple echoes to each splash and pat confused her brain, making it harder to concentrate on the necessity to immobilise him.

But they enabled her to creep closer without him hearing or suspecting her presence.

Then she paused, suddenly unsure of her strategy. It lost her the advantage of surprise because he looked up and glimpsed her through the gloom.

"Don't be angry - you were gone so long I was dying of thirst. I knew you came this way for water, so off I set on hands and bum." Then, realising his light hearted tone was out of key with her mood, he quickly changed tack, "I know you think I'm thoughtless, selfish, shouldn't be here pursuing water therapy and trying to restore strength to my legs when you might've been injured in that earth tremor. I heard thuds of rockfall and the tunnel shook a bit, but some sixth sense told me you weren't hurt." He seemed to brush aside the horror of what had really happened remarkably easily, "I thought you might be pleased by this water cure. In fact," he had the audacity to add - and in a mildly injured tone, "I'm surprised you didn't think to try it earlier. But then," and this was actually sarcastic, "the secret nature of your water supply comes before everything."

Was he bluffing? Could a bang so monumentally deafening reduce to a 'thud' simply by passing through fifty metres of rock and earth? Hmm, she could hear footsteps from the col, much further away…were acoustics *so* variable? Or could it be down to their different ability to hear, since he never noticed the fainter sounds she did. Perhaps his computer experiences had robbed him of the acuter perceptions, whereas her way of life had encouraged them.

"I haven't touched the main lake," he gestured casually at the central reservoir, "so no worries. My dirty, unproductive body hasn't contaminated your drinking supplies. I don't see well in the dark, as you know, but I did gather this pool was the place to paddle. And you now look - to a half-blind, half-man - a remarkably real woman standing upright like that."

She ignored the transparent flattery. "That was no earth tremor. It was a man-made thing, and it blew up half the moraine! I…I think it's killed everyone… Certainement the young couple who just arrived, probably Zin - and Fin's cave's caved in, so I doubt they can've survived. I'd guess the bang could be heard from Mont Blanc at least - yet, somehow, *you* couldn't hear it."

The spark of humorous enjoyment faded, replaced by a seemingly genuine expression of shocked concern. But she was an inexperienced judge of human sincerity.

"An incendiary bomb? Or a missile?"

"I don't know. All I saw was rocks thrown in the air, a great cloud of smoke filled with dust and stones and some kind of dirty smoke that smelt sour, stung my eyes and made it difficult to breathe. And now there's a crater near Fin's cave and the small water reservoir's been opened up. But…no sign of survivors."

"If it *was* a missile there'll be more on the way. That's a typical invasion tactic: instil fear, then swiftly ratchet up to terror proportions. Those missiles'll be drones. Let's hope they're not programmed," he glanced anxiously at the untroubled surface of the reservoir, "to seek out water. Usually they're heat seeking - to home in on human hideouts."

"It must've homed on the young couple then. The blast was exactly where they were divining for water, and the guy big enough to give off the heat of six times you."

"My mobility's improved from the water - plus the headroom to stand up," he tried to look at her without a hint of reproach at the slight on his stature - if slight it was. "I might manage to drag myself outside at long last, and might be able to judge what happened from the damage caused."

"Pah!" she shook her head. "That might be precisely what you want - the opportunity to get outside and signal to your friends."

Immediately she neared the burrow exit, the soft, downy hairs on the nape of her neck alerted her to a hostile presence and a faint, unfamiliar smell confirmed it. Crouched at the lip of the exit, her eyes roved everywhere but she failed to notice Cormorant because his silver jumpsuit blended, chameleon-like, into the background. All she eventually saw was the tiny, darker grey radio transmitter, and the fug of moisture his breath had formed on the visor of his oxygen mask. These were sufficient clues to gradually tune her eyesight into perceiving the elusive, shimmering outline of his sleeping body.

She kept the man deliberately trapped behind her, her body blocking the exit route. She knew her physical superiority would not last much longer, not if he continued to regain mobility and strength, but for now the threat of her claws and his ignorance of the outside terrain should keep him compliant. Son 'chip' ne doit rien transmitter - c'était de rigeur.

She whispered a description of man and machine, using a less than technical vocabulary.

"Radio communications are seriously low-tech, so good news there. It'd be useful to know how he arrived though - hopefully not by projectile or infra-light."

"But is he from your organisation?"

"No. Or…well, I doubt it - we avoided communicating by radio. The waves are so easily intercepted or interfered with - even a marmot whistle could jam them! But he'll have radioed for reinforcements already, so there's little point jamming them now."

They sat in silence, puzzling over their independent interpretations of this newest invader, and the implications it brought. She kept one eye on the masked man, but another on the unmasked one - who was also masked, but in a different way.

Her mother had repeatedly impressed on her that only a mere handful of survivors clung to life on a dying earth, all of them cavefolk or burrow-dwellers who wore furs and dieted on roots, berries and raw meat. Quelle absurdité! Now she must readjust to the concept of organised armies with technological know-how and technological equipment aiming to colonise her forgotten outpost, along with the disparate bands of independent rebels (Fin's group and the tipi lot) who had already arrived.

Why had it suddenly happened now - after being so long incommunicado? It was difficult not to point a finger at the man, the first of the influx to arrive...

"Human societies've always failed," he said, using his most grandiose manner. "Power, greed, feelings of superiority. I was taught I belonged to a super-race bred to rule the world - or what was left of it. And by 'belong' I mean appropriated by, not born into (it's too a long story, so not for now). We were taught the apparent causes of the GD but they just didn't ring true - at least not for me they didn't. So I secretly belonged to a cell of revisionists who knew that the 'special ones' of the pre-GD era (refered to as BGD) had been lusting after world domination for a very long time. They'd grown impatient with their habitual methods of reducing the world population through wars, famine, global diseases, and by owning and oppressing everyone financially - and then lying to them via their total control of the media. They therefore devised a mega-disaster that would kill everyone off, once and for all.

Except for them. Having planned and engineered it, they wouldn't be taken by surprise. They already had an escape route - to somewhere, maybe on another planet even, I don't know, where they could live out the deadly dark times while the earth remained inhospitable. Once the poisons had lost their zap, they'd return.

The organisation I was attached to - for simplicity I'll call them the 'Browns' - were not the real brains, those top dogs who'd got clean away but would one day return to knock them off their perch. They were just ground troops, gate keepers. In charge until such time as the megas, the-powers-that-be, Kratos, decided it was propitious to return and re-establish command." He suddenly lost his proselytizing tone, as if at the flick of a master switch, "We'd better hope that's not what's happening now."

"How'm I to know you aren't just having a laugh at my expense? Next you'll say there are parallel universes, and I'm imprisoning you in my pre-iron age one..."

"Listen, I admit I've made some thoughtless allegations, used the term 'primitive' once or twice, been a bit contemptuous of your technological ignorancey - but I've been propagandised from birth, don't forget. You've been able to develop independent thought. Your mother of course influenced you, which is a kind of propaganda, but at least you managed not to believe it some of the time. And she didn't kill you for disagreeing."

"Well, you weren't killed either."

"Others were," he retorted, and a shadow fell between them. He looked away, "My co-conspirators...I managed to escape - you know the rest."

"I know virtually nothing," she retaliated sharply. "Perhaps you'll tell me more."

"I might. But I'm still programmed to secrecy - yes, you find that very convenient, and you're right, since there are still things I don't want to think or talk about."

She held a finger to her lips. Not because she had heard the roll-call of excuses before, but because her intuition warned her of another unfolding drama that took precedence. She then peered anxiously downwards, misled by past experience into imagining that the danger came from below.

9

Motte was wrong in assuming that the silence and absence of both Fin's and Murchadh's groups meant they were all dead. In truth only some had died (along with a third of the marmot population - occupants of the lower burrows nearest the site of the explosion).

Murchadh survived because he was not in the tipi when the dynamite exploded. He had wandered back through the col, leaning heavily on Eartha, in order to study the lay of the lower lands and work out how best to defend this, his new mountain fortress, from any Custer-type attack. He now decided it was tailor-made for them to plot a Sitting Bull style ambush, but unfortunately left them vulnerable to attack from higher ground. So it was lucky he had kept his counsel earlier, he reflected, because this, his new assessment of the terrain, completely contradicted his former one!

Without warning, he and Eartha were violently hurled to the ground, the explosion having sent a shock-wave hurtling through the col - like a tunneled sandstorm, but loaded with stone splinters instead of sand. Their Hunkpapa wool-woven capes were ripped by these shards and liberally flecked with their blood. Momentarily being winded, though, was actually a blessing in disguise because they breathed in less of the sour smelling, dynamite-filled air.

It shook their brains so forcefully they were momentarily dazed and disorientated, and once Murchadh's brain re-engaged he was seized with terrible guilt. What use was his clairvoyance if it failed to kick in at the hour of need? What a fool he'd been! He had suspected Layla was a loose cannon, realised Samson was putty in her hands, and now knew just how stupidly wrong he was to have imagined that his ancient chunk of dynamite was too old to work - in fact already useless back when his granpa gave it him.

Eartha's brain recovered simultaneously with his.

> "You still alive, Murchadh? Bloody hell! I *told* you to ditch that death-powder ages back. But no, you must've smuggled it secretively - and now it's gone and blown up the mountain you swore would be our saviour. Poor young Layla and Samson were right in the brunt of it. They'll never have survived."

"Owww-uch!" Murchadh's attempt to deflect her anger was overly transparent, yet he persisted in pitiful moaning punctuated by grunts and gasps whilst he struggled over onto his backside, "That 'poor young' Layla must be the one who set it off. Didn't she just nip in to fetch those flint stones? I should've had my wits about me - asked her why she needed them. She wasn't about to roast an eagle."

"Well - now you've killed *our* golden goose. Let's face it, Samson was the only one of us with brawn as well as brain. Marty'll've been killed too, though that might be a mercy since he was fading fast, what with his festering wound and chronic depression. So it's just us; a fool of an old man and an old fool woman. How d'you like that?"

"I didn't bloody do it by purpose, did I? OK, I'll take the blame... fair cop I guess. But...what about that cowboy chappie we saw on our way up? D'you think he'll've survived?"

"We're only alive through a sheer stroke of luck - from being this side of the pass. I doubt anyone the other side will've been so lucky..."

Murchadh forced himself to face the fact he had more than blood on his hands. Sound travels far - and farther still in a silent world. A boom of that magnitude must bounce from island to island, so doubtless the entire archipelago of the Alps would be within hearing distance of it. On top of which Samson had recently mentioned his fears of huge carrier ships, like complete floating worlds, lurking in the fog far out to sea and equipped with listening devices. If that were true he had as good as told them where their mountain was and that it did support (or had supported, prior to the blast) human life. Making him a traitor as well as murderer.

Unless, by good fortune, they mistook the blast for a volcanic eruption... At least with the density of cloud around they could not spot the lack of débris jettisoned skyward that a real eruption would cause. So there was, surely, a slim chance they would never come to investigate. And that Samson was out to lunch with his theories. After all, he had believed in aliens and Layla, for starters.

They felt too bruised and shaken to move, so spent the night exactly where they were. Thus they had an unimpeded view of the arrival of Cormorant as he gently floated earthwards.

"A modernized animikii!" Murchadh's eyes widened in awe. "A symbol of something - only I've clean forgotten what! It's a mammoth responsibility to try 'n retain all the old wisdom of forefathers. In them olden days when people lived in communities, they could share knowledge and pool understanding. Some of 'em even wrote it down so's not to forget. How I wish my great great granps - or even batty old great great granma for that matter - were still alive and with us now. 'Cos I can't bloody remember if the sight of an animikii (or is it actually a wakinyan?) is good or bad news... Though I've a sneaky feeling it's of course bad."

"Looks bad. Why's he wearing that silvery outfit so the colours get swallowed by the mountain if he isn't being sneaky? And why that idiot mask - as if he's too refined to breathe our air?" She spat disgustedly, "He's a goddam punk with a superiority complex, and we'd better get praying he doesn't sniff us out."

Murchadh dozed fitfully, unable to settle on the sloping, stony ground, tossing and turning so that he inflamed the scratches on his back. He pulled his woven cape over his head in a futile attempt to blot out the radiation and the reality of what had happened - well, he should man up to it, what *he* had caused. Dynamite was not a Hunkpapa tool. It was handed down through the white-skinned Scottish branch of his family, which in truth was the main trunk of his bloodline (whereas his link to native American blood was the mere slenderest branch through his maternal great great grandmother). But, since she was worth more than the rest put together, her blood presumably had most power.

The woven patterns somehow worked their way into his brain and fed his dreams. Dreams in which a marauding flock of animikii flew down to roost on the rocky crags of a bowl-shaped canyon, and their piercing cries were unearthly sounds - like the screams of witches burned at the stake in the long distant past of human punishments. They smelt of death, hardly surprising since they threw back their sinewy necks whenever they swallowed the severed limbs of those killed by the dynamite blast, and the stinking gases from their revolting, death-lined stomachs were thus released. When jolted awake by the horror of it, he was relieved that the scream he thought he had emitted was only a silent one. It must have been, because Eartha was still peacefully asleep beside him.

It had nonetheless been a prophetic dream because when he looked towards his Capricorn ridge he saw that six more thunderbird-types had landed in the early morning. They were just setting off in different directions to explore their new playground.

Gently he nudged Eartha awake.

"Enemy on the prowl! They won't see us if we slide down to the old dry river bed, though my instinct cries out we ought to make for higher ground - but there's no time now."

"Who *are* these guys?" he whispered, a little later. "Damn 'em, I wish they'd go back where they effing came from."

"Well, that bang must have roused their interest somewhat."

"*My* fault they're here you mean. But they can go now, can't they? I don't hold with invading other people's land - I'll bet they have a distorted view of it, like all land-thieves always had. 'A land without a people for a people without a land', that stupid catch-phrase those latter day invader-types trotted out to justify their theft, yet even with the puny population in the current world there's probably barely a single island left uninhabited by someone. Or, they pretended their God had given it to them as a homeland, or that they'd once lived there thousands of years into the past and needed to reclaim it! Yet did the native Americans ever get their land back? No Sireeeee!"

"Well," Eartha said thoughtfully, "we only just got here ourselves. I hope you're not starting to think and act like the place belongs to you. What about that cowboy - this time around, he got here first!"

"Bloody women!" Murchadh muttered irritably. "Never let a man get worked up into a lather - always wanting to tone it down."

"It's a time for caution, Murchadh. You'll see."

Fin felt equally guilty. He should have exerted firmer control over Zin instead of letting him pursue his own madcap agenda. And even if he did nothing else, he should have expressly forbidden him 'spying'. Poor mite could not possibly have survived being smack in the bull's eye of the explosion; last time he looked, Zin was sprawled atop the actual rock that blew up, and that rock sure as hell did not exist anymore. Bloody bitch must have been some kinda suicide bomber, but venting anger onto her did nothing to diminish his misery. Because he was a goddam traitor to his own family. It was as if his darkest subconscious wish had been interpreted in the most vicious way possible. There he was, happily lauding the virtues of Bernina while having a moan to himself about Hon, almost wishing something bad onto her (but only something minor) when suddenly all hell breaks loose and terra firma explodes!

How he escaped being crushed by the imploding cave walls and the collapsing roof was a total *no comprende* thing, and had Bernina not chosen that exact minute to slip her lovely slender form behind the gashed recess she would have been crushed to a pulp along with everyone else.

He must not dwell on such images. He must blot them out or he might start howling aloud his misery like a chained hounddog. All his littl'uns, poor wee cherubs, crushed under tons of fallen rock and so thoroughly buried that he could not begin to search for them - even if he still had two good arms, which was not the case.

His wrist was swollen like a puffball, yet he felt so numbed by shock and the ache in his heart that all pain was nullified. Poor Bernina sat vacantly staring at the slanted slabs of rock that had fallen every which way, shocked, speechless, and motionless.

Then they heard it. A tiny sound, like an olden-day mouse creeping surreptitiously behind wainscoting. Then the faintest moan imaginable, quieter than his rasped breathing, just loud enough to give him a clue to its location.

"Is that you, poppet? Tell papa where you are!" he cried, hardly daring to expect an answer.

"Here," came a whimpered response, immediately recognizable as his youngest baby girl, Lhotse.

"Daddy can't see you yet sweetie, but I sure am comin'!" he yelled. "Comin' right away!"

Bernina emerged instantly from her zombie-like state. She sprang across the new arrangement of rocks - piled like a giant's game of spillikins - and began to tug at one the size of a Stonehenge upright. It refused to budge even a millimetre, but she kept at it, rocking gently from foot to foot to give herself the illusion of something moving.

"Speak again sweetie, it's the only way we can find out exactly where you are. Once we know that, we can shift the right rocks and get you out," her voice trembled with the effort of sounding optimistic, as if what she suggested was the simplest procedure possible.

"Here!" Lhotse sounded indignant, as though they were dragging their heels and ruining the spontaneity of her game of hide and seek. "Down here you dummies!"

Hours later they were still straining to shift the same massive slab, their hair matted with sweat and their faces haunted with the horror of failure. But throughout that time they had heard nothing more from Lhotse, and no longer needed to invent soothing lies of imminent rescue.

Fin had strained every sinew to breaking point so that his body shook with exhaustion. Eventually though, he resigned himself to the impossibility of rescuing Lhotse and began, instead, to pray that she had simply fallen asleep and died peacefully, spared being frightened of the dark, the pain, her loneliness or death itself.

Pre-GD people had expected to live, and live until a ripe old age, like sixty years or more - some even made it to a hundred. But not now. Now, death was prevalent, life the rare exception. Lhotse wouldn't have been thinking like that because she was too little, but she knew about death. Both Bernina's babies had died, and Holg had too, very recently. She wouldn't have been afraid to die - he clasped onto that as a solitary crumb of comfort.

Then he kicked the rock with vicious fury. He hated it for its hard, soulless intractability, and fervently wished that trees still graced the landscape with their beauty, their changeable qualities of growth and their seasonal shifts in colour or foliage, not to mention the wonderful texture and resinous smell of felled wood which you can saw, carve or chisel. Wood was beautiful and alive. In times past you could even burn it for a glow of warmth, or to cook a juicy hunk of meat on.

He had always detested rock. But never so bitterly as now.

The clouds did not precisely part. But they again proved themselves porous when the six silvery, phantom-like shapes that Murchadh saw floated down, passing through them as easily as a hand can carve a path through air - without any bruising from the impact.

Motte looked upwards when she heard a faint hum or hiss of air from that direction, and her first glimpse of the six silvery forms, which due to the nature of the silvery material they wore looked transparent, made her initially assume that dust particles still floated in the air after the explosion, and this explained the strange vision.

Her mother used to say humans once toyed with strange concepts of what lurked above the cloud barrier: black holes, supernovas, and dead or dying stars - which they believed occupied the outer space area of the universe. But throughout man's history he had changed his view of the universe so many times it was obvious to Motte that he never did - and probably never would - get it right.

As a child she considered even the idea of invisible lumps like the sun, moon, stars, and meteors weird enough. Early man had been so inspired by their moving in perfectly precise paths that he had called them gods (plural for some, singular for others), or else the shining spirits of his dead ancestors. Having buried her mother, however, she knew a dead body went into the earth, but she had always liked the idea that a person's invisible essence, which some called their soul, escaped to float away. It gave her the comforting notion that her world was not so limited and prison-like as it seemed.

But now, the idea of enemies living up above the cloud barrier, able to pass through it at will in either direction, was truly horrifying.

She rubbed her eyes (not an easy operation wearing marmot pelts) and looked again. They were still there, closer, closer with every second, and gaining in size as they approached - proving they were real because they obeyed the laws of perspective. Unlike eagles, their wings were not fixed to their shoulder blades but floated like unfurled umbrellas above their heads. All six landed neatly upright, so gently they barely needed to flex their knees to cushion the impact. And no sooner had they landed than all six reached into their right breast pockets, withdrew their shiny radio transmitters, and in unison barked:

"Condor 6 to Alpha Ipsilon, Condor 6 to Alpha Ipsilon, can you hear me?"

"Nah, it's no echo man - we're all jamming together! I'll get t'others to turn off and I'll yap solo. Simpler, don't want to confuse yer mate."

"Right, me on me tod now. Well, what can I say? Landed safe and sound, not yet linked up with Cormorant but I can see his ugly mug a bit downhill from where we are, sound asleep! No sign of other life at the mo. What a flight we had - seriously hairy to begin with! Speak soon. Over and out."

Their leader, self-appointed it would seem, pocketed his transmitter and slapped hands in celebratory fashion with the other five. Whereas Cormorant had been wary these lot exuded confidence, but that was natural enough because he was the pioneer, and the fact he had already survived for more than twelve hours without mishap showed the place must be benign.

"A word in your shell-likes before we explore and assess. Directive is to take stock of all current amenities and the potential to start cleansing from here. If we come across life forms - animal or human - then no killing, apparently. Capture's the aim - unless they put up a fight of course, in which case no holes barred! Use your Taser 309s.

If there are any primitives still alive they'll be valuable as gold dust. They'll know how to survive in this god-awful, inhospitable place, plus where to find best sources of food and water. And, vitally, they'll have inbuilt immunity to the radiation, viruses and what-not which we'll have to extract by transference. Got it cozes? Rightyho, let's meet back here at," he (or she, for at this stage the voice had become quite trebly) consulted a gadget on the pad of his/her little finger, "17.08, 250 PGD, OK?"

They wore chunky boots with chubby, caterpillar-grip soles that enabled them to walk over rocks as effortlessly as tread on air, but deprived them of sensitivity to the ground underfoot, so they would fail to pick up on its vibrations. There could be an earth tremor and they would trundle on, oblivious. Cormorant's suit inflating into an airbed had already suggested these sky-invaders liked their creature comforts, now the boots confirmed it. Motte hoped this might prove their weakness - and they must have the feeblest lungs if they could not breathe without masks.

It was encouraging that they had orders not to kill on sight, but 'potential to start cleansing', 'capture', 'Taser 309s' were less reassuring. Later on she and the man must discuss them, but for now she would focus on watching - and listening - especially to their conference so precisely booked for 17.08, 150 PGD.

They nudged Cormorant awake and all seven spread out across the terrain. They air-walked through the col, across the moraine (she noted with satisfaction that their boots struggled to gain purchase on the shale) around the lip of the crater, and over the flattened remains of Fin's former cave and the erstwhile enclosure for Mary-Lou's crops. Instead of seeing with their naked eyes they looked through a tiny object, which every now and then flashed like a bolt of lightning - or how Motte imagined lightning. Thunder, she knew, closely resembled the explosion.

Eventually they returned to their landing platform, a flattish area 300 metres below her burrow entrance. At that distance she could see them clearly, but because of the chameleon-like quality of their clothing they drifted in and out of visibility so, if she took her eyes off them even briefly, it was then a struggle to relocate them. Their reporting was part verbal, part a sharing of images on their viewers.

"There's a honeycomb warren of marmots all the way up to the ridge, but most're hibernating at the mo. Not much visible sustenance, yet they must tuck into something 'cos they sure-as-hell shit!"

"There's rows of maize corn, carrots and alfalfa planted recently. GM 2,000 type seeds, origin can't tell - but the seeds were harvested at least four years back. Dunno what that suggests, unless they can only manage a harvest in four year cycles."

"Approx 2 mil. cubic litres of water in an exposed deposit near the veg. allotment - a real tops A gold medal find. Rocks've been blown away, must be the blast we registered, so now it's open to air and needs re-covering. Water's clean."

"Human remains scattered far and wide from that mega-blast. Not a fun find - detached limbs, severed heads and other puke-worthy stuff. Already part-feasted on by a beaked bird, prob. an eagle. We'll watch for its return, 'cos it'll def. return to finish off the scraps. I'm pining for my virgin taste of bird flesh - are we seriously not allowed to kill any wildlife?"

"No word on birds, so we could plead ambig. instructions. Veto's for mammals and humans, needed for medicinal and info. purposes. There's theories we might find cross-breeds, *revoltoso* animal-human cross-overs. And the humans'll be retrograde most likely. That ancient philosopher - Dali was it? Darwin? Perhaps Dionysus 'cos I think he was a Greek...or maybe a Brit, and poss. an anthropologer not a philosopher... Anyway, he'd've been right chuffed to find them!"

"Take a squint at this! Buffalo-hide according to my attributor, and buffaloes've been extinct since way, way back. What's more, they only ever existed on one continent, North Amurka if I'm right, or poss. Vietnam - can't rightly recall. Either way it's a jewel discovery."

Motte reluctantly tore herself away from their conference because the man was thumping like a buck marmot on the tunnel wall behind her, desperate to gain her attention. He worked through the entire gamut of persuasive tactics to bend her will into allowing him a sight of the outside, but she held firm. Whilst his chip stayed put, so must he, because his incomprehensible 'desuetude' argument (who knows what *that* meant) was not even flimsily convincing. His eyes alternately flashed and pleaded, but without resorting to physical force he was powerless. For the moment, at least.

Cormorant was last to join the group. The others seemed to share a buddy understanding but he, perhaps by nature, perhaps design, appeared to operate as an individual. He climbed slowly, taking care not to jolt something very delicately cradled in his arms.

"Got a semi-live one! A young primitive, male I *think* but too mashed up to be sure. Runty thing, malnourished and skinny as an antennae. On the way out too - just the faintest pulse poss., which when you tally the degree of damage it's suffered is no surprise. Primitives must be physically beef even if mentally rabbit. Take a look - burnt back, multiple fractured ribs, no legs below knees and mere stumps above. Plus the face's been rearranged unless that's their normal placement of ugly features - yet still breathing! Did you guys bring medical correctives?"

"Yeah, but basics only. Anaesthetics, soft and hard tissue transplanters, skingraft wraps, infra-red tectiles - that kind of Premier Aid stuff but nothing that needs an operating theatre. I could patch it up better than the original if you think it's worth the bother. If it can talk afterwards - that'd justify the op., but we know effing zero about their lingo capabilities. At least we've got some truth enforcement posses., should they happen to speak in proper, joined-up prose!"

"If it wasn't so subhuman, I'd almost feel sorry for it. But 'those not with us are against us', as the maxim goes. D'you want the medi-pod inflated?"

"Whenever you're ready coz."

It could only be Zin. Motte felt torn between fear and empathy. She had somehow always recognised him as her nemesis - but, le pauvre petit was still only a child.

10

"He should grunt," was the man's suggestion. "That's all they expect from a primitive. Then they'll soon give up, I know these types - no patience."

"How do they 'enforce' the truth? Les drogues?"

"No. Or…it depends. They usually measure pupil dilation (that's that black dot in your eye) and the smell and consistency of sweat, and …certain reflexes. It's an elementary, non-invasive process."

They laid his battered, truncated body on a silver sheet while they prepared the operating theatre inside their medipod. He was deeply unconscious, she could tell. Perhaps a rescue plan would miraculously occur to her, but it must wait until after their medical intervention, since his injuries were far too grave for mere moss to mend. In the world she inhabited, he would never survive.

"Are they space travellers from another planet?" she asked, wide eyed in spite of her aversion to the threat they posed. "Did men *really* walk on the moon?"

"Like everything from the past," he sighed, "we have no idea what was true. Some say men flew to Mars and back, even that a pioneering group spent sixty trial years on the moon (preparing for the GD, perhaps), but others - whom I trust more - maintain that entire narrative was bullshit. Pure propaganda, promoting a scientific brilliance they didn't yet have; and a useful ruse to siphon off huge sums of money from a gullible populace, on the pretext of needing it to win a non-existent 'space race'. One counter-theory claims no human or computerized equipment could possibly pass through the Van Allen belt without being radiated, fried to a charred crisp, and thus all so-called 'space journeys' were in reality nothing beyond a little jaunt in orbit around the earth, outside earth's atmosphere, but safely inside the Van Allen belt.

This lot, though… Well, my gut feeling says they're from somewhere pretty close to earth."

Motte's mind, bewildered by this plethora of indigestible words and ideas, slipped thankfully away into a private reverie...

Her mother always maintained that the reason human intelligence progressed so very slowly (if indeed it progressed at all) was due to its obsession with seeking unnecessary answers to totally unnecessary questions. Far too much time was wasted arguing about: How did the world begin? How will it end? What's the purpose of life?

These three questions were fought over by three distinct factions. Motte could still, even now, recite what she was taught in parrot-fashion : First the scientists, who pretended to work with 'facts'; then the philosophers, who claimed to use 'logic'; and then the religionists, who decided to deal in 'belief'. It all flooded back to her like an old-time wave on an old-time ocean, although she might have remembered the sequence back to front - perhaps religion came first.

It was only when her mother had a pang of guilt about her (Motte) spending too much time with marmots, while she (Motte's mum) spent too much time trying to breed with different men, that she trotted out these awful educational lessons that were meant to widen Motte's horizons. There was a professor somewhere in their ancestry, supposedly, who had married someone linked to the Parc National de la Vanoise, and this was the reason - apart from assuaging her guilt - that prompted her mother to foster these academic studies.

As far as Motte remembered, the philosophers spent their time pursuing what they called knowledge by vacillating between two slightly different premises. And these were (in paraphrase):

1. Nothing can ever be proven to be either true or possible unless you can first prove it then disprove it. (Motte had tried to unravel this bizarre reasoning numerous times but never succeeded. It was the brainchild of some father figure called Poppa).

2. We might or might not exist at all, and thinking either proves or disproves our existence - plus an analogous parallel compares us to cows. This one (possibly the brainchild of a Berkeley-Hume collaboration) clearly made no sense whatsoever, but her mother insisted that that had been the whole point of philosophy. Motte was not a keen fan, except in the sense (or non-sense) that it was only a thought process and as such had never done excessive harm; not caused wars, disasters, diseases etc, and probably had no causal connection to the GD.

Not so the other two, science and religion. They were massively more dangerous and culpable because they did indeed try to make sense. They were not merely a thought process but actively attempted to mess with (as opposed to simply confuse) people's minds.

The scientists split from religion. This happened (of course) over the hugely controversial issue of how the world began, compounded by further heated disagreement over how the world would end, plus plenty of disagreement, naturally, over all the interim drama betwixt and between.

The scientists thought it began with a big bang. A giant explosion of heat and light with rocks flying into space and eventually cooling down, and gas and water also part of the whole kit and caboodle. It would end, inevitably, with a whimper - everything weakening, fading and slowing etc. into infinity (or was it oblivion?)

These eager-beaver scientists spent the major chunk of their time peering at tiny things through microscopes, or staring at distant things through telescopes. None knew what the ultimate purpose of it all was, and it was precisely this lack of macro-understanding that prompted some to return to the religious fold, admitting that there might be some kind of unseen, unknown power behind all that mysterious complexity. (They called their ideas theories, eg. The theory of evolution, the theory of relativity and the chaos theory). Of course, the language of 'unseen' and 'mysterious' was bang central to the mindset of religion, that being the precise reason certain scientists scurried back.

The religionists were divided into so many groups that they were really difficult to quantify (which might/ might not be an apposite word, because from the lexicon of philosophy). None agreed on much, although you could simultaneously argue they all totally agreed with each other, since they all borrowed (or stole) each others' stories. Any, or none of them, might therefore be right. They particularly squabbled - just like the scientists - over how the world began and how it would end.

Religionists quarreled using fancy words like creation, immaculate conception, crucifixion (not to be confused with fiction - unless you were a non-believer), revelation, heaven, hell, limbo, paradise, theology, meditation, prayer, yoga, kamasutra, reincarnation, and of course the primary one : God. Some had several gods, including animals and women, while others were happy just with the one. If they only had one it was usually male, and very occasionally merely a spirit - which had to be called 'it' because of non-indulgence in sex (except in other people's dreams).

This religion thing was far more dangerous than philosophy because people became exceedingly heated over it. They even killed and died because of it, demonstrating it was used as a fig leaf (what did her mother mean by that?). And this necessitated the introduction of a whole new grammar: infidel, chosen, bible, torah torah, holy war, shaman, yahweh, insurrection, blasphemy, infant sacrifice, purgatory, sin, conversion, gaia, goyim, gurus, holocaust, anti-semitic, inquisition, democracy, terrorism, suicide bomber, all the hallmarks of al quaida, and, of course, invasion.

Religionists dressed up whereas philosophers and scientists tended to dress down, trying to blend in with the masses. In fact, the religionists did their level best to look eccentric, plagiarising magicians with their wardrobes and fashion accessories: black cloaks, goblets, crosses, yamulkas, wimples, menorahs, skull caps, togas etc. for the sole reason they abhorred blending in. Au contraire, they aimed to be respected, feared and revered - otherwise they risked failing to convince their audience (sometimes called flock, as in sheep or bird, because humans assumed birds and sheep followed the leader without thinking.)

Eh bien, perhaps that's the intended lesson, Motte deduced, finally snapping out of her pupil-recall session. To warn me not to behave foolishly, like a flock, as in blindly following a leader. Is the man trying to be my leader?

"Now that my strength and...well, not yet my virility...seems to be returning, it's time I told you..."

"Pas besoin," she interrupted irritably, "You already have. You're not attracted by my claws. 'Men can't do it unless they want to,'" she mimicked him using an exaggerated nasal whine.

His voice grew thick and heavy. "It's not...that. I told you, if you remember, that my co-conspirators were killed. What I didn't say was...," he made a determined effort to clear the sudden lump from his throat, "one of them was my...my partner, my wife if you like. And of course they killed both our children too, to underline our monstrous error in defying their absolute authority." His voice became bitter and he swallowed painfully. "I should have told you this sooner - not led you into thinking it was just a personal issue with you. I know that."

Motte stared at him in stunned silence. His emotion was so palpably genuine this time that she felt deeply ashamed of her former niggardly suspicions.

Cormorant kept a slightly different routine to the others. He slept near them but not amongst them, and performed his daily tasks - reconnoitering, scanning, eating, abluting etc. a few minutes ahead of their synchronized schedule.

On this occasion he stood up while they continued their siesta and immediately activated his radio.

"Cormorant to Alpha Ipsilon, Cormorant to Alpha Ipsilon, can you hear me?"

Only on the third attempt did he link up with his base (or space station, cloud city, whatever it was).

"At bloody last! Signal's patchier now and you got me worried. Anyways, today's update: still but one primitive in custody, not a useful one either, owing to dire and hideous injuries which we've yet to repair. It should improve post-op - if it doesn't die in course of.

We've now picked out possible caches of others but nothing confirmed - only low range oscillations. Both sexes it seems - and boy-oh-boy could we use some female action! But no full penetration, of course - they must be crawling with diseases owing to total sanitation lack! But onto more imp. matters…exposed hydro source is currently fenced off, but suspected other major source detected on master scanner still stays elusive, dammit, - yet shouldn't be long before we locate it."

"No mate, not a twitchy. Signal's fading. Gotta go. Over 'n out."

The other six began to stir. Lurching to their feet, they fumbled for their scanners. Even though Cormorant had arrived before them he was evidently wearing a superior mask or was physiologically stronger, because they (but not he) were increasingly showing signs of maladaption. Perhaps their oxygen supply had depleted faster, or they were suffering more from the altitude - certainly their movements were less fluent than before. Motte noticed a mist blurring the inside of their masks which must surely cloud their vision, but the man told her it was merely the moisture in their breath.

Releasing the reservoir water *could* be beneficial. It might change the micro-climate, he now suggested - even to the point of bringing the miracle of rain. Then straight away he threw doubts on this idea, admitting he knew nothing of weather patterns, claiming the idea would never work in any case because of something called a 'coriolis effect'. If she understood his explanation properly, it meant that because the earth itself was moving, the rain would inevitably fall elsewhere, instead of back onto them.

Motte spent the remaining darkness-hours crouching at the mouth of the burrow, waiting for the moment to carry out her rescue raid. The man suspected their scanners were kinetically powered, so the ideal time to strike would be just prior to them waking, when the power was at its lowest ebb.

Zin's injured body, post operation, lay folded into a kind of bubble capsule to the right of the still sleeping spacemen. This meant he would be easier to carry - providing the bubble weighed next to nothing, otherwise she would struggle to shoulder his weight, despite his thin, under-nourished frame and horrifyingly truncated limbs. She could not risk dragging him like she had the wounded man because the scraping noise would betray them.

She had only moved a few paces when a blinding streak of light pierced the clouds, pinpointing the skymen encampment with spot-on accuracy. Had her gaze not been focused on the ground it would have burnt her retina, but luckily she was merely dazzled by a succession of white, pink, lilac, green and blue flames licking at the lashes of her tightly squeezed eyelids. The flickering lights were a malignant version of the colours she sometimes saw in her dreams. And the multi-colours illusory because the light was purely blue.

Robbed of her powerful night vision she crawled back to the burrow, groping blindly with outstretched, trembling fingers.

"Laser weaponry," the man opined grimly. "Or plasma, or maybe even particle beam - classifying military weapons was never my thing. But I'm surprised the cloud barrier didn't misdirect it by 'blooming' and I thought the technology for it was discontinued years ago. Well, that's what we were told... Seems somebody out there doesn't like our new spacemen friends. I wonder who. Did it kill them all?"

"I don't know. After the flash I couldn't see anything - and still can't. This blindness better not be permanent... I don't regret their deaths, but *why* didn't I rescue Zin earlier?"

"You had no opportunity to. And, realistically, what possible chance did he have with such chronic injuries?"

"I could've said the same about you."

He grunted. "You'd been alone for so long. Probably the novelty of human company persuaded you to give it a try."

"I gave it much more than a try."

"I know, I know. I *am* trying to earn my reprieve by being useful. So, either we have a new enemy out there, with greater armed sophistication. Or the weapon was launched by their 'superiors', because they'd served their purpose and their time was up. Perhaps they were just too hopelessly slow finding the water, or..."

"Murder, you mean? Friends killing friends?" She was perplexed.

"Of course. It happened often in so-called advanced societies. Where I'm from, it was the norm. Why else did I escape? I don't know why you're surprised - you've told me your mother was even prone to the odd murder, convenience driven."

"Survival driven."

"Well, that'd be their justification, had they ever needed one. Murder's easy to pass off as suicide or natural death, and heart attacks were a favourite method. Simulated with a miniature laser charge, an electrode, radiation… Don't get me started - I could go on and on."

11

Murchadh shielded his eyes from the blinding laser beam, his expression one of ecstasy mingled with pain. His previous blathering about the animikii (or was it Wakinyan?) had come with a strong dose of wishful thinking, but this was surely the real deal! Genuine animikii behaviour: a bright blue lightning flash so powerful no cloud barrier could obstruct it, then deafening thunder claps worthy of that old Greek madcap, Zeus himself.

The fact that no thunder rumbled failed to dent his soaring spirits or cause him one iota of doubt. If he were younger he would have danced in celebration; instead, he groped for his peace pipe in the deep recesses of his leather trouser pocket. It gave no more real comfort than a baby's dummy or placebo drug, seeing as no hallucinogen or potent leaf of any sort had been lit there since his great great great grandma, Nahimana, had been a teenager - when smoking was still hip. Family lore told that her second son, Macawi, had grown some lethal, hydroponic stuff in the empty basement of a terraced house in Glasgow, during the cushy era when electricity was commonplace, and running water taken for granted.

But the dwindling supplies ran out more than a century ago, since when the faint seductive smell in the pipe bowl (it was a family heirloom, like the dynamite) had truly faded into extinction. Yet he still enjoyed puffing it, and his mind still wandered into areas of extraordinary delight, so that during these brief moments his faith in the Wakan Tanka was almost restored, and he could halfway imagine meeting a proper Wakanpi.

The first thing to temper these idiotic feelings of euphoria was the sight of his bête-noir, the cowboy, stomping towards the col like a man demented. Although the man's cowboy accessories (he wore some form of grungy leather chaps) were a serious turn-off, Murchadh felt tentative admiration for him in this wildly delirious state, because Sioux teachings equated madness with spirituality. He therefore decided to approach and exchange greetings. After all, some white Americans were a cut above total trash, and Wovoka had always advocated making peace with white folk. And, to tell *tha honest trooth*, he himself was more Scot than Sioux!

Eartha was still blissfully asleep. It would be sheer cruelty to wake her, so he thoughtfully flipped his share of the torn, blood-bespattered, Hunkpapa cape over her and began to climb the dry stream bed.

Pre-GD, he reflected, most humans had lived collectively in gargantuan cities - consequently they had been easily wiped out. Nowadays, the paltry few survivors were the misfits and odd-balls; they alone were capable of living in isolation, lying low, being stealthy and keeping quiet. (Not to mention the obvious fact that their ancestors must have been either high mountain dwellers in the first place, or high on a high peak at the hour and day when the GD struck).

Sadly his dynamite had now broken the carefully nurtured silence and caused deaths. Since it was his fault, he must make amends. And, just possibly, renewed collaboration might be the answer…

His progress was terribly slow. The altitude made breathing a struggle - and sucking on his peace pipe had certainly not helped. Soon the rasping, whistling complaints from his clogged windpipe forced him to rest, whereupon he began to reflect on the former wonders of the universe.

Firstly he contemplated the mystery of circles. Everything that mattered was a circle, according to ancient Sioux wisdom. The sun, moon, earth, seeds, egg yolks, tree trunks, wombs, women's breasts, birds' nests, the perpetual circle of life and death, and - especially designed to emulate all these magically rounded things - the circular tipi.

This current landscape, however, was obdurately linear. Not a single circle - not even a bird's nest (the eagle's eyrie must be discounted owing to its scruffy shapelessness). No wonder everything was in such an alarming state of decay.

He sighed wistfully. Circles were not the solution. Even though the earth must still be rotating and revolving in a roughly circular (OK elliptical) path or nothing would be functioning at all, even badly like it did. Or could its revolutions have gone askew because it *was* no longer round (or roundish), so that instead of spinning in its historical position viz-à-viz the sun and moon, it was now careering off through space into unknown territory?

Abandoning circles, he progressed to musing over the magic Sioux numbers. Four and seven. Four : four seasons; four winds - north, south, east and west; four parts to living plants - roots, stem, leaves and fruit; four stages to a twenty four hour day, and to human life itself (though Shakespeare for some daft reason decided it was seven!). Aha seven: hmmm, that was harder.

Seven…days of the week, deadly sins, White Buffalo Woman's seven sacred rites… Stumped for more examples he moved hurriedly on to the most important number, the sum of both sacred numbers: twenty eight. The lunar month, the menstrual cycle, linked marvelously to the ocean tides…

His exuberance, which had begun to mount again, suddenly checked, fell back - and this time its deflation was terminal. Who'm I kidding, he demanded angrily, spitting a disgusted globule of phlegm onto the threadbare toe of his ancient, worn out moccasin. I don't believe these things, not deep down, so why'm I clutching at a faith best left shrouded in the mists of the past, that was never truly mine in the first place? The native Americans expressly warned white man not to abuse the rivers, forests and plains, and not to slaughter the sacred buffalo, or the balance of nature would be lost for ever. And it has been. They didn't bloody listen.

So how could the spirits of the former world exist in this one? Who am I fooling when I cheer myself up with idiotic visions of screeching animikii and rampant capricorn? Get real Murchadh, you're a stupid old man stuck up shit creek. You'd get yourself blind drunk down the local pub to escape reality if you only had that chance, which is the very fate those white men foisted onto the native Americans, what with their humiliating stamps only redeemable in thieving reservation liquor stores.

Perhaps that cowboy has the right idea; no false spirituality nonsense, and no stupid stiff upper lip either. Just run around, angrily kicking at rocks like a loony.

Motte could tell where the man was from the sounds he made: the gentle shallow breathing; the soft knocking of heart against ribs; the licking of moistened tongue against teeth. Then of course a faint whiff of what was almost, now, an agreeable smell. But she could not see him. She was still blind.

He said she must not panic - her blindness would be temporary. Apparently many a rich, reckless person suffered this impairment back in the snow-days. When the sun glittered brightly on the ice crystals, and they forewent the wearing of designer sunglasses lest the evenness of their suntans be compromised, they, too, were afflicted with the dreaded 'snow blindness'. And invariably recovered within a day or two.

Same thing after watching eclipses of the sun without a smoked glass lens (but this affliction hit the awestruck poor more than the rich and reckless). Her eyes, he told her, due to living in perma-twilight and being adjusted to see in what was total darkness to any normal mortal, were bound to react adversely to any strong light stimulus. He, after being subjected to so many forms of artificial light, would be less vulnerable.

"Perhaps now's the time to introduce the tender arts of love making, since you're stuck in the burrow until you recover your sight. And it used to be said that love is blind."

"Mais qu'est ce que tu dis?" she gasped, aghast. "I thought you wouldn't, couldn't, and… Why now?"

"Don't get me wrong - *I* won't be involved. I'm not suggesting mating! Just for you to learn the basics about your own body. After all, those of us who lived communally, well, we exchanged what facts and wild rumours we picked up, then we experimented. Whereas you, from being alone and always wearing animal hides, totally missed out."

"Mon dieu! I may not know my body but I think I know my mind! Anyway, isn't it natural and instinctive? I'm sure animals don't get instructions, or practice sessions - nor need to talk about it beforehand."

"What sort of parallel is that? Animals don't talk as we know it anyway - whatever the circumstances."

"They communicate. They just don't waste words."

"OK. It makes no difference to me. I had the best of intentions - to distract you from your blindness at a time when your other senses must surely be heightened. It wasn't meant to benefit me."

She closed her blinded eyes so as to better relive those moments during childhood when she might have felt emotion, or might have wondered about sex; not that her mother ever suggested there was a correlation between the two.

The only emotion she could clearly remember was fear. Connected, pas besoin de le dire, to her mother. Fear of losing her; fear of being trapped forever with her. A longing for greater closeness; a longing to never see her again. She had briefly believed she loved her half-brother, but always knew he felt nothing for her - apart, ultimately, from a slither of guilt at abandoning her. Perhaps she had only grown hard afterwards, from living alone.

Lured by the seductive smell of dampness and the need to escape her burrow lest the man challenge her again to self-explore, she groped along the tunnel towards the main reservoir. Presumably, now that Cormorant and Co. were dead, their planned 'cleansing operations' would be cancelled. Unless, of course, they had been murdered by their superiors as the man suggested. In which case they might go ahead regardless. The idea heightened her wariness, so she frequently paused to listen for unfamiliar sounds.

Perhaps she had exaggerated in her own mind how much she could normally see on this route, because being blind made very little difference to her bearings.

It was only when she noted the acoustic change from tunnel to high vaulted cavern that she realized her eyesight had actually returned. What she saw, though, was so strange... In the distance, beyond the gleaming sheen of dark wet rock and the shimmer of its watery reflection, crouched a small, naked, baby-like figure with such milky, alabaster white skin that it was almost luminous, and such ash-blond hair it seemed made of thistle fluff.

It must be an ethereal being, she thought at first, or a ghost. It looked exactly how she had always imagined the fairy characters in the bedtime stories her mother recounted (very infrequently), the cringingly sentimental ones where every alpine flower had a fairy buddy who wore its petals as a pleated skirt, and spent all its useless life sprinkling magic pollen on the ground to make unhappy children dance.

Motte hated those stories with a vengeance. They meant her mother had sunk into a depression that might last for days if not weeks, and they concealed a message too - don't you dare pick those genepi flowers without my permission, or their fairy buddies will exact a horrible revenge.

She approached the creature walking upright. It looked sweet, innocent and frail - but looks can deceive. It was a female fairy, squatting on its haunches as if the man had planted it there for the sole purpose of giving Motte a graphically diagrammatic lesson on female genitalia, so carefully defined were they in their strangely swollen state against the darkness of rock.

It was only when she drew close that she realized her ridiculous, fanciful mistake... She was looking at a child she had met before! Lhotse, Fin and Hon's youngest girl who was probably four, or five at most. She stared at Motte with huge, haunted, disbelieving eyes. Both seemed to share the self-same thought - that this was a mystical meeting, on some mythical river or lakeshore separating life from death, where you waited for the ferryman to cruise in and forcibly make you embark. He was called Charon, Motte seemed to remember.

She noticed a shoal of bubbles effervescing beneath the surface of the water, and suddenly grabbed Lhotse's shoulders lest she be snatched into the watery depths. The child gave a soundless cry of terror when she saw Motte's claws brush her skin. Then her body slumped limply, her eyes closed, and her mouth blew pulsating kisses that were not affectionate or even kisses but really a desperate gulping for air.

Motte walked for as far as the high rock ceiling allowed, but once she re-entered her burrow tunnel was forced into her habitual loping marmot stride, carrying the dead weight of an unconscious Lhotse clamped against her chest. The burden grew heavier with every step, yet she dared not tighten her grip for fear of suffocating Lhotse in marmot fur.

"*What…?!*"

"I found her by the reservoir. I know what you're thinking - that's she's an alien child from outerspace planted there as bait, but I swear that's not so. She's Hon's littlest girl. She must have crawled there through one of the narrow marmot tunnels. She was conscious when I found her, but then…she fainted."

"You'd best rest your arm. I'll hold her. I've more practice at comforting little girls."

Before Motte could reply he took Lhotse in his arms, murmuring some kind of nursery nonsense that sounded reassuring, but was neither French, nor English, nor anything she understood. It seemed ironic that there she was, desperate for a child and he abhorrent of the very idea; yet she had handled Lhotse fearfully, whereas he held her tenderly, naturally, and their mutual bonding was clear to see.

Murchadh noticed that the cowboy had at last stopped kicking rocks. He now sat with his head sunk in his huge hands, a picture of grief. The important thing for he himself, right now, was to avoid schadenfreude at all costs. No gloating. No truck with his erstwhile wish to see a grieving cowboy. This guy was no Custer, nor he anyone to be proud of, least of all Thathanka Iyotake (Sitting Bull in white man's talk). He must show compassion. Feel it in his heart to forgive.

He struggled purposefully up the rocky slope and laid a comforting hand on the man's shuddering shoulders.

"Brace up mate!" he urged cheerfully, "nothing's as bad as it seems. It's usually ten times worse!"

"Thanks for the sympathy man, but it's the very worst it could be. The wife and littluns all dead 'n gone, crushed under them rocks. Whoever set off that goddam bomb needs a megablast up his ass. I've never killed no-one, but I could strangle that guy with my bare hands."

"Och yes, well…That Layla's dead already, so there's no-one to take yer vengeance on. Damn fool chit of a girl."

"Well, wasn't she with you though? I saw the five of you arrive. Group responsibility, huh? Why's it just *her* fault?"

"'Cause no-one else knew she had a bomb, did they?"

"Oh," Fin sighed, his anger snuffed more easily than his sorrow. "Any male survivors 'part from you? I need a mighty strong hand to shift some boulders…"

"Na, 'fraid not. Young Samson's a goner, so it's just me an' Eartha. On account of me bad back, lungs and gammy leg I'm not what I was at lifting weights. Eartha's a powerhouse though."

Fin calculated the density of the slab which he and Bernina had failed to move, then shook his head. "No matter. Lost cause I guess," and his head promptly sunk back dejectedly into the bowl of his clasped hands.

12

Motte clambered down to the lip of the glacier, where the rocks retained a vestigial memory of their frozen past and reacted more sensitively to atmospheric fluctuations. They were her faithful barometer.

Mingled smells of rock, earth and stunted bush hung in the cloud-heavy air, while faint stirrings of sleepy marmots flickered the stillness with an almost inaudible subterranean murmur. Overlaying these subtle sounds were occasional stronger ones: the creaking of a rock reacting to the fading shock waves of the explosion and intermittent tremors from human feet, hands and quiet tongues. Evidence that others had survived the blast was clearly audible now that the seething, whirling dust of the explosion had settled and she could move freely again because the skymen were dead. The comparative peace was unlikely to last, but it was a welcome respite.

She found Bernina first, sitting cross-legged where the gateway to Fin's stockade had been obliterated. Her eyes were tightly closed and her twitching hands rested palm upwards on her knees as if in supplication.

"Fin?" But when the ensuing silence informed her it was not, her eyes snapped open in alarm. "Oh, you…!"

"I came to see who survived. I didn't mean to startle you."

Bernina groaned, "There's just me and Fin left, and it might be my fault… He kinda *wanted* Hon to die, y'see, in the back of his mind. And all the kids got killed too, poor li'l mites. I'm thinkin' it musta been God's wrath all because of me, or maybe Merv..."

"Mais non," Motte assured her. "That blast was a manmade thing."

Bernina jumped to her feet in renewed alarm. "Then where's Fin now? I just had this horrenderest nightmare he got killed too, that that old injun' fella from the tipi slit his throat in one great gash… Oh we never shoulda come here! Have…have you seen him anywheres?"

She seemed strangely elated, but Motte assumed shock must be the cause of it, not a murderous delight at the prospect of Fin dying. Reassuring Bernina that muted male voices could be heard near the col she set off to check whose they were, puzzled why Bernina, who had been a staunch believer in Mother Nature - calling her Gaia - before the blast, now suddenly seemed to rebelieve in God. Perhaps it was because God and explosions had prior association - being the two contradictory theories of how the world began.

Motte had, however, recently lost confidence in the Big Bang scenario because a rival argument fatally undermined it: 'Matter can neither be created nor destroyed, only transformed'. Well, if this 'matter' saying were true then a Big Bang could not possibly have begun everything (or anything), simply because there *never was* an actual beginning if this matter stuff had always existed, and always would! The man (who championed the 'matter' argument) kept insisting that the 'transform' element was absolutely key and what unriddled the riddle so to speak, but her doubts had taken root and refused to be easily satisfied.

Gradually her pace slowed and her gait lost its light-footed agility. A monstrous granite boulder of guilt weighed heavily on her, biting into her shoulders and bruising her conscience. There was no excuse to justify why she had kept it secret that Lhotse was alive and left Bernina to suffer unnecessarily. *Why* had she done this? Because she wanted, like a lowdown child-thief, to keep Lhotse for herself? Or because she wanted to use Lhotse as a tool to prise out more of the man's past?

Whatever the reason it was unforgivably cruel. If there was a God he would know, and assuredly punish her for this evil sin.

Murchadh began to delicately delve into Fin's earlier life to distract him from his misery. He learnt that an Alpinist great great great grandpa (who must have been a near-contemporary of his great great great gran from Glasgow - who had luckily not been in Glasgow when the GD struck, or his lineage would have ended there and then)... Hey, concentrate on Fin, Murchadh, not your *own* past!

Fin had a hazy memory of his childhood which he painted in an unrealistically favorable light, coasting quickly past adolescence to his romantic first meeting with Alpha, whom he immediately recognized as his made-in-heaven mate. They quickly settled into a boulder home (laboriously constructed by Fin) a short hop from his parents' boulder home (laboriously constructed by Fin's grandad) at the head of the former Moretratsch glacier. However Alpha was none too keen on the parents' eating habits, which were primarily animal kill but would stretch to human meat if serious hunger gnawed. Fin was intentionally vague about whether they deliberately killed their human prey or just took advantage when someone happened to expire. Alpha was mainly a berry eater, meat only an absolute last resort to avoid starvation. This caused considerable tension in the extended Fin family, and gradually he and Alpha saw less and less of Fin's parents.

Then came children, but at this stage in the narration he grew distressed again so Murchadh switched hurriedly from past, to present, to a fragile, potential future.

> "I propose a pact mate, a kinda loose arrangement of cooperation. I've got one or two skills, mainly premonition and planning, Eartha (that's me woman friend) has a million more, especially producing food from thin air and making me see sense. You - well you look a strong lad an' fer sure a dab-hand at stockades, and I know you've still got one woman left 'cos I'm the one with the ol' clairvoyance, eh? How about we combine our strengths and cancel out our weaknesses, as far as possible that is? How about that?"

> "Well gee-thanks. I don't reckon as Bernina'll have any objection to that kinda arrangement, but I guess I'd best ask her first, 'fore we shake hands on it. She's kinda shook up at the moment, but she'll come around."

Fin left to try to enthuse Bernina with the idea of collaboration, which he was hopeful was indeed what Murchadh had proposed. The reason he was unsure was the difficulty he had understanding him - partly on account of the whistling sound he emitted due to his shortage of teeth, and partly because of his strange, impenetrable accent. It had underlying elements of a Scots brogue, but plenty else besides.

Murchadh sat down to once more contemplate the universe, but must have fallen asleep. How else did he get talking to a thumping great marmot that had somehow crept up on him unawares, sat boldly beside him on its haunches and proceeded to discuss all the important issues of the day?

Beavers or marmots were not normally associated with visionary ideas or prophetic symbolism. That was the exclusive domain of eagles, wolves or elks; but when the world changes, so, perhaps, do the spirit-figures that co-exist with us, forming fateful links. This marmot chappie was a genuine breath of fresh air! Knew the mountain back to front and spoke a fount of good sense, in fact voiced all the positive plans that had been half formulating in his brain shortly before they got talking. Sort of crystallized his thoughts from fluid droplets to solid diamonds, so that he dreamt he was nodding in agreement to everything it suggested.

When it had gone he felt weak at the knees, shivery even. He had had mystical encounters before, of course he had, but never anything as intimate as being seated literally side by side. The closest he had been to such an animal-spirit before now was at least two hundred metres, whereas this time he had felt the warmth of its breath and smelt the living quality of its fur! Incredible!

Eartha did not seem to fully appreciate his euphoria. She faintly disappointed him at times like this, being too damn sensible and down to earth, too grounded in the practical, mundane side of life. Groundhogs are awful lazy come wintertime, she pointed out, and they invariably carry fleas. Their beaver brothers are good at buildings dams, granted - useful had there happened to be a gushing river in the immediate vicinity. They'd have made a great animal companion some two centuries ago. A little too late now though. And off she wandered to scrape off some lichen she had spotted growing on some rock, and damned if he didn't hear her softly singing 'Nothing so tasty as groundhog pie, groundhog pie, groundhog pie,' to the tune of 'Nothing so tasty as Lenten pie', which he had a hunch was a hit tune way back in William Shakespeare's day!

Motte wandered back towards the burrow entrance. Her reconnaissance trip had given her a glimmer of hope, which she clung to, desperately, as an antidote to her guilt. Four survivors, both sexes equally represented so a neat balance there, although no new male stud because the Murchadh character, now that she had seen him close up, was well past his prime, and no longer an attractive mating prospect by any stretch of anyone's imagination.

He had, however, eagerly agreed to all her conditions for peaceful co-existence. On top of which he had volunteered - without any prompting - to take on the physique and spirit of an eagle, and to fly above the clouds to spy out the enemy airship that must be anchored somewhere overhead, as well as overfly the entire area of the former Alps to check the lay of land and sea. In response to her private, unspoken doubts about his capability, he had assured her that the skill was in his blood.

Back inside her burrow, the man and Lhotse looked as happy as sand lizards sheltered in a sandstorm. He was rocking to and fro on hands and knees as

Lhotse's horse, while she was mounted gleefully astride him, giggling, smacking his behind and urging, 'Giddee up, faster, *faster*!"

When he noticed Motte he looked mildly shamefaced.

"I'm amusing her so's to keep the hunger pangs at bay."

Motte went wordlessly to her cache of dried ibex meat and her leather pouch of dried myrtle berries.

"Here," she said, "bon appetit, ma chérie."

But when she stretched out her arms towards Lhotse the child shrank back, shielding her eyes with her small hands.

Motte shrugged, discouraged, "She'd have died of starvation down there, if I hadn't found her."

"It's your claws, Motte. Any kid'd be scared. She'll've been fed stories of cruel, killer animals - mums still tell them, the habit persists despite no books anymore. Your mother did too, I'll bet."

Motte nodded. "But I'm not paring down my claws, just when a whole new spate of digging's needed to open up the blocked burrows, and maybe new routes that might become necessary. She'll have to learn not to be fussy."

"It's not 'fussy'. It's fear."

"Supposing…I had a child, my own child, would it cringe from me too?"

"It'd accept you because you'd be familiar from the beginning. You're not…pregnant for God's sake, are you?"

"Of course not! I was just wondering. It's just…well, I need my claws. They took ages to grow, hours and months of concentration."

He frowned. "Are you suggesting you *willed* them into existence? You weren't born with longer, stronger nails than the rest of us?"

She stared at him, astonished. "Of course I willed them! I might've had strong nails naturally, but I worked to improve them - with mind and diet. I've told you to do the same with your legs. You're not putting enough effort in."

"Hard as nails," he muttered with a resigned shrug.

Then he turned to Lhotse, pushed her gently in the stomach, whinnied and tossed his head defiantly.

"Horse tired of being ridden. Child rider too lazy. Horse want eat food with animal friend," and he crawled closer to Motte and snatched the piece of ibex meat with his teeth, not bothering to check whether Lhotse was even watching.

"Psychological games are nothing new to me," he whispered, "and I've been experimented on more than most," he added darkly.

Despite the fact that he grossly overacted: smacking his lips, chomping his teeth, making slurping sounds with his tongue, even belching and farting like a horse who had gobbled his grass too fast, Lhotse was easily fooled. After a short while her fingers splayed open and her wide open eyes could be seen peering curiously through them. Then she dropped her hands and sat quietly watching as Motte, a reluctant actor in this absurd pantomime, dropped berry after berry into the horse's gaping mouth. She disapproved of over-indulgence and pandering to a child's irrational fears, but the man seemed adamant he knew best.

"Don't be so harsh, Motte," he whispered. "She's only four or five and gone through traumas - a terrifying explosion, being lost underground, losing her parents. She might or might not realize they're dead, but she obviously knows they're not here. She *needs* an escape from reality. Go on, get on my back and I'll show you just how much stronger I am."

Motte had no choice but to accept his challenge - otherwise she would have felt obliged to confirm - or deny - his assumption that both parents were dead. Fortunately he had merely a vague knowledge of Fin's group and their respective names, so if one man and one woman had died he deduced they were Lhotse's parents. Added to which, he had no reason to suspect Motte would be so reprehensible as to keep a young child and her already grieving father apart, each thinking the other dead.

It was such a wicked deed Motte was herself astonished she had committed it. She hated and despised herself for it - but lacked the courage to face up to it. It was as if someone else, a manifestation of herself that she had never known before, had acted surreptitiously without her consent.

Later, she told herself. But with each passing moment her shame grew and it became progressively harder to admit to her deception.

Seated astride the man she could indeed feel that the muscles of his back were firmer. It was extraordinary how the awkward, deformed, shuffling invalid of such a short while ago had transformed into a crouching creature capable of supporting her weight.

"Giddee up," she cried, aping Lhotse who was watching in astonishment, "faster, faster!"

Suddenly she was catapulted sideways to bounce and roll over onto her back, the speed momentarily taking her breath away and spinning her thoughts into a whirl. She could hear Lhotse clapping excitedly in the background, then the man's triumphant face loomed over her.

"You OK? I threw you off onto your good shoulder, so I hope it didn't hurt."

"I'm not hurt, but why do that?"

"It's what wild horses do. They hate humans controlling them so they buck and throw them off. Now you can stop taunting me that I haven't tried to heal myself and regain my strength. I've some way to go, but I'm getting there…"

Motte sat in troubled silence, watching the man feed Lhotse. In a few hours her world had crumbled. One minute she had been climbing the shale towards her burrow entrance congratulating herself on her skill at uniting her little 'flock' of four; Murchadh, Eartha, Bernina and Fin, boastfully convinced she was Queen of the Mountain, the only one who knew the area inside out so held the key to their collective survival.

Next minute she had been dethroned, discarded. She had stolen a child who secretly knew she was an evil imposter, the man had suddenly reversed their positions of power and proved himself nobler and stronger than her (quite apart from his superior knowledge of the world). Both he and Lhotse shared something special, something which isolated and rejected her.

Even in her worst moments of lonesomeness she had not felt this depth of desolation. She had had the confidence, then, of being a moral person, a person with honour and self-respect.

But she had lost that now.

13

Some French words had seeped into the English language, Motte discovered. They were having what Fin called a 'Parley'; a mangled word in Motte's opinion, meaning (for him) a chat about what to do and how to do it. The venue for it astounded her even more because, prior to her slump into self-disgust and sudden loss of authority, she would never have allowed it. They were in her most secret, sacred location: the vaulted cavern of the reservoir. The man had chosen it on the grounds it had sufficient space for everyone to sit, plus the flecks of light mysteriously thrown up by the water provided a feeble, fitful glow. But she was unhappy with it.

Outside on the mountain would equally have been a venue of comfort and visibility, but out of the question due to the triple dangers of radiation, airborne invasion and observation by satellite. She did accept that rationale.

Lhotse was the sole absentee. She had been left in the burrow, happily playing with the strips of ibex hide that were waiting to be sewn into leather bags to hold berries, bone fragments and useful tools. Motte had cunningly contrived this by insisting adult talk would bore her and unknown dangers lurked in the deep water of the reservoir, but of course neither were the real reason for her not to be there.

Disappointingly, Murchadh no longer talked with bravado of flying over the archipelago of the Alps to snoop out enemy spaceships, but only in basic, practical fashion about what they could or should do, and who should or could do it. Motte listened apathetically, melting shadowlike into the background, increasingly convinced that despite what anyone said or wanted, ultimately the man would get his way. In private he showed her an affectionate concern and a degree of humility, but faced with a larger audience his leadership qualities burst out in full force.

Under the guise of sharing and getting better acquainted, he probed for revealing details of the others' pasts. Motte was too distracted to absorb much of their stories, but she gathered that Fin's group had sailed over from the sizeable Mont Blanc/Grandes Jorasses island because Holg had somehow, and quite unexpectedly, acquired a seaworthy boat. A totally miraculous occurrence, seeing as they had been marooned in the one place all their lives! He had been told her island bore the healthiest tinge of green in an otherwise grey world; or at least it did on those rare days visibility improved enough for it to be seen from distance. If he wanted to cure his disease, was the advice, that's where he should go.

Fin and family joined Holg and Bernina's expedition simply to keep them company - and to get the hell away from Mont Blanc at long last! Reiterating what they had already told Motte, they had firmly believed her island was virgin territory, uninhabited, because rumour claimed it was encircled by a killer current, or a sea serpent, or some other ridiculously fantastical deterrent. Granted, the jagged ridges of the mountains that had once stood 3,650 metres high or thereabouts so were now submerged, did make sea landings perilous, but they were the only shoreline dangers she believed existed.

Murchadh's experiences were utterly different. He was born at sea and fully expected to die there too - on a daily basis! His father was a mad sea-dog, forever sailing one moth-eaten seacraft after another in a hopeless quest to find a non-existent island called Aproximedes. His mother, from whom he (Murchadh) inherited his slender percentage of native American blood (but major amounts of spiritual, mystical heritage) was the practical one who managed to keep them alive. Well, some of them...

The name 'Murchadh' was chosen by his father. It meant 'sea warrior' in Gaelic; but his mother always called him Chayton, Sioux for 'falcon', and sometimes Napayshni, meaning strong. Which he had been, when younger.

She was the navigator, armed with compass and old, worn, torn map of Europe, a treasured gift from her father. She had cleverly contrived to designate the new sea-mass area by using the altitude lines (it was a physical map with all the proper contours) as her guide, colouring the sea area with a red berry dye so that the mountain islands leapt out at one in stark relief.

He reckoned they had criss-crossed from one to another so many times their routes would resemble a spider's web, had his mother ever felt an urge to represent them in thin, black lines. Which she never had.

To cut a long story short, he met Eartha only when already an old man, on the Rimpfischhorn island, and they'd been together ever since - but how long that might be he couldn't say because, as was the way of things these days, he hadn't kept track of time. He'd recently chosen Motte's mountain as a destination because it was a place of power, the Wanblee (eagle, in white man's talk) had told him so - and guided him there too. He realised Motte had preserved it and cared for it in the native American way, showing respect and living in harmony with nature. He was therefore all the more deeply, profoundly sorry for the damage his dynamite had wrought...

Eartha had nothing to add at this juncture.

"What does my life matter?" she demanded of the man, "I reckon we'd best focus on the here and now, and what to do next."

"Any ideas what force that silver clad commando belonged to? Murchadh asked. "I've only heard talk of The Browns and Kratos."

"There's a Kratos uber-force - but I can't say more. I have this internal device that'll zap me dead if I utter certain key words too close to the truth, or which might more precisely identify them. It's a cunning way to ensure no-one plays traitor to their cause."

Motte wondered if this were true - or simply his own device for being secretive, and simultaneously garnering sympathy. If true, it was odd he had never mentioned it, so it was likelier a smokescreen to avoid revealing too much to almost perfect strangers.

"It'd help to know why they came." Eartha mused. "Could be for the water supply, or to investigate the explosion. Could even be that we're the final human survivors on the whole of earth, who by coincidence are all in the same place at the same time, so they grabbed the golden opportunity to kill us off, once and for all!"

"Nicely nutshelled my dear," Murchadh gave an appreciative grunt. "But why were they killed by that light beam? D'you think they got chatting about your uber-force and were zapped for that?"

When the man ignored this question Motte recognized his crafty tactic. He had basically censored them by claiming *he* was censored. This ensured he controlled the topics of conversations and, by virtue of his secret knowledge, the upper hand in everything! But then he had been taught these methods by experts at mind control - as he had admitted. So he shouldn't have any difficulty manipulating a little band of uneducated, undernourished, ignorant cave dwellers, bien sûr.

"If only we knew more about the past, it'd help us figure the present. Surely you've got some useful insider knowledge of the GD?" Murchadh probed. "Natural catastrophe? Or man-made?"

Obviously this question was directed at the man, who set about a ponderously lengthy explanation.

"The official line declared it a combination of natural disasters; a meteorite impact, (or impacts) causing earthquakes, in turn triggering a massive rupture of the magma. But that won't be the truth - or not the whole truth anyway. Plenty of alternative theories circulated in secret, some plausible, some away with the fairies. A quickfire selection of the more credible: their experiments with climate control went disastrously wrong; mega-nuclear explosions intended to obliterate a troublesome sector of the world ended up obliterating much more than anticipated; the Kratos uber-force actually *wanted* a massive disaster so's to destroy all records and basically memory-hole the past, plus purge the world population - particularly of those 'lesser' and 'troublesome' races they abhorred. Without permanent records they could reinvent history and start again with a clean slate. And, vitally, a brand new population; of them, and a manageably small slave populace to serve and service them."

"Hmmn… Possible, possible… But what I don't understand," Murchadh admitted, "is how in hell the sea got so ginormous. How could it flood the whole friggin' world, all them countries and everywhere, right up to nigh on four thousand feet??! It's…well…it's just impossible to create so much water. It'd take years and years of non-stop rain! I can't believe it - yet me eyes tell me it's true. Water everywhere, with just a few poxy islands sticking out like hillocks of bogweed! *Water, water everywhere yet not a drop to drink* - such premonition from old Samuel T., the Coleridge geezer… See what drugs can do to stimulate an inventive mind, eh?" he added, glaring accusingly at Eartha.

"Didn't that Noah guy have the same kinda problem?" Fin chipped in.

"Nah mate - he was given warnings a-plenty before his flood. Enough time to build an ark and round up a load of animals, for starters. According to me great, great (etc.) grandma, they got no bloody warning whatsoever. But then anyone who survived was high up a high mountain at the time, so perhaps there were warnings - which never reached them."

"We can't be sure," the man countered, "if it did affect the whole of earth. We only categorically know about Europe. Perhaps the cataclysmic event lifted the earth's crust in one place, but depressed it in another. All we can be sure about, vis-à-vis the remainder of the world, is there's been a deathly silence from it ever since the GD. Maybe the southern hemisphere isn't sea, just an empty, uninhabited dustbowl… because it's got a burning sun and cloudless skies and we've got… Well, we all know what we've got," he ended bitterly.

Silence ensued. Each retreated into their own, private thoughtworld so that only the faint gurgling, fizzing, suspirating sounds of the water were audible, magnified by the acoustics of the cavern and faithfully recreating their earliest forgotten experience as an embryo floating in a womb.

Motte, whose hearing was more acutely tuned than their's, froze for one terrified moment thinking she heard the distant cry of a child, but when it was repeated it more closely resembled the hunting cry of an eagle, and she could relax again. She leaned back, imagining the eagles picking futilely at the clean bones of the space invaders, wondering why humans had devised weapons that dissolved the flesh so fully and so fast. Was it so they couldn't be eaten?

Eartha was first to break the silence.

> "No more shooting the breeze - best get back to work. I want to repair the tipi, I'm sure Bernina's aching to see those seedlings inch upwards, and Murchadh has a lot on his plate, not so m'dear?"

> "Full circle," Murchadh's eyes were closed and he wore a beatific smile, "nothing'll progress until we come full circle. And we almost have!"

> "Ah, off on a trance," Eartha explained. "He'll snap back to reality soon enough."

> "Is he really an injun?" Bernina asked in hushed tones.

> "Depends on the point of reference. Blood, spirit, DNA, physique or sheer wishful thinking? He qualifies on some - but don't let it scare you, that's my advice." She chuckled softly as she rose to her feet, manoeuvred herself through a slender aperture, and disappeared.

Motte hurried back to her burrow in case that scream was not an eagle. To her relief Lhotse was fast asleep, curled up on the mound of fur pelts that was the man's 'in-tray' before he tailored them into something else. Motte felt weary; a deep ache gnawed at her stomach. Presumably caused by hunger pangs yet she had no desire to eat, in fact the idea of food made her nauseous. She fell asleep beside Lhotse, her hands folded protectively across her flat, sore, empty belly, her wrists hooked over the sharply protruding pelvic bones.

The pain persisted through sleep. As if something blunt were clawing at her stomach lining. There was moisture, too, sliding between her thighs. Perhaps she was simply imagining sex like the man had suggested, at last acknowledging the femininity that ought to suffuse her consciousness. Her body was too angular, too slight. She had noticed that although Eartha and Bernina were thin because of the scarcity of food, they still had curves gracing their overall shape. In fact Eartha, despite being skeletally thin elsewhere, still had a rounded bottom - it positively bounced and nodded gleefully at every step!

Not wanting to wake Lhotse, she stifled the urge to moan. Sexual dreams were supposed to give you ecstasy, but although the dampness between her thighs was increasing the ache in her belly persisted and pain overrode pleasure. Or truthfully there was no pleasure, only a faint smell of metal with an overtone of death. She lay perfectly still, eyes closed, waiting for the flush of excitement as the nerve endings in her birth passage sprang to life and lust as they apparently should, but no such warmth or pleasure came.

Very slowly her brain whirred into proper functioning and a fading memory clicked into focus: I've experienced this before. This is no new miraculous thing called an orgasm; only the old, moon-tide pull of 'my time of month' or what is properly called 'la menstruation'.

Immediately she sat up. Nervously - in case her dozey state had misled her and really she was bleeding to death from a ruptured ulcer or a burst appendix - she opened her legs to explore the texture of the blood trying to glue them together. It was as she suspected. The gentle flow emerging from her birth passage, the dull ache caused because the special tissue to wrap a baby in its pre-birth cocoon was being ripped from the wall of her womb and discarded; both confirmed that, at last, she was bleeding again! What a blessed, blessed relief! Even if she never became pregnant and never, ever gave birth to a living child, at the very least she could identify herself as a proper woman!

She crawled across the burrow and squatted by the water urn, ravenously gulping water. It explained, now, why she had felt gloomy and overtired lately; her body had been preparing for this. Before shedding blood and one (or two) unused eggs, the unfertilised body tensed in disappointment because it could not nurture an embryo, and must push out the unused shell of one. It was forced to participate in this process of death. Somewhere in amongst the blood must be a minuscule, pinprick sized egg that would never become anything. But perhaps the next month's egg would have a different fate...

"Mummy... mummy," Lhotse murmured, half-asleep.

Motte leaned over and stroked her hair. "She's not here. Remember what happened? Mummy died, so now she's gone to somewhere beautiful and peaceful, and you're here with me."

Previously she would never have contemplated promoting the heaven-myth. But what else could soften the blow for someone so little?

"Motty?" Lhotse intoned it curiously. "Motty, Motty!" Then she wriggled onto Motte's lap and nestled against the marmot fur which still covered Motte's torso. "Where...where's my daddy then?"

Motte shrank back, aghast. Her equanimity shattered in a split second. What kind of selfish, senseless world had she been sucked into...? No, what depths of cowardice to pretend herself a victim of outside forces - when she had acted so very intentionally. She had stolen Lhotse, plain and simple. No excuses. She was not the dotty old woman in a story her mother once told her. The one who took leave of her brain and sought out the forgotten pram in the attic, dusted it off and pushed it round the park, mouthing sweet baby phrases to an empty pillow - pretending the child she lost to illness forty years ago was back alive. She knew what she was doing. Even if she could not explain her motive - nor why she ever imagined she would get away with it, because of course Lhotse was bound to ask the dreaded question. Sooner, or later.

Not only had Lhotse's memory not been wiped clean, but the man, now that he had met Fin, would be bound to find out, in a conversation or merely by putting two and two together. He was no slouch at that. She was a fool, a liar and a thief. She had seen with her own eyes the misery Fin was suffering, and yet had sat through the meeting in a daze of her own making, saying nothing. Cruel, horrible, hateful...

Tears flowed down her cheeks as steadily as the blood between her legs. Tears even entered her mouth, and she coughed and spluttered at the surprising taste of salt.

"Motty?" Lhotse was still waiting patiently for an answer.

Motte again stroked her hair, struggling to articulate, her voice midway between whisper and sob, "Your daddy's...fine. He'll want to see you right now, I bet."

She could not face Fin. He must be still in the reservoir cavern - the exact same location where she had abducted Lhotse, who would be sure to recognise it immediately. Eartha might be willing, however, to act as a go-between. And she would be busy mending the tipi as near to its original pitching place as was safe - without literally falling down the blast hole. Praying those satellite spies were not watching her, she set off with Lhotse an awkward, deadweight load curled inside the sling she normally used for transporting moss.

Eartha was seated under an overhanging rock. Post explosion and post skymen it was a case of balancing the risks: be crushed by falling rock destabilized in the blast, or shot by a light-weapon out in the open. She watched while Motte approached, her bone needle firmly gripped between her teeth. Even when Motte produced Lhotse - like an olden day magician whisking a rabbit from out of his hat - she remained motionless, forcing Motte into breaking the silence.

"Lhotse is not...my child. I found her lost in the reservoir and...she's Fin's. I want you to give her back to him. Please. J'ai honte de la faire." Motte's eyes flitted nervously from the ground to Lhotse.

"Pour moi," Eartha replied, after an elongated pause, "il n'y a aucune problème."

The authenticity of her accent aroused Motte's curiosity, but being desperate to avoid a cross examination of her own behaviour, she was effectively muzzled from asking questions. Lhotse began to fidget, suspecting a hitch.

"Daddy's gone," she declared dramatically.

"Non, non, ma petite. Eartha'll take you to him. Now. Tout de suite."

However, a mere few paces further up the scree Lhotse wrenched her hand free from Eartha's grasp and stood, glued fast, refusing to enter the dark interior of the mountain with a total stranger. It made Motte realise she should have returned her herself. Her cowardice was an added betrayal.

"Come on littl'un," Eartha coaxed. Then her tone assumed a sharper edge as she spoke to Motte, "Other folks coming here was never going to be a straightforward thing."

And suddenly, both were swallowed up by the wall of rock.

Murchadh was no longer immersed in his trance. He was now in transition, a deeply contemplative state but safely back within the zone of rationality. In this mindset he felt convinced that the flecks of light in the vaulted cavern were indeed phosphorus, and the effervescing bubbles enlivening the water were caused by volatile gases ascending from the bowels of the earth. Water, fire, earth and air - all four elements combining in a subterranean cave-world which had an atmosphere of perfect peace. Yet, also, a brooding menace.

The organisation that sent those techno-punks in their swanky suits was massively superior to them in hi-tech efficiency and advanced surveillance methods, but couldn't history point to some banana skins on which so-called superior forces slipped up? Sadly, he could think of none. Better weapons had after all allowed the white man to annihilate the native Americans, (Custer may have lost one individual battle, but his buddies indisputably won the war). Same way as imperial might had soundly beaten the Aborigines, the Maoris and every other primitively armed peoples. Those Romans didn't do badly either, expanding their empire thanks to their fancy javelins and finely-crafted metal bludgeoning tools. Right up to the era of bombs and chemicals. Power meant victory, sooner or later.

Thankfully his mad-cap father had enjoyed brief but fairly regular interludes of sanity when he forgot all about his mission to reach Aproximedes. During them he managed to impart a limited version of the history of warcraft, some highly specialised scientific knowledge relating to physics and chemistry, and several verses of Coleridge's Ancient Mariner which he could recite by rote. His lessons of Gaelic, much to his bitter chagrin, had played second (if not third or fourth) fiddle to his wife's Sioux teachings, so right now the only Gaelic word he (Murchadh) could remember with absolute confidence was his own name!

But back to dogs and underdogs…Even that story of David and Goliath, which he had always believed the perfect example of underdog triumph, was nothing but a whopping lie - or so the man had just now told him. In reality Goliath was a puny little wimp, the man claimed, whereas David was a huge strapping lad just like Samson (their one, not the Bible one). However the guys who penned that particular Chapter of the Old Testament (late on, well after the New Testament was written) were secretly David supporters so they simply reversed the roles, describing David as an innocent wee child and depicting poor, unfortunate Goliath as a giant psychopath!

Perhaps all he had ever heard and learnt was arsewise forward… That would involve a total rethink - it would be a disaster! Because then he would have to redefine Custer as honour personified and Sitting Bull as a devious bastard, see white men (yes, even those pistol-happy cowboys) as saintly, but indigenous peoples as rude and graspy as rats with their *This land is my land* selfish way of thinking… Clearly they should have been more inviting and welcoming to those who came to steal (oops, force of habit, I mean *share*) it. Should have willingly offered up their wives and daughters to be gang raped; their cows, buffalos, goats or camels to be milked and gobbled up; and finally their own throats to be slit so that when they fell their corpses could be trampled on, just like some ceremonial red carpet, by their honest, upright victors…

Och Murchadh - where're you goin' with all this? Contemplation me hat - you've got sidetracked back into the past, as per usual, when you're meant to be forging ahead to the future, or at the very least working on the present predicament. Visionaries need to concentrate better than that, you bet.

Get back to those four elements, Murchadh, therein lies yer source of power. Rock: a firm foundation - or to crush to death; water: to nourish and refresh -

or drown if necessary; air: to breathe - or gases to behave with volatility, to poison, explode or mutate to liquid form; and finally fire. In those early myths fire had been the magical force, a gift of the gods - so the Greeks believed. Or perhaps not strictly a gift because somebody sneakily climbed up Mount Olympus and stole it from them! Anyway, however man got his hands on it, it made a huge difference. He could at last cook his meat, bake his bread, heat his cave, melt and forge metal things and...destroy forests, burn enemy crops, burn whole cities...and then collect the insurance payout!

Well, which was dynamite? Earth, gas, fire? Same with the bombs: atomic, napalm, nuclear, white phosphorus, neutron and that newest one, the filthiest, deadliest of all, whose name escaped him? Presumably, conglomerates of gas and fire...

Gradually a bit of the basic physics and chemistry his father had taught him hovered on the horizon of his understanding, viewed through his Sioux lens, of course. He recalled that yes, the secret of both creation and destruction lay in *fusing* elements. Some fused with a sigh of pleasure, an act of love; some however, had instant loathing, and their confrontation was explosive. Amongst the latter were lightning, thunder, electricity, internal combustion engines, nuclear reactors, nuclear bombs, dynamite and war, war, and more war.

So what about this phosphorus stuff and his dynamite then? Compatible or antagonistic? (And yes, he still had some dynamite, Layla had not purloined the lot). She had nicked the only flint stones, agreed, but he found it hard to believe there was but the one type of stone in the whole range of stones worldwide that was capable of sufficiently heating up to create a spark. (Steady on Murchadh, we're marooned on a wee mountain island surrounded by the poisonous waters of an endless sea. We don't exactly have access to the world's supply of stones).

Using phosphorus and dynamite they could perhaps create...something. Perchance those air bubbles fizzing in the water could be extracted - might be the missing ingredient to the phosphorus/dynamite compound. Or was he being stupid here, because water always contained air, or how had the fishes managed to breathe? A chemistry experiment would be a monstrous risk, and blowing up the mountain a prime example of sawing off the branch you're sitting on, but desperate times need desperate measures. How the old clichés fitted like a glove! Still, sometimes a dangerous leap of faith was needed...

At last he opened his eyes, and sighed. It was all well and good being a visionary, but it was less fun than others seemed to think. Mainly it was frustrating. Because every effing genius idea that popped into your head got mashed and mushed and churned until you hadn't a clue what was which or where to turn. Full circle. Full cycle. Gets you bloody nowhere.

All through that deep-thinking time he had been aware of low voices murmuring in the background. Now that he looked up, he saw there had been a change. Eartha had returned, Fin was swaying ecstatically back and forth rocking a tiny blond child who he clasped in a bear hug, and the little child was thumping him on the back and grinning like a chipmunk. Eartha was watching them with an air of contentment; only the man seemed less engaged in the scene of blissful reunion. His expression was not unhappy, but it was certainly pensive.

It made him wonder if the man could also be a source of danger.

14

Motte lay with face buried in the burrow floor, the usually reassuring tang of earth and roots bitter to her nostrils.

Padding sounds told her the man was approaching up the tunnel from the reservoir. By now he would know the truth about Lhotse. She kept her head down, willing him to go away without noticing her - but sadly his darkness vision had grown too good for that. Soon he was squatting alongside, feeling for her wrist pulse, trying to rotate her body so that she lay on her side and could breathe freely.

"What's up? What've you done? There's blood on the floor Motte! Is it yours?"

She explored the earth with her hand, momentarily mystified, then traced it to its source. Amazingly enough, the darkness of her shame had swept away all memory of the most momentous event in her recent life - the return of her bleeding cycle. But she no longer gloried in it now. She swiveled onto her back and stared bleakly up at the ceiling.

"It's that woman-thing that happens, once every moon cycle it's meant to be, in a healthy world. For me it's only once in a blue moon. But now, after I've...I've..." She couldn't put into words what she had done. Tears of self-pity welled in her eyes.

"Listen. Doing wrong is being human, get that into your skull. No-one's perfect like you expect. I've been trying to tell you how damnably flawed we all are from whenever it was you coaxed me out of my coma. It's no harm done in the end - now that they're back together. And Lhotse played ball so well she didn't even let on that she knew me! Only you, Eartha and I know the truth."

"Yes, the three people I don't want to see me in a bad light. My soul and my conscience know it too, and they'll never let me forget it."

"Well, that's the whole point. If you forgot you'd do worse next time, and the time after that worse still - until eventually you'd have crossed a threshold and would no longer care. Believe me, I know what I'm talking about - I've seen it, been part of it...myself. You're the lucky one, holding onto your innocence for so long. You see, it's only when you live with other people that you can learn the truth about humanity. Welcome to group living Motte. It's no picnic."

He massaged the small of her back in a gentle, clockwise movement which must surely come from experience of another woman's period pains, probably his ex-partner's. It made her wonder, along with his pensive mood and the practised way he had distracted Lhotse, whether he were reliving something from his past. For the first time she noticed occasional grey strands in his dark hair, just like her mother's shortly before she died.

He sat down and took up his sewing, squinting into the gloom and pursing his lips like some petulant old grandma as he tried to thread a length of gut into the narrow slit-eye of her bone needle.

"I'm running low on skins," he remarked, "let's hope an ibex or two die soon."

"Hibernation time for the marmots should nearly be over. Some of the old ones never wake again - it's how I get my skins."

"That's too much work. The bigger the pelt, the less I've to sew. And I'm ambitious - I'm aiming for a tapestry of life on earth that can turn into a boat should we need a speedy getaway vehicle!"

Motte frowned. Was such fantastical nonsense meant to cheer her up? She wasn't a three year old who could be easily tickled into forgetting her troubles. Or was there a method to it, introducing the concept of escape when she felt too ashamed to object?

"That device you said they planted in you, the one that'll zap you dead if you talk about who's truly in control, does it really exist?"

"No. They're obsolete, after malfunctioning one too many times. I only mentioned it as a feeler - for all I know one or more of our new comrades might be a plant."

"A *plant*?"

"Not the growing type. A spy, mole, or sleeper working for the enemy."

She said nothing, seeing as she had long harboured such suspicions of him, as well he knew. It was therefore obviously intended as a bridge to some new suggestion, and she was not wrong there...

"Motte you're not alone in wanting peace. But it merely needs one group to lust after control over others for the pattern of wars, deaths, and invasions to recur ad bloody infinitum. It's been so since the beginning, as I've always said, so it's naïve to think it'll suddenly end now just because we want it to. Humans early on made up stories to explain the presence of wickedness, like the Garden of Eden being ruined by a devil, or the Greek Pandora's Box version. And there're no shortage of others."

"OK," she sighed, "I understand we all have evil in us now. But why does it always have to win?"

"It doesn't fully. That's why the struggle's perpetual. Listen, I know you needed to be single-minded, well - blinkered perhaps, in order to survive so long alone. You don't know how much I admire you for that!

Omit the flattery. It's off key right now, owing to my guilt-stained conscience. And don't patronize me either. But instead of voicing these thoughts like she used to, she simply listened like a good little malleable student. Or a marmot, sniffing the evening air for what's afoot.

"Now that you know the world isn't what you thought - not just a dying one where the struggle is merely to survive and breed, like it is for animals, but a complex one plagued by war and competition, political planning and devious intrigue, murder and plunder still on the agenda, what d'you want to do?"

"I still want to live the best way I can. I'd rather not be caught up in the political struggle for supremacy, if that's what you mean."

"It's too late for that! You *are* involved - by virtue of the fact your mountain's been discovered. Those silver men died, OK, but others'll replace them. So, d'you want to live in permanent hiding, stuck underground, subsisting on dried berries until you starve to death? Or do you want to fight, in the open of necessary?" A revolutionary gleam unexpectedly flared in his eyes.

Motte promptly closed hers, hoping for a glimpse of subconscious soul wisdom to guide her beyond the pettiness of the present - or put it into perspective. He was talking sense, or what made sense in one dimension (there might be more!). She had wrongly assumed she could be alone on the earth, wrongly obsessed herself with having a child which she blindly assumed would be a panacea. How she had despised the former inhabitants of the earth with all their doctrines of religion, science and philosophy (and a whole other load of bunkum). Probably wrongly too...

Eat, sleep, and breed was a fine life for an ibex. Not enough to satisfy a human though, she could acknowledge that now. The fine line of separation between them being...hmmm, there she was stymied. Perhaps it was the ability to debate ideas, to think rationally and irrationally, in fact to spend an inordinate amount of time thinking, as well as having a conscience and a soul.

Also to talk…oof, how could she have overlooked the talking? A major, major pastime, and the man just relished it like no-one else!

"D'you want to fight these uber-forces because otherwise they'll kill us? Or because you want revenge for what they've done to you?"

The gleam in his eyes flickered fractionally. "Both," he admitted, "having no ideology I can't use it to justify killing like they do. Of course I burn with resentment - but killing to survive is self-defense. Your mother did it, animals the same."

"It's a slippery slope, but I guess, depending on the situation, I…could kill."

"Good, good. But sometimes the choices are fight or flight. What if the only way to survive was to leave this mountain, go someplace else. Would you?" There was an edgy eagerness in his voice.

"You never let up do you, Mr Inquisitor? Enough for now - just let me be."

This time the gleam in the darkness was not his eyes but his teeth, smiling. "Have I ever done other than let you be? Yet Eartha accuses *me* of being an oppressor, even daring to imply I'm verging on being a paedophile manhandling a young child!"

"Paedophile?"

"Means an older person who preys sexually on a child. Hah - tout au contraire! Little does she know *you're* the sexual predator here, and me the helpless, hapless victim unable to oblige owing to impotence from paralysis! But don't you worry, I kept your lustful secret safe."

Motte looked horrified, "How old does she think I am? I'm not a child at all!"

"Seventeen, or thereabouts. Apparently she's good at assessing these things… Don't be upset Motte, it still means you lived alone for six or seven whole years after your mother died. It may not be the twenty eight years you sometimes estimated, but it's amazing nonetheless."

Murchadh always found readjusting to normality an anti-climatic let-down after the thrills of hallucinatory experience. On this latest occasion he had traversed the entire globe floating weightlessly on a comet's tail, dipping and rising as if on some inter-galactic roller-coaster ride, fighting nausea with every flip and dive. It wasn't a question of partying whilst the others worked though - his hallucinations always had a purpose.

Hence he now knew not only more about phosphorus, but more still about gases. Yet, depressingly, nigh on zero about the properties of dynamite and precisely how predictable (or not) it was. He had a hunch how to launch an armed missile, yes, but then again essential details such as how to bullseye it onto a given target, its range, its aerodynamic properties (and so on and so on), all remained unknowns.

How he wished he had paid finer attention to ol' grandad's wafflings about twenty first century wars and warcraft, instead of dreaming about the sadly extinct species of pretty freckled girls in body stockings, who apparently used to frequent the late night bars in Glasgow before the sea submerged it all. They had apparently worn Tam O'Shanters (unless that was a far earlier fashion fad) which sounded racily saucy but perhaps were nothing of the sort. Items of female clothing were difficult to gauge on name alone. Sporrans were strictly for men, he did at least know that.

But back to the subject of weaponry... It all became remote controlled well before the GD - so no-one needed a good aim. They could sit comfortably in an air-conditioned office far away from the dusty arena of war. It was like a kids' computer game for the killer, though not, of course, for the victims who really did die. The killer simply used a screen to simulate reality (which ws a real place, filled with real people they wanted to kill), a camera in lieu of eyes, made sure the target slipped into some central circle delineated by a death-cross (called *locking* onto your target, if he remembered rightly) and bam, fired whatever weapon it was (bomb, missile, drone). And got a nice shiny medal for bravery!

It was anyone's guess what developments were made post GD. Spade loads of technology had been lost and destroyed, that was a given, but those silver men had techno-gadgets, and died from a techno-gadget. Eartha reckoned the men weren't human at all but remote controlled robots, but Motte had seen their charred bones, so perhaps they were cloned humans; Samson used to swear aliens encircled the earth in a perpetual merry-go-round while Bernina thought benign and evil spirits cluttered the air above the cloud barrier. So, plenty of theories to pick from...

The only apparent certainty was that there were enemy invaders in the near neighbourhood up to no good, and some other lot got rid of them for some reason or other. And the only person who doubtless knew far more than he was admitting was Motte's man. He was friendly and voluble enough - but an underlying tension suggested he was guarding a dark secret with his very life.

The US had been obliterated, that much the man had conceded, so whoever the uber-forces were, they weren't Americans based in the USA, although they did (the man again, revealing tidbits - of minor consequence) primarily use English as their Language of communication. It was sheer prejudice that made him harbour suspicions of Fin, since the CIA must be as obsolete as the North American land mass.

Still, who got us in this fix Murchadh? You. Yes, you with your damn' dynamite! So don't cast aspersions on others when you set the rot in motion.

Bernina gripped Lhotse's hand as they groped along the shore of the reservoir to the shelf of flat rock that was their new home - for the moment. Motte had suggested it as a safe place away from the harmful air plus out of sight of enemy surveillance, but Bernina was unconvinced. Sounds here echoed uncannily, and there were times when the water seemed frenziedly alive. Lhotse swore she had seen a sea monster basking on a distant rock, but Lhotse's imagination had been whipped into overdrive by the experience of getting lost in the dark underground innards of the mountain.

> "Oh you was jus' dreamin', sweetie. Honest to goodness you didn't live in no earth cave with a bear all that time! You were gone so long Daddy got very worried."

> But Lhotse stood firm. "Did so. A big brown one an' a mummy bear. An' I got to eat funny meat and wrinkly berries. I wasn't dreaming 'cos I wasn't asleep."

She led Lhotse across a series of sharp, slippery rocks - much like the barnacle encrusted ones kids used to scramble over when shrimping in the carefree days before the GD - and vanished down a narrow tunnel into total blackness.

> "Are we tryin' to find my mummy and the others?" Lhotse's normally robust voice quavered fearfully.

> "No sweetie, only bad folks go *down*. They're up above the clouds, I bet."

> "If we was to die, will we be goin' up or down?"

> "Lawd's sake Lhotse...you're talkin' wat too much! I've gotta' concentrate else we'll get ourselves lost..."

Motte scurried upside down across the burrow ceiling, her claws gripping into its earth roof so lightly she was virtually levitating. In this position blood and thoughts flooded her brain as she pondered the unwelcome prospects of unequal war. Their unit numbered merely seven - and effectively only two. Murchadh being too old to fight, Lhotse too young, Bernina some kind of vegetarian pacifist, the man still partially paralysed and unsteady on his feet, and she hampered by her incompletely healed collar bone. The only robust ones were Fin and Eartha, and the only healthy one Eartha... What a fearsome force!

In sombre mood, Motte accepted that if she delayed her expedition for moss until she was better, it might by then be too late. Moss was essential to heal injuries, and in war injuries are inevitable.

"What *are* you doing Motte?"

His tetchy tone emanated from cramped fingers after too much sewing, fuelled by his habitual disapproval whenever she moved in an animal-like manner; his patronizing one from the yawning age gap between them. He was in his mid-thirties. Meaning - *if* she were still a teenager as Eartha surmised - he was twice her age!

Naturally it affected the balance of power between them. Age aside, it had already tipped in his favour owing to her moral slide and his returning strength and mobility. Then access to a larger audience had significantly boosted his mental confidence, augmented, no doubt, by the subservient way they listened raptly to his monologues on ancient and modern history, geo-political intrigue and each and every pocket of knowledge ever possessed by man. She did not resent his intelligence or knowledge but they made her wary. Partly because she had a hunch intuition and local knowledge, her strengths, would ultimately prove pivotal; and partly because the more persistent he was in getting his way, the more suspect he seemed of being the enemy within.

"I'm exercising my climbing muscles. We need more moss."

"We also need you to stay alive, Motte. Please take care."

"Who's 'we'?"

"Same as your 'we' I imagine," he huffed, "primarily you and I, and secondarily our merry little band of six and a half humanfolk. Who else?"

"I'll go the day after tomorrow. And it goes without saying I'll take care. I always do."

Several hours later she quietly tiptoed out into the dark obscurity of night, in contradiction of the plan she had told him. It was of course blatantly more dangerous to climb in the dark but it was a deliberate decision. If he were in the business of communicating with the skymen (or their enemy, or any other enemy out there) his information about her trip would now be wrong.

Conversely he might not be a spy but could be transmitting recorded conversations unawares - having truly believed his microphone was long ago switched off and his transmitter destroyed. Either way, they would not be expecting her out on the mountain until later. If all went to plan, she would be safely back in her burrow before they trained their satellite eyes on the rock pinnacles, aiming their missile to kill her.

Satellite eyes were not always vigilant, not according to him. They circled the earth too, just like the sun and the moon, so coverage of any one particular spot was an on/off thing - unless there were a series of them to take up the surveillance like the handover of a baton in a relay race. And he doubted they had many left, not after something had happened - something apparently too scientifically obscure for her to possibly understand.

They might pick her out using infrared technology, but would have to be below the cloud barrier to do so accurately. And how would they know what was moving? It could be a marmot, or an ibex. She was, as it happened, wearing a modified ibex pelt because marmots never climb rocky pinnacles, whereas ibex are masters at it.

They also might hear her. Some process called ultrasound, sodar or sonar, but he claimed it functioned best underwater. So many of these weird machines had once existed it was no wonder pre-GD man shut his eyes and ears to the world around him! What madness made her think they had all been destroyed? And even as she asked herself that question, the answer leapt out at her. Ma mère, bien sûr.

In some ways it was safer to climb blind. As a child she often did so for fun - but not on the vertical pinnacles forming 'les dentelles' of the saw-tooth ridge splicing France from Italy, she was never that mad. Being blind channeled greater sensitivity into hands, fingertips, claw-nails and toeholds - all the vital climbing tools. Balance was vital too, and the flexibility to curve one's body into whatever shape preserved balance. There was even a mystery force, a kind of magnetism generated by an inbuilt trust in one's ability to stick to the rock that prevented one falling. Fear could break it. Even a lapse in concentration, however fleeting.

The moss favoured the northern facet of the pinnacles. From habit perhaps, since no sun's rays had struck the south-facing slabs since the GD - unless there was some substance within the rock only on the north orientation that fed it, like the brain being split into lobes that performed different functions. Switch off your emotional lobe, Motte, it'll not help you climb. It'll make you more paranoid.

Paranoid…rhyming with asteroid, rhomboid, void, avoid. How her vocabulary had expanded lately - like the universe straight after the first Big Bang (if that was the correct theory). Listening to the man had educated her a millionfold. But more words did not necessarily mean more wisdom. And more English words interfered with her fluency in French; that alone might be a subtle form of propaganda.

Look to the positives, Motte, dwelling on negatives is paranoia to a tee. Under the man's influence she had advanced a millennium, où peut-être plus. Whereas previously she had been stuck in the Paleolithic or Neanderthal age, now she had hurtled forward into a medieval understanding of the world, maybe even an eighteenth century one! Give her a few more days, weeks or months in his company and she would be right up-to-date with whatever date they were currently at. It must be at least 2,180 AD by now, although no-one seemed to have kept a tally on dates.

Nearly there. Hand over hand, foot over foot, like an agile spider-monkey in a jungle tree. But why an animal comparison when humans gave greater inspiration? Marie Paradis, for instance, the first woman to climb Mont Blanc way, way back in 1808, and - by happy coincidence - a teenager too, eighteen at the time. Then Josune Bereziartu, a Basque so not strictly French, but revered by her mother despite that because she spoke French and climbed in France. She was the only woman to ever manage the most difficult category of rock climb, ten on a range of ten. Motte felt deeply humbled by that. What rating might these perpendicular pillars have?

Her real hero of the past, however, was the 'spiderman', Alain Robert, the grand master of 'buildering'. He was not a mountaineer at all; instead, he shimmied up all the famous skyscrapers. But far from applauding his bravery he was treated as a criminal. The police would invariably turn up to scoop him off the skyscraper summits in their helicopter, then arrest him for reckless trespass. This didn't stop him, however. Oh no, he climbed every tall building in the whole world! He had been skinny and light as a feather, just like her. You had to be, how else could slender fingers bear the weight of your entire body and also lever it upwards, against the pull of gravity?

Men somehow persisted in prefering women with plumper, more curvaceously rounded bodies, even though starvation had reduced everyone to skin and bone. It must be their failure to engage with reality… Similar to women like her mother still hankering after men without beards, when who (apart from the skymen and other techno tribes that might exist, which her mother didn't even know about) could manage to shave these days?

At last she felt the prickly texture of moss. Lowland moss used to be softly green and velvety smooth, apparently - yet killed the instant it invaded garden lawns. But the current alpine variety was markedly different: brittle, with a greeny-grey tinge in the daytime half-light. Once a year, very briefly, it flowered in a miraculous halo of tiny star-like flowers which had hints of lilac and pink if you strained your eyes to aching point. It had no roots and literally sucked its lifeblood from the rock - until she and the ibex sucked their lifeblood from it.

15

Climbing down was a sterner test. Up was simpler because groping fingers could feel the way and balance was natural; down was a descent into the unknown. Bare toes had to explore the hidden drop for tiny footholds, and sometimes these could be found only through leaning slightly outwards, losing one's centre of gravity in a poise of imbalance, heart in mouth. And then the total darkness, the utter blindness was no blessing but a curse. Without visibility you had no memory to remind you of your route up - although the route down could never replicate it in any case, since sequences of moves simply did not revert.

It was no coincidence that historically more climbers died on descent than ascent, even in the easier era of gadgetry with ropes, metal clips and abseiling techniques. Down was when you were tired. And sometimes foolishly overconfident, due to your premature sense of achievement at reaching the summit. In the euphoria of conquest people somehow forgot that real success was to remain alive.

While climbing down she switched off all extraneous thoughts. Concentration. Silence. Darkness. A simple mantra. Hand below hand, toes stretching and searching…for grip, a ledge or fissure to support the body in order to make another move. The head being the heaviest part of the body should never lean out too far, and should never encourage hurried moves.

Surely she must be close to the base of the pinnacle by now? It seemed as if her feet had been stretching for footholds the whole night through, yearning for that moment when they touched firmer, leveler ground and relief could flood through her. She began to doubt her route. Had she become disorientated in the dark and somehow traversed the ridge into Italy? On the French side the dentelles reared up from the head of the old glacier, but on the Italian they merged with an almost sheer rockface which she had never descended, but because it was invisible from the ridge must end in an overhang - then a long, fatal drop into the valley far, far below. The fact that the night was still impenetrably dark prevented her knowing whether this had happened - but also proved she had not been climbing that long.

All she heard was a sudden *tat*, made by a tiny pebble striking rock at high velocity. The point of impact was some distance below and to the right of where she was, poised in the midst of a complex chimney move, so she blocked it from her mind lest it disrupt her concentration. Next she noticed a faint, unfamiliar smell. And then a dryness spreading through her mouth and throat, as though all the saliva had been hoovered up, and something similar was stripping the mucous from her nose, making it tickle. When she coughed her eyes smarted, but instead of drying they dripped wetly - yet she had no idea whether what dampened her cheeks was blood or tears because her hands were gripped to the rock and could not explore.

At first it made little difference being blinded by her flooding eyes because she had been climbing blind all along. What made a difference though, a drastic one, was the swimming sensation in her brain. A dizzying, nauseous sense of vertigo. Try as she did to cling to the rock, impaling herself on her claws as if they were coat hooks and she a gossamer light summer raincoat, the strength and purpose quickly drained from her fingers and they metamorphosed into useless appendages stuffed with an oozy jelly.

Then her whole body melted into this jellied substance so that she slid, slowly, then picking up speed until she hurtled like an olden day bungee-jumper down the final thirty metres of rock pillar.

She landed with a muffled plunk on the steep shale slope, and in her swollen, jelly-filled state rolled over and over until a ledge of rock trapped her legs and anchored her. There she lay sprawled on her back, hanging partly upside down because her feet were higher than her head, unable to move at all.

Hearing seemed to be her only active sense. She listened, bewildered, to the churning, thwacking sounds of waves thundering onto a pebble beach, and the rasping noise as they clawed at the pebbles, pulling them forcibly back into the sea like a ton of marbles funneled into a tin. The sounds were so magnified and distorted inside her head that she would normally have flinched from their agonizing volume, but could not move so much as one burning eyelid. Her eyes were aflame but could just as easily be freezing because the rest of her body was certainly frozen solid.

Now a storm was approaching. The clouds swirled and massed behind the mountain ridge, slanting rain spattered against the rocky shale and a huge herd of ibex came galloping, heading for cover into a massive cave and hotly

pursued by a horde of men shouting strange, guttural battle cries. Thick
swarms of flies queued up to buzz in after them, lusting for blood. A faint,
high pitched scream suddenly cut through this whole cacophony of angry,
rumbling noises, but ended in a wheezing, fluttering sound that slowly faded
to absolute silence.

"Stop making such a fuss," someone uncannily like her mother tutted,
"it's nothing to worry about. Just a sore bloody throat."

"Paralysis," someone corrected her, "infantile paralysis. Let's put her in
this handy wheelchair to take her out of the ward. Hey, watch where
you're walking."

"Talking you mean. She can't hear nothing so it doesn't matter what we
say, deaf as a post and dumb as a mutant. Turn off life-support I say."

The grassy knoll she now lay on squirmed, shuddering like a landscape in the
making, then flattened to a desert-like expanse of sand. Occasional mounds of
sand dunes blown out of their perfectly conical shapes alleviated the pancake-
flat terrain, and they sprouted withered clumps of faded purple flowers which
seemed out of place. They must surely be dying from lack of water.

She sat up so suddenly that her ibex pelt ripped, then strode away at
considerable pace, her hand shielding her blinded eyes from the powerful,
near horizontal rays of the rising sun. She was only moving eastwards so fast
across the now sloping landscape, she realised, because the ground was itself
rushing towards her almost as fast as the planet was spinning anti-clockwise
round the sun. And then the sun vanished again. It wouldn't revisit for another
so-many thousand years, for God's sake.

"Motte," she heard a faraway voice say, "flutter your eyelids to show
you can hear. Try." It might be Bernard, he was the first person to call
her Motte.

"Motte…," Possibly it was the same voice, but some while later. "Take
deep breaths. Breathe iiiiiiiiiiin, then slowly ooooooooooooout. Now
try agaaaaaaaaaaaaaaiin." No-one would talk in that stupid sing-song
way unless she was a young child.

"Motte…," the annoying, invasive voice refused to let up. "Listen.
They've somehow drugged…. (At last it faded, and she gained a long,
welcome pause. When it resumed it was sometimes audible, sometimes
drowned by the persistent sound of avalanches crashing from the
overhanging ridge where she was standing, for she was high on the
Aiguille Grise again, although for some reason she called it

Kangchenjunga). "Chemical… overwhelm you… hypersonic… muscarinic… hallucinogenic…now. Can you?"

She had of course no idea whether she could or couldn't. Nor where she was, nor why. At long last the final fly left the cavemouth with coagulated blood coating its outstretched proboscis. It whined mournfully in her ear before perching on her forehead, stopping there to preen something dry and dusty from the delicate hairs on its front legs. She must have recovered her vision, she realized, because she could see it as clearly as an old-fashioned botanist scrutinising it through his special magnifying lens. It had unnaturally pointed fangs, rainbow colouration on its wings, and its proboscis was a dark crimson-brown from the blood that had dried into a scab. Might it be her blood? Probably not, because her body was still formed from a clear jelly substance, except that a pins and needles sensation in her arms and legs hinted at returning circulation.

"Now, try deep breathing: iiiiiin, 1,2,3,4,5; take the air dooowwwn into the pit of your lungs until you feel it pressure your diaphragm. Good! Now expel it very, very slowly. Slowwwwly does it."

Much as the incessant voice grated her nerves and she longed to escape it, she must have performed in accordance to its wishes because gradually it became less nasal, brittle and edgy and more soothing and cooing - until it was ultimately cloyingly sickly-sweet.

Since its timbre had the exact quality a hypnotist would cultivate she sometimes tried her hardest to flout its suggestion, but disobedience only worsened her headache, making black spots dance across the curve of her eyeballs. She had been taken prisoner, she supposed. Meaning after the hypnotism would come the torture, then the solitary confinement, more torture and, finally, the intensive brainwashing process.

She prayed for the solitary confinement stage. It would usher in a period of blissful silence in which she no longer had to hear the irritating voice, or had to suffer a headache, get fixated on flies, and be urged into slowly breathing iiiiiin and oooout.

A small herd of chamois grazed languidly on the steep grass pasture below the ridge, their tawny butts twitching with the pleasure of eating so much fresh green grass - or perhaps swatting off imaginary flies with their imaginary tails. None of those high mountain grazers such as ibex or chamois possessed tails, perhaps because tails interfered with their balance or got in the way of their rutting. She had no tail either, nor could she remember whether marmots did or didn't. Some of her claws were mangled and damaged by some recent event or other, but her headache got in the way of remembering what. Her headache got in the way of more or less everything; any movement, any thought. There was always the danger that that persistent voice, once it had successfully cut into her consciousness, would soon split open her very brain.

She could hear it even now in the distance, on and on, part of an endless loop, sometimes complemented by another voice...

> "Several hours ago. No, not precisely. I'm hoping it's a 'non-persistent' type, but I know precious little about what biological or chemical weapons are still extant. She's improved a fraction and that gives a glimmer of hope. Her pupils are dilating, albeit sporadically, and her breathing's more regular. But she hasn't a clue where she is, or what's happened, who I am - nothing..."

> "Surely water'd flush out or dilute whatever she's inhaled?"

> "No, it could be disastrous - some drugs stimulate epileptic fits when combined with water, or worse. It's obviously intended to confuse the brain and interfere with the nervous system, so an antidote's required - which of course we don't have. I'm scared she'll sink into a coma so I keep on talking. But there's no sign she understands any of it."

> "I'll try singing then. And deep breathing in sync. with her. Soothing things - as much to keep me busy as in hope they'll help..."

The clouds closed in again, their pink underbellies highlit by a dying sun yet their upper slopes and ridges an ugly, leaden grey. A huge bird flew down and probed along the shoreline for sandworms. When it wandered disturbingly close to her outstretched arm, its beak cruelly sharp, she tried to manoeuvre her hand out of its way but found it so swollen - like a water-filled balloon - that she could not move it. The downy feathers beneath its folded wings were matted together where a rash of red, eczema type scabs wept with a milky looking pus, but the bird settled to preening its wing plumage, seemingly untroubled by its itchy, mattering skin - or by the parasites busily chewing it.

She tried to follow its example. Ignore pain, preen what's uninjured. Forget your throbbing head, your eyes making everything circulate in harrowing, narrowing circles, the dizziness, thirst, ache, nausea, numbness. Preen your feathers instead, because 'feathers' must be code for the mind's ability to fly free of its shackles...

Something or somebody was stroking her huge bloated jelly belly. She was a jelly fish, repeatedly flipped over by waves, hoping to avoid maroonment on the sand where dehydration spelt death. Bubbles incandesced as the umpteenth wave somersaulted, propelling her head over heels with all the flotsam of seaweed, foam and sand particles, upside down, inside out. The impotence of being a jelly fish was the lack of limbs and complete loss of independence; she was helpless, limbless, brainless...

Now a something or somebody was pushing her belly, then sweeping it round and round. It might be a curious sea animal, or a sexual predator, or a predator full stop. Even a torturer. Well, they had started too soon because she wouldn't be able to talk if that's what they wanted, and it always was what they wanted. *'Who are your friends? Where are they hidden? What are their weapons?'* The salt sea water and the circling made her sick.

> "Quick - lift her head or she'll choke on vomit, Murchadh being once a bit of a drinker I know the dangers. I'm sure it's a good sign, the poison has to come out and this is surely the quickest way - so long as she doesn't vomit blood. That's the major danger. We don't want liver or kidney failure, or any internal haemorrage. Hey Motte, it's OK..."

Blood, blood-red blood. They might mistake her menstrual blood for vomiting blood and give her the wrong operation. An old fashioned means of torture was to drip water onto the top of a victim's skull for hours on end to send them mad. She, however, would welcome water: cooling, soft, without salt. But they wouldn't give her water because she was foaming at the mouth, which they would diagnose as rabies.

> "I'm wracking my brains. I don't think it's ricin, but it could be any of so many others: dopamine, thorazine, acetycholine - I wish I'd learnt more about the nightmares of neuroscience... It could be a fiendish combination - disorientating, hallucinogenic and whatever else, to totally incapacitate brain and body. Poor Motte."

> "Hmmm. She's suffering the horrors, that's plain enough to see. The drugs are to blame for the physical effects, but the psychological ones, perhaps, have another explanation... You know what I'm getting at. No-one else knew she'd gone on this climb. Just you."

> "But I didn't know! She slipped out hours in advance of when she said she'd leave. She told me she'd be setting off round about now."

> "Huh - I wonder why!"

> "You're playing right into their hands Eartha! Nothing they'd like more than us suspecting and mistrusting each other, so unable to mount any kind of co-ordinated resistance."

Suddenly the jelly fish expelled all its jellified innards in one glassy looking, foul smelling puddle, and the children on the beach shrieked in dismay, and ran off barefoot over the ridges of sand created by the outgoing tide.

16

Bernina groped along the hidden, eye-slit tunnel she had secretively explored a few hours previously, feeling her way in the darkness with one hand, the other tucked behind her, trailing Lhotse. After worming past a protruding bulge in the wall of rock, she stopped abruptly.

"Close your eyes, sweetie. You get three guesses as to what you'll see. Ready?"

"Er- erm. Mummy bear's cave and the naughty man!" Lhotse giggled in tantalised anticipation.

"Oh do be serious, huh. We're inside a mountain, not a fairy tale."

"Errr, ummmm. A Mr. Dragon with his pila gold!"

Bernina was silent for a moment, "Well, it so happens you're not too far off, 'cos it's a bit like gold, in a kinda way. OK - final shout."

"Erm, Missy Goldilocks eatin' yummy porridge!"

"Now you're bein' a sillybilly - an' honest to goodness, you're too stuck in that one Fairy Tale! Still, you deserve a kiss for getting' so close before. Right - open up those eyes!"

Lhotse stared glassily into the gloom, disappointment furrowing her brow. Whilst her eyes adjusted to the mysterious grey shadows of this new cave, eerily backlit by a slender gash in the rock - resembling an arrow-slit window to the outside mountain, she could see nothing of interest. No gnomes, dwarves, dragons or bears. No gold, jewels or meadow flowers. No mummy in a carved wooden casket like daddy swore he would build for her. Just junky ol'rock. What was Bernina on? Her mummy once said she sometimes went juju, gaga or ape-shit, so perhaps she had now.

"Sweetie, this is a cave fulla goodies, can't you see?"

Lhotse shook her head sorrowfully.

"Look there - the finest jewels this side a' paradise! Glitterin' pinks, swoony purples; way better than the gemstones stuck in an oldenday Queen's crown!"

Finally she did notice some layered veins of colour threading through the rock to one side of the cave; pink, peachy slices sandwiched between the normal slabs. The dim light rendered their colours uncertain, fleetingly hinted at rather than assuredly seen, as if a mere trick of the imagination. A geologist would identify them as pink quartzes and purple fluorites, but there was no geologist around.

"And that's not all. Look right there. There's two ol' sacks fulla food – mightn't be fit to eat but I'm sure hopin'. Cans and ol' cookies and I dunno what!"

Lhotse felt obligated to act pleased. Privately though, she thought the rusted cans not remotely attractive, and although they might have been edible once upon a time, that time had passed long since. Due to her giving the cans a thorough, detailed stare, however, she came to notice other, more ghoulish objects emerging from the gloom behind them. Bleached bones, stiffened, wrinkled swatches of leather, frayed clothing material - even something closely resembling the button that once belonged to her great-grandma, which her mummy used to keep stashed inside her special 'memento box'. These bones-folk most probably died from trying to steal that food. And the same fate would surely befall herself and Bernina.

"Oh let's go," she whispered, yanking at Bernina's hand.

"Sure. But we've gotta get some of them cans first."

"No!" Lhotse shouted, the echoes reverberating until they blended into a single roar, much like an avalanche. "Them cans're spooked! Look at the skellingtons they've killed!"

Bernina had previously noticed nothing beyond the broken sacks of food, but suddenly her fortunate find of jewels glinting in the dark - like a benign beacon of hope - lost its lustre. She had instead unwittingly entered a sepulchre of death. An irrational fear crept up on her: she was surrounded, penned in in fact, by the accusing corpses of Alpha and the children, although of course common sense should have reassured her they could never be reduced to skeletons in a mere few days. She slumped backwards in a faint, almost crushing Lhotse's toes in the process.

"Oh I wanna' go... *Please* wake up, Bernina!"

Again, echoes imitated and multiplied the tones of terror. Her supplication resounded eerily - as if the skeletal remains of all eight Italian mountain guides, along with the twenty five Americans, Britons and escaping French resistance fighters who had died in that fatal avalanche in April 1944, and whose original burial place had so recently been rudely upended by the violence of the dynamite blast, were joining her in a ghostly chorus.

Eartha was torn by indecision. One half of her insisted she stay with Motte, who was so severely intoxicated, so close to death's door that to leave her even briefly might be tantamount to a final goodbye. But the other half realised that, like the man said, only an antidote could save her now. And she, Eartha, knew what it was and where to find it.

Charcoal (according to Murchadh) was the sole efficacious remedy for poison, so she cursed herself for having wasted precious moments singing pointless lullabies instead of remembering it sooner. Murchadh kept a few lumps of it amongst his minimal collection of personal treasures. He had sworn it was a Sioux miracle cure for just about everything (poison foremost), but then he had foolishly eulogised dynamite in similar fashion, so perhaps the charcoal was useless, or actually dangerous, not curative at all. Still, without an alternative it was a risk worth taking - even though fetching it entailed leaving Motte alone with the man, completely at his mercy.

Initially, Murchadh acted weirdly protective. His whole ancestry and belief system were seemingly tied into each ugly, dusty lump, and he clung to them like a limpet its rock - until, at last, a graphic description of Motte's condition plucked two lumps free from his grasp. Eartha hurried back with them, so intent on the need for speed that although she thought, in some subconscious zone of her mind, that she could hear a tiny, plaintive voice filtering from beneath the earth like a spiral of mist from an Irish peat bog: '*Motty, Motty, please come!*' she dismissed it as sheer fancy.

Back inside the burrow she pounded the charcoal to a fine powder before dissolving it in water. Motte by this time was limp and deathly pale; even the man, as if through empathy, had adopted a very similar pallor. There was a noticeable slump in his energy level too, suggesting Motte was involuntarily poisoning the atmosphere with each and every exhalation. Moreover he actually seemed happy to obey her (Eartha's) orders - in complete contradiction of the personality she assumed him to have, and of his attitude thus far. Possibly the poison or drug was one of those mind control substances that rendered its victim one hundred percent pliant - in which case she would soon succumb...

Motte no longer had strength even to vomit. But judging by the amount of liquid already expelled - evidenced by the sizeably soggy stain on the earth floor, she had parted with more than was safe to lose. Unnaturally bloated before; now she was wrinkled, shrunken and gaunt - like an ancient, mummified corpse.

The sharp beaked bird still dabbled in the shallows. Motte recognized him by his trademark, three-pronged footprints in the wet sand - which faded when the water washed over them. He casually smashed a sea snail against a rock and swallowed the slippery snack, his thin gullet bulging as it travelled down his spindly neck. Then, without warning, he swivelled at snakelike speed and prodded a hole through her jellyfish body, puncturing it so its jellified filling poured out in one liquid gush.

All that was left of her now was an empty smear of transparency - like some olden-day sheet of rumpled clingfilm. It was a relief to have shed all that jelly, but strange to be so very feather-light and insignificant. *'Plus ça change, plus c'est la même chose,'* her mother's voice whispered tauntingly in her ear.

These creatures were attempting to reliquefy her. Bucket after bucket was hauled from a bell-shaped well in the centre of the beach, their contents then carefully strained through a sieve into a beautiful blue glass flask. They had evidently chosen the flask specifically to mask the disgusting appearance of the water, which was a vile, swirling black colour - darker than the well from which it was drawn. They poured it down her by the bucketful, chattering excitedly about the ingenuity of their methods. Then each drank their own bucketful, smacking their blackened lips as though it were a five star witches' brew straight from hell.

Although she seemed scarcely a sixth of the size and weight that she had been, she did feel magically better - mainly because her brain-splitting headache had receded into nothing more than a dull soreness in the forehead and temples.

> "Of course! Miraculous charcoal!" the man celebrated. "How it managed to slip my memory bank I've no idea…but well done Eartha! And thanks, of course, to its discoverer, the genius pharmacist Touery who blew the minds of an entire collective of the French Academy of Medicine, back in eighteen hundred and something or other. In a brilliantly crazy move he risked his own life when proving its efficacy as an antidote - by glugging down ten times, (yes - TEN TIMES!) the lethal dose of strychnine (one of the most virulent of poisons ever), followed by an equivalent dose of charcoal (three tablespoons, if memory serves me well.) And felt fit as a fiddle afterwards!"

> "Listen. How come you've got all this high falutin' knowledge always at your fingertips? You're a walking, talking encyclopaedia, while the rest of us are ignoramuses - or I s'pose it's 'ignorami'," Eartha grumbled. "I don't understand you. Stuffed with too many facts and figures... Whereas I happen to value reasoning more highly – adaptability too. Shut up and put up is my modus op."

"Well…." The pause was lengthy, the disclosure at first hesitant, reluctant: "unlike the rest of you, I'm…well…you could use the label 'manufactured'. When still just a child I was targeted for 'Intelligence Plus'. Meaning they created more NMDA receptors in my brain and, hey presto, my memory was enhanced by whatever percentage they'd calculated. The technique was first pioneered on mice by a fellow called Tsien back in the early 21st century (do excuse the plethora of facts, Eartha, I just can't seem to avoid them. Sorry.) Now even old artificial me knows memory doesn't equate to intelligence - but it does for their purposes. Or, I should say 'did', because I'm trying to develop my *own* intelligence now. But old habits die hard - one of the sixty thousand clichés I'm burdened with knowing."

The silence that followed was so lengthy Motte decided the creatures had fallen asleep at last, drunk to the eyeballs after emptying a surfeit of brackish water into their throats. She continued to lie on her side, eyes closed, listening to the distant murmurings of the sea meeting the shoreline.

None of her other senses functioned, except her hearing which had grown discernibly more acute. She could now detect the humping of earthworms under the sand, the singing of the sea in rounded shells, and a tiny, fairylike voice calling her from deep underground. 'Motty, Motty,' it urged. 'Please come - I'm lost *again*'. She half-recognised this voice, just as she half-knew something dangerous had occurred. It left her feeling mildly half-sorry for the both of them, and half-grateful to the two (or more) drunks who sat on the beach beside her, busily detoxing themselves of her poison.

Fin had meanwhile been immersed in stone masonry, or perhaps it was more an act of sculpture. He frenziedly banged and chiselled on a rockslab, while Murchadh sat hunched in the shadows nearby, quietly ruminating. To an oldenday time traveller - had such a personage ever existed, they would doubtless resemble two cohabitees of an open plan office: Murchadh the boss owing to his utter lack of observable output, and Fin the manual worker working like a dog. But instead of resenting his inferior role, he relished the chance to wallop and punish those rocks.

He was making a memorial stone for Hon and the kids. Hunched over the slab, gouging out grooves and pummeling protrusions, he was so intent on engraving a neat capital H that he forgot the passage of time. Only when he had finally chipped out the crossbar of the H did he look up and realize the half-light was already fading, yet there was no sign of Bernina or Lhotse.

"Bernina!" he yelled, "Lhotse!" Then, remembering there might be enemies with microphones hanging out of the clouds, he added at a more subdued volume, "Daddy's comin' to get youuuuuu!"

He listened, heart in mouth, for cheery voices emerging from a dark forgotten corner of the reservoir cavern where Bernina might be telling Lhotse a bedtime story, but none came.

Motte could hear a familiar voice murmuring from the direction of the sea, accompanied by a tingling in her ears which sometimes drowned it out, yet sometimes accentuated it. The tone of this voice was what she registered as familiar, not the words, nor even the language they were couched in. It seemed a hybrid one, perhaps of northerly origin. Certainly it wasn't French, which she might have understood, nor did it sound particularly Latinate. Still, whatever it was, she absorbed the sounds as if they were a melody sung to a steady rhythm, but they had no meaning.

'I sense, Motte, that you can hear and understand me. Oh, I hope I'm right! I promise I won't blather on for hours, but I desperately want - well, need - to talk to you. I'll try to make it brief, though you know what I'm like…

Listen, I said a few things to Eartha in the emotional turmoil that were seriously indiscreet, which is why I must tell you - otherwise you'll only learn it from her, twisted and contorted. She's somewhat anti-me, you see, judging by her 'paedo' insinuation, plus the inevitable post-feminist, post-racist prejudices that always rear their heads. D'you understand, Motte? Stupid question, of course. You can't let me know either way…

Before I admit to my indiscretion though, let's focus first on you. About the chemical attack. I'm no doctor but I know dribs and drabs about neuroscience. Some of the noxious inhalations won't have a lasting effect and'll wear off soon. Then, any persisting ill-effects - and let's pray, keep fingers crossed or whatever good omen trickery you've got up your sleeve (excuse my stupid, cliché'd manner of speaking that's so plainly at odds with reality, of course you don't wear *sleeves*) only time'll tell. There's no-one stronger at self-healing than you. And no-one knows what medicinal herbs are to be found here better than you. You brought me back to life - that's proof you work miracles!

The risk of lasting damage (I know you want me to be honest, not downplay it) are to your immune system, kidneys, liver, nervous system and brain. And by brain I mean cognition, impulses, personality (if they used that fiendish dopamine you'll be plagued to hell by paranoia), memory and motor control. I don't want to get all technical - I just hope against hope (what a *bizarre* tautology) you'll experience no permanent disability.

Not wanting to tire you, I'll be more succinct. So, as I said, the numbness in your body, like a temporary paralysis, should quickly wear off. It's just a means to incapacitate you really. Whatever made you swell into a balloon - I've never seen it take such a virulent form, but that might be to do with your natural, chemical-free life up 'till now, meaning you had a more powerful reaction than most - I don't know what drug caused it, but we need to soothe your skin now. It's raw, inflamed and weeping as if it's been burnt - I guess the moss you brought down'll help, so I'm going to soak it in water to soften it, then apply it. Can you move your eyes to tell me that's OK? Or a tiny pressure from your thumb? - I felt it!

Where was I? Ah yes, the swelling into a balloon was arguably a fantastic plus because otherwise (I don't know how far you fell, I'm guessing far) you might've broken every bone. As it was you were encased in a balloon 'packaging' like old fashioned bubble wrap, so I don't *think* you've got any breaks. Though of course we can't tell yet because you can't move and have too much pain, I imagine, to locate where any of it originates. Am I right? That charcoal beverage will've cleaned out your system, it magnetises the harmful drugs, and being sick rejected them too, so you have the best possible chance...

I wish I'd stopped you going! Still, you've brought enough moss to keep a whole hospital busy for ages, we should thank you a thousand times for that. And, by the way, you might have hallucinations too - that means seeing all kinds of crazy visions. But don't worry, they'll wear off.

I can tell you've heard enough about drugs now. I'll shut up, let you rest...

OK if I continue? I suppose I must move on to me now. I've been delaying it, naturally. By your definition I'm *mostly* human. Human in that I was born from the natural sexual pairing of a male and female 'human' (in so far as the society that reared me ever produced humans). All individuals were to a certain extent genetically modified though, including my parents. Our society was made up of what's defined as 'post humans'; we were kind of a later model of the 'post modern' society that existed just prior to the GD. (Our great great great grandparents' era, more or less). Those twenty first century guys were anyway fast losing their humanity, I can tell you! By their standards you lot (and by that I mean Eartha, Murchadh and you, though I'm less clear about Fin and Bernina) are almost pre-human, except that sounds derogatory. Perhaps I should say 'early human' or, better still, 'genuinely human'.

What that means is we were all in different ways tampered with, altered, in their view 'improved'. I was singled out (well, not truly 'singled' because I wasn't the only one, there were two others treated alongside me. Language is so fucking imprecise at times it gets on my nerves!) for what they called *Intelligence Plus* intervention. They adjudged I was anyway intelligent, so decided to augment it - d'you understand the idea? No?

I'll try again… When I was eight my brain was operated on. Then a second time at twelve. They fiddled with my brain receptors amongst other things, fancy things called NMDA and other pathways - which were never discussed with me either before or afterwards, so I remain pretty ignorant about what parts of me are really *me*. The net result was I ended up with a phenomenal memory and what was classified (loosely) as a 'super-human' intelligence. Please don't imagine I'm proud of it!

This intelligence was not meant to be a fun thing, allowing interesting thoughts, inventions, fuelling imagination etc. Oh no. A million times no. It was solely meant to advantage them in their battle for survival and total control. Any problems, particularly communication or computer-related, I ought to be able to solve. Plus I was their human (OK, almost human) walking bloody encyclopaedia, their fount of knowledge about the past, if you like - just in case all computerised knowledge vanished in a massive delete.

I'm sure your main interest, though, is in knowing what else they altered…ie. am I programmed like a robot to perform their dirty work under all circumstances, even now when I've escaped their sphere of control? Do I have any independent will of my own? Can I be trusted - or am I still 'owned' by them and their evil machinations?

You're none too fussed by me seeming smarter than you, are you? Surely not - all you want to know is can you trust me, or am I a traitor to your - well, I'd like to think 'our' - cause?

Now I'll take another break. This time, not because you're getting tired (I'm sure you are!), but because I need one. I'm knackered! Never was good at confessionals, better at self-promotion than self-examination it has to be said. Rotten at asking forgiveness - well, I'm not asking for forgiveness because none of it was my doing or my fault. I'm explaining something that I arguably should've explained very early on. That I didn't is partly because I never thought you'd understand (I can imagine you snorting in derision here as I excuse myself by means of a put-down, *very* convenient I hear you say). And partly because I felt I'd been reborn as a real human thanks to you - and don't argue, I'm convinced the old, 'programmed' me, if that's how you'd describe it, died from a blow to the brain falling off the ridge. I know how fatally far I fell. Well I'd like to think that blow blew out all the artificial receptors!

So…now I'm intent on regaining (or it could be retaining) my free will. I'm working hard on it… But unfortunately I can't be certain I've cut out all connections, all subtle forms of their control. How can I know? I can only hope…

I promise you Motte, that although the incursions by enemy forces are inadvertently down to me - from them tracking my escape route to this mountain because of the chip - I've not communicated with them once since then. I've cut the cord, emphatically. Slashed it to shreds. The paranoid feelings you're sure to be experiencing that I lured them here, that I told them you were climbing the pillars, when and where, all that, it's not true.

It's natural you mistrust me. After all, you lived alone so long and your mother taught you to be wary, as a means of self-protection. And that mistrust has been further fuelled by the massive charge of dopamine released in the chemical bearing missile that struck the rock…

But don't listen to your paranoia, Motte. Listen to your instinct instead. Trust your instinct…

17

Eartha lay restlessly awake, staring at the vaulted ceiling of the reservoir cavern. Her insomnia was of nervous origin, or more precisely the nervous fallout lingering in the air after Fin's panic - which was arguably her fault because she could have pre-empted it had she only recognised Lhotse's cries for help when she first heard them.

Luckily his frantic panic-attack was quickly quashed, peace being restored as soon as the two young errants reappeared, well before she did. And the furore over their vanishing was then forgotten in the excitement over their discovery. A pile of rucksacks, chockfull of World War 2 emergency provisions!

Verification of this astonishing find had yet to take place, however, so possibly Bernina's account was exaggerated. So far, the only samples her somewhat credulous audience had set eyes on were: one tin of hickory flavoured spam, produce of Austin, Minnesota (attested to by Fin, despite the fact he had never learnt to read anything, food labels included - but the torn, faded picture of a pink slab of meat on the disintegrating wrapper was the giveaway); and one cigarette lighter, identified as such by Murchadh - who could not stop drooling over it, even now, whilst he slept and snored.

Before he fell asleep he had whispered to her, in tones of awe, that it could easily pre-date that World War 2 - might even be up to a thousand years old! Then he had hummed and hawed, having a vague memory tobacco was still an unknown commodity in Europe that far back, having only been 'discovered' when some exploring Brit or Scot brought it back from the Americas (North or South, he was not sure which - it could even have been Cuba, where they apparently fancied it for cigars). What he *was* sure about was that its history amongst white invaders was more recent than amongst indigenous peoples, since the Mayans and native Americans had been happily chewing and smoking the stuff for over three thousand years.

Eartha tossed and turned and finally woke him up.

> "Sorry, my mind's buzzing. That man of Motte's troubles me no end. He's admitted to being a *programmed* person. They've fiddled with his brain and upped the capacity of his memory - who knows what the implications are. Probably he has perfect recall of conversations, plus a

detailed brain-map of this mountain-islandscape - and poor Motte's now a helpless vegetable, putty in his hands. Come on Murchadh, rise and shine and don your thinking cap! We can't leave her at his mercy."

"Oooh, give us a break Eartha. Must be the bloody middle of the night - though it's hard to tell when daylight comes in this infernal cavern. I miss my tipi!"

"Well I don't like to keep mentioning it, but you've the lion's share of the responsibility."

"So *everything* that happens from now on's my fault?"

"No. Only direct cause and effect. Dynamite causes bang. Bang invites curiosity - in form of investigative incursion. Need for self-defense becomes paramount, fighting likely so Motte climbs to get medicinal moss, is shot at with chemical warhead resulting in near death. Man possible suspect... Got the picture?"

"Yes - but your whole sequence is arsewise forward. The man, your major suspect, got here first. Before us, before dynamite blast. So answer this woman - how'm I bloody responsible for the man or his enemy army? Your logic's cooked!"

Eartha sighed longsufferingly. "Well, damned if you haven't still got a brain! OK, I accept you emerge pure as driven snow once was. But all the same, I'm off to help Motte. Someone's got to."

Just before she reached Motte's burrow (via the interior tunnel) she could hear the man's voice in full flow:

"...same techniques you used on me. We're going to work on your brain now. Did you know you have around one hundred billion neurons linking all the little parts of it? Ah! Your eyes are rolling about like glass marbles telling me you didn't, and couldn't care less. That shows me the drug damage is already part-wearing off, so now we need to focus on the sharp shake-up when you fell. That can damage the frontal lobe, or another lobe (there're four in all) - not forgetting the cerebellum which vitally helps you move and climb. So, I want you to imagine those neurons linking up in a silver chain. Though perhaps 'chain' and 'silver' don't give you a picture. Let's try droplets of water joining to form a fluent stream... "

Eartha could not help but eavesdrop and watch. Despite her misgivings she found herself warming to him - he seemed so tender and caring. Perhaps she had him wrong? But his next words ushered back all her suspicions:

"I carried you back, you know. Didn't see you fall but managed eventually to struggle my way outside when you never returned, limped all over searching, searching - finally found you at the base of the pillar. Struggled to carry you - you were a balloon-baby, then had to drag you down the tunnel, sorry - there was no other way. See how much better I've become that I could manage that? Well, you'll be better faster seeing as you're not in a coma like I was. You can hear and move your eyes already."

Eartha's mind whirled. So, Mr. Pitiable Paraplegic could suddenly walk carrying the weight of a human (Motte was light as a feather, normally, but in her 'inflated' state must have weighed more). Mighty strange! Plus, who knew the true trajectory of that weapon? She had assumed it was fired from above since that was where they presumed their enemy to be based, but there was no proof. It could as easily have been fired from the ground, by the man himself. She tried to shake off this interpretation, but it couldn't be discounted. It was a more likely scenario than his sudden 'recovery'. How could someone recently semi-paralysed from the waist down recover full mobility so quickly?

He must have sensed her perturbed thoughts and accusatory stare, for he suddenly glanced up to see her waiting at the juncture of tunnel and burrow. He gave a reasonably proficient performance at acting pleased to see her.

"Your charcoal has sure done its stuff! She's miles better. Her eyes are focusing, as far as I can judge, and they're tracking movement, she's breathing fine and even - just now - shown she can move the fingers of her right hand. I'm more sure than before she can hear and process parts of what I'm saying."

Eartha knelt beside Motte, struggling to suppress an involuntary gasp of dismay on seeing her at close quarters. Her skin, until now so carefully protected by the constant wearing of pelts, had previously appeared as fine and delicate as a baby's. But the chemical cocktail had had a violently corrosive effect, burning through it to the underlying flesh which was weeping, blistered, and brightest red. Motte lay perfectly still on a specially prepared carpet of moss, and Eartha hoped that she had no sensation in her body yet or the pain must be excruciating.

"What could've caused such burns? Napalm? White Phosphorus? The bastards! I'm a pacifist but I'd happily throttle them without a qualm... Motte honey, how can we help? Some of my special tea'd do you good - stone cold of course since fire's a forgotten luxury. I brought some up (she caressed a little animal-gut flask, shaped much like the famous sausage folks used to eat with knife and fork in olden times). I'll help you sip it. Murchadh swears it chases troubles away."

She cradled Motte's head, lifting it a fraction so that a thin trickle of tea dribbled down her throat. Then she began to hum soothingly, something between a lullaby and a blues, until Motte's eyes flickered closed and her breathing slowed, suggestive of sleep.

"Have you looked for broken bones?" Eartha whispered hurriedly. A shake of the head was the response. "Then we should check her spine, especially her neck. I realised it the moment I lifted her head - we might be doing the exact wrong thing in ignorance. I accept you were right - in a way - to concentrate first on the brain. But not everyone values intelligence above mobility," she added sharply.

"Well, the brain happens to control everything, mobility included. Despite what you think, I'm trying my best for Motte - not least because she saved my life."

"Fine. Then help me now."

Eartha inwardly shuddered at the task, for Motte reminded her of the skinned mountain hare her father had forced her to eat raw as a child, when they had had nothing but leaves and twigs for weeks on end. Whoever once said the eyes were windows to the soul was spot on, because humans in sleep more closely resembled their animal brethren. Murchadh was a soft-bristled badger, especially when he snored - though no doubt he would optimistically identify with a fleeter creature like an antelope, or a fiercer one like a buffalo. She was - well, a more docile farm animal came to mind, a pig or cow, except they were reared fat, for eating. She had no firsthand knowledge of any of them, so perhaps Murchadh was closer to a fighting cock. He sure as hell stirred up trouble! The man - hmm, she just hoped he was no snake-in-the-grass who'd pick them off one by one with his poisoned barb.

Coincidently, Murchadh was indeed pondering stirring trouble. He had been visited by spirits in his sleep and now considered a pre-emptive strike was their only viable course of action. So far, there had been several hostile probes: the parachute landing from above; the laser-type weapon which killed the sky-men; and lastly the chemical warhead aimed at Motte. It would not end there, though, not judging by past lessons from the history of warfare. The world had ever danced to the tune of the war makers, and the current disaster zone that was earth hardly suggested the ushering in of a new era of peace and plenty where things would be different.

So, he had plans. No longer visions or pie in the sky plans, real plans. They were still in an early, developmental stage but Bernina's fortuitous discovery had lent them legs - in the shape of raw materials. Those World War 2 guys had such a wealth of possessions it was difficult to believe they had been not only embroiled in a war, but furtively crossing a mountain frontier under cloak of night at the time of their deaths. Their backpacks yielded goodies galore: cigarette lighters by the dozen (the cigarettes had long since sadly disintegrated), litres of lighter fuel, army biscuits, tins of food, more than a handful of hand guns (mainly Berettas, and Smith and Wessons - had he been a gun nerd who recognised such things), hobnail boots, a field radio listening device (this mystified him), and even some neatly folded parachutes, showing a few of those escapees must have been airmen.

Fin was magnetised by the Nestlé chocolate bars and tins of boiled sweets.

> "Tempting as Eve's apple," was Murchadh's assessment, "but dangerous as the devil himself. We canna' trust food - stuff in tins breeds all kinds of toxins, and stuff out of tins the same. The boiled sweets might be OK - but now't else. We'll not tell the others or they'll come creeping down when hunger gets the better of their judgment."

> "But Bernina already spotted that tin a' spam. How'm I gonna keep her in check?"

> "With a firm bloody hand," Murchadh growled. "Or, say it's got botulism."

> "What's that?"

> "Haven't a clue mate. But it dunna sound healthy."

It took Murchadh and Fin hours of intensive work to extract, sort, prioritise and transport what they deemed the best pickings. Only once were they interrupted - when Bernina and Lhotse pleaded for a few of the finest pink quartzes. And all the while Murchadh's dream of launching a pre-emptive strike against the uber-forces was gradually crystallising in his mind's eye, and he was avidly learning all about World War 2 weaponry (resistance fighter style, not battlefront) and 1940s climbing gear - so much so that he could have given a lecture on it, had not all forms of academic studies totally obsolesced.

Eartha would definitely be grateful for the tarpaulin groundsheet, the three woollen blankets that had managed not to rot, and the tin mugs, plates and cutlery - if she deemed them hygienically safe with all their incrustacions of rust. But she would hate what he was planning, so he intended on keeping it secret.

The only occasion that justified fighting to kill, in her view, was when your life - or the lives of your children or loved ones - was endangered. He on the other hand had learned from history. The suppression of his people (not the Scots, who were among the worst colonialists, but the Sioux), along with the suppression of all oppressed peoples everywhere, had convincingly taught him that if you waited until then it was too late. You would have already lost.

Every inch of Motte's body was sore, a glowering headache throbbed back and forth across her skull, while breathing cut her throat more sharply than a knife blade. These two people whom she knew from before even though she could not remember the context, were constantly cooing and fussing over her as if she had just been born, the first rare birth in ages of a sorely endangered species. But they had at least moved her away from the beach now, to somewhere darker, shadier and kinder on her headache.

The motherly one bent over to pour a torrent of words in her ears:

'Lying still, eyes closed, is best for healing, I agree. But I want you to listen carefully, and show me if you remember anything at all. Not in words of course, I know you can't speak with your mouth so burnt. But we need to establish how much you remember to see how well your brain's working.' (Now that was ominous. It was the classic way interrogators started off. Plus she had switched from 'I' to 'we' which was equally typical of hostile questioning. They tried every which way to confuse you.)

'Sometimes our memories go walkabout after a head injury, yet if we exercise them, they improve. So here's what we'll do. I'll talk about what's been happening - and you let me know, say by squeezing my hand, if anything rings a bell.' (A 'bell'?)

'Right. Well, Murchadh and I arrived on your mountain not so long ago.....'

(This story was resoundingly boring. Fortunately the woman realized and started on a different tack, but not before another voice interrupted saying it should do the talking. It was a dab-hand at that, it claimed, and had already held her attention brilliantly up 'till now. But she must have waved it aside because it was she who continued). 'I met you for the first time at the reservoir, and was totally bowled over by what you'd done. Me - I wouldn't have the courage or nouse to live alone and incommunicado for more than eight whole days, I swear!

Anyway, after us talking a heady mixture of fine sense and total codswallop, we went our separate ways. And the second time I met you was when you brought Lhotse down…' (Now that was a name she knew. It conjured an image of a fairy child, white, white skin and fluffy white hair and a grumpy ill temper - so perhaps not fairy-like after all.)

'Hah! Thought you'd give me a squeeze at that! You'd found Lhotse a couple of days earlier and, I guess, planned on keeping her. Now I'm not judging you, but I've a gut understanding why you stole her. I reckon she struck a chord, like she was you when you were a little child. Maybe you got lost yourself, and taking her was a means of travelling back to your own childhood. Am I a bit right? Yeah, and maybe you not liking Fin that much was another factor, a golden opportunity to exact…'

The second voice interrupted at this juncture, berating the woman for her lack of tact and sheer bitchiness in taking advantage of someone unable to defend themself. But the shouting back and forth between them hammered Motte's head so brutally she shrank back onto her moss bed in a bid to disappear. They must then have noticed her distress because the volume plummeted in a flash, the row grumbling on in hoarse whispers: accusations, acrimonious counter accusations, swearing, pacifyings, grunts - everything characteristic of a fight bar the sound of a physical slap.

Finally the woman got her way. 'You've got me wrong man, I'm showing her I do understand and don't go blaming her, and that's what any mamma would do. How can you be a mamma? Plus, she needs to get that guilt out of her system to be at peace with herself, I'm telling you.'

When the woman resumed, she had undergone a dramatic change. Now she was relaxed, at ease and quietly expansive:

'Hey Motte child, where was I? Oh I'll leave all that crap, 'cos I want you to know a little about me, help along our mutual whatever-it-is and since you're such a lovely listener - I tell you, I get the feeling you listen like no other person I ever met. So, you must be wondering what the heck's a black woman doing on this mountain, 'cos us blacks never were a mountain climbing bunch, that's for sure. Well, my great great greats were the exception - just *crazy* about high mountains smothered in pure white snow!

They had this anniversary thing to celebrate, so what did they do? Only came to Geneva, Switzerland and shimmied up a whole long list of peaks. Every mountain higher than four thousand metres, they wanted to get the better of. So they were right there, on the top of that famous Matterhorn one, when the GD struck. Fancy that! On nothing but a toothpick of rock falling sheer down into what quickly flooded into a raging sea! Knowing nothing about mountain survival either - and yet they bivouacked for more than a few months surviving heat, wind and starvation, 'till they finally got off safe in a raft they'd lashed together using the timbers from the Matterhorn mountain refuge, to switch to some better place in the Bernese Oberland, which was a classier island with more of everything.

I guess there was inter-marrying after that before I came along, I don't rightly know the details since my parents died before I was full grown, but in the whole of my life I ain't met another black person so I could truly be the last. I'm apparently a 'throwback', though that sounds a nasty kind of expression.

Well, I've done my bit to keep our race going, had five kiddies in all - but God knows where they've gone now, trying to spread out and reach the four corners of what remains of the globe. I'm still here, and Murchadh's a good guy to be with - when he's not up to some crazy scheme or other. He identifies with them native Americans so he's no white supremacist or nothing. And what kept me going through the hard times (and still does) was not wanting to let my great great greats down. After all, what was the point in them suffering as they did if I were to give up? I owe them bigtime. Just as you owe yours. And that's why we've a bond, I guess.'

Motte knew who this woman was now, having heard the softer timbre in her voice and seen the paler, palm side of her hands. She could even backtrack her mind to an impact noise and an artificial smell, but doing so plunged her into a violent sensation of nausea as she relived ingesting the wafting, corrosive mist - even via her skin, despite the ibex hides that would normally protect it.

At first she felt grateful to be still alive. Until she remembered the after effects of chemical warfare. She would be barren now, unable, ever, to have a child. Tears oozed from her eyelids to run in burning rivulets down her blistered cheeks.

"There you go. Have a good old cry. It'll do you the world of good."

"Some mamma - just a mean bitch."

"Not so, Mr Big Brain - them saltwater tears are the best way to flush poison from her eye ducts, you'll see. Crying clears away the toxins and the stress."

Fin had spent hours ferrying Murchadh's selected booty up from the dark cave to the reservoir cavern. He now sat exhausted on a slab, Lhotse astride his thigh. At first, sorting everything inside that death cave continuously forced him to confront the horrors of being buried alive, because despite knowing nothing of the avalanche that crushed the life out of the skeletons, it was obvious death had taken them by surprise. But after a while the sheer physicality of the work boosted his spirits and he began, at last, to see a reprieve from sad days spent in the doldrums, stifled by family bereavement and personal guilt.

He reckoned Murchadh was an old nanny over the food. The whole point of canned goodies (or tinned, their non-American name) was for them to last. Otherwise folks would have eaten them fresh! He was nevertheless conducting a safety test; nibble by nibble he was munching his way through a chocolate bar, and so far - not a single ill effect.

He would be guinea pig. Then, if still safely fit as a fiddle, he would get sharing with Bernina and Lhotse. He was not entirely sure why he held off giving her a boiled sweet when even ol' nanny Murchadh had passed them as safe. Maybe she needed to earn her way back into his good books, or maybe he was waiting for the right moment to reward her. He was actually testing her now. If she patted him, her trusty horsey who had galloped her across the fluffy clouds to the Grand Canyon (apparently once a famous place in the ol' US of A) then she would get her treat. But if she regretted once more that Motte hadn't come to her rescue this time around, she'd sure as hell miss out!

"Hey there sweetie-pie, open your mouth and close an eye," he sang in a booming baritone.

"Can't close one eye without the other one closin'," Lhotse protested.

"Then close 'em both."

As her just reward for a few half-hearted pats on his knee-cap a lime-flavoured boiled sweet was temptingly placed on her outstretched tongue. Quick as a lizard capturing a fly, Lhotse flicked it back onto her epiglottis, whereupon it blocked her windpipe and instantly shot out. Despite a long, meticulous search they could not find it again, so Fin substituted a cherry flavoured one.

"Be real careful this time."

Lhotse sucked it thoughtfully for a minute before declaring, "This one's way sweeter and yuckier. *Please* can I have another like the first?"

"Well you gotta' be super-good and daddy jus' might oblige."

"Uh-huh," Lhotse answered distractedly.

She had had a brainwave. It might be a route to being adjudged 'super-good', or it might make her daddy mad, but because it involved stealing something from Bernina she could hardly ask Bernina's advice. Her conundrum: Bernina had secretly taken one of them pistol things from the cave. She had hidden it down her clothing, confiding that it was a mighty dangerous thing, not suitable for a kid. But Lhotse knew where she had hidden it. Should she squeal? Or guard Bernina's secret? She just wished Zin were still alive to help her out over this, but of course if he had been, she'd have given him the gun...

Fin failed to notice her preoccupied state, being beset by thorny problems of his own. Did he dare sample the tin of hickory flavoured spam, which mere contemplation of set him dribbling? Despite his tally-ho attitude towards Murchadh's cautionary approach, the nearer he came to actually opening it, the more misgivings he felt. For meat, especially in composite form meaning it was part-fake, was infinitely more dangerous than a mere can of beans.

Not only did Murchadh's botulism warnings still echo in his ears, he also recalled Hon had warned him off the occasional rotting carcass using equally fearsome sounding names: Mad Cow Disease or Ecoli somethin'.

But boy, was he sick an' tired of munchin' twigs an' berries!

18

Silence descended on the burrow after Eartha left. The man leaned against the far wall, his brow furrowed in concentration, to resume his sewing. To an outsider it might have seemed a genuine scene of peaceful domestic bliss.

"How could I have neglected it?" he suddenly burst out. "Moss - to cure your headache, it worked wonders for me!" Expertly he shaped a wad of moss to the contours of her skull and held it there like a molded swimming cap until she fell asleep...

She was a younger, healthier version of her current self, walking across an unfamiliar landscape where banks of swirling clouds were reflected in dark shadows scudding across the bleached grasses, and the mountains had shrunk to rounded, rolling hills dotted with umbrella pines. It surprised her to see not one single grey rock projecting from the soil, but she supposed that they were nonetheless there, a hidden armature of strength beneath the surface, upholding the soft layer of earth and vegetation like a skeleton supports the muscle-bulging skin. She lay on the grass and stroked it, reveling in its softness.

Then she entered a strange chapter of this dream. Whereas she had plenty of previous experience of dream-wandering in pre-GD places where the earth was properly alive and the sky possessed an electric vibrance, she had never before entertained feelings of eroticism. This time however, as she lay on the soft, caressing grass she *knew* there was another naked body lying alongside, brushing firmly up against her, and her skin tingled warmly wherever their bodies touched. She kept her eyes closed so as to heighten the tactile sensations that flooded through her.

Gradually the motions of stroking became more overtly sexual until his (it seemed to be a him, but not conclusively) hands probed everywhere, gently cupping or encircling her breasts, fondling her upturned nipples and exploring ever deeper between her thighs. She wondered, briefly, if she should protest; but once she had allowed the possible moment of rebuttal to pass she found herself no longer able to impose her will on anything or anyone. She was in a state of helplessness…or was it bliss? Truthfully, she could not in that moment distinguish one from the other.

Then she heard a gradual crescendo of faster breathing, like the panting of an animal exerting itself either in excitement or distress, but she had no way of telling if it came from her lungs, her unseen, unknown companion's or from some frightened animal they had thoughtlessly disturbed.

Eventually even those sounds receded and she lay perfectly still, enveloped in a cocoon of seeding grasses that tickled the underside of her legs, wondering if her mother or brother would come to find her - as they sometimes did in dreams. She was unsure whether to act defiant or embarrassed if they did. She had the sensation of being flushed and re-energised, and she now seemed to be lying still naked but at least alone. In the distance she could hear someone calling her from the valley below, but her throat was too sore to answer. She managed with difficulty to heave herself into a sitting position.

> "See!" he crowed delightedly, "Look what the moss has done - up on your butt again!"

She was back inside her old, familiar burrow, with that ever-present man she had rescued what seemed several lifetimes ago, and her body had mercifully returned to a sort of normality. Her pounding headache had resolved into a mere bruising soreness that was perfectly tolerable. The injuries yet to heal were almost insignificant now: her mouth, nose and throat still felt acid-stripped and raw; her arms weak and shaky; her skin burnt and blistered; but she could manage to move a little. Even her brain seemed thus far capable of certain rational thoughts, but as for the hidden effects - to her internal organs, especially the digestive and reproductive ones - well, only time would tell. She managed a feeble smile.

> "You've shrugged off those noxious, mind-splicing drugs, dopamine or scopolamine, or maybe it was some fiendish new hybrid they've concocted." He smiled back, a touch sheepishly she felt, "God - what a nightmare!"

> "For me?" she enquired, her whisper virtually inaudible because her burnt tongue rasped her burnt mouth, "or for you?"

> "For you, of course!" He frowned, "and for me empathetically - I hated watching you suffering. Don't you remember what I said about trust?"

It was inadvertently poor timing that he brought up the subject of trust at the very moment she recalled the extraordinary sensations of her dream. When she fell asleep, she could swear he was leaning against the far wall, whereas now he was right beside her on her moss-bed. But when she glanced again at the sheer untouchable hideousness of her inflamed skin, which had effectively been stripped of its entire epidermis - unlike in her dream world, she realized how ridiculous it was to entertain such absurd thoughts. No-one, not even an entrenched 'paedo' at his perverted worst, would be tempted in her current state. To entertain the idea was insanity.

"You know best how to heal your body, all I can do is help you recover your mind - and your personality. They use drugs routinely as a method of control, you see - and I'm talking from years of personal experience. They'll have aimed to render you confused and submissive (assuming you managed to survive, no mean feat in itself). That entails blending a cocktail of drugs giving muscarinic, nicotinic, paranoiac and hallucinogenic effects. The paranoia's the very devil because it makes you see danger and deceit in everything and everyone. That's why I'm obsessing about trust - because their aim is to rob you specifically of your trust in me, so you don't believe what I tell you about them. That way, all my advice and warnings'll go unheeded and they'll roll us over easier than a line of ninepins!"

"I need to sleep," she whispered, avoiding looking him in the eye, "until my skin heals and I can move properly. My staying awake is a waste of everyone's time."

"Well, don't trust your dreams - and don't go getting hooked on them either. The drugs infect them too!" were the final words that rung in her ears as she sunk into a deep, deep sleep.

When Eartha returned to the cavern the place was fundamentally transformed. Compared to the monotonously rugged, steeply slanted stone-scape outside it had always had its own beauty; its spacious, high arched ceiling imparting the same lofty feeling as those eerie Gothic Cathedrals of old that made people more truly convinced they believed in God; the quiet peace that emanates from a still lake - even though its waters could swirl and eddy mysteriously, sending spirals of part-luminous effervescence tumbling over each other; and the strange, distant sound of water turbulence that rumbled from its depths. Now, it looked like an Aladdin's cave or wizard's den - or, unromantically, a charity jumble sale in the local church.

Murchadh and Fin had cordoned off a salvage collection area with a stretch of stout climbing rope. In fact the 100% casualty count of the avalanche victims was due to them being roped together with this very rope, even though normally you would expect the sensible precaution of being roped to be your salvation.

All the victims had been huddled together near the col, sheltering from an icy north wind after the effort of climbing in a wild April blizzard. They neither saw nor heard the avalanche until fractionally before it hit, and those on the outer edges who were flailing and struggling to escape it were instantly pole-axed by a massive snowfall from the corniche - which plummeted with the force of solid concrete. There were so many crushed skulls that Murchadh assumed they had been killed by falling rock, since his impression of snow was as something benign, light and fluffy.

Within the cordoned area Fin had carefully stacked the separate piles of goods while Murchadh had purloined his own private inner den area. There he sat, the image of an ancient alchemist, watching as steam rose from his sorcerer's brew with the eager expectation that a gold elixir would soon emerge. He had constructed a cage around his single burner kerosene stove, amassed enough lighter fuel to power a year of hot dinners and was spooning, stirring and distilling like the future of the world depended on it. If the alchemist comparison was wide of the mark, he could have possibly been mistaken for a friendly master-chef of the TV era - except for the World War 2 gasmask that transformed him into an evil alien concocting something devilish. And Eartha was in no mood for poisonous substances, having just seen firsthand what havoc they could wreak on a human body.

"I hope you know what you're doing," she barked, "it doesn't look to me like a nourishing bowl of berry soup, which is what we do need."

Murchadh replied with a cheery wave to acknowledge her return - and to indicate he could hear nothing inside the self-contained world of his gas mask. He pointed excitedly to the heap of treasure trove set aside for her. And momentarily she forgot her negative take as she inspected its wonders: woollen blankets, a tarpaulin groundsheet, a teetering pile of rusty tin plates, mugs, cutlery, a First Aid Kit, alpine socks, leather boot laces (handy for repairing the tipi) and three pick axes (technically ice axes, but only an old-style mountaineer like her great great greats knew erudite details like that). Even iron tablets to ward off anaemia!

Fin was curator of the weapons collection, cordoned off with rope to demarcate an absolute no-go zone for Lhotse. He gazed rapturously at the modest collection of hand guns, ammunition pouches (still loaded with cartridges), a couple of rifles, and something truly bizarre - which was in fact a hand grenade. There was even a canister of gun oil to help restore the weapons to proper working order, though it was glaringly obvious the rifle barrels were far too squashed or distorted to fire straight - if at all.

He explained to Lhotse exactly why she shouldn't come near.

"Nasty, bangy things. One blast and you're goddam' dead."

"Like dynamite?"

"No sweetie, bullets are made a' lead and lead's - well I guess it's made a' metal… Just take it from me you're not to touch 'em. Else daddy 'll get mad, OK?"

"'Never, never let your gun, pointed be at anyone'."

"Huh?"

"It's a rhyme Bernina learnt me."

"Well I don't rightly know why she got talkin' about guns, but the message is spot on, 'cept these here crooked ones can't be pointed anywhere safely. So stay away, yer hear?"

"Yeah. You already said."

Lhotse wandered off to join Bernina at polishing rose quartzes, which, according to her, were brilliant at curing heartache and helping you forgive someone who'd done or said something reprehensible. Lhotse decided to hide one crystal away somewhere safe in case she might need forgiveness in the future. It seemed like ev'rybody did, she mused, at one time or 'nother. Her daddy needed to forgive himself over her mummy's death, since he'd a' been dead along with her if they'd not been rowin' at the time, so's he went out to 'do what a man's gotta do' (whatever *that* meant). Mostly it meant pokin' Bernina, far as she could tell…

She sauntered yet further in, where Eartha was busy stripping off wrinkled berries from a twig to plop them into this new pot called a 'billy can'. Better still was a 'Ghillie kettle'. Apparently it whistled, just like boys used to long ago when they'd spied a pretty girl, whenever its water boiled, so she hung around until it did exactly that.

"Can I see Motte with you, next time you go? *Please* Eartha…"

"No Lhotse, she's very ill and mustn't have visitors. Soon as she's well enough I'll let you know."

"Hey, look at that baby bear come to your whistle, he must think he's a dog! He don't look none too well either."

Eartha assumed Lhotse's imagination was embellishing the truth, at first seeing nothing unusual in the gloom. Eventually she perceived the indistinct outline of what must surely be a marmot. It was up on its hind legs swaying dizzily, while flecks of creamy white foam demarcated its mouth - as if it had lathered itself in shaving cream.

"Don't go near. It looks sick with the rabies. Let's go tell Murchadh. If he reckons it's healthy, we could soon be savouring marmot stew."

Eartha battled to gain Murchadh's attention. His localised atmosphere was so intensely hot and humid he was enveloped by thick, billowing clouds of steam. He looked ready to melt - or vaporize into a peasouper fog. When he finally noticed her flailing arms through the misted lenses of his mask, he conveyed - through frantic gesturing and pointing - that he could not possibly stop now, mid-experiment. She had to summon all her patience while she watched the steady flame transform each element into something else: solids became liquids; liquids converted to gases; and gases liquefied! Perhaps, had he not mucked up so disastrously with the dynamite, she would feel more confident he was in control of these chemistry exploits. Plus, if he hadn't been so deeply secretive about the desired outcome, she might have gunned more wholeheartedly for its success.

At last he seemed satisfied with a tiny, metallic-looking nugget the size of a pea, which to Eartha would have been a serious anti-climax after all the wizardry of steam and flying sparks. He ripped off his mask and grinned.

"Right, now I'm ready for anything. What's up?"

"A dopey looking marmot's come visiting, foaming at the mouth. I'm thinking it's had a dose of Motte's poisons, else it's disease-sick. Or, could you be poisoning the air in here?"

"No way! Ah, you're thinking that's a chunk of uranium, are you? Well, close enough, I'll give you that, but no-one's ever got radiation sickness from that little pellet, I swear on all the Sioux and Gorbals' wisdom. So, where's this marmot chappie?"

Eartha had yet to air her major worry: why was the cavern heating up? Could it conceivably be from a couple of flames burning for an hour or two? Surely not, otherwise in olden times with all the chuffing trains, the revving combustion engines, power stations, jet planes and home fires burning, they would have been toast long before the GD destroyed them.

She wiped the beads of sweat from her forehead, now wondering if, perhaps, the increasing heat was merely illusory - simply because the human brain had learnt to equate flames with heat. If only those poor avalanche victims had carried a gadget called a thermometer, she would be able to gauge if the temperature truly was mounting. Or, if Motte were ever active again, being so familiar with every minute detail of the mountain and its underground tunnel network she would know too. Also about what ailed the marmot. Possibly he had merely woken up from hibernation ahead of schedule, and was simply disorientated...

'Motte, me again. Not meaning to interrupt those dreams you're doubtless having and quite probably enjoying (but beware the sudden descents into *les cauchemars,* intended to stifle you), but verbalising's the way I keep myself sane. I bet you talked to yourself during those lonely years, didn't you? Otherwise how could you have kept in the loop with language? You use it well enough, believe me; even if subtlety's not yet your forte, and your vocab. ceased expanding at the age of eleven.

I've been thinking. Kratos haven't come here solely to recapture me - I'm not that important; nor because the dynamite explosion whetted their curiosity in this area. It's for something else. You could suggest the water supply, like Eartha. It's an unparalleled cubic volume of clean, fresh genuine water that anyone would covet, but I don't believe it's the reason either. Or not the major one.

So, I put my phenomenal memory into overdrive, searching for links to this area; mineral, geological - anything that might attract them. I'll run through my findings, OK? But first, a wee intro., as Murchadh would say, to the subject of climate tampering, in order to set the scene...

Long ago, well before the GD, they had the ability to meddle with weather and weather patterns. I won't throw complex details at you, but seeding clouds with silver iodide flares, fiddling with the ionosphere and creating electromagnetic fluxes were the most common forms of manipulation. Although of course I could be wrong because no information or theory can ever be trusted, and I might have been deliberately steered off course by a theory that was nothing but a *conspiracy theory.* A conspiracy theory (in case you're wondering) is any theory that undermines the master theory (the master theory being the one proposed by those in power). Believe me, I'm trying to keep this as simple as possible.

Right, back to the main narrative... So, it *is* possible that although the potential to manipulate climate was there, no-one, on high moral grounds of conscience and religion of course, ever used it on a grand scale. Just as the witches of the past denied causing hurricanes and floods (and yet were invariably burnt for allegedly having done so) so did the governments around the 2000 date deny causing weather change (and stayed in power because of it). The fact that we now have a 90% destroyed planet, a twisted and contorted landmass (well, not much land, so not exactly a *mass,* more precisely a water/sea mass interrupted by dotted islands of barren land, or so we've been led to believe) no rain, no visible sun, is of course not their fault at all.

Probably it was witches again. Or weather terrorists. Or aliens, jealous of our erstwhile pretty green planet.

Climate per se was not their only plaything, either. They were just as happy to toy with the subterranean areas below the earth's crust, where the mechanisms that trigger earthquakes and volcanic eruptions reside. This was a better place to play being hidden from the eyes of the masses. Plus these particular beasts (popularly known as natural disasters - even though skeptics suspected some were far from being 'natural' occurrences) could have massive effects on the atmosphere (eg. ash clouds blocking out the sun) and on the land (tsunamis flooding lower lying terrain etc.). I promise we're closer to the crux now. I'm well into the business end of your intro....

They would argue until blue in the face that if any earthquakes or volcanoes were triggered by man, then it was absolutely accidental, 100% so. By 'accidental' they would be alluding to the various instances of deep drilling for oil or other mineral or gas deposits, or geo-thermal vents far underground that might set off a chain reaction; and the same for the burial of nuclear wastes, underground nuclear tests (very popular) etc. etc. These could certainly trigger earthquakes or eruptions, but cause and effect would be hard to prove, and most people's energies were channelled into rescue and rebuilding in the aftermath, so no-one had time, nor will nor means to look into the underlying causes of such disasters. Much the same as with wars and so-called terrorist acts...

And they controlled the news media anyway, so finding out truthful information was a difficult feat; then trying to disseminate it an even harder one, bound to get you discredited, or killed, or both.

Using the rationale of needing the capability to predict volcanic eruptions and earthquakes so as to avoid being taken by surprise in the future, they energetically researched the underlying structure: the core, mantle and hidden areas below the surface crust, especially those deep ocean beds. They got very excited by the discoveries of certain 'super volcanoes' whose historic eruptions had apparently just about crushed or destroyed the planet long prior to the advent of humans. They had a bizarrely fatalistic fascination for scenarios of mass deaths, mass interments and catastrophic destructions. It's called the 'Moloch Syndrome'.

And this is where I finally get to my main point! *Why* they might be interested in this area… It just so happens that one of the biggest supervolcanoes of all time left its traces not far off eastwards - just south of your favourite Mont Blanc. I know you prefer the islands which once belonged to France or Italy, and this one arguably won't take your fancy because it's split between Italy and Switzerland so nothing to do with France, but still, it is (or was) the second highest peak in the Alps after Mont Blanc, called Monte Rosa (so in name more Italian than Swiss).

Well, far back in 2005 certain Italians discovered they'd been sitting on the most enormous crater of a monstrous super-volcano filling up La Sesia valley, without having noticed it before - perhaps because it was so big that they didn't join up the evidential dots!! Imagine such carelessness! Still, who am I to scoff, I hear you thinking, since back then folks weren't being treated to artificial interventions such as *intelligence plus,* they were mere genuine, fallible humans. But still, even so, it's dumb as hell - but I grant you they (the Italians) were indeed brilliant at art, sculpture and creativity with pasta. Even if arseholes at volcano crater spotting.

So what was learnt about the secrets of La Sesia Valley super-V…? Well, the crater had last blown in eruption 280 million years ago, long before humans even existed (or so we're told) and it had devastating results. It made traces of the event as visible as it could, the entire innards of this volcano having been turned on end when the movement of the earth's crust caused the African and European plates to collide and buckle, but even so humans walked over these tell-tale rock formations for millennia without realizing their significance. Imagine not noticing a super-V until 2005!!! It's difficult to understand how not one single bright spark of a geologist managed to, but the fact is, they didn't. Once they did, they found it showed them fabulous curving tunnels swerving downwards into the bowels of the earth through which the bubbling magma forced its way out, like an underground piping system leading down into the area of hyper-hot.

But so what, you could be thinking. That La Sesia Super-V is over fifty kilometers away. And although Monte Rosa still rises boldly out of the turgid seas, its crater remains submerged, so what possible connection makes them interested in my mountain?

Well I'm afraid I can't be sure here; it's guesswork and conjecture, nothing concrete, nothing convincing. Sorry Motte. But strange things are happening. The temperature in the reservoir cavern is mounting, gradually and discernibly - in ways that can't be explained by Eartha cooking the odd soup and Murchadh busy with a single burner flame. What's more, the upvent of water, which has always created swirling bubbles and strange oddities - according to you, is distinctly tepid now. A geyser in the making. Baby frogs and slinky salamanders might soon slither out! So we're left with why...

Well, you ought to know, I'm certain you're thinking. What's the point of your vaunted *intelligence plus* if you're stymied by this? How can you crow about the idiocy of Italians and other myopic geologists when you yourself are stumped?

Are you groaning, Motte? You're usually so silent I find it haunting and have to check - heart in mouth - that you're still breathing. Then you groan and I flinch at your pain, or you moan and I wonder at your pleasure - although from my own drug experiences I can imagine what's afoot...

Perhaps if I fully understood the past I'd be more able to decipher the present. But lamentably the GD itself gives rise to conjecture but no causal clarity whatsoever. I assume it was a provoked catastrophe that got out of hand, way out of hand. I assume they played with fire and got burnt, that they tried to manipulate nature and it thumped them back, good and proper. I've always thought they wanted everyone to die except a select few (themselves) - who would ultimately inherit a cleansed and purified earth to redevelop all over again. But maybe not. Maybe they want to destroy everything, including themselves. Fire and brimstone. With them, that degree of madness is honestly possible.'

Motte could hear her daily morning talking-to rumbling in the background. It was comforting - like an age old, familiar passage of music, but she absorbed it without consciously taking it in. The foreground action demanded her full attention...

She was possibly eight or nine, she guessed, since her naked body was taller than a toddler's yet still an undeveloped child's. She was locked inside a transparent cage of glass about the size and dimensions of a squash court; well not *locked* because there was no sign of lock or key, yet she knew she was trapped there. The 'audience', primarily men, surrounded her on tiered, plush-red cushioned seats, leaning forward with rapacious eagerness. She was high above them, clinging to the slippery glass walls of the cage at about their halfway height, alternately mounting a few metres higher as her bare feet and hands managed to gain purchase (or suction) on the vertical walls, then sliding down the same few metres as she lost grip. She knew she would not manage to keep herself suspended for much longer; that the strength was slowly seeping from her limbs and her eventual fall inevitable.

The audience loomed ever closer, gripping the edges of their seats, cat calling, mocking her lack of femininity, cursing her flat, pre-pubescent torso squashed flatter by the glass, then screaming out the latest lowest odds to the latest bets. She had no inkling of the exact rules of this game, only that there seemed to be an even split in its betting element. Half had wagered on her falling, the other half on her winning the round, so the frenzied excitement came from the immense fortunes imminently due to be won or lost. A 'round' must presumably last a specified time, and the mounting tension suggested they were nearing the end.

The floor below her seethed with small, bright green and doubtless deadly poisonous snakes. Their cold-blooded scaly bodies sent draughts of chilled air upwards, whilst the sweat and tension from the audience warmed the exterior side of the glass walls until a sheen of mist rendered them indistinct - and at the same time increased their slipperiness for her.

When a shrill whistle cut the air the countdown yelling began: 15,14,13... She closed her eyes to concentrate on keeping her grip, 8, 7, 6, now her sinews were so taut they trembled and the slow slithering down began. Then, suddenly, all her strength evaporated and she plummeted down, but before she felt the squish of trampled snake and the harder impact of solid floor she realized the counting had completely ceased, superseded by a deeply pregnant silence. Until a volleying of angry shouts broke out.

"Fuckin' landed after reaching zero. I swear!"

"Effing didna'! Let's watch the bleedin' replay. You'll see her feet touched base before that zero flashed. Consult the rules you punk - you'll see who's right!"

"I don't need no second viewing. I know what's freeze-framed to my very eyes. The bitch's won me a thousand million drams - so swallow that!"

Motte felt dazed, especially as the green snakes had mysteriously vanished - seemingly into thin air like witches' familiars, leaving only a smirch of blood where she had dissected one on landing to testify that they were not imaginary, or metaphors for something else. Meanwhile the argument raged on outside the tank, so violently it shook the misted glass walls until they rattled, and their vibrations opened a glass door, invisible up until then, through which the snakes must have fled. Should she follow them? Or were they waiting round the corner to inject her with their venom?

Too tired to properly weigh the dangers she slipped through the inviting doorway and found herself in an empty, ill-lit corridor where blobs of well-chewed chewing gum adhered to the concrete floor, and the sharp smell of chlorine showed someone had tried in vain to clean it. The corridor was a cul-de-sac though, its only outlet back into the glass tank area, so she waited, hoping for a burst of inspiration to come to her aid. She was still bereft of ideas when two men with sweaty bare chests and purple jogging pants came marching out and yanked her roughly to her feet.

"It's fifty-fifty whether you won or lost, so we gotta resolve it one way or t'other. And the way the guys've voted is to give you one last chance to prove you won - in a speech. You've five minutes to prepare it."

Her mind went blank, desolately blank. She had no powers of persuasion, no sense of argument, not one idea to support her cause. Had she even 'won'? And if so, what? It couldn't be her freedom because she was still a prisoner under their control.

"Time's up," the men came to remind her, and led her like a reluctant dog on a lead back to the glass tank.

Except that when they did file through the doorway it opened onto a different room altogether! This was no gladiatorial sports arena where overhead projectors flashed frenetic last minute betting odds, but a sombre, enclosed room lined with wooden benches, an imposing raised dais dominating its far end. It could only be a courtroom, and she was thrust unceremoniously into a pulpit-like seat reserved for the accused. Three judges lined up behind a high table, each nursing a glass of clear, sparkling water.

"You are charged with living, masquerading and behaving as an inferior species, thereby disrespecting the civilized mores of the human race," growled the first.

"Consorting with mountain rodents and aping their bestial mannerisms for a sustained period of fifteen years or more," snarled the second, tugging irritably at his beard.

"So, what impertinence have you to say in your defense?" demanded the third.

Despite their overbearing manner Motte was relieved they only required answers to specific questions. She was used to that, it was almost conversation-like and far, far preferable to delivering a maiden speech. Her only uncertainty was where to look. At the floor, to demonstrate subservience which she knew they craved; uniquely at the questioner; or at all three judges in equal measure? She knew nothing about courtroom etiquette except that long words were de rigueur.

"I lived in the manner my mother taught me. I was a child so legally a minor when she passed on, therefore had no reason or authority to change my ways." Unable to impress with the correct, jurisprudential vocabulary, she was trying her hardest to sound exceedingly humble.

"Skulking underground, a mud-burrow your despicable place of habitation, scratching earth, growing *claws*?" He blew his nose noisily, wiping its effluent on the voluminous sleeve of his black gown.

"The radiation was deadly strong out in the open, even people living in caves died from it. My mother was about the only survivor, so her methods must have worked."

"A diet of mud, roots, bark, berries and other similar filth, no toilet, no washbasin, no hygiene - even, (vile, revolting, reprehensible behaviour) - drinking urine! Crawling on all fours, a rat in flea-bitten fur. How *can* such animalism, such reverse-anthropomorphism, be justified in any court of law?"

"There was... no other way."

"Then tell us why not!"

She knew her last reply was feeble, but his final response was equally lame, leading to her realisation - hopefully in the nick of time - that both trial and charges were staged affairs. A ruse to gain information, nothing more. They would rapidly have progressed onto questions about the water supply and alpine moss, and she, like an unsuspecting fool, might easily have given all the mountain's secrets away, along with revealing the presence of her supposed allies, the man, Murchadh, Eartha, Fin, Bernina and Lhotse. She trembled at the fine margin of her escape - she had so nearly fallen into their trap!

Her next realization was equally unnerving. She stared intently back at the judges, hoping that by locking eyes she could anticipate their next planned manoeuvre in this tactical game, and found herself looking into the unmistakable faces of Murchadh, Fin and Holgathon! In uncanny unison they stood up, looming over her, their demented eyes fixed on her naked body which, thankfully, was still a youngish child's. Or maybe not thankfully, since she would be so much the weaker and less able to resist...

19

'Breathe deeply Motte. It's a drug trip, none of it real. Come on, *please*, b-r-e-a-t-h-e d-e-e-p...

That's better! The drugs lessen their grip when your breathing rhythm's slow and steady. It might feel like everything's against you, but that's provoked by the blend of hallucinogens and depressants, with those hallucinogens already a volatile mix of psychedelics, dissociatives and deliriants. You're doing fine; they're gradually, gradually wearing off.

I want to encourage you with how you've improved physically. You've slept so long you aren't aware of it, but all that time you've been healing. There's a visible, centimetre-long halo of hair growing back on your head now, your cl...nails are re-growing strong and long - except for a few twists and turns that is, and your skin's reforming before my eyes! It's still covered in scabs at the moment, of course, but don't be discouraged - they'll fall off. You might be left with some scars, but barely noticeable ones, especially in this penumbral world we inhabit'.

The voice was startlingly interrupted by the sharp report of a gun. It reverberated through the cavern, ricocheting off granite-hard surfaces so many times it sounded like machine-gun fire. Immediately the lone eagle flew up from the ridge in alarm, and the jarring of the soil jolted waking marmots out of their wintry slumber.

"Ne me tirez pas!" Motte implored, "je vous en prie."

"Oh God!" gasped the man, "and I was halfway expecting it!"

He set off at a bent-double run towards the reservoir. On having hurtled through the twisting, turning tunnel and emerged into the cavern, he was met with sounds of complete bedlam, yet the echo chamber quality of the cavern made it impossible to locate where the screaming originated. It was female screaming, that was obvious. But from where and who was not.

He managed to pinpoint Eartha's voice attempting to restore calm somewhere beyond his line of vision. Approaching in trepidation, he confronted the very scene he had already anticipated and was dreading - Fin spreadeagled, eyes glazed, staring sightlessly upwards. Lhotse was clambering over him, hugging him frantically and sobbing, while Bernina stood like a statue, frozen still. It was her gaping mouth which gave vent to the hysterical screaming.

"Making that hullabaloo'll only help the enemy," Eartha remarked wearily. "And leave him be, Lhotse, give him space to breathe. He needs air and calm - not this hellish noise. Try to quieten Bernina if you want to help."

"Can't," sniffed Lhotse miserably, "she's flipped."

"You've sent her into shock, that's all. Where's Murchadh when you need him?" Then, aware that someone had materialised behind her, she twisted round. "Ah. You. Just in the nick of time. Shot in the foot - but no time to expand on the why or wherefore. What a shame we've no Motte to help, with all her healing expertise. Fetch me the First Aid Kit - it's by the stove."

The man's initial fears were blatantly wrong - this was no suicide attempt. Shooting one's foot was proverbial folly but unlikely ever to be fatal. It must be a plea for sympathy therefore, or an outright accident; either way Fin's lack of mobility would pose a gargantuan problem. Plus put a serious dent in the escape plans he (the man) had been quietly formulating...

Fin's eyes remained closed, yet he was conscious of the hive of activity around him. He had lately sunk into such a deep trough of self-pitying despair that this sudden, acute physical pain was honestly a godsent relief. It meant he could stop blaming himself for all his family misfortunes because this mishap assuredly proved him the victim of bad luck. How many times had he impressed on Lhotse the danger of guns? It must be a dozen, at least.

It wasn't completely her fault though. She probably thought she was doing the right thing bringing him the gun, and had she not accidentally slipped on that rock, it would never have fired off.

He frowned. The only reason Bernina had for secreting a gun must be jealousy. Recently, whenever he wanted a moment of closeness, she rebuffed his advances by claiming there was this tiny, miniature version of Hon sitting coquettishly on his shoulder, coyly crossing and uncrossing her legs. And this fairy representation of Hon always waggled a forbidding finger at her - that's why she couldn't manage to respond to him. Well, maybe she had been planning to shoot the fairy creature... And if so, he might have been genuinely lucky. For who could deny it - she might have *aimed* atop his shoulder, but erroneously shot him, bulls-eye, straight through the heart!

His mind retreated, sluggishly now due to the pain, into a more distant past, trying to pinpoint when his relationship with Hon first started to deteriorate. Was it when they met up with Holg and Bernina, and Holg and he experienced this spicy, male bonding typa thing? Before that, he had never talked dirty, nor seen broads as a whole different species...Holg and he had sure shared some mighty fine jokes - but without getting smutty themselves, they weren't low down bum chums or any such thing. Still, it had all the same placed a widening wedge between himself and Hon.

Him making out with Bernina didn't help much either. Even though in her better moments Hon saw the sense in unrestrained breeding, vital to keeping some vestige of American presence in PGD Earth, as she used to say. Then, when he got the hots for Wolf-woman (100% egged on by Holg - in his defence) this truly rubbed in the salt and painted him as a real heel in Hon's eyes, her being so busy mothering the kids. It made him wonder how life must have been in the good old days BGD, when there were so many broads a guy got driven nuts! Mind you, there were so many more guys then too, so a surfeit of competition as well as choice.

He was about to sigh, but swallowed it just in time. He wished to reminisce in peace, and attract maximum sympathy meanwhile. It was actually about time folks gave him some proper attention, instead of deriding him as a cowboy or CIA operative (whatever the hell that meant) instead of seeing him as the well intentioned guy he really was.

Zin was another troublemaker. Such an independent, arrogant kid (again, 100% egged on by Holg). He would so like to retain only glowing, loving memories of his eldest, but could not sweep aside the image of his mouth constantly curling in contempt, or those taunting, angry eyes disrespecting him for everything he said and did. Poor Zin, if ever there was an illustration of *pride comes before a fall*... He could not even bring himself to conjure up the others, because they hadn't stood a chance and none of it was their fault - unlike Zin's.

"He's coming round," Eartha declared, noticing his fluttering eyelashes. "Go get...oof," she exhaled deliberately slowly, "no, don't be getting anything, Lhotse. Just sit right here and hold your daddy's hand."

"You...feelin' OK?" Lhotse's voice shook like a treefull of Autumn leaves.

"Uuurghh," he groaned, "I think some eejit, gun-totin' bandit just shot my foot!"

She swallowed awkwardly, choking back a sob, "It was...me, daddy. I didna' mean to... Gun went off by itself." Her hand wormed into his ham-sized fist.

"Not to worry, sweetie, I'll still be able to hop. Hey, did I never tell you 'bout a cowboy hero called Hopalong Cassidy?"

"No. Or, I don't remember..."

"Well, guy got shot in the leg so came to be called Hopalong. Hey, you could be my best mate, Speedy McGinnis, howd'you like that?"

Lhotse hesitated, "Don't rightly know about *Speedy*. Eartha says bein' too speedy is what makes you muck up."

Eartha wiped the sweat from her burning forehead, placing the scalpel for excising snakebite venom on a nearby rock. It was a stroke of luck that somebody's army had thoughtfully equipped one of their soldiers with just such a tool. Perhaps its former owner had been warring in Africa or some place hot before ending up in occupied France, or else it was standard gear in his army, Eartha had no idea either way. She used up the entire tube of anti-venom, hoping it would disinfectant the wound which was peppered with bullet lead. Although this must be removed and the shattered bones reassembled, neither could be done while Fin was conscious. And even then, only Motte was capable of conducting such an operation.

Wiping her brow yet again, she noticed Bernina still in a state of petrified shock.

"You're to snap out of it, Bernina. Don't think I don't sympathise, I do. I know you've been through hell and feel guilty as sin, especially since Hon got clean away and seems an angel now, just through dying, whereas you're left with the mess.

None of us is pure as saints and none can choose our ideal partner anymore - if we ever could. We've just got to cope with whatever fate slings us - including people. Who knows what'd cement us here into any kind of loyal group in any other situation but dire necessity - but dire necessity's the only theme these days. So, the bald choice is: cope or fail to. And the plain truth: if we can't treat Fin quick-sharp you'll have his death on your conscience too. You get me?"

Bernina nodded, holding up her hand in a gesture Eartha optimistically interpreted as *count me in.*

"So, we must have Motte here to operate, if she's strong enough to come down. She knows most about anaesthetics, antiseptics and broken bones. All you've got to do is keep Fin company - and an eye on Murchadh while you're at it."

Again Bernina nodded, so Eartha struggled up the tunnel. She had little faith in this errand. Realistically Motte needed days, even weeks of rehabilitation before acting as an operating surgeon who would not do more damage than the bullet already had. Silently she cursed the god-forsaken breed who killed or maimed by proxy, aiming poisonous weapons at an unarmed girl harmlessly climbing her mountain. Assuming they truly were the perpetrators, that is… Her body had been horrifically burnt, her brain jolted and her insides flooded with toxic chemicals. How on earth would she manage to wield a scalpel with perfect precision, then set the intricate mesh of bones that were split and splintered, probably beyond repair?

The man had hurried ahead, so she anticipated firm resistance.

"She's potentially at greater risk than Fin," he pulled her aside, out of Motte's earshot. "If it's a toss-up who survives, there's only one choice for me," his voice hissed aggressively. "I know more than you how seriously ill she's been."

"There's more to health than the physical. I'm not so deft with words as you, but, to put it bluntly, I reckon it'll help her. Call it karma if you want, but 'what goes around, comes around' works just as well. I'm none too sure what happened between them before, but something made her dislike Fin enough to let him suffer, believing Lhotse dead. So, to make amends, she has the chance to give him back his life - and I say 'chance' because, well, it may not work…"

"You vindictive, spiteful…! - I suppose you're thinking karma got her burnt?"

"Of course not! All I'm saying is: she'll feel better in herself for helping Fin. Call me bitch or cow if you want, but I'm a woman first - I know these things."

A sultry, humid heat rose from the cavern. The goggle-like eye holes of Murchadh's gas mask had fugged over completely, leading Eartha to secretly hope this had prevented him making any further progress on his fiendish experiment. The very word itself was loaded with danger. Implying an unknown, unpredictable outcome. Planet Earth was doubtless some other

Murchadh's experiment, and their goggles had clearly got hopelessly misted over a long, long time ago.

"Budge over," she gave Murchadh a half-affectionate shove in the ribs. "Your workshop's the flattest area here, so we're requisitioning it for our operating theatre."

Murchadh awoke with a start. At first he satisfied himself he had not continued fusing or separating anything potentially explosive during his catnap, but once reassured on this account he was co-operation personified. He not only tidied the area purloined for the operating table, but volunteered to be the anaesthetist, first emptying the hip flask of cognac (found amongst the avalanche flotsam and surreptitiously confiscated for his private use) down Fin's throat, then sitting firmly on his legs to immobilize him during surgery. An ashen faced Bernina offered to take charge of the medical equipment (scalpel, iodoform gauze, bandages etc. all from the First Aid Kit) leaving Eartha free to make a root-bark soup.

Thus the stage was set for Motte's operation. The remaining doubt only whether her painfully thin arms had sufficient strength for precision control of the scalpel, her eyes the ability to focus after so many days shuttered in a comatose shadowland, and her brain sufficient normality of function to understand what must be done. She appeared to comprehend the situation and her role, but had yet to speak an intelligible word to anyone.

After several raucous renditions of the chorus of 'Bury My Heart at Wounded Knee' (Buffy Saint Marie version) followed by the 'Hopalong' song ('Here he comes, hoo-hoo-hoo-hooh, here he comes, Hopalong Cass-i-deee'), Fin finally passed out. At which point, Bernina and Motte launched into action.

It was a long procedure. The bullet, fired at close range, had the arch of his foot, torn through flesh and bone onto rock, then bounced back into the arch where it was still partially embedded. Motte extracted it fairly quickly, using her claws and various oddments Bernina found her for leverage. The major problem, though, was that fragments of leather-hide from his shoe, and tiny splinters of shattered rock had both been drawn into the flesh wound. If she failed to extract them infection would spread, surtout la gangrène. Her brain was managing to think lucid thoughts, (using the left frontal lobe, just above the left eyebrow, so the man had told her) but they were, for the moment, always in French.

She was so frail that precise incisions could only be done in short bursts followed by frequent rests, while the flickering light of the kerosene lamp strained her eyes, weakened already from long, dark days of recuperation. Even had she been strong and healthy, the operation would still have been difficult without X-ray technology and a state of the art operating theatre. And, to cap it all, Fin's drunken stupor would not keep him comatose for as long as was needed.

Yet these external pressures helped clear her mind of its drug distortions.

Lhotse was charged with the task of monitoring Fin's breathing. It should stay slow and steady, Bernina reminded her.

"It's raspy - an' it smells of that licker-stuff," Lhotse's nose wrinkled in distaste.

"That's not a problem." Bernina fired back.

"Not for you, you're at the other end. Wanna' trade?"

"You're at the important end. Breathing keeps folks alive," Bernina's spirits had discernibly lifted from having to assume a responsible role. She was anticipating Motte's moves now, and alert enough to support her each time she slumped.

"Eartha come," she beckoned urgently, "Motte can't carry on, I don't reckon. She's pooped and can't see straight. Wound's clean - it's just a few bones and stringy things still need fixin'."

Eartha snapped off the heat beneath her simmering soup. She stared in dismay at the mangled foot and felt any confidence Fin would walk again slipping away. Had she known feet contained in total 26 bones, 33 joints and 100 muscles, ligaments and tendons, she would surely have despaired. As it was she brought Murchadh and the man into the fray as consultants.

"You're the dab-hand with needle and thread, according to Motte, - and while you're up in that burrow fetching it, she could do with more moss. I'm not being bossy - just acting interpreter while she's too tired to speak, or not yet able to."

"Eyes're openin', he's comin' around!" Lhotse yelled, just before Fin emitted a bellow of pain.

"Hey Hopalong, you gotta be brave," Lhotse coaxed, while Murchadh, in response to Eartha's gesturing, reluctantly handed over the very last dregs of cognac he had been hoping were surplus to requirement.

Motte had had experience of single broken bones, in the lower arm or leg - those were relatively straightforward to reset and splint. This damaged foot, however, served to cruelly illustrate the greater violence and speed of a gun fired at close range compared to a sling shot or bow and arrow, and she was out of her depth medically, never having imagined the mechanics of a foot could be so intricate. Her eyesight clouded, bloodied flesh swam like a purple clotted ocean across her field of vision and she lent helplessly on Bernina to prevent herself toppling onto Fin.

"Je ne peux plus," she whispered, "en plus, je ne sais pas que faire."

She lay back, alternately shivering and sweating, gazing vacantly at the damp sheen on the rocks, as if they, too, were sweating... A veil of steam hung over the surface of the water, which was lapping rhythmically against the rocky shores of the reservoir - except at the back, where the waves were livelier. Here a whirlpool spiraled showers of bubbles, and the steady sussuration of churning, swirling water could be heard from somewhere deep below the surface.

Sporadically a louder, gurgling sound was emitted, followed by a sudden upswelling dome of water which rose nine or ten centimeters - as if the head of a basking whale were bursting through the surface - before collapsing, sending tiny waves radiating outwards until they merged into the sheetlike surface of the stiller water. She had seen these phenomena before. But they did now seem, as the man had suggested, more insistent, more powerful, and more alarming.

The temperature had dramatically soared, higher than the body heat of five people permanently living there could possibly account for. And somewhere, back in the distant recesses of her memory, she seemed to hear the voice of her mother's friend Bernard chattering excitedly about the existence of *une fumerolle mystérieuse*.

She became transfixed by the 'bathing' pool. Reflecting the light of the still-burning kerosene lamp it was softly flecked with liquid gold, its allure so potent she instinctively crawled towards it. It looked warm and soothing, like runny honey or some rich, dark, nourishing oil, and her desperation to immerse herself in it was fuelled by a sudden, maddening itchiness, as if she had been smitten by a virulent attack of eczema.

Lhotse gave a start of terror. The walnut brown scabs adhering to Motte's body - coupled with her exhausted, crawling gait as she struggled over slippery rocks and slithered into the water - were, in her imagination, the very image of a slinky alligator! But she bit down on her incipient scream and glued her eyes back onto Fin, who was slipping in and out of consciousness.

"We've done the best we can, but his foot's gonna hurt like flamin' hell when he does wake up," Bernina had said. "And if the first thing he sees is your little face, he'll feel way better." So Lhotse made sure her face stayed plumb in the middle of where his eyes should look. And because he was unaccountably cross-eyed after all that alcohol, this was no easy feat.

Motte lay blissfully submerged in the blood-warm water. When she emerged, she had somehow miraculously metamorphosed, as if from chrysalis to butterfly. All the dessicated scabs and scaly patches had peeled away, courtesy of the mineral and sulfur-rich water. Now the real Motte was revealed once more, perhaps a little *too* freshly pink where the new skin needed more exposure time to settle, but virtually her old self again!

20

Motte squirmed inside a crevice from where she could observe most of her old, familiar view - yet safely remain hidden from the enemy satellite that supposedly lurked overhead, eyelessly watching for them. Her ears buzzed from the endless discussions thrashed out between the man and Murchadh, who cheerfully disagreed over virtually everything.

The satellite was one such bone of contention. In order to 'deal' with it they had to identify type and orbit. It could be a geosynchronous, a Molniya, a Tundra, even a Low or a Middle Earth one - Motte felt a mixture of pride and exasperation at actually remembering the weird and wonderful names the man bandied about as if they were as commonplace as moss or rock.

Exactly what should be fired, and how, was another hot potato. Here Murchadh held the upper hand - their sole chemist, physicist and deadly weapons expert. Although the man fully accepted Murchadh's superiority in these fields, he had privately told Motte he thought the crucial measurements too reliant on the magical Sioux numbers of four, seven and twenty eight. But since Murchadh had no way of measuring anything (liquid, solid, or gaseous) with any precision whatsoever, Motte reckoned it was ultimately irrelevant what numbers he hit upon.

A mega-argument was lined up for that very evening. All were expected to attend, plus (except Lhotse) participate and cast a vote. The venue: Motte's burrow. Concensus had been reached a few days previously that the heat in the cavern had crossed the Rubicon, so Motte's burrow had replaced it as their communal home. It was an essential change for Fin in any case, since nothing encourages infection more than hot, humid conditions.

What to do next? was the motion under debate, and Motte's maintaining a watchful eye on the outside world her way of preparing for it. Murchadh was pitted against the man, so a mighty philosophical tussle between logical positivism and philosophical freedom on one side, and visionary mysticism and applied science on the other, was in the offing. Motte, despite the fact that her English was only shakily returning, (or, possibly, she feared, because of it) had been made chief arbiter.

The mounting temperature was their most imminent worry. Without risking revealing herself to the satellite, Motte leaned out as far as she dared. True to the man's claims, wisps of grey vapour were indeed wafting upwards from two new fissures. Steam or smoke, Motte was unsure which.

The marmots were jumpy as jack-rabbits. Become any hotter and the substrata rocks would surely warp and crack, ruining the careful structure of their burrows. It would kill the plants (called 'xerophytes' according to the man) which were already exhausted from their long battle to adapt to dry, rainless conditions; and it would spell the end for the ibex too.

The eagles were the fortunate ones, free to fly away. Yet the fact they kept returning to nest suggested their lack of any alternative refuge. She had only heard of the Karakoram and Himalaya ranges, where the highest mountains in the world once reared to an awe-inspiring altitude twice that of Mont Blanc (if you persisted in measuring altitude from the old sea level, that is.) But those mountains might no longer exist, for the man said they were fatefully positioned in a place constantly plagued by invasion, pillage and war, all part of the frenzied anti-Islamic fervour BGD that was whipped up by Kratos to fever point and beyond, so most likely they had been destroyed. Or overheated - a precursor to the ongoing scenario here. If planet earth was indeed reduced to a lump of scalded rock it would be back to square one again - exactly how it originated (*if* those scientists were right, of course...)

She could have sought solace in an escapist flight of fantasy, but until she had completely cleansed the drugs from her system she dare not indulge. At times she honestly mourned the loss of her dream-state. Not the nightmare segments - just the exciting, erotic interludes that punctuated them. It was a deliberate strategy of course, the man had explained. They swamped you with pleasure interspersed with pain and terror in order to weaken your resistance, but at the same time enable you to carry on and be tortured again. Be very wary of the pleasure interludes, he kept insisting. They are perniciously addictive, leaving you profoundly dissatisfied with reality. It's called *Love Bombing*. You need to resist it, Motte...

Huh, she thought, her thinking repopulated with English words once again, who knows if you're right? Not me. At least if I die now, it's not as a virgin. My mother won't be shamed. I've well and truly...hmmn, the exact word escaped her. But the feeling or sensation didn't, and that was what she craved. It's called *Disinhibition* he warned, another mind control ploy they love to use.

Lhotse was free to fantasize but of course her world of imagination was an innocent, childish one. Or not so innocent, if Murchadh was the judge.

"What's this effing malarkey 'bout that 'Hopalong' character? Granted he was never a real man, just a fictional one whose portrait started out rough and rude, so more accurate. But your daddy's taken the later portrayal of him as gospel, the sanitized TV nonsense that plugged him as a superhero. I'm telling you Lhotse, not one of those cowboy characters is worth admiring, not even for their silly hats. D'you know the truth behind the lying legends? They were murderers and thieves. They robbed the native Americans of their lands, lives and buffalo. Sixty million butchered buffalo! So please don't mention Hopalong in my hearing ever, ever again!"

"Don't you go threatening her," Eartha scolded. "It's meant light hearted - as a way for her to feel better about her daddy's lameness."

"There's no excuse for condoning cowboys. Come over here Lhotse, sit down on that ol' sack, so your dotty old Uncle Murchadh can tell you the story of how Wanblee Galeshka, the Great Eagle, saved the day for the human race during the first Big Flood that tried to destroy earth. How about that?"

The bickering, squabbling duels between Fin and Murchadh were nearly as frequent as the man/Murchadh jousts. On a positive slant they helped pass the time entertainingly, but on a negative they exemplified yet more of the sinister 'mind control' techniques the man had warned Motte to fight against. Namely: *Rejection of Old Values; Confusing Doctrine*; and something she didn't fully grasp: *Metacommunication.*

The penultimate technique: *Removal of Privacy*, would surely have upset her in the past, but ever since her close brush with death she had become more tolerant of others. In fact the man was experiencing more difficulty sharing her burrow than she was! Nevertheless, she was now sitting almost in her old favourite spot, looking down over her grey-tinged world and indulging in private, personal thoughts, so clearly she did still need time and space for solitude.

As conference hour drew nearer, the increasingly tense atmosphere could have been cut with a Swiss Army knife - had Murchadh not left it behind, tucked beneath his stone pillow in the over-heating cavern. Tomorrow was the appointed day to recover all essential food, clothing, apparatus etc. from there, and already Eartha was worrying this retrieval mission would be too late - woollen items might have already shrunk, and food ingredients already steam-cooked and started rotting.

It was Murchadh's turn first...

'You all know I have this affinity with native Americans, more specifically the Hunkpapa and Lakota Sioux, and more specifically still, one particular man - Thathanka Iyotake. Or Sitting Bull, as white people know him. Besides being a great leader, he was a medicine man and a visionary. Now I'm sure you'll've noticed I am no sort of leader, nor am I especially wise, nor even remotely medically savvy, but I *am* a visionary in the sense that I do have visions.

Before I elaborate, there's another thing I have in common with him - my slowness. When he was young his nickname was *Hunkesni,* slow, because he was never impulsive or hurried but thought deeply before he acted. I'd like you to see me that way. OK, that dynamite blast was anything but thoughtful, I'm sure you're all thinking. I admit it was a hugely regrettable accident for which I'm prepared to take my fair share of the blame. Eartha would like me to take an unfair share...but that's a private quarrel.

So...visions. Try not to see me as a nutcase here... I know some might say (he looked sharply at Fin and Bernina) I only see them after a toke on my empty peace pipe, but it's empty as a white man's heaven I tell you! I don't even need to do the Sun Dance to get my visions - they just come. I guess those with facts at fingertips (here his eyes gravitated to the man) know that Sitting Bull had a premonitionary vision before the Battle of Little Bighorn.

He'd done the Sun Dance (a smidgin of self-torture and near-death experience), then had a vision of white men falling head first from the sky. And straight after this, what happens? Well the white troops, huge numbers sent to clear the Black Hills of *injuns* because they wanted to get their grubby paws on the gold - despite their written covenant never to do so, went and attacked those who had joined up with Sitting Bull, on account of him being a generous host as well as a man who defended his people's land and rights. But he whooped them good and proper, every man-jackass of 'em!

And it'll happen just like that, all over again! The signs've been coming thick and fast - the golden eagle who circles four times before alighting on his eyrie; a Capricorn calf (or fawn, or perhaps kid - I never could rightly remember which) silhouetted atop the ridge; Motte in accordance with Sioux teenage ritual going on a vision quest (you might argue with that interpretation, Motte, but it's close enough to be more than mere coincidence); then Motte experiencing a symbolic death, followed by a symbolic rebirth in the sacred pool of the reservoir. And finally my vision: scores of Kratos falling head first from the sky!!!!

So, well, here's my proposal. This mountain (Motte'll agree with me on this) is a blessed place, a spiritual haven and - compared to the other island deserts rising from the oceans of filth that surround us - a place of plenty with enough natural resources to support our community just fine. There's never any

173

excuse for invaders to steal land and kill native populaces, so we need to stand firm and defend ourselves against the hi-tech bastards from the sky. They'll lose - my vision told me so.

But what about the scorching rock, the boiling waters? I see these questions forming on your lips and floating through your minds. Yes, yes, I'll grant you, it's a desperately thorny problem. Here the man and I do agree - an eruption is imminent and we must take evasive action. Motte tells me there is (or rather *was*) a warren tunnel leading all the way beneath the former glacier to the mountain flank on the other side. Of course it might need a wee bit of repair and rebuilding, even resizing (it was built by marmots for marmots) owing to total lack of use these last ten years. But Motte's game to repair it as best she can. I suggest we decamp via this cunning tunnel to the adjacent mountain until the eruption's over and the enemy dispatched, then return in triumph to our future mountain stronghold. A wee little eruption won't be getting the better of us lot, no way it will, you'll see.

It took his audience a few seconds to realize he had indeed finished and they were free to ask questions. They shuffled, cleared their throats, wracked their brains, yet still hesitated. Should they raise hands to signal a desire to speak? Was it Motte, as arbiter, who decided who spoke and in what order?

Motte's ears, meanwhile, were quivering from the intensity of her concentration, for she had been on the lookout throughout for the final mind control technique: *hypnosis*. The man had explained its rudiments. The key thing was the 'voice roll'. A patterned, fast paced style of speech that set up the so-called hypnotic or trance-like effect, the words delivered at a rate of 45 to 60 beats (ie. syllables) per minute, thus approximately equating to the beat frequency of a human heart. Apparently lawyers BGD had frequently used this 'voice roll' technique when desperate to lure the jury onto their side.

The trouble was though, as soon as she had tried to count the beat-frequencies in Murchadh's speech she realised the futility: she had no means to calculate a minute! Plus, whenever she focused on counting she lost comprehension of meaning; and how could she arbitrate an argument she hadn't understood?

At last the questions came:

"Sitting Bull got his premonition of victory before the Battle of Little Bighorn, agreed - but what about his arrest and death at Standing Rock? And the massacre of his people at Wounded Knee? Didn't he have *any* premonition of those?" This was of course the man.

"Er, no - not as far as I know. I get your drift, I think. Implying he only got warnings of the good things, not the bad."

"This vision you had of Kratos falling, how d'you know they were dying, not flying down to attack like the others did? - You know, the ones who got killed by the light weapon?" Bernina's nose had wrinkled thoughtfully.

" 'Cos they were falling head first, just as they had in Sitting Bull's vision. The skymen landed feet first - though I admit they died pretty quickly afterwards."

Murchadh had launched his peroration with zest and confidence, but the question and answer section left him visibly deflated. Still, Motte thought, it was the argument not the arguer that needed to be persuasive, and so far it was neither better nor worse than any other. Up next - the man.

It was the strangest thing. He had scarcely begun to launch his argument when the burrow walls began to sway left to right, then billow outwards, loom inwards - as if its tunnels were rhythmically contracting and expanding like a birth canal desperate to push a baby out. She first mistook it for the early throes of volcanic eruption - until she noticed that the others continued to sit listening in rapt attention to the man's words, clearly oblivious to her private, pulsating world.

Then the scenery changed to a long, stone flagged passageway lined with overbearingly imposing gilt-framed portraits, opening at the far distant end onto a grassy mound where a row of tall poplars swayed in the breeze... Her dreamworld had returned to entrap her.

She ran headlong down the corridor, eager to escape its stale, rancid air pungent with the sharp smell of burnt onions, and the teeth-on-edge scraping sound of something abrasive attacking an encrusted pan. Once outside she stumbled and pitched forward onto her stomach, immediately inhaling the reassuring tang of moist earth and squashed white clover flowers, blissfully luxuriating in the softness of the closely mown grass.

Almost immediately she felt those familiar firm hands fondling her buttocks, stroking the tops of her thighs, then pressing a little too insistently against the small of her back - as if impressing on her that resistance was futile. It caused just enough discomfort to break through the passive state of sexual indulgence that had overwhelmed her in the past. She sat up immediately, jerking sidewise as though forcefully struck on the cheek.

"Laissez-moi! Je n'en veus plus!" she entreated.

175

When she resurfaced inside her burrow world Eartha was bending over her, while in the background the man's mouth gaped open, arrested mid-sentence. His eyes expressed alarm and, more surprisingly, genuine bewilderment.

"I guess she's heard enough," Eartha opined, a touch smugly. "She's the arbiter so it's well within her rights to halt proceedings."

"Heard enough? Or had enough?" There was a fractional hesitation.

"Not sure it makes any difference. Let's give her space though. Here Motte, drink this. You almost fainted there and you're paler than pale."

Motte sipped gratefully from the water pouch. Beads of chilled sweat trickled down her face, her hands were clammily cold and her inner thighs moist - but this might be, embarrassingly, from arousal rather than fear. Had his speech patterns been hypnotic, was that what had resurrected her hallucinogenic dream-world? She had not even had sufficient time to count to 45 or 60 beats, or gauge the ebb and flow of his emotional thrust in the hypnosis test that he had taught her, although she knew that he could modulate his words and change the pace of delivery in a clever way to attract and hold people's full attention.

Perhaps there was a more innocent explanation, however. Perhaps, because she had heard his voice endlessly lilting in the background of her delirium as if it were an integral soundtrack, they had somehow fused and by sheer association one induced the other. *Could* such a thing happen? And if so, how could she ever free herself from it?

Best to find out straight away…

"C'est bien," she smiled at Eartha in a convincing way. Then, turning to the man with much the same smile, "Pardonnez-moi, tu peux continuer."

But her dramatic interruption of his talk had somehow clipped its wings. A certain halting eloquence fitfully returned but he remained unusually subdued, sometimes genuinely hesitant, and it was obvious he was making an immense effort to tone down his naturally fiery, polemic style.

Motte turned deliberately deaf ears to both the rhythm and melody of his speech in order to concentrate on the content. And, apart from one isolated wobble, she felt no dizziness at all! Before long, however, her mind strayed even from the argument - this ought not to offend him, she felt, since she had heard it many times before. Instead of bothering with the effort of close listening she relied on occasional words fluttering through the cavities of her brain to assure her he was still on track with his familiar discourse: *Monte Rosa...Kratos...megalomaniacal...total annihilation.*

Whilst he ploughed on she sought solace in private reflection. Before the arrival of others she had always relied on her instinct - and survived. How could reason ever manage to solve an unreasonable situation? She should do exactly as the man had urged, so frequently that his words resounded in her head like a holy mantra: *'Don't listen to your paranoia. Trust only your instinct'.*

It was strange that he of all people should promote instinct when it was ostensibly an animal characteristic. Up until now he had openly denigrated animals as inferior beings, and was contemptuous - if not downright disgusted - by her affinity with them. Possibly Murchadh's Sioux spiritualism had softened this attitude, or he had found a way to flout his Kratos indoctrination; but if not, it could only mean she *should* listen to her 'paranoia'!

He might be an arch deceiver, feigning the role of ally but secretly operating as a double agent; or, he might be genuine. Reasoning, however, could not determine which, whereas animal instinct could gauge whom to trust by the very simplest of methods. Smell!!!

"Any questions?" He challenged.

"Yeah. Fin overheard those skymen talkin' about cleansin' the valley and stuff. Well, if they planned to set up stations on this mountain, surely them now wantin' to destroy it by volcano makes no sense. Are you sayin' they went and changed their minds?" Bernina's debating skills were blossoming by the minute.

The man gave her a frosty stare. "A good question. I reckon the skymen were a splinter group working partly to their own agenda - that's why they were terminated. Kratos've always hankered after a fiery destruction. Smoking mirrors. Smoking islands. The flood was more of an accident - a bi-product of the fiery end they'd intended."

"Why've they waited so goddam' long then? More'n a hundred years after the flood to get to the real intended thing? Doesn't sound like they're all that powerful..."

"You can't apply logic to their thinking. They're nihilists."

"Are there any women in the higher echelons of power?" Eartha's question seemed genuinely rooted in curiosity, but might equally have been an attempt to catch him out.

"I don't know. I was never allowed to snoop further than my remit. We were merely cogs in the grand machine - but don't take that as an admission of androidism! I'd guess full knowledge of the 'master plan' is highly restricted, to no more than two or three top dogs."

Motte would have liked to have smelt him there and then but events intervened. Suddenly she felt a shuddering vibration feeding upwards through the roots of the mountain, followed by a faint humming sound. The marmots were mumbling concernedly, and Murchadh's preoccupied expression showed he had detected it too. As arbiter it was her role to interject.

"There's no time to talk," she said, "the mountain's warning us. We can't wait to collect things from the cavern - we've got to go now."

The urgency was such and their preoccupations so overwhelming no-one actually noted that she had spoken not in French, but in English. Leaving Lhotse to keep Fin company, they hurried down the juddering tunnel towards the reservoir, praying they were not heading straight into the path of molten magma and inevitable death.

The cavern was a cauldron of hot, steamy air, where clouds of vapour billowed from the churning, sizzling water, itself flecked with sickly, yellow-tinged foam clotted into chunks of froth that slowly circled round and round, like a slow motion gyroscope. It looked like volcanic vomit, the disgusting impression intensified by the pervasive stench of rotten eggs.

"Sulphur dioxide!" declared the man. "It'll asphyxiate us if we're not careful - we ought to be wearing masks. And there'll be carbon dioxide too, which we can't even smell but is just as deadly. And monox---"

"Tie that across your face," Eartha slapped a wettened rag over his mouth and nose. She handed similar 'masks' to the others, "Hopefully these'll stop us talking too. A measely extra minute of delay could be the fatal one."

They groped through thick smog, the lack of visibility a serious impediment because instead of using sharp eyes to choose the most essential items, they had to rely on the vagueness of memory as to where they might be stashed, and solely the sense of touch to relocate them.

Murchadh sought only his scientific apparatus (such as it was) and attendant raw materials, and an extra pair of boots; Bernina as much clothing and as many blankets as she could sling over her narrow shoulders, along with a jumble of boiled sweets mingling with polished rose quartzes inside her bundle of rucksacks; and Eartha headed straight for her kitchen. There she split what had most likely survived steam immersion between herself and Motte, begging the man to shoulder the remains of the tipi and all the lightweight parachutes. After less than five minutes in the hell-hole of hissing, belching waters, cracking rocks and swirling, whirling banks of fog, they formed into a neat line and re-entered the tunnel.

Eartha's wet-rag-muzzle might well have saved their lives, for less than a minute after they had quit the cave an ear-splitting *crack* sent shock waves throbbing after them, and the ensuing booms and thuds suggested part of the cavern ceiling had thundered down. Fin had no danger of dying from spam poisoning now, for the two hickory flavoured tins he had coveted and secreted in his bedding lay buried under half a ton of rock.

Lhotse was shivering when they returned.

"I heard guns go b-bang!" she stammered, "Wh-who's got shot?"

"No-one sweetie, it was just them rocks snappin' in the heat. We've gotta move on outta' here, but Murchadh says it ain't as desperate as it sounds so don't you worry none."

The man and Murchadh agreed that volcanoes rarely had major blowouts without several days - even weeks - of heightened seismic activity. Rumbles, bangs, cracks, spewing smoke and venting gases were all typical of eruptive foreplay. They would of course be stupid to rest up and assume they had months of safety ahead of them - but they should be able to count on a few more days. Unless, of course, provoked eruptions did not conform to established patterns...

"Of course I'm not bloody fantasizing!" growled the man, when Fin appeared sceptical over his concept of man manipulating nature. "One of your breed of Americans, ie. a white European import, but a brilliant, super-brained one called Nikola Tesla - perhaps you've heard of him? No, well...he it was who suggested and tested the possibility, way back in 1912. He correctly predicted one could combine vibrations with the resonance of the earth itself (which is 8 Hz, and came to be called the Schumann resonance - in case you're curious) to cause absolute havoc.

And don't imagine his ideas weren't deveoped further... Although not all of them of course, since he discovered a way to garner free electricity from the earth, and no way would the limitless greed of Kratos tolerate such a horrific loss of future revenue for centuries to come! So please don't fire that tired old chestnut of *conspiracy theory* at me, or I might just explode in rage, prematurely setting off the volcano!"

Fin, having lost his mobility and independence, had no option but to now swallow his pride. He could hardly go hopping along a marmot-sized tunnel, so they were aiming to transport him on an improvised stretcher (part of the tipi and two of its poles). And because the man would be the 'horse' subserviently dragging it, Fin had to be extra-specially polite to him.

"Why d'you go getting mad at me all the time?" he fretted nonetheless, "I never said one word against no conspiracy theories. And I never got to go near the ol' US of A, did I? - So it ain't my fault they got themselves took over by your wicked Kratos lot. I don't rubbish others' theories. Fact is, I reckon there's no smoke without fire - but it ain't a clever time to be using that expression!"

Eartha grinned at the man, "Huh, you got told!" She slapped him almost affectionately on the shoulder, "Let's keep it calm, eh? The mountain's anger's enough, and seeing as most of us lack your *intelligence plus,* we need you on our side."

Motte crouched, leaning against the earth buffer blocking access to the old, defunct tunnel, hoping her memory was not playing tricks but truthfully recalled taking this route as a child. It was the man's idea that the earth they scraped away to reveal the onward passage be stored nearby in order to close the route again - like shutting the back door behind you. It would block off the sulphur gases, even the fiery flow of lava or molten magma, or any other deadly thing that might snap at their heels as they sought to escape.

For someone who strongly valued brain over brawn it was surprising he had undertaken the most strenuous job - clearing and storing the earth; while she and Bernina scraped and scratched, deftly plaiting any plant roots left dangling from the curved ceiling so as to reinforce it. It needed to be strong. There was no point fleeing a fiery death merely to be buried alive by a tunnel collapse. And all the while the mountain continued its shaking and shuddering as if aiming to ruin their handiwork.

Eartha stared in amazement at Motte's 'larder'. She had always wondered how Motte had kept hopes and spirits alive during the years of lonely vigil on her mountain. Now she knew. She had collected and hoarded with a magpie's fervour. Or perhaps it symptomised more closely a mother in a crisis, stockpiling emergency rations for her little ones; or a squirrel amassing nuts before a lean, starving winter. It was crystal clear she had needed to believe there *was* a future.

There were several half carcasses of ibex, preserved in something grainy and hung to dry; numerous pelts (marmot, ibex, and one seemingly a wolf's); gut-bags of berries; skin-sacks of twigs; tiny bulbs hanging off hooks; water pouches; and of course a healthy mound of moss stashed in the darkest corner. She had stockpiled enough food to last their group for several months and Eartha felt anguished at the thought of abandoning any of it.

However, it was the task Motte had set her... Whatever was nourishing, light and compact enough to carry could go; the rest must be forgotten. Eartha sighed at the tragedy of wasted effort and slumped forward, her head heavy in her hands. Sometimes the blackness of despair swamped her, until she remembered that people, especially *her* people, had always suffered - so who was she to give up? For the sake of their little group she must soldier on now. But it made her realize yet again that had she been alone like Motte was, she would never have had the strength to persevere. She would have lost hope and died a lonely death before the very first week was out.

Lhotse's little hand patted hers comfortingly.

"Feelin' sad, Eartha? I get sad, sometimes..."

"Well, we all do. Even when life was hunkydory people still got sad."

"Is it...is it true, like Murchadh says, that earth's been flooded before? An' that Wanblee Galeshka rescued a beautiful girl like Motte from that flood, then flew her up this mountain an' ...*did it* with her. Eurrgh! I don' reckon birds outta do that - an' I sure don' want no bird husband!"

"Don't you worry. That was long, long ago."

"But how'm I ever gonna' find a boy-husband?"

Eartha chuckled, "There's no huge hurry yet."

21

The drugs refused to fully flush from Motte's system. Sporadically, so usually unexpectedly, they would well up again, as if a thousand chemical bubbles were bursting in her brain to flood her mind with bizarre images and the strangest of scenarios. Her lack of mental clarity was not what disturbed her since she had never pretended to an abundance of it; what did was the suspicion those drugs were a means to infiltrate her psyche, making her a pliable tool to service someone else's purpose.

The 'excavation' team, ie. Motte, Bernina and the man, had already managed to restore almost a kilometre of tunnel. At intervals its ceiling was high enough for the man to sit without needing to stoop, so wherever this blessed extra height occurred they scooped out extra width as well, creating bowl shaped 'rest areas' where they could ready themselves for the next segment of claustrophobic crawling. And if, during the crawling stretches, they happened to imagine themselves as obscene lumps of human excreta squeezing their way through the elastic walls of the sigmoid rectum towards the anus, then - this was pretty much *exactly* what they were! The faint but pervasive sulphurous smell served only to heighten the awful verisimilitude.

> "And to think oldtime folks used to go pot-holin' for *fun*," Bernina exclaimed - after one particularly violent lurch seemed like a deliberate attempt to expel them.

All the while, Motte tried to picture the terrain on the far side of the former glacier. As soon as the tunnel began climbing, she kept probing its righthand wall, for marmots always took the precaution of providing emergency exits. These could act as fresh air vents if the dioxide densities worsened, but would unfortunately allow twoway traffic - out and in, so the burning heat and toxic gases they were trying to avoid could also seep in.

> "Why's higher ground safer?" she suddenly asked the man. "Doesn't the giant fireball shoot up before it crashes down - and the same with all the burning rocks and smothering ash?"

> "Well...," from this one word she sensed his inner tension. The warring stance between his knowledge of volcanology pitted against his desire

to reassure them and gloss over dangers. "It depends. There are lots of different eruptions, depending on what's thrown out and how violently. The weakest are Hawaiian, Strombolian and Vulcanian, (I'm discounting the Surtseyan, Submarine and Sub-glacial because they simply don't apply here). These three 'friendlier' types kind of bubble out and burble along for ages without doing anything catastrophic. So one of them would be ideal - except it won't happen.

Then there's (and we're getting progressively super-loud and super-dangerous) Pelean, Plinian and, the most fiendish, *Ultra* Plinian. They're mega blasts which detonate so forcefully they can be heard a thousand kilometers away. In fact when Krakatoa exploded back in 1883, some prize fool of a British Commander on an island 400 miles from it heard the bangs, assumed the local rebels were firing guns from just around the corner, and ordered his soldiers to march against them! But apart from silly stories like that they aren't particularly funny. Not for those directly involved...

And I'd know much better what eruption to expect if I only knew what Kratos were up to..."

When they returned to the burrow Murchadh sat, a bedraggled lump, hunched over in private gloom and bitter misery. His acute suffering was not, as they first assumed, him pining for his precious Sitting Bull outfit with its magnificent feather head-dress - which he had intentionally left behind. And nor was it private, either, because Eartha knew all about it.

"He's only bloody gone and forgotten a tiny but *crucial* element, rendering the whole experiment a no-go event!"

That night, Motte had one of her aberrational experiences. She might or might not have been asleep, while the man might or might not have been talking to her. Whether he really was whispering in the dark so that the others could not hear, or whether the whole thing was imaginary, an invention of her sickly brain, the following words somehow floated through the unknown, inner world of her auditory cortex:

'Although your burrow's a communal area now, meaning we're never alone anymore, I can't suddenly stop talking to you, Motte. Not after us living in such intimate seclusion during all that time before. And I've grown used to talking to you, I'd feel deceitful if I kept a lid on my thoughts.

Like I said, Kratos' motives are key to what'll happen. If the filthy scum fancy 'redeveloping' your mountain into a viable earth resort they can use, they'll aim for a mild eruption. There's a measurement scale for eruptive potency called the VEI (Volcanic Explosivity Index). It rates eruptions on a scale of 1 to 8. That Krakatoa bombshell I mentioned wasn't the biggest boy on the block at 6, so imagine the force of a full-blown 8! I think Monte Rosa was one, and Lake Toba too. Toba blew about 70,000 years ago, plunging the earth into cold and darkness (known euphemistically and far-too-prettily as a 'volcanic winter') for at least ten years. And, thereafter, it created a 'cool period' which continued for an entire thousand years.

I do admit these 'facts' are mere guesswork however, since nobody was precise in their notes and record taking that far back - as you can imagine! Along with the problem that history constantly gets rewritten anyway...

A mild eruption could even be beneficial, especially a one off. Hot air venting upwards can cause storms - lightning and rain, rain being the one they'll be after. But instead of refreshing, nourishing, clean rain, it'll be harmful, acidic rain, sadly. The stuff that damages plants and, in turn, whoever/whatever eats them. Everything, I tell you, has a positive and negative outcome! (I know you feel my arrival on your metaphorical doorstep is a prime example of exactly that...) Ash clouds are the same: positive and negative. The positive: over a longer period they enrich and fertilize the soil; the negative: in the short term they destroy vegetation and wildlife, make the air dense and difficult to breath, and spread themselves all around the world, cooling everywhere.

Murchadh's optimistic vision insinuates just such a minor eruption, with the mountain fit to re-inhabit immediately it's over. I'm not saying that's impossible and I'd love to believe it'll happen, but the odds are stacked hugely against it. As they are, too, with the poetic death he envisages for Kratos - floating down to die like snowflakes fluttering from a leaden sky. Too beautiful a death for those ugly bastards! (Although of course I know such pre-cognitive visions aren't meant to be understood literally).

Beauty - volcanoes wallow in it! Power, energy, light and fire; gold flames licking at an ink-black sky. Artists and painters've always been inspired by the flaming sunsets and smoldering crimson clouds they've caused - you might even've heard of a famous one (but English, sorry to say) called J.M.W. Turner? Well, his doting admirers ranted and raved about his vivid imagination in creating such wild, almost impressionist-style sunsets. Yet all he was *actually* doing was faithfully reproducing the colourful after-effects of the mega-eruption of Mount Tambora in April, 1815 (a 7 on the VEI)!

I shouldn't be flippant though - it was beautiful for those far away, yes, but utterly horrific for those involved, its death toll more than 70,000, I think. Always, always the negative…

We must face up to the possibility of a powerful eruption here, I'm afraid. This Mt. Tambora type of hyper-hyper destructive conflagration sits perfectly with Kratos' taste and style. Wow, do they just love death by fire, the ultimate cosmic holocaust! It's exactly what their ancient, bloodthirsty prophesies have always proposed. I can very clearly imagine them over-flying the burning wastes of planet earth, the sounds of their celebrations resounding through the stratosphere. If that *is* their plan, to decimate the last living archipelago of islands still hanging onto survival and be rid of earth for ever, then they must have found a viable alternative place to live.

Unless they intend to die too in the apocalyptic conflagration. I wouldn't put it past them.

I wish I had a crystal ball, Motte…'

There then ensued a lengthy silence, during which Motte could open her ears (complete with their tiny anvils and hammers, he had informed her) to other sounds. The mountain's rumblings had momentarily ceased so that Murchadh's wheezy breathing had become the loudest noise, until Lhotse whimpered a little in her sleep, cringeing away from something to her left so that she wriggled closer to Motte on her right. They were packed into Motte's burrow so tightly that any movement from anyone impacted onto somebody else, and the one who had to be most careful was Bernina, who must not disturb the delicate propping of Fin's injured foot.

They had made a protective 'cage' to envelope both foot and ankle, but all the same, even the slightest contact with his lower leg made him gasp in agony. She checked the injury as often as she could, but the frequency had dropped off now that the tunneling had precedence. Fingers crossed, the wound seemed to be healing with no signs of gangrene. But his foot was twice the size it ought to be.

The scufflings of marmots had receded from the area near her burrow. They had evidently understood the danger and were busy hollowing out new tunnels away from the central core of the mountain. If only Motte had still been a free spirit, she would have joined forces and shared tunnel excavation duties with them. But she knew there were too many long seated, anti-animal prejudices to be whittled away amongst present company before that were possible.

She was certain the ibex would have already fled.

Just as she was drifting into sleep the voice resumed, this time softer than the after-echo of a whisper…

'Your hearing's so acute, I'm sure even this volume's audible…

You know Murchadh's counter-attacking weapon is short of a vital screw or two. I'm wondering if it's my fault - I'll explain… I admire and support his ideas, of course - madcap though he is, he's quite brilliant at times, and his first intention was to produce a kind of defensive, counter attacking weapon. Then the chemist's excitement must've taken over his saner judgment, and the amount of explosive force he calculated was necessary ran amok into double, treble, no - how *could* I forget? Everything gets measured in fours, sevens or twenty eights! Let's say he miscalculated by four then, because seven would seriously get my wind up. Well at this point - as you can imagine - I began to harbour strong misgivings.

When we all went to rescue the final belongings from the cave, I found myself wishing Murchadh would forget the…shall we say *most* inflammatory element. You may remember I helped him locate his laboratory area because he couldn't see a thing in all that steamy fog, then I came back to hunt out the tipi for Eartha. At some stage my *wishing* burgeoned into *willing* that he'd forget the…you know, hyper-volatile element I mentioned already (sorry I'm not naming it, but I'm bound to a promise of absolute secrecy, and all the Sioux curses be upon my head if I dare utter the relevant word to you or anyone). Understand I neither 'lost' it on purpose, nor distracted him intentionally at the exact instant he was packing it; all I did was *will* him to leave it behind.

And, in case you're worrying, it still won't blow from where it is (where he left it) even in an eruption, since it needs something else as a catalyst.

At least we now have the chance to charge the weapon more modestly. We don't want anything near the range of a VEI 8 eruption from a handmade rocket for God's sake! I hope you don't disapprove of my manipulation - if that's what it was, and I hope you'll keep an eye on Murchadh whenever he next takes out his apparatus. At the moment he's too disheartened, but he'll recover. The man's a survivor and has his ethics intact - that's what I like about him.

It's not the first time I willed something to happen, though. The first was for you, that you'd recover from the chemical attack. It all makes me faintly uneasy. Of course pleased and overjoyed about you, but uneasy nonetheless. The power of the mind is unknown, spooky. Telepathy, thought transference, mental matrixes, morphic resonances - they're all deeply disturburbing, just like 'intelligence plus' is, for you. What I hate is the thought that my mind isn't...well, 'mine'!'

They were groggily half-awake when the mountain jolted so violently Lhotse was catapulted out of her blanket onto Motte's legs, yet Fin emitted such a roar of pain they first assumed she had landed on his. The jolt gradually decayed into mere shuddering, but it was more than a minute before the vibrations of rattling teeth, jostling possessions, and glugging water stoppered into skin pouches settled into something nearer true stillness, and their confused minds could correctly identify what had happened as an earthquake of considerable magnitude.

Bernina, quick as a flash, smoothed a damp cloth onto Fin's forehead and returned his leg to its cage-perch, whereupon his roaring was reduced to moaning.

"What d'you reckon - the presage of doom we've been waiting for?" Murchadh asked, after several seconds spent anxiously exploring his mouth with his forefinger to check if he had lost more teeth.

The man nodded. "I guess so. Earthquakes are precursors to eruptions, although there can still be days of delay before they finally do blow. I don't think we should risk it though. Let's go!"

"*Why* do there have to be volcanoes?" Lhotse asked tremulously.

"To let the heat out, sweetie. Otherwise down under the earth gets too hot and black, like burnt toast."

"What's *toast*?"

"I dunno - it's just an expression," Bernina replied absent mindedly, removing her hand from smothering Fin's moans.

Their evacuation procedure may have been hazy and under-rehearsed, but its early stages had been carefully planned. Everyone knew which shoulder to burden with what sack, bag or pouch - all meticulously packed by Eartha and her more slapdash accomplices, Lhotse and Fin. The job had fallen to them by default, Murchadh being always too preoccupied and Bernina, Motte and the man too busy carving out the escape route.

Motte headed the column, being the most skilled tunneler, followed by Bernina, the man - dragging Fin on his tipi-sled like a trap pony through the dark corridors of a subterranean coal mine, then Lhotse, and finally Murchadh and Eartha, who brought up the rear so no-one would witness her pyrophobia.

"Aren't we there yet?" Lhotse soon wanted to know.

"Not long now, though *there* ain't much different to *here* - we've still gotta dig out the end bit. You can help if you don't make no fuss."

"I wanna see that volcano spoutin' fire," she declared. But the tremble in her voice suggested otherwise.

The ground periodically shuddered from after-shocks, and one super-loud 'crack' was fortunately muffled by the density of subterranean rock and earth, or it might have deafened them. Eventually they reached the end of the restored tunnel where they had dug a circular, igloo-shaped area with just enough space to sit in a circle, backs to the wall and feet touching (except Fin's). Murchadh and Eartha had by then fallen far behind, so the others spent anxious minutes trying not to connect this to the 'crack' - which suddenly developed all the characteristics of Murchadh's bomb detonating. At last they caught up though, wheezing and gasping, the whites of Eartha's eyes bloodshot and bulging from their sockets.

The rest space was feebly lit by a gashed opening to the outside, one of the occasional air vents Motte had located. This arrow-slit opening was illuminated by a flickering orange glow, but Motte was the only person (apart from Lhotse) slight enough to crawl along the outlet tunnel to reach it. After much struggling, craning, and contorting, she eventually manoueuvred her face through the aperture until she had the mountain in view.

A rim of gold silhouetted its western ridge against the coal black sky beyond, while the dark form of the mountain in the foreground was broken up by flickering gashes of flame that ran vertically upwards, like pleats of light on a funereal skirt. Sometimes the flames licked brightly and the atmosphere cleared, then belches of smoke puffed out and the flames faded behind a grizzly mist, and there was a turbulence in the air like a mirage.

It was a vision of hell and heaven, simultaneously.

Lhotse wriggled back and forth between Motte's window and the others' den like a manic yoyo, energized by the flying sparks and glowing incandescence after so long pent up in the dark. A giddy excitement had banished her fears and the magic of fire bewitched her. Even Motte, although she understood better the deadly consequences of the destructive force she was witnessing, was strangely exhilarated by its mesmeric beauty. Blood tingled in her veins, and she had to swallow her strange, ill-judged elation before rejoining the others.

"Is it bulging? Any change in its shape?" the man lent eagerly forward.

"It's difficult to judge with all the flames flickering. It *might* be thickening around its waist, at the height of the reservoir. Why?"

He became sombre, "Because swelling's a sure sign of pressure from the magma as it rises up the chamber. Those slits, where you saw flames - they occur where the upward pressure finds weak points through which it can shed some magma load. The rest carries on up like smoke through a chimney, and when it pours out the top it's called lava, not magma anymore." He sighed, "I'd been hoping for an effusive, not an explosive eruption, though I knew it was only a pipe dream. Now we'll have to *will* the magma not to be so darned full of gas that we get a Plinian, or worse. Hold my hand Lhotse, and we'll make the wish together."

Now that the prospect of a central vent eruption loomed, the man channelled his thoughts into preparing for it. He had hoped for Murchadh's input, since whatever he lacked in factual geological know-how he more than made up for in leaps of imagination and guts - but sadly both Murchadh and Eartha were wholly preoccupied by their constant battle to keep breathing. What would happen when the inevitable ash cloud clogged the air he dreaded to think…

On the plus side they had already left the volcano behind - to an extent. Their current position was under the northern flank of the neighbouring mountain, La Aiguille Verte. Also they were safely underground, shielded from rockfall and boiling streams of lava.

The main danger though, was not lava but pyroclastic flow. A brutally terrifying, killer beast of big eruptions, a hellish compund of superhot liquefied gases mixed in with rock particles and ash that whooshed out at such a speed no creature could possibly outrun it. Temperatures could reach 1,000 Centigrade, and speeds more than 200 kilometres an hour! Flows had been known to travel more than 50 kilometres from their volcano source because they were avalanches of fire and pulverized rock and somehow immune to the laws of friction - they could even travel across the surface of water like super-powered speedboats from BGD times!

And if Murchadh's pipe-clogged, asthmatic lungs could only breathe with wheezy, choking difficulty now, and Eartha already struggled to breathe with whatever fears had constricted her throat…well, actually they would fare no worse than anyone else, because a pyroclastic flow inflicted instant suffocation even on the healthiest, purest lungs like Motte's and Lhotse's.

189

In the self-same way that the tiny space of the den restricted his physical movement, so did the lack of others' knowledge of volcanic phenomena limit his ability to bounce ideas off them and think outside the box. The only person he could talk to properly was Motte.

"Viens avec moi," he urged, "c'est très important."

"Where?" she asked.

"Couldn't you widen the route to your window? Oh I know I was against it earlier - but now I *must* see out."

Motte scratched and scraped, enlarging the offshoot tunnel and creating an alcove beside the slit window where she could stash the surplus earth - to later plug the window against the force of the full-blown eruption. Lhotse transformed into a little mole, her hands flapping like flipper-paws to sweep aside the earth, her energy sparked by the volcanic vibrations that seemed electrically charged. At last the man could squeeze through to the window.

"Central vent it is," he declared sorrowfully. "The mountain's visibly swelling around its neck and torso. We'll know it's on the verge of erupting when the peak itself expands and there's a curved, upswelling lid right at the top. When it blows, Motte," he seized her hand in a gesture of emphasis and solidarity, "it'll have more force than an atomic bomb. We *must* keep constant lookout from now on, and prepare our defences against the torrent of terrifyingly hot gases and finely pulverized rock that flows out like molten liquid, carbonizing everything in its path. I told you about it, remember? Like burning breath from hell! We must blockade ourselves somehow, keep out the heat and poisoned gas as best we can…or, well, we've no hope. That's why we need to keep watch and anticipate the explosion. What…what *are* you doing?"

It was the first decent opportunity she had had to smell him without the mingled smells of others confusing the potpourri of odours. Now, in the close confines of the window bowl they were thrust firmly together, so she could inhale every nuance of his breath, skin, sweat and hair.

"Are you *mad*?" He shrank back but had nowhere to go to escape her twitching, inquisitive nostrils. He tried to laugh it off but his voice betrayed a flustered nervousness. "I'm not at my best, hygiene-wise. No water, no way to wash, no means to swill my mouth out - it must be the perfect breeding ground for halitosis…! Not to mention the sweat from earth moving, crawling, dragging Fin. Motte *stop* it! It's darned undignified!"

"Undignified? I don't think like that. I'm following your suggestion - using my instinct. Smell is the best judge of character."

"Huh! Well? What've you concluded - beyond me smelling like a skunk in fermented pickle?"

"I've found…you *can* be trusted, but not fully. Also - there's a disturbing quality to your smell."

"I wish you'd stop! I actually wish Lhotse would barge in on us so you'd have to, and *that's* a first. So…what's disturbing?"

"Your smell was in my dreams. It's the smell of the spectral figure or form, or whatever it was, that aroused me."

"What the hell are you implying? That I *raped* you when you were ill and defenseless?"

"No. It was never anything like rape. I don't know what it means, I only recognize the smell. And I'm not mistaken."

"Well it's a vile, fiendish accusation! I was there by your side all the time, caring for you, never taking advantage. *You* had the dreams, they came from *your* subconscious (OK, drugs a major input too) but if I appear in your dreams it's not *my* doing, is it? How can it be?" His anger shifted into something else, self-satisfaction possibly, perhaps even an element of cunning. "It must simply show you fancy me, I guess. After all, you've been desperate to get yourself pregnant throughout. Your dream was presumably a product of that basic desire."

She gave it a long moment's thought. "I suppose you could be right. But you've been puzzling over your growing psychic powers, your ability to will things into happening, haven't you? And you have intimate knowledge of those drugs. You're capable of cleverly manipulating…" She sighed, "I should've kept my thoughts to myself."

"Yes you should've. This is no time to pit my so-called paedophilia against your apparent nymphomania, or whatever inexact labels defunct BGD sexual psychologists would stick on us. We've a pre-erupting volcano to contend with, Motte! Post-Freudian analysis can't combat that. And Freud, quite frankly, was nothing more than a meddlesome charlatan in the first place!"

22

Kestrel and Griffon were studying the dark underbelly world beneath the cloud barrier through their light-intensifiers, all other readings having unequivocally assured them they must, by now, be hovering almost exactly above the soon-to-be volcanic rupture site.

At first it was difficult to distinguish rock from sea, let alone one rocky island from the next rocky island, in this shadowy, slate-grey limbo space between the old, dying world and the new. But eventually their onboard attributor spotted a spiral of misty, vapoury substance seeping from a rocky cone, and the higher temperature readings at low altitude immediately above it confirmed the find. Buzzard's attention, however, was fully attuned to the display panel, leaving him no leisure time to study their aerial view. Yet he had the sharpest eyes by skymen standards (myopic by Motte's), and would surely have additionally noticed the licking tongues of orange flame - had he had the chance.

> "Park it here, Buzz. Right here. That gives the best perspective. Aha - summit's bulging like a birthing shicks - so it's too late, now, for a Caesarian op. rescue, even if we'd wanted one. And, while on the subj. of old-style birthings, if retrograde primitives *are* in there, still alive - which I profoundly doubt, they'll anyway be roasted-toasted in a tick."

> "Best solution in the end then," Griffon assumed he was agreeing, although Kestrel hadn't actually expressed pleasure or displeasure at their probable demise. "Elim. all contacts with the past is jewel news in my opin. I never did cop the rumpus over precious Mister Historyman's apparent vanishment, not from first off. You've got to plough ahead, haven't you? The past's a arse-pain."

Buzzard noted the gradual build-up of water vapour misting the pod's visibility screen. He vanished it with the de-vaporiser, but irritatingly it straight away refugged. It was his first time, ever, of experiencing moisture on a visibility screen in a whole lifetime of flying! He had to fess that mostly he had flown in the upper zones above the cloud barrier where bone-dry atmospheres prevailed, but he had descended through the cloud on two previous occasions. And then, even though the humidity level rose several digits above zero, the air had not once wept visible moisture.

The rotar blades were similarly being defected by this unexpected steam-clog. Their vibratations were a distinct decibel or two louder than normal, and not quite as perfectly, purringly smooth.

"We shouldn't hang about vertically over the volco-vent, it's asking for trouble," he warned his two companions. "I intuit Jellyfish doesn't like it this hot."

"They wouldn't send us on a mission impossible, matey. These pods are impervious to any and every," Kestrel snapped his dislike of any type of whinging.

"Well, all the same... Tell me the instant you see that swell-belly chamber about to pop. We don't want to be dead centre above the chimney draught, not when it blows a megaton. That's just asking for malfunctionings."

"I'll quiz them about poss. probs we might encounter then, OK? So's to set your mind at rest, Buzz. Right: 'Griffon to Alpha Ipsilon, Griffon to Alpha Ipsilon, can you hear me?'"

Several tocks later Griffon's voice was discernibly huskier, after repeating the same old fruitless formula to no avail.

"The pooping pykies! Either we're clean outta coverage - else they can't be arsed to bloody yap!" he grumbled.

"No. It won't be that," Buzzard corrected. "Blame instead the gases from the vent. They cause electrical oddities and interfere with radio waves. That's the prob with our low-tech., backward communi-systems. I *have* aired my negatives before. Still, we can't be monitored either, that's the bono. Let's get real *rebellious,* shall we? Let's party on seditious goss.!"

"Not on my watch," growled Kestrel, taking him seriously. "We've a mission to achieve, you guys. Mister Historyman might still effect a break out, and if he does, we swoop into action even if your pesky Jellyfish is melting to syrup. Gettit? And if he doesn't, then we still stay here to carry out the rest of our brief. No shirking. No xcuses. Gottit?"

"OK mate," they cho)rused dutifully.

"You ought to lighten up. Else you'll get ulcers," advised Griffon.

"Didn't they tell you - Armageddon's *partytime,*" Buzzard smiled wrily.

For a few secs Kestrel tried to keep his irritation private, but it soon burst forth.

> "I'll have to pull autho. then. You can't quibble - you knew it when you signed. We stay put, centrifuging and subterfuging right here, until it blows and we get a max. temp. readout and photo the blow."

Buzzard stared at the irregular, twitching displays before quietly replying.

> "You've autho. for the mission, yes. Can't argue. But as captain of this pod, I've autho. to act how I see fittest to keep it airborne and preserve it, not smitherene it. And I'm informing *you*, right here we're smack in the path of a mega-bomb. I don't think you understand the certainty of science. What's the point in data and photos no-one'll ever bloody see?"

Far below them, Fin lay awake in the new dugout, glorying in the miraculous absence of pain. It was so extraordinary he first had to check he was still alive, because up until now every movement of his injured leg had sent bolts of agony ripping through him; pain so acute he had literally ground down his teeth, and smoothed off their useful cutting edges from constantly gritting them to stifle moans and groans he could never otherwise have suppressed.

Now though, the only sensation to suggest he still possessed a lame foot was its icy numbness. And that in itself was a welcome relief from the mounting volcanic heat. He celebrated by falling asleep - another pleasure he had been deprived of since Lhotse shot him and the pain kept him continuously awake.

Motte was silently watching, waiting for this exact opportunity. Healing so shattered a foot was never likely to be easy, she had known that all along. On the last time she inspected it, the circulation problems were glaringly obvious. Painstakingly, she detached the protective cage and removed the moss 'bandage', briefly confirmed her suspicions and headed straight down the tributary tunnel to where the man was doing his turn at duty-watching the volcano.

> "There used to be this saying '*A watched pot never boils.*' I'm adapting it so's to stop the eruption in its tracks. What d'you think? It's not got any more imminent has it, under my watching brief?"

> "Mais non - the magma bulge does seem temporarily stuck. It won't go conveniently back underground, though, not after getting this far. But…we've other problems."

"Oh Motte, don't go back there again!"

"It's Fin."

"Are you winding me up?"

She frowned perplexedly. "I don't know what you mean. His toes've turned black which means they're dead. I can detach them, it's quite an easy thing. But if the gangrene still spreads higher and we have to, er...in French c'est dismembrer, I think you say amputate...higher up, above the ankle..." Her face blanched and the hand that touched him trembled violently, "I can't do it. Just to think of it gives me the horrors. I'll deal with the toes now, but *you* must cut the leg - if it becomes necessary. Please."

He stiffened. "I'd like to see the damage now, before you sever anything."

"That's why I came. Because," her voice turned bitter, "I know you're infected by Eartha's thinking - that I want to disable him out of malice. Quelle bêtise!"

"Not intentionally, Motte. No. But...don't be angry here, such a thing *can* happen, subconsciously, so that even you aren't aware of it..."

Motte dithered over the best procedure. Before the avalanche victims' gift of fire and knife blades she would have used a gut tourniquet just as her mother had done. But now their medical resources had advanced from pre-historic to Roman era, and cauterization possibly was the better means to stem the flow of blood and create the boundary between living and dead flesh. It was no use consulting the man over this dilemma - unless another lengthy revellation on the medical breakthroughs and philosophical forward leaps of intelligence by a certain Aelius Galenus (sometimes called Claudius), from back in AD 129, was really going to help determine anything.

She eventually decided to cauterize, then cut. Murchadh could immobilize him and Bernina act as nurse once again.

"What? Murchadh? With his dodgy breathing? When I've been the one dragging the guy around..."

"Someone has to watch the volcano," Motte reminded him coldly.

"*Why* do we have toes?" Lhotse asked worriedly. "Will he...will he still be able ta walk?"

Motte's nerves jangled, partly from his unfair mistrust of her (outrageous after all the careful doctoring she had done for both injured victims - and primarily the man himself), and partly her mistrust in him, which ebbed and flowed without ever fully evaporating. They also seethed uneasily over the certain knowledge Fin would be lucky to survive, let alone ever walk again.

But then, with the gathering venom of the volcano, so would they all…

Eartha at last began to emerge from her black-hole, fearful state. Lhotse was the catalyst, hurrying to tell her five of her daddy's toes had been chopped off.

"*Jus'* because they was black!" she declared indignantly. "How comes you have pinky toes and pinky hands, when the rest of you ain't that colour, Eartha?"

Eartha gave it serious thought. "Well, my daddy used to say it was because the soles of our feet and the palms of our hands did the most work, and never got a look in from the sun - when there used to be a sun, that is. But I don't rightly know - best ask that know-it-all man, I guess. He'll be sure to have some half-assed theory about it."

"I reckon being black's way better," she ruefully inspected the smudges of earth smeared all over her sweating white skin. "It don't show up the dirt like mine does." Then she brightened, "Let's make somethin' to eat, shall we? I've been chewin' earth ever since you got sad, after Motte said it wouldn't do no harm. Murchadh's took the only stove though, to make his ol' rocket-bomb."

"Oh, it surely can't be a bomb," Eartha protested.

But there was a falter in her voice nevertheless. Secretly she blamed the man for drawing elusive parallels between his Kratos and Murchadh's all-time bête-noir, that dog of a George Armstrong Custer, since Murchadh had never been attack minded before.

Murchadh, meanwhile, sat ruminating beyond the bend in the tunnel a little ahead of their communal resting place, an area Motte was in the process of excavating as an onward route. He had only just begun breathing freely again, after ejecting a monstrous globule of earth-tinged phlegm the size of a gobstopper.

With the augmented oxygen rushing in, ideas ran riotously through his mind and his lidded eyes saw wild, explosive visions.

His native American folklore gave no guidance on volcanoes. Its archives were confined to a soppily romantic legend of Popocatepetl (a brave and handsome male lover) and Iztaccihuatl (his female love interest and, naturally, a beautiful princess) in Mexico - which was anyway an Aztec domain so not strictly the same heritage. These two cosily adjacent high volcanic mountains were once forbidden lovers in a scenario not hugely dissimilar to that of Romeo and Juliet. It was a pretty enough tragedy, but gave him no help whatsoever. Scientific know-how being what was needed, not a tearjerking fairy tale.

Thanks to the man he had grasped the distinction between a pyroclastic flow and a pyroclastic surge. The *flow* rushed pell-mell downhill whereas the *surge* could go anywhere, uphill or down. Meaning it was worse - for them anyway - since at their current altitude on the adjoining mountain they should avoid the likely path of a flow but a surge could swamp them with ease. In the past people had tried (unsuccessfully, it had to be said) to build barriers against lava flows, but pyro. flows were unstoppable. Like liquefied superheated hurricanes, they burned, flattened and buried like a grim reaper pumped full of methamphetamine.

His plan was simple enough, in essence. Fight fire with fire. Create a blast hotter and faster than a pyro. flow and fire it to collide head-on! As an *idea* it had legs but would it work in practice? Those innovators of old were able to test their theories a thousand times over before fine tuning them to maximize the chances of success and minimize the possibilities of failure. He, sadly, had but one chance.

His head was a frenetic war zone of battling opinions. Several contemptuous inner voices derided him as foolish beyond belief. What he proposed, they scoffed, would effectively double the damage - like a head-on collision between two fast cars, or a multiple nuclear blast. How they booed and taunted! Had there been tomatoes to hand, he would be pelted to a pulp!

But the dreamer segment of his brain, the lyrical consciousness inherited from a culture of story telling, myth and imagination was more optimistic, suggesting that such a miracle could indeed happen. Huh, his saner half retaliated, those old legends were mere metaphorical interpretations of possible factual events simplified down to the level of a small child's understanding. Plus, they had been warped through the constant retelling, an oral tradition as fickle as the game of Chinese whispers, spreading and shifting amongst a people as simple as they were illiterate.

The weirdest thing was that the man, despite being the product of a society in total thrall to knowledge, order, authority and control, was an eager supporter of his mad leap of faith! This was the straw he clung to, and yet…how could a flimsy straw truly save a drowning man? The saying was clearly a trap, not a truth. Plus the caveat was darned obvious. If the man was a traitor, still acting as a tool for Kratos having never 'deprogrammed' himself at all (and if they were as all-powerful as he claimed, how could he have busted their programming with the pathetic help of alpine moss, Motte and his own manufactured-by-them brainpower?) then his encouragement played plumb into enemy hands.

All he, dumb old Murchadh, would be doing was to magnify the colossally hot explosion of end-of-planet-earth which they would applaud from some safe altitude up in the sky. The whole conflagration was probably planned to benefit their stupid new planet, or re-power their crafts that were doubtless running low on juice…

The man had also seemed to say that, alternatively, they might actually want to burn themselves up in the whole bonfire in an act or pact of mass suicide, either to rise again like a phoenix or perish in an inferno simply to satisfy the correctness of their ancient prophesies of Armageddon.

Humans must have been stupid from the word go if that truly was what they had in mind. Survival was supposedly an inbuilt urge. How could they change it for a death cycle? He sighed deeply. At his age he was more than ready to die, but what about poor wee little Lhotse? What chance had she had in her short little life? Or Motte?

"Goddam' pain's back. I had a fine lil' interlude without it. But now my toes are fair killin' me again."

Bernina was no adept at keeping secrets. She had struggled to keep Holgathon's for long enough, and felt more at ease, now, after at long last unburdening herself to the man. Fin anyway ought to know the truth because - according to Motte - his best chance of healing was to engage in self-help.

"Can't see as how that's at all possible, Fin honey, since they ain't there no more! They was all rottin' away so had to be cut off, before the gangrin climbed higher up your leg. Motte says you've gotta' stimulate your circulation down to your foot or it won't work. You gotta' think blood into your foot, Fin, otherwise the rot climbs higher."

Fin's eyes registered alarm. "How much is gone already, godammit?"

"Jus' the five toes. But if you don't get the blood pumpin'…"

"OK - I've got the picture. Perhaps if you was to kiss it better…"

"Gawd a'mighty, you're onto sex faster'n a jack rabbit come Spring! I can't be kissin' while other folks're near, now can I? And you gotta help yourself, that's Motte's whole point," Bernina reminded him sternly.

Motte clawed at the rock-clogged earth beyond Murchadh's chemist's lab, working blind since any faint glimmer emanating from the window slit where the man still watched was blocked out by Murchadh's bulk.

She was working on the hunch that, by contriving a corkscrewing tunnel that spiralled downward, this would delay and confuse the pyro. torrent soon to be their nemesis. Her reasoning - the intense heat, having once made the mammoth effort to rise from the burning inner core out onto surface earth, would never seek to return via similarly narrow passageways, back into the underground world from which it originated. Same as a baby, once having traumatically exited the birth canal, never thought to clamber back into the womb and rejoin itself to the umbilical chord…

And yet - that was what her brother hankered for! Obviously not *literal* rewombing. Merely to rewind time so as to be reborn in an earlier, happier era, before the present bleakness strangled the fragile existence of hope.

She joined the man at their cramped lookout post.

"My turn to watch now. Yours to dig," she informed him.

"But I know best what to watch for!" he wailed, "and I'm rubbish at digging."

"Fair's fair."

"You know full well it isn't. 'All's fair in love or war' was the more apt saying because it licensed serial cheating and admitted nothing *is* fair, which is of course the truth." However he reluctantly ceded her the window space. "Did your mother never mention Mt.Vesuvius?"

"A volcano?"

He nodded. "Its most famous blow-out was in CE 78 when it buried Pompeii and Herculaneum under nearly three metres of pumice, and they weren't dug out until seventeen hundred years later! Imagine - with everything preserved under the hardened pyro. flow precisely as it was at the moment of live burial. Figs and peaches half-munched on plates, smears of wine staining goblets, screams and gasps for breath still contorting the faces of the mummified corpses, lovers lying in bed clinging to each other for comfort or in the last grasps of passion. And, those fastest to react already running down the street in a hopeless bid to escape."

Motte sighed. "Are you trying to tell me we have *no* chance at all?"

"No. Or not conclusively no. They died because they didn't foresee the power of the eruption. It was a Plinian, the first-ever because the name itself comes straight from the man who described it in detail, Pliny the younger. He was eighteen years old at the time, perhaps the same as you! Coincidences... The other one being it vented an ash cloud the shape of an umbrella pine six to eight hours before the eruption. Haven't you spotted our umbrella yet?"

"Mais oui," she admitted sorrowfully. "It must mean we've only six to eight hours before the cone blows."

"Well, they might not be copycat eruptions after all. But if you look carefully at the peak, the central cone's already bulging upwards. Such a blatant, in-your-face symbol of male arous..."

"The ash cloud makes it difficult to see."

"Difficult to breathe, as well. I must go and warn Murchadh. He's planning to increase our oxygen supplies using an ultra-risky combination of water, salt, two buck-ibex horns and earth's natural electrical charge! Sounds crazy as a wedge, I know... Keep watching like a hawk, Motte. The pyro. flow is our enemy number one."

"I thought that was Kratos."

She was too fixated on the burning fires consuming her mountain home to look at him, but she heard him take a deep breath. Several deep breaths.

"I wish I could tell you the substance of Bernina's confession, but now's...well, not the time. All I'll say now, is no-one can *invent* an eruption from thin air, it can only happen because of pre-existing conditions. You told me Alessandro mentioned 'une fumarole mystérieuse', plus, it was hotter when your mother was a child, and you often noticed tremors and minor earthquakes - all of them classic volcanic symptoms. Unsurprising, since we're on the plate boundary where the African and European plates collide, and have volcanic regions from the distant past as neighbours: the Auvergne area off west, Monte Rosa out east, our Roman friend Vesuvius down south, not forgetting Etna and Stromboli in Sicily, or thereabouts.

Kratos will simply have stirred your mountain's dormant fires, like baiting a fighting animal to rouse its aggression."

An unwelcome, unwanted memory of when she had found him splashing in the reservoir waters after the dynamite explosion suddenly reared up in her mind's eye. Paranoia or perspicacity - it could as easily be either. But who else could have accessed the 'fumerole' to stoke its fires?

> "I'm sure they'll be confidently thinking we're still holed up in the fiery depths of your mountain, long dead, so they might get over-cocky… Hmm, I can see you thinking that description's me to a T but no - I'm how I am from trying not to be brow-beaten, downtrodden or humiliated beyond all reason." A volcanic fire flared along the glassy curve of his glittering eyes, "Not by them - nor by you."

> She raised an eyebrow. "My stance is self-protection, same as you say is yours. Except I've much less experience at recognizing the boundaries between a friend, a false friend, and a true enemy." This time she held his gaze.

> "There's no certain guide, take it from me."

> "I thought you championed instinct." Her smile was heavily sardonic.

After he went to talk tactics with Murchadh, Motte watched the mountain so unblinkingly that its flickering flames and belching smoke banished all other optic receptivity. Even when she turned her back on them, they superimposed themselves onto the earth tunnel walls like some filmic form of kinesthetic wallpaper. She seemed to have lost the ability to perceive any distinction between illusion and reality.

It actually made her wonder if this whole volcano thing, this impending eruption drama, was nothing but a drawn-out sequel to the tests and trials the drugs had encouraged her to believe were real. Like a scene several episodes later on from the glass tank and frenzied betting hall. In reality (if indeed such a thing existed) she might simply be thirsty, so hallucination translated that parched, hot, thirsty feeling into…a volcano! The man had himself drawn the parallel between the upthrusting magma flow and an erect penis ready to discharge, so there again was a direct link to the other, the sexual aspect of her dreams.

Soon she would be discharging her own flow of magma and panting with the breathless warmth of it all. And then she would wake up on a sandy beach and see the man and Eartha ladling buckets of brackish water over the steaming geysers, and that bird with the vicious beak would want another prod at her jelly!

"Lhotse," she called softly - in case Kratos were still busy sound-monitoring despite being convinced they were dead. "Come and look!"

"Ev'rybody wants me today!" Lhotse purred happily.

"D'you...d'you see...*people* crawling around near the peak? Those dark specks moving oddly, just below the crater fire?"

Lhotse stared intently where Motte pointed. "*Can't* be, not unless they're devils crawlin' outta hell. Normal folks'd get burnt up so close to fire. Them specks are prob'ly just rocks burnin' and rollin' about 'cos of the slope."

Murchadh chomped on his pipe stem to subdue his chattering teeth. Now that the man had left, he was assaulted by the fear he might have made crucial miscalculations, all flimsily based on half-knowledge about physics, explosives, and which gases were compatible, which not.

He vaguely remembered being told that the Hindenburg disaster (a famous, hot-air zeppelin-style balloon that combusted in a mighty fireball) proved the out and out incompatibility between hydrogen and some other gas, oxygen most likely, and it was his failure to remember the details that nagged at him now. Equally unfortunate was the fact his knowledge of chemistry came from a single, limited source, subsequently filtered through the conduit of his father, who was undoubtedly insane.

This source was a distant past great, great, great who worked as a demolition expert in the days of high-rise buildings. The dynamite was his parting gift to his son who presumably planned to follow in daddy's footsteps. But since all high-rise buildings sank below the sea in the GD before this son's career in demolishing them could get properly started, it was never put to use. Thus it became a precious family heirloom and made its way into Murchadh's hands. (An alternative family theory claimed dynamite was superseded by something much better long before the GD, so the 'gift' was really more of a put down, from a dad who despised his son).

Never rely on a single source was a golden rule in Science, yet here he was openly defying it. For the first time, too, he fearfully questioned the limitations of using four, seven and twenty eight as the sole basis of his calculations. Everything he was relying on might be no more substantial than a will o' the wisp!

At least, he comforted himself, even though he felt guilty now, knowing how fully responsible he was for everyone else's lives, he wouldn't in the future feel any guilt when he failed and his explosion backfired - because he would be dead, and so would they. It was the waiting that agitated his nerves.

If the lesson from the Hindenburg crash was that oxygen and hydrogen gas should be kept apart at all cost - unless you wanted a fireball, that is - then he had taken proper precautions. Cue in the two ibex horns, specifically employed to keep the two enemy gases forever separate. But gases by definition were the most volatile and unpredictable of things. They acted up, always did the unexpected, were usually invisible, only made a bang when it was too late to warn of danger, and often deceived you by having no smell at all, nasty or enticing.

He was not even precisely sure what gases lay encased in the magma, and whether they exploded on reaching the outside air because of contact with oxygen (most likely), carbon dioxide (least likely) or nitrogen (somewhere-in-between). Damn' and blast his ignorance! (Or, on second thoughts, omit the *blast*. Too stupidly tactless an expression under present circumstances).

This pre-eminent stage of eruption was like a woman in labour. The contractions were happening, the waters had broken (that would be the fire visible around the neck of the womb or crater) and the head was fully engaged. When the midwife shouted 'push' then out would pop the baby. And this was precisely where his silly comparison came unstuck. Because there *was* no-one to shout push, so no way of knowing when the magma would burst out and the detonation happen. Even the crowds of geologists and volcanologists who would have been swarming all over the area in times past, measuring the seismic levels of tremors, gauging the viscosity of the magma, taking temperature readings, photographing this, that and the other, *never* managed to predict the exact moment of explosion!

And *their* experts? Well, they were relying partly on Motte, who had a close and instinctive relationship with her mountain and would notice the minutiae of changes; and partly on the man, who had an encyclopaedic knowledge of volcanoes as well as just about everything else. And, to complicate things further, Motte had recently changed from a self-reliant survivor with acute observational skills into a drugged-out automaton wandering around in a daze; while for all anyone knew the man already had his finger on the detonator and, just prior to pressing it, would strap on his flying wings, ignite his solo-rocket and whoosh into the clouds to rejoin his mates!

That's what waiting did to Murchadh...reduced him to a bundle of nerves who saw the worst in everything. The one good thing, though, about this thinking bout, was it had boosted his self-confidence, a highly desirable state prior to putting a dangerous experiment to the test.

After all, he had begun by blaming himself - and ended up finding a way to pin some of the blame onto Motte and the man!

23

Eartha stirred the cooking pot with a steady hand. While watching the steam rise, the thought seeped into her mind how horrified her soul sisters from way back would be that she had so completely abandoned their crusade of feminism.

In their total ignorance of the current world situation, they would be aghast that she had voluntarily undertaken all the menial tasks - gathering herbs and roots, cooking, cleaning (well, not too much of that!) and comforting others. They would angrily condemn her for undoing all their hard work, undermining centuries of hard earned progress and huge sacrifice; and insist she should be out there, active and on the front line…making a bomb, or some equally destructive statement!

Well, she had utmost respect for the pioneers and early campaigners. From the stories she had heard, they had had a very genuine axe to grind. But the latterday lot swung the pendulum far too far, became worse than the men they wrested power from - or certainly no better. Because if they had been better, how come the GD happened after they took the upper hand?

Unless, of course, the stories she had heard were littered with lies, and women had indeed united in a thrust for universal peace to prevent the GD, and to undermine and topple Kratos. Her ignorance over this was the reason she had asked the man whether any of the positions of power in the current Kratos hierarchy were held by women. And it was apparently the one and only thing he did not know!

Suddenly her thoughts fizzled out as the earth shook like a terrier breaking a rabbit's neck. She almost fell forward into the soup cauldron, so far forward her shrunken breasts skimmed the surface of the soup, while Bernina's head jerked back against the tunnel wall, and Lhotse fell sideways onto her lap.

Something far more catastrophic nearly happened in Murchadh's lab area, but by sheer good fortune, or from Sitting Bull's blessing or cunning intervention with the Wakan Tanka, Murchadh's shuddering hand caught hold of it just in the nick of time. He hardly dared to breathe for two full minutes, and only then because he was on the verge of coughing. And that would have been fatal.

"Easy does it," he whispered encouragingly to the two ibex horns. "Steady my beauties. You'll soon be free, galloping with the wind…"

"Kind of the eleventh hour," Motte called from her observation post. "Magma's level with the peak now. If it carries on at the same pace we've one hour left."

Her voice tailed off when the earth lurched sideways for a second time - as if the African plate had finally freed itself from the overlapping European one – causing her to bite her tongue. She licked it to subdue the pain, wondering if these restless, jerky movements rippling through the ground were her mountain's last struggles of resistance to the magma plug that was inexorably climbing upwards and out, a reverse act of rape.

The man gripped her shoulder as he squeezed alongside in the aperture, wanting to assess the magma progress with his own eyes.

"An hour's very accurate," he agreed approvingly. "What an amazing vision of fire-power - I so wish we were watching it through a telescope from a safe distance, and that I believed in life after death." His thumb pressure on her shoulder blade was pleasantly reassuring.

"If you knew for certain you had only one hour left to live, how would you choose to spend it?"

He was uncharacteristically silent for a while. "Well, for starters I'd choose to be elsewhere rather than stuffed into this hot hole, in such a hideous, hostile world…"

"I mean, accepting the present situation is a given, if you didn't have to occupy this final hour futilely planning your and our survival because you knew it was pointless, how would you make the most of your last sixty minutes of life?"

"Motte, why're you saying this? We shouldn't be indulging in idle dreamers' talk while there's still a slender chance of survival. It's like we've reversed roles! You were once the sensible, practical one, completely ruled by your survival instinct… Don't let the drugs change you, and don't sink into apathy. I rely on you as my only ally you know!"

"Apathy? Is that how you describe digging tunnels, watching volcanoes and operating on rotting toes, all around the clock? I was only asking what wish would you like to fulfill in your final hour of life. If you could have or do anything you wanted."

"Well, I already said I wished I was watching this fiery scene from a safer distance. I didn't say with you by my side, but I could have."

"Me, not your wife? Are you sure?"

"Yes I'm sure. Your turn now…for your wish. The truth, the absolute truth. No watering down allowed."

"I would want…c'est embarrassent, tu sais…to change from a girl to a woman. I'd like to die a woman, having known a man."

"A man, or a specific man?"

"You know which."

"But I want you to say it!"

"Well of course it isn't Murchadh or Fin. You."

"Because I'm the only viable alternative to Murchadh and Fin, and the only one not already linked to a mate? Or because I'm me?"

"I don't know. How can I know what it's like to have a choice? We have no choices. Yes, I *might* have chosen a younger man whose mind had not been tampered with, who wasn't repulsed by me in the beginning, who was honest from the word go and I trusted from the first moment - and by now could trust completely. It's very possible. Possible, not certain. But…as you say," she became suddenly flustered, aware that she had arguably said too much, too soon, or maybe too late, "we shouldn't waste time in dreamers' talk. We've been thrown in with each other into…how d'you say it?...into the lion's cage I think it is, so there is…err, are…bound to be feelings in common, that we share." Her eyes moved away from him to the mountain, "I know I should be thinking of surviving, not of what I missed by dying young."

Had he been able to view her face instead of the back of her head and half-profile, he would have noticed tears sliding down her cheeks, illuminated by the dancing volcanic fires rimming the gradually distending summit aperture. Hot tears, like molten lava. It would have disturbed him. An emotional Motte would be weaker in a crisis, when their predicament demanded strength. Everything depended on split-second timing. If Motte wept over the futility of her unfulfilled life her misted eyes would miss the moment just prior to detonation, and all subsequent plans depended on fractionally anticipating it. Murchadh needed three to four minutes' countdown time. Nothing less would do.

"Watch like a hawk," were his final words as he retreated into the side tunnel. "Shout '*Now!*' when the magma dome's just proud of the peak. You'll see the curve of molten gold, like the rising rim of the sun - although I know you've never seen it. Then plug the hole with the speed of lightning and hurry to the depths of your corkscrew tunnel, closing as much behind you as you can. Do exactly what we've planned.

207

Remember - I'll be with Murchadh helping him launch his anti-pyro.
gadget. We'll join the rest of you if and when we can."

Motte watched and wept. She would have immeasurably preferred to be a
voluptuous Pompeiian woman, indolently munching sweet ripe figs and juicy
peaches, savouring a final goblet of mature red wine before sauntering off to
bed with her ardent, loving husband, muffling the sounds of their passion so
as not to disturb the children who lay fast asleep in the adjoining room, an
embroidered curtain's width away. Blissfully unaware, bien sûr, of her
impending fate.

Instead she was this frightened creature crouching in an earth tunnel waiting
to be burnt alive by her own saviour mountain, still a barren virgin except in
deceitful, drug-distorted dreams.

Deal with it. Don't even *dare* feel sorry for yourself. How can you tell Fin to
do one thing, but fail in doing it yourself? Imbécile! You used to be strong, a
survivor, someone with determination. Snap out of your sentimental state of
self-indulgence and put up a fight! All you have to do is watch and listen,
nothing difficult or daring. Child's play compared to climbing pinnacles in the
pitch dark.

The man had said that if they had a ten percent chance of surviving, nine
percent of it would be lost at the first hurdle (which meant immediately) if she
failed in her job of calculating detonation point minus two seconds. How
could she flush away nine tenths of their chances to live? Translate the
equation into human lives and that would be condemning six of the seven to
death. And *who* would be the lone survivor? She could not bear to
contemplate it…

At last she suppressed all straying thoughts and desires. Her old art of
listening for every sound and watching for every movement returned with the
force of a healthy ocean wave as she crouched behind the slim aperture,
absorbing the swelling neck of the mountain with all her senses except the
tactile. The air was dry, hot and prickled the skin (although that could be fear)
and it smelt of burning rock and sulphur fumes, the taste curling her tongue
with bitterness and furring it with a sickly slime (which also could be fear!)

The mountain creaked and groaned, emitting sharp tat-tatting sounds under
the pressure of the rising magma. Fountains of hot steam jetted skywards with

a shrill hiss from the former reservoir, its waters now boiled away into misty vapour that intermingled with the pungent smoke.

She watched intently for the moment a golden arc obtruded above the rock, the first glimpse of the rising sun. This symbol of a new dawn had not escaped her, it lent a glimmer of hope.

She must stay calm. Should she warn them prematurely, Murchadh's weapon would discharge too soon and the pyro. surge evade it and engulf them; if too late, they would be engulfed before he could act. The magma was viscous, the man had said, it would first bulge to form an almost imperceptible arc, continue swelling like a giant bubble, then burst. She had to catch the exact fleeting moment midway between arc and bubble. She must on no account let the awesome, hypnotic beauty of it tempt her into waiting for the burst...

Fin lay on his tipi-sled in an elbow bend above the final descent of Motte's corkscrew tunnel. He could not be carried further because of its narrow, spiraling design, for he lay stretched flat out, strapped to the tipi poles like a medieval torture victim tied to the rack. He had been dragged there by the man in advance of the explosion. Once Motte gave the signal, Eartha, Mary-Lou and Lhotse would hotfoot past him down to the platform below, carrying all the emergency supplies, while the man would be joining Murchadh in his cramped lab-space. No-one would have time to deal with him then.

He was a burden, he knew it only too well. Despite so recently being the guy everyone could count upon to carry the heaviest load, dig Bernina's veggie patch, singlehandedly build the corral enclosure, service both women-folk and treat the youngsters to a piggyback when they got tired and frettin'. God A'mighty, he sure had come a cropper!

If being so goddam useless persisted, well, he'd do the honorable thing. Lower himself onto a sword like them gutsey Romans used to (except, not having a sword, he would be obliged to use the flick-knife from the avalanche victims' cave, now stuffed uncomfortably into his backside pocket). He fished it out, preparing it for its possible future task by sharpening it on the overhead rock, scattering clouds of rust but hopefully honing the blunted blade. Alternatively, he could somehow get his hands on Motte's amputation knife, whose sharpness made him wince with part-remembered pain.

His suicide wasn't a done deal, not yet. He might still prove useful in the future - if he could combat the gangrene rising up his leg. The man had tried to boost his morale by lavishly complimenting his manly upper torso, claiming what was needed after the explosion was a real tough cookie like himself to hack at the solid sheet of pyro. deposit that would imprison them in.

Apparently it would spread across the entire terrain like a solid layer of cement (which olden day buildings were once made of, after the eras of stone, mud or wood, so the man said). He was the very typa tough guy they needed to belabour this cement with the ice axe; it didn't matter that he couldn't stand because he'd be hacking from underneath, so could be lying or sitting, whichever he favoured. This cement-like stuff might itself be overlain with some kinda glass substance (another classic material in them olden day houses). And this glass stuff could cut sharper even than a knife, so he might end up slitting his wrists with it…

But he had to keep this cement-hacking prospect a secret, owing to conserving morale. No point worrying others with future scenarios of doom when they hadn't yet got through the preliminaries. Bolstered by having a future and a concrete plan of action, he lay back contentedly, eyes closed. Following Motte's instructions, he tried every-which-way to 'think' blood into what remained of his left foot. Somewhere the subliminal messaging went awry though, because low and behold he ended up with a massive erection instead - which it was only polite to massage. At least that blood had gone somewhere it could throb with energy, instead of staying there, festering in his heart like before.

"Ain't we gonna eat the stew-soup now, before the mountain pops?"

"No sweetie, there's no time. Plus half of us ain't here. Also, Murchadh don't much like the association of havin' *The Last Supper.*"

"Is that 'cos after it, somebody died?"

"That happened, I think. But I'm guessin' he's more worried it'd mean there's a traitor in our midst."

"Well, that'll be the man, I bet," Lhotse wrinkled her nose perplexedly, because sometimes the man made her laugh and she would prefer him not to be a baddie. She couldn't remember if baddies were sometimes heroes too; in fact she had almost forgotten how to recognize a hero it was so long since she had heard those Hopalong stories. She probably knew way more about Wanblee Galeshka these days!

"The man says really olden day folks used to think volcanoes were angry giants gruntin' underground." Her voice became more subdued, "Well, sometimes I think them groany noises are my brothers and sisters moanin' from under the rocks where they died. D'you think they're angry at me, for bein' still alive?"

"No, no," Bernina laid aside the pouch of soup she had just filled and stoppered to give Lhotse a heartfelt hug. "They'd be happier than a chipmunk at the return of trees to know you was still alive and well. You make us all feel better, truly you do."

"Amen to that," Eartha murmured.

Murchadh sucked on a preserved gentian stamen. It retained the vaguest hint of its former sweet nectar, but Motte assured him that was enough to suppress a cough. Either coughing or sneezing would be fatal. In fact the gases were so-o-o-o volatile the man hardly dare open his mouth for fear of altering the air balance in their cramped chamber. A single outbreath increased the carbon dioxide ratio infinitesimally - and too many could trigger catastrophe. So they worked with bated breath.

Four, seven and twenty eight. Why had he worried about these sequential numbers? All of a sudden he saw them geometrically, or perhaps pictorially was the apposite word: they represented the perfect outline of a stand-alone volcano (which this one wasn't, being part of a range!). *Four* corresponded to the diameter of the cone or caldera, *seven* the wider section at the base of the cone, and *twenty eight* the broad base of the volcano rising from the volcanic plain - across which the volcanic deposits were strewn come eruption time. Without doing so consciously, he had not only devised a scheme to fight fire with fire, but to fight volcano with volcano!

The man and he worked wordlessly, manouvring their apparatus into position as if it were fashioned from precious gold and purest diamonds, preparing the stage for the terrifying moment of ready, aim, and fire. Murchadh was so protective of his secret 'bomb' recipe that not even the man, his closest confidante, knew its exact ingredients. All he knew was the theoretical chemistry behind it, the principal ingredients that must be kept separate at all costs, and that any mistake would annihilate them. He suspected, though, that for all Murchadh's bumbling-old-fool act and lip-service pretence of adhering to Sioux tradition, at least one of his forebears must have been either in the military service of a warmongering nation, or a canny false-flag 'terrorist' who knew his explosives like the back of his hand.

Murchadh had firmly denied this however. "I am inspired by Sitting Bull," he insisted, turning uncharacteristically solemn, "and helped by the Wakan Tanka. That's why I'll destroy the destroyer."

At some stage during her vigil, Motte's perceptions intensified from human to animal. Foreseeing was not a gift of the eyes, it relied on the greater acuity of the sixth and seventh senses.

She effectively *became* her mountain, and then the penetrating magma was nothing like rape. It was akin to hot vomit rising towards her oesophagus, ready to stifle her or be ejected with the violence necessary to expel a virulent poison. Unlike the beauty of the volcanic fire which co-existed along with its deadliness, this sensation had nothing of beauty. But it was crystal clear that the instant she began to gag and retch was the moment to warn Murchadh.

The first sign was her stomach convulsing, as if she had gorged on unripe berries, or gobbled putrefied meat. Then a lump rose slowly upwards through her oesophagus, threatening to pierce the narrow bottleneck of her throat in a reverse tracheotomy. Only when she actually began to choke on the heated bile did she realize - to her horror - that articulating whilst retching was physically impossible.

> *"Now!"* she tried to shout, the sound no more forceful than the faintest suspiration of a summer's breeze through poplar leaves. And then she lost all power speech while she jettisoned everything she had eaten in order to be strong for the stage ahead. Finally she whimpered from the sudden weakness she felt throughout her now hollow, empty frame; and from the terrible realization that she had completely failed them at the crucial last moment.

> "Motte says *NOW!*" Lhotse bellowed with the strength of an ox demanding attention from a distant pasture it had grazed to barrenness. She did so with the same strange conviction she had had when, trapped in the jewel cave with an unconscious Bernina, she had cried out, 'Motte, come find me, I'm lost again!'

The risk was that no-one would believe her. That they would presume she was over-excited from the strain of waiting, like an overwrought athlete pipping the starter gun. Luckily they assumed no such thing. They simply reacted on auto-pilot to the established signal and immediately set to work in their pre-arranged ways. Eartha and Bernina, assuming she had heard the signal better with her younger, sharper ears, handed her her share of the food and water rations, grabbed theirs and hurried towards the corkscrew tunnel. The man and Murchadh primed their weaponry in total silence, their ears attuned and all their senses waiting in suspense for the deafening detonation that would come any second now. Fin crossed his fingers and muttered a quick prayer to whoever might be up there in the guise of any God. Right now he would not object if the only deity about the place was that ol' Wakan Tanka spirit - so long as it was on their side.

Only Motte lay motionleass, a limp and crumpled rag, unable to fulfill her second vital task of blocking the small window opening against the incoming pyro. surge.

Until an inner voice urged, 'This isn't a dream, Motte! Move - and fast. Remember Pompeii!' It was enough to spark her into life. She barely noted the obnoxious puddle dissolving into the rockbed or caught its sour, sulphurous smell; instead she stuffed the moss-woven, mud backed shutter (similar to ancient daub and wattle) that Bernina had constructed into the window opening. Then headed for her corkscrew 'stairwell'.

The volcano blew just as she reached the elbow bend, and - remembering the man's instructions - she threw herself face down onto the steeply slanting floor.

"Fuckin' hell!" Fin howled. "Right onto my broke-up foot!"

"Oof, pardonnez-moi," Motte murmured in the politest of tones, so out of key with their current emergency that she might conceivably have been a guest at some olden day cocktail party, having inadvertently spiked her host with six inch stilettos.

Once the vibrations from the detonation began to slacken, she gently returned his foot in its protective cage to its tipi pole prop, her ears straining to detect what exactly might be happening. The man had explained that the explosion itself, caused by the incompatible gases within the magma, would immediately launch a thunderously black vertical cloud of ash, and then, from under the skirts of this cloud, would rush the deadly grey pyro. flow (or surge), whirling and frothing into a thousand somersaulting tributaries that uncannily resembled the heads of cauliflowers (some kind of garden flower, she supposed).

But the reverberations were so confusing it was impossible to identify the different thunderous drum-rolls of upventing ash, burning gases, shuddering rock and - hopefully - Murchadh's counter-attacking pyro. rocket successfully being launched. If not, it must have fizzled into anticlimactic nothingness, a damp squib of failure, because Motte had already counted to more than a hundred seconds, yet no secondary explosion had riven the mountain apart.

One hundred and twenty one, twenty two, twenty three...one hundred and thirty...forty... Had the danger that Murchadh had bungled his bomb-making really passed? Did she dare to hope?

"Yippee-yih!" yelled Fin. "Come *on* you mother fuckers!"

She was lying closer to him than she had realized, for his breath blew like a hot gust funnelled against her neck. But instead of sharing his jubilant celebration it injected her with a sudden doubt... Gas was not always deafening and violent, it could equally be silent and deadly. In the misgivings of her imaginary eye, Murchadh and the man lay gasping, enveloped by a green-grey poisonous mist of their own making.

"Restez ici," she told Fin (as if he had another choice), "I'm going back up. To check on everything."

With increasing trepidation she crawled towards the lab., waves of heat searing her face and a constriction clutching at her throat, trying to asphyxiate her. Either gases from the pyro. surge were seeping in through their primitive defences, or it was the poisoned stew of Murchadh's chemical miscalculations.

24

Buzzard surreptitiously engaged the vertical ascend function, in slow motion of course, or Kestrel would instantly be aware of it. Fortunately he was so preoccupied with filming and recording that he failed to notice their gradual ascent, although it should have been blatantly obvious from the motions of the autofocus.

They were rapidly running out of wiggle room, however. Overhead Buzzard detected six other craft drifting in a perfect hexagonal formation; so the only way through this star of David-style cordon would be to drift upwards dead centrally - right through the eye of the hexagon, as it were. But he grimly suspected the inevitable layer of command. Whilst their task was volcano watching, the task of the six overflyers was to watch *them.* Consequently there would be no way through. And Griffon and Kestrel would unite against him anyway, were he to try for one.

"Inferno cooking up OK?" Griffon enquired of Kestrel.

But Kestrel was locked inside his specialised world of micro-calculations, whispering into his memorizer what sounded to the ignorant other two like mystic incantations. But then they could only overhear every third word, now that the volcano was beginning to roar and rumble, spitting fire like a scalded cat, so probably what he said made perfect scientific sense - to another scientist.

"Rhyolitic, not Andesitic I rec...submicron particles... pyroclasts, yes...orifice gargantuanising...azimuth 40...pizza oven."

"Well, that last phrase makes perf-sense, even to me," Griffon said smugly. "Must be max. 350 Celsius, I intuit - if it wouldn't ruin a pizza. And that's not seriously hot-hot."

"Huh, he can't be temp-reading the caldera, in that case. Look at the bugger... I can measure heat by eye-scan, simple fashion, just by applying colour clues to the incandescing rocks. Orange to yellow equals 900 degrees or plus; bright cherry red signifs 630 degrees - plus or minus a fract.; and a red glow is approx. 480 degrees, enough to already over-crisp your pizza. And, since I detect a predom. of orange, I'm guessing it's in the hyper-hot range." He smacked his lips, but not from any satisfaction. "We're in a gruesome place ourselves, but clover compared to the ground crew, poor mugs. Fired, glazed *and* cindered."

"Protective clothing's meant to *protect*," Griffon objected.

"Hmmm," was Buzzard's response. He had long ago learnt that such a vague voice-noise was not identifiable as a dis-crime; if it were, he'd have been zapped long, long ago.

"Wow!" His eyes bulged in awe and horror as he caught sight of the magma rising with a sudden burst of speed vertically below them, gleaming like a fount of thickening, liquid gold, or a salivating animal's tongue thrusting apart its rocky jaws studded with sharpened fangs. "Wait for it...she's about to blow!"

First came the *boom* of detonation, like the pop of a champagne cork sprung from the bottle by the pressure of a thousand gaseous bubbles, but magnified a billionfold. Then followed the shock wave, pummelling the underside of their craft like a boxer's steely bodyblow to their ribs; and finally the upthrust of tephra and ash which whooshed like a Roman candle firework, only instead of a jet of light it smothered them in the blackness of a chimney sootfall. Buzzard tried in vain to steady the bucking, splintering, disintegrating craft.

"Thanks a bonanza, Kestrel," he cursed, "Effing lame last words - bloody told yer so."

Motte immediately noticed the drastic rearrangement to the cramped lab. area. There was now a gaping gash in the far wall which illuminated nothing since, if anything, outside looked darker than in. How could the volcanic fires have been so rapidly snuffed?

Then she saw their bodies, slumped one across the other. The man (who sprawled on top) must either have been rescuing Murchadh, straining to pull him further from the hole, or else aggressively restraining him from reaching it. When she was within touching distance of them she saw, despite the poor visibility, that their faces bore a strange, blue-greyish colour, while a faint tinge of green encircled their mouths.

Although unconscious, both had a pulse. Blue skin...? She had an inkling people turned blue when they drowned, for she remembered her mother saying they were difficult to locate in the olden day sea - which was blue itself on a sunny day. Humans definitely turned blue when extremely cold (if they were white to begin with, presumably not if they were dark like Eartha). But coldness was inconceivable in this heat. And also, when blue flames were hotter than red, yet red skin hotter than blue, the relationship between colour and temperature was an unreliable guide.

Think Motte, think! Stay focused on what you *do* know of the human body...

Can't be digestion. Nor heart. Could be brain; most likely lungs though - they handled breathing, and gases were the solitary topic of conversation between the man and Murchadh ever since the volcano surged into life. Et bien...blood returning to the heart appeared blue in the veins, but bright red when freshly pumped. So did blue mean less oxygen?

She was floundering, she sensed - confusing the blood system with the breathing system. Oxygen and carbon dioxide were to do with lungs and breathing, not heart and blood circulation... If only she had paid fuller attention to the man's monologues on gases! She *did* recall several carbons, most of them poisonous - especially monoxide. But since she was still breathing, albeit with increasing discomfort, she could rule out monoxide. It killed instantly, didn't it?

How slow her mind was! And further slowing - perhaps whatever air imbalance existed in the lab would soon turn her blue, add her body to the growing pile. She had better 'smarten up' as Bernina would say. Climbers of old used to slow down at high altitude because of oxygen starvation. The unlucky would shut down altogether - the exact reason some wore masks. So, perhaps oxygen was the key after all, it being the common factor in two possible diagnoses.

Pursuing this thread she focused attention onto Murchadh's 'apparatus', principally the curling ibex horns acting as chimneys. The stove beneath it was turned off so she assumed it should stay off - if unpredictable gases lay in wait, turning it on might invite an explosion. She remembered Murchadh had been aiming to *increase* their oxygen supplies, but dare not experiment in case hydrogen was lurking. Best close the gaping hole to the outside, where noxious gases must be leaking in. And take no risks - stick to what you know.

All these thoughts tumbled out in rapid flurries but her movements were increasingly laboured. How long had she been there? How long could a human survive when scarcely able to breathe? She had a hunch magician-types could hold their breath for five minutes, your average person roughly two, and someone like Murchadh, who constantly snuffled and wheezed, less than one. Yet she must have been dithering ineffectively for up to ten minutes - and they were already blue when she arrived. *Depêche-toi, Motte!*

More valuable time ticked fruitlessly away while she plugged the hole with whatever came appropriately to hand, she still needed to be selective because there might be a secondary eruption, and a follow-up pyro. surge. Meanwhile their facial tones shifted ominously from blueish grey to a deathly grey and flecks of foam seeped from the corners of Murchadh's mouth. Then the man's body shuddered suddenly, as if in final resistance to whatever was poisoning it.

Her time had run out to find cause, illness and diagnosis. There was time only to act. Instinctively she repeated what she had once seen Alessandro enact with someone in a state of shock - the *kiss of life* he had called it. First, no doubt subconsciously, she chose the man. Superimposing her lips over his, ignoring the lurking suspicion that she had possibly done this before (but only in an unreal world of hallucination), she tried to suck his poisons out. Then she released her breath into him, pumping his shuddering chest, hoping to re-inflate his shrunken lungs with a better balance of gases. *What doesn't kill you makes you stronger,* her mother used to say (in French, of course) when she set about an unorthodox form of treatment. Like sticking back a lump of flesh that had been detached, a whole limb once, but she naturally didn't succeed with that…

Again Motte repeated this *kiss of life,* then again, again and again. He shuddered less, but his breathing was not noticeably stronger.

She must not forget Murchadh, much the frailer of the two. He equally deserved his chance… She fought her way past the dense entanglement of whiskers that guarded access to his mouth, trying to forget the yellow foam she had noticed earlier, had just locked her lips onto what seemed to be his and was sucking in through his almost toothless gums, when she heard a sound close to her ear.

"No! No…*no Motte! I'll* do it. We're mates in this together, he and I. Let me…"

Although he looked a sickly, blanched-white colour now and was far from steady in his movements, he managed to nudge her aside and usurp the *kiss of life* duties for a few feeble attempts. Without any success.

"Not working," he gasped feebly, collapsing backwards.

"Of course not," Motte interposed herself again.

She tried five times in succession, and was very near to reeling with exhaustion, on the point of giving up when, pausing for breath herself, she heard a weak cough. Weak - but very obviously Murchadh's familiar, rasping peace-pipe cough. He coughed again, spat feebly, so feebly it dribbled foaming down his chin, then managed to whisper:

> "Did we do it? Did we make that pyro. bugger turn and run? Someone, please, tell me I'm not in hell. Then, beers all round…!" but the rest of his utterance was swamped by a further bout of coughing.

At this point Lhotse, invisible due to the darkness but instantly recognizable from her voice, peeped into the lab.

> "Hey," she said, suddenly gleeful, "We was all awful worried. But here you are, just havin' a li'l chat. Ain't you gonna come on down? Eartha says we can't eat nothin' 'till you guys come."

They spent five whole days incarcerated in the inner den. The man insisted such a lengthy interval was essential to allow the air outside to clear, the pyro. heat to diminish and the aftershocks to slacken. No-one else had sufficient earthquake experience to disagree with him, and they knuckled down nearly as obligingly to his second proposal:

> "Let's get sewing in the interim. Eartha brought the six nylon parachutes with her - light as feathers, as you'll soon appreciate. We've got to stitch them together with gut to fabricate a huge balloon. It's our escape craft."

> "Well, we could always sail away in the boat us guys arrived in," Fin offered, "it's a real classy one - Holg got given it."

> The man's right eyebrow leapt so high it vanished into his hairline, Motte noticed. "It'll've been obliterated, you'll see," he answered quietly.

25

Having emerged from their underworld after the prescribed five days, they stared, open mouthed, at the brand new landscape which revealed itself during fleeting moments of fog-free atmosphere. Visibility shrank to nothing whilst dense clouds of billowing smoke and ashes drifted lazily past - as though some hidden hand had drawn a filthy lace curtain to purposefully block out their view. But when the air momentarily cleared again they could see far into the distance in perfect, astonishing focus. It was this teasing *now you see me, now you don't* trickery that heightened the surreal qualities of the scene.

Motte stood transfixed. It was as if her tunnel had taken them not onto the eastern flank of the Aiguille Verte, but to some unknown location on the far side of the earth. Or even another planet. She had always had a marmot's ability to stand stock still, a frozen statue. It was the pose she adopted now.

'Her' mountain, once a proud peak rising more than four thousand metres high and adorned with a gleaming cap of snow in the long ago past, had been totally blown apart! Instead of looking up at it, she now looked *down*. The ridges and rock pinnacles had vanished into dust-filled air - in fact they were literally breathing them in! There was no summit, no glacial features, no moraine, no col, no underground reservoir.

Way below, the newly hewn ridge of the crater formed a huge encircling rim, perhaps half a kilometer in diameter. And the slopes of this new volcano bore no resemblance to the surface clothing of the valley she had known since birth. It had never been fertile by any stretch of the imagination, but it had had variety, in its own limited fashion. Formerly there were gradations in rock, both size and colour, plus scatterings of different vegetation - hardy bushes, dwarf shrubs and, below the olden day tree line, the greying, withering remains of tree trunks (which Fin had dragged up for his corral).

Now it possessed just a lifeless, ghostly uniformity. Its outer slopes were draped in a deep layer of powdered rock, pulverized into a fine grey dust exactly like olden day cement, then further overlain by a thick layer of ash. Its inner slopes (descending into the crater) might well have looked the same, but they were still shrouded in wafting smoke and black ash particles that continued to spew upwards even though all the fires and flames had been extinguished. There seemed to be a glimmer of green-grey lake on the floor of the crater from which rose hot plumes of steam and jets of seething, boiling, sulfurous water, but this might have been an illusion caused by poor visibility, or her desire to find *some* vestige remaining of her old friend the reservoir.

Because, with the top half of the mountain blown away, all her childhood haunts had vanished: her burrow, the marmots' network of tunnels, Fin's cave, the burial sites of everyone who had ever died and been buried there from olden day climbers, the escaping avalanche victims during the war - down through the years to her father (if that story were true), mother and, most recently, those who had died in the dynamite blast. Reduced, in stark, literal fashion, to dust and ashes.

From what felt like an immense distance away and in a different time zone, she could hear the man patiently explaining that the mega-eruption of Krakatoa in 1815 had similarly reduced its altitude by a thousand metres plus. It had also discharged a phenomenal *eleven cubic miles* (his tongue wrapped itself around the labial consonants with audible relish) of volcanic ash into the atmosphere! On cue, his captive audience gasped in awe. To top that, he continued, the shock waves it generated had actually stopped clocks on mantelpieces as far as one hundred miles away! (No gasps ensued; his audience had zero knowledge of mechanical clocks or mantelpieces). Not to forget the monster 120 foot tsunamis it had unleashed on the high seas, he added, making them considerably *higher* seas!

He had the sense to leave her in peace, realizing she was unlikely to appreciate any resumé of volcanic history at this precise moment. Lhotse was rendered speechless. She fiddled with her grubby fingernails and stared in astonishment at the gaping crater far below, coughing whenever particularly noxious particles seeped into her lungs. She joined Motte, as dazed as any somnambulist, slipping her little hand tentatively into Motte's not much larger one.

"It's all gone, Motty. Bang…pfff. I never knew mountains could *do* that."

Murchadh's curious eyes appraised the smoking abyss. But, unlike Motte, he was searching for specific signs and had a vested interest in the details of the destruction.

The symmetry of the crater bore witness to a massive blow-out from the central vent, so presumably his home-made, rocket-propelled bomb had only limited responsibilty for this really drastic resculpting of the landscape. He prayed so, anyway. He had no wish to be just like Kratos - able to harness earth's power, but hopelessly powerless to control it. Nor did he wish to draw comparisons between himself and an olden day toddler, irresponsibly armed with a full box of matches and left gleefully to his own devices in a tinder-dry pine forest. He prayed the collision between 'his' contraption and the pyro. surge had simply steered the latter off course, so that it veered safely away from their hideout, as was always (well, originally) intended...

Trouble was, his eyes were too bleary to see properly. When the man had finished his harangue he would hopefully be ready for a private debrief, though where to be private on this narrow observation ledge teetering on the brink of a landslide was problematic. The Aiguille Verte had survived intact, granted, but when you looked at it closely it was cross-hatched with as many faults and cracks as the wrinkles on his careworn face, so an injudicious step risked the whole rocky edifice hurtling down into the sludgy sea far below.

Despite the fact he was exhausted by the constant battle to survive, he didn't want this mountain to be his *Wounded Knee*. No - he had got that wrong. Wounded Knee was a tragedy for sure, but Sitting Bull had not met his death there. It was at Standing Rock that he was double-crossed and killed. Ignominiously shot by...well, no-one really knew who fired the fatal shot, but it stank of treachery and the 'enemy within'. It was possibly the outcome of a misunderstanding, a bungling mistake, a miserable anti-climax in lieu of the heroic death such a great man deserved.

But then the man (Motte's, not Sitting Bull) would say *that* was precisely the intention. All strategic deaths of all charismatic 'enemy' leaders always followed the same old pattern. It was the means to belittle and humiliate them. It had in fact become an over-much-used ploy in the run up to the GD (apparently), but the naïve and credulous populaces hoodwinked by Kratos failed to see through it - despite the numerous repeats that should have aroused their suspicion. Instead, they invariably fell for the propaganda (evil tyrants, despotic dictators, bla-bla-bla) and revelled in each and every assassination. Except for the very, very few with sharper eyes and minds.

Murchadh looked upwards, hoping for a positive sign of cheer from that direction - there being none from any other. It struck him as decidedly wrong to feel so flat, so dreary after their incredible success - against all the odds - at cheating death. Why did he not feel elated? The man seemed chirpy enough...

Perhaps this was no more sinister than the simple truth that different people react to shock in different ways. To his eternal shame he remembered giggling irrepressibly when his mother died - but in his defense he was barely a teenager, and the sorrow hit hard a few days later. The man's upbeat mood was actually more understandable than his own; nevertheless, it struck a sour note when you saw Motte's distraught face. And wee young Lhotse had never been so down in the mouth.

"Should we risk being here, in open view? Eartha asked. "It's madness, surely - after all our earlier care to stay hidden, and all the effort surviving the eruption unscathed, to get so stupidly careless now."

"You're spot on," the man approved. "Let's go inside, prontissimo. At least we've seen the new lie of the land now, which'll help us make the next move, so there was method in our madness."

"Are you lot still bangin' on about them Kratos? I 'spose you reckon they'll be roller-bladin' up and down that ash cloud, yellin' whoopee-yih-yo?"

Fin packed all the sarcasm he could muster into that utterance, owing to feeling bitterly let down by the man. The lying rat had promised him the all-important job of hacking through this massive layer of concrete-lava, but all he'd actually delivered was a total bummer of an anticlimax. Because Murchhadh's rocket-bomb had snatched the work right out of his hands! It had already scorched a path through to the outside; all he then had to do was shove away the mish-mash of stuff Motte had used to plug the gap against the pyro. surge, widen it a fraction, and hey presto - job done! Easier than a rat's tooth through candyfloss...

His anger was further inflamed by the unwelcome prospect of yet another 'parlee'. The reason for it: they must reach a concensus about where to go and how to get there. The whole parlee process had lost its shine for him, mainly owing to the fact their previous one featured Murchadh's preposterous belief the eruption would be a mere baby; a weeny puff of smoke and a gentle oozing of organic fertilizer. Well full marks, Murchadh, he muttered contemptuously to himself, you really got that right, sonny boy!

As far as the forthcoming parlee was concerned, although he could not predict the precise arguments that would surface, he could pin his faith on one certainty - the goddam man would monopolise it. What's more, he'd have Bernina slobberin' over every word of his fancy elocution.

"Monte Rosa would be my first choice - if it were down to me. But let's pool our knowledge of the viable alpine islands left intact. There's no point considering further afield, say the Himalayas or Karakoram, since that area must've been destroyed long ago. Fin, what's your take on Mont Blanc?"

"Hell no. It was splittin' apart and dry of good water 'fore I left. Water saltier than a croc's tears."

"Murchadh?"

"Lauterbrunnen Breithorn wasn't bad, but nothing compared to Motte's mountain here - before it erupted, of course. And it might've deteriorated since then. Everywhere might've, if the doom scenario has hit."

"Eartha?"

Eartha closed her eyes as if deep in thought. "I'm easy - well, not quite true, being terrified out of my wits by volcanoes and such. But I'll fit in with the majority decision."

"There ain't no majority," Fin growled, "jus' one guy playin' us like puppets."

"You *was* asked your opinion, honey. Ain't his fault you've not got one. I don't fancy goin' nowhere, but I know we've got to. I'll go along with whatever Motte thinks best."

Motte looked surprised by this vote of support. "I've never been anywhere but here. My gut feeling tells me we should go East rather than West, that's all."

"Why?" Fin snarled, "You've been listenin' to biased views blamin' the West for every damn' wrong there ever was. Everybody takes a pop at Yanks these days."

"*Please,* honey. You ain't normally so sour. West means more than Yanks. It includes all Europe, so probably we're all Westerners here. It's only the man don't have no national background, having been bred for some other purpose..." her voice tailed off, uncertain what that purpose was.

"None of us are nationalists - though I'll confess to having a soft spot for Glasgow. We're co-survivors. That's our allegiance now - to each other."

"But 'sposing we can't agree. How do we decide? A vote, like in a democracy?"

"Hmm. Democracy failed because Kratos took total control of it from behind the scenes. They bankrolled it for starters, then bankrupted it. Have you never heard the saying 'Democracy's two wolves and a sheep deciding who's for supper'?"

"Well there's six of us," Fin persisted, "Just 'sposing three want one thing, three another. How do we sort that out?"

"*Six?*" Lhotse cried indignantly. "You've forgotten me! If it's three 'gainst three, I'll get to decide!"

"But you're too young to vote. In all them countries long ago nobody got to vote until they was around sixteen, eighteen or twenny one. They had to drive a car first, 'fore they could vote," Bernina explained.

"Oh," Lhotse looked deflated. "I could've driven a car, I bet. What *was* a car?"

Conversation petered out while the stew-soup took centre stage and the water pouch was passed around, everyone sipping thriftily to eke out the dwindling supplies. No-one, in any case, could see anything would be gained from resuming it, since they all knew Monte Rosa would be their projected destination. For lack of an alternative, and lack of a champion to propose one.

Fin's ill humour gradually dissipated as the conversation moved to the mechanics of escape. He was quietly confident Holg's borrowed boat would still be seaworthy, consequently he its undisputed captain - despite the man's lavish complimenting of Murchadh's balloon.

"…fifty odd miles should be well within its range."

Eartha gasped in disbelief, "Says you - I guess he hasn't come clean on the other time he tried? The thing floated happy as a bubble for a minute or so, then dropped like stone for no apparent reason."

"There was a glaring reason," Murchadh retaliated hotly, "and I've put it to bed. This one's twenty eight times better."

"Well - you've thoroughly set my mind at rest there… So, how soon do we fly? I need to know our baggage allowance before I start packing." Her mouth set in a tight, thin line of controlled sarcastic fury, but she could not impose the same degree of discipline over her agitated hands.

"The flying stage is a last resort," the man hastily reassured her. "First off, we try to float - for as long as that works. And before anyone objects, I've checked the availability of our seafaring craft. Pumice. Anyone heard of pumice?"

"I *might* have," Bernina replied. "Isn't it that pale grey, stoney stuff folks used in them olden days, for scraping off rough bitsa skin from the soles of their feet? My great, great…"

"Exactly!" the man cut in. "It's formed when the extruding hot lava contacts colder water. It's been shackled together to form rafts before - so a precedent exists, and it's been proved to float as far as fifty miles. From Krakatoa, I think. With our combined weight it might not manage the full distance to Monte Rosa, so that's where Murchadh's balloon comes in. Also, if there's a tsunami bearing down on us - airborne we'll have to go!"

Everyone was silent, absorbing these remarkable, hitherto unsuspected future scenarios. Surviving the eruption should have been a cause for wild celebration - but now it seemed that that outburst of nature's fury was merely the prelude to more, and still more, terrors to come. Eartha's mood turned truculent. In total contrast to her normal, motherly persona, she sullenly refused to allow any second helpings, even for Lhotse.

Only Murchadh recognized this mood, and feared she might soon plant her feet like a mule, flatly refusing to go with them.

They had to wait again. This time for the dark plume of ash cloud to slacken its venting before they set off, or they might succumb to its noxious fumes. The man insisted that meanwhile they practice emergency landings. If the balloon basket (a patchwork of rucksacks being cleverly adapted and lashed together by Bernina) plummeted down faster than intended, they must pitch out at the last minute and perform a series of forward somersaults in order to decelerate momentum. Lhotse and Motte were easily the most adept at this, the man average, while Fin for obvious reasons was spared the exercise. Of the remaining three, Bernina lost her bearings halfway through and skewed off sideways - each time to her bewilderment; Murchadh never tucked his head in properly so fell back again, risking a broken neck; while Eartha refused to try.

"I value what little's left of my dignity," she declared firmly. "I never did get the hang of somersaults, even at Lhotse's age."

"Oh I wish you were my age now. Well, I wish *someone* was. Might there be other kids on Monte Rosa?"

"We'll have to…"

"Wait an' see!" Lhotse's wild shout reverberated unnervingly along the tunnel, as if it were a threat maliciously repeated over and over by evil lackeys of Kratos.

Eventually there was a lull in the post-volcanic action; it was the window of opportunity the man had been waiting for - they must start the climb down. His previous argument about the blackness of the ash cloud harming their respiratory systems was suddenly, conveniently, forgotten; now he suggested it was the safest time to move - while the pall of darkness shrouded them from prying eyes. In response to Fin's mumblings and grumblings about 360 degree turnabouts of mind, he merely trotted out his usual cliché of positives versus negatives. He had become their self-elected leader, no doubt about it.

Motte was lead climber though. Being familiar with the Aiguille Verte, she would recognize where new fissures had opened up, or the rock rendered dangerously unstable; which gulleys could be trusted, and which evilly enticed them onto impossible overhangs and certain death. She would also recognize the route of the dry stream bed fed by the melting glacial waters in long ago summertimes, and at what point they must deviate from it - because it fell abruptly, a lethal eighty metres of vertical drop, where a waterfall had once thundered down and attracted multitudes of camera-toting tourists.

The trouble was, they needed an experienced climber to bring up the rear too. They were roped together, so if anyone fell the last climber must be able to anchor the rest. As it was Motte had to double up, sometimes leading, sometimes belaying at the back, depending on the differing perils of the moment.

Secretly she was hoping to see evidence of ibex or marmot survival. But since both were high altitude dwellers, the lower they descended, the less likely it became. What she did come across, however, was as unexpected as it was unpalatable: *human* remains! She waited anxiously for the man. He was third back in line (after Bernina), still dutifully dragging Fin on the awkwardly imbalanced tipi sled - a perilous, more exhausting, harder task even than Motte's.

> "Over there - can't you see them?" she asked. "They're burnt and blackened but you should still notice the bones where they stick out of...*pouah*, I guess it's flesh. Or was. They're scattered all across the slope. Could they...could they be the avalanche victims, thrown out from their burial place yet again by the force of the eruption blast?"

Even as she spoke she realized that impossibility. The avalanche victims had died more than two centuries ago, had become skeletons draped in frayed clothing. Whereas these must have only recently died - in spite of their scorched, mummified state, superficially giving them an appearance as old as the victims of Vesuvius in ancient Pompeii.

Bernina instinctively covered mouth and nose to ward off the stench of death, but the intense temperature had of course sizzled away all bodily fluids, and therefore all smell. The man stood stock still, momentarily transfixed. Then, very gingerly, he approached the nearest corpses - as if he feared they were feigning death and would suddenly bite, or maliciously plunge a knife into his heart. He motioned Motte not to follow him, then was swallowed up by a wafting, spiralling cloud of dense blackness.

Motte waited on tenterhooks while she guided the rear-markers down. Lhotse behind Fin, then Murchadh - whose wheezy breathing was audible long before he was visible, and finally Eartha, who turned out to be surprising agile on a rockface (presumably inherited from her Matterhorn climbing great great greats).

They were beginning to wonder how they would survive without the man, and whether anyone would ever recognize Monte Rosa from the air and thus prevent them flying into sheer emptiness, or outer space itself, when just as suddenly as he had left he returned, a grim expression etched into his face.

"A whole platoon of Kratos scouts - and what a richly deserved death for those scum. Murchadh - come verify it for me please, or I'll be doubted, scorned and forever pooh-poohed."

But Fin (the principal pooh-pooher) was in no position to scoff, being completely reliant on the man's strength and goodwill to get him down the mountain - unless he chose the suicide route of course. He *had* given it further thought. He had actually devised a fancy manouevre to make it seem entirely the man's fault, either a deliberate act of murder or dumb negligence at the very least. So far he had put the plan on hold because the prospect of a balloon flight had him in thrall. The strength in his manly upper body might yet prove a lifesaver...

Murchadh and the man eventually rejoined them, conversing thick as thieves. Motte had never doubted that Murchadh would back the man up. They had, after all, been co-conspirators for a long time now, privately assembling rocket bombs and secretly planning balloon rides without anything more than token consultation with anyone else.

It was astonishing how rapidly their group cohesion had disintegrated. Blown apart, just like her once-so-solid mountain. Suddenly they were a squabbling, back-biting, faction-riven bunch - no better than her traitor-brother's boat crowd! Where had it gone, their mutual feeling of friendship, solidarity, even, perhaps she dare think it - love?

The man had scavenged some minuscule objects (so severely scorched they were honestly unrecognisable as anything in particular) which he defiantly exhibited as clear 'proof' the dead bodies were truly allied to Kratos. Murchadh returned empty handed, but in lieu of exhibits he babbled excitedly, describing these bizarre, extraordinary, futuristic fragments of wreckage from their flying crafts, but sadly located in such a tricky, dangerous place they simply couldn't be recovered…

The find seemed to roundly confirm his theory that they (said crafts) were powered by a mysterious combination of forces, *centrifugal* and *solar* were mentioned repeatedly, but it was beyond Motte's realm of comprehension. The more excited he became, the more his speech was indecipherable, but she nevertheless gathered that the 'crafts' had crashed partly due to the extreme velocity of the shock waves, and partly to the clouds of volcanic ash. Murchadh would have happily awarded his rocket bomb the accolades. But that would be a lie.

The disputes and controversies were a distracting sideshow for Motte. Her mind drifted back into the past. She wanted to remember her mountain as it used to be, and in her mind's eye she could conjure vivid images of all those animals it had nurtured. She would never see them again, she knew that - not in reality. Even assuming some had survived, this pumice raft would not be able to repeat history by transforming into Noah's Ark.

They reached the shoreline close to where she once stood, a lifetime ago, to watch the receding speck that was her half-brother disappearing without trace. Then her eyes had ached with the effort of trying to see something that was no longer there; now they smarted from the pollution - yet managed to see well enough to realise the man was right about the pumice. Strange bubbly clumps floated everywhere on the mildly choppy waters, emitting slapping noises as the water hit their undersides.

The man sprang into action despite his exhausted state. He waded into the shallow waters to prod and poke at these clots of flotsam, shepherding them en masse back onto the beach like an olden day farmer chivvying his sheep. Then he instructed Eartha and Bernina how to shackle them together, several layers deep, so that they formed a raft with dimensions of approximately five or six metres (length) by three metres (width) and a single metre deep.

He calculated that their combined weight would almost immediately sink it by half of this metre, which he declared was exactly the right amount to have stability in the water - sit too high and they would likely capsize, too low and they would sink prematurely. It would gradually sink in any case, he warned, since this pumice-stuff was not truly boat-worthy - it was too porous. Once it sank to a point just before total submergeance, well, Murchadh's balloon would have its moment in the spotlight!

Everyone listened to him in silence since there was nothing to be said. Their fate seemed sealed and words futile.

26

They managed to board the raft without undue fuss. It was only when they were sitting comfortably that the most important aspects of sea travel needed addressing - how to persuade the raft to move, and how to master the direction it moved in. Despite the man's phenomenal knowledge and undoubted possession of *intelligence plus*, in the chaos of avoiding death and masterminding their intial escape he appeared to have overlooked the crucial 'after embarkation' stage.

For a while they sat patiently bobbing up and down, going nowhere. Bernina assumed it a deliberate strategy of his to get them gradually used to feeling queasy, before the full force of seasickness hit as they skimmed the waves at speed. Eventually, Lhotse broke their deadlocked thoughts:

"We oughta move - else we'll never get there."

"Goddam' right," Fin agreed, "we've gotten marooned already!"

The man lurched out of his deep reverie.

"Shit - I wasn't thinking straight…or was I thinking *too* straight? This craft's the perfect shape for cresting a tsunami but not for getting from A to B. It needs a prow and stern to forge ahead through water, and a means of propulsion, too. Yet we can't mount a mast strong enough to set a sail (even though the balloon material would make a brilliant one), so we'll have to paddle, using the two shortened tipi poles from Fin's stretcher as makeshift oars. Since we can't build oarlocks it'll mean paddling canoe-style. Fin - this is where your fantastic upper body strength will really save the day!"

"Jeez, count me in!" Fin grinned delightedly, "hand me that oar, folks!"

But Fin was too quick off the mark and the error instantly obvious. A craft of three metres' width was too wide for a single canoeist, so all that happened from paddling on the one side only, was they performed a neat little circle from A back to A. Two paddlers were evidently required, closely matched in strength and reach. After a quickfire auditioning process, Bernina proved to most evenly balance Fin's power and technique. Motte and the man already knew about her hidden strength from their tunneling efforts, but it came as a bombshell to Fin.

"Wow! Fancy that! Jeez…you're a Trojan, babes - or Amazon, is it? Watch out Monte Rosa!"

"Please make it go steadier, Bernina," Lhotse pleaded, "or I'm gonna be sick."

"Stick yer head over the side," Fin advised. "We don't want no vomitin' in this proud ship. Let's christen her. I'll start the ball rollin', you guys have a go, then we'll vote what's best. My proposal's *The Intrepid*." He eyed the man challengingly, "See? You ain't the only one as can use a sophisticated lingo!"

But the naming game had to be suspended because a further problem emerged: how to forge and maintain a die-straight East-North-Easterly direction. If they didn't succeed in that, they risked bypassing Monte Rosa completely and - if the man could picture his map of the world with faultless precision - have to travel over open sea for hundreds to thousands of miles before they hit another island. And he wasn't fully sure he *could* picture the map of the world.

"We're going too East-South-Easterly at the moment," Murchadh stared unblinkingly at his compass. "You must be tiring, Bernina. We could try you swapping sides with Fin for the exact same number of strokes you've done already. *Might* do the trick," he added doubtfully.

"I just can't picture it clearly enough. What's happening to me? Maybe the *intelligence plus* is unravelling… I can't, can't, CAN'T remember the topography of those countries around the Black Sea like I should…!" the man sounded fraught, panicky - even deranged.

"You're overtired," Motte suggested, "you've overdone it - helping Fin down, collecting all that pumice singlehandedly, straight after being ill. The brain shuts down when it's too stressed. Take it easy for a while."

What next ensued no-one could have predicted. It was truly a bolt from the blue. The man seemed about to sensibly follow Motte's advice and have a lie down when suddenly he changed his mind. Leaping to his feet, he seized a minuscule something from somehwere and - his eyes wild and what they assumed (afterwards) to be an evil smile of triumph on his face - shouted into it:

"Evacuation complete. Seven survivors in all. Fire and Brimstone to Watery Grave - and don't play with me you fuckers, just give me back my *intelligence plus*!" before tripping over his own agitated feet and falling face down on the gently pitching deck of their pumice-boat, now temporarily known as *The Intrepid*.

Murchadh was no slouch in an emergency, despite his advancing age and asthma. In a flash he had him neutralised with a lightning combination of right knee and left foot, while Fin more ponderously grabbed both the man's hands, pinning them into the small of his back. Within two seconds he was totally immobilised. Eartha was stunned speechless, Motte and Bernina's mouths gaped open in unmitigated horror while Lhotse screamed long and piercingly. No-one had the calm presence of mind to prevent the oar Fin had dropped from drifting off into the misted wastes of the sea, or to notice where Murchadh had placed the precious compass.

In this extreme state of shock they continued to shackle him, or perhaps truss him up better describes it. Yards of gut (intended for the balloon and basket) soon swaddled his body so that he could barely move a muscle, their only hesitation coming over whether or not they should bandage his mouth. In the end they left both mouth and nose free, suffocation being unnecessary because a simple shove overboard would be all it would take.

And meanwhile the raft continued to drift aimlessly off course.

"So, what next?" Fin asked, panting heavily, "torture the truth out of the rat? Fuckin' double crossin' traitor!"

"For starters he can't spill a bean while he's unconscious from that smack you gave him, but...well, we'll deal with him later. First off we should make waves and *move*. If any Kratos bastards got that message of his they'll home in on us any minute now, having located *exactly* where we are! Get rowing!" Murchadh yelled.

It was then that they discovered the missing oar (or tipi pole). And, simultaneously, Murchadh almost suffered a panic attack until he succeeded in locating the compass, which had slipped between his legs and almost slithered overboard. He closed his eyes and took a long, deep breath.

"I'm afraid *The Intrepid* no longer fits the occasion Fin," he remarked wrily, "I propose *The Ship of Fools*."

No-one felt moved to contradict him.

They rocked gently on the turgid sea and spun slightly left, then slightly right, but because of the lack of decent visbility it was hard to know whether they had moved appreciably in any direction, right or wrong. After some time Murchadh regained his wits enough to offer some suggestions.

"I think the man was spot-on saying this here raft's the wrong design. You can't go *anywhere* on water in an effing box! Let's attempt a wee rebuild. Nowt dramatic. Just a pointy projection up front, what should be called the *prow*, plus a bit of tapering in the rear or stern and Bob's your uncle! - Or would be if that oar hadn't gone bloody walkabout!"

"Let's scoop up more pumice then, for modelling the prow and stern." Motte had also recovered an element of practical thinking, but her voice was distinctly forlorn.

"And cut the tipi pole in half," Fin was a trifle sheepish, having lost the other in his desperate fervour to neutralise the man. "I'll just hop if we ever reach land again so's we won't need a second one, and we can't build a tipi anyways with only two poles."

"I *still* feel sick," Lhotse whimpered.

"Doin' things'll take your mind off it, sweetie. Here, grab hold of this while I get more."

"Kratos folks don't even care enough to kill us," Bernina confided quietly to Eartha while they collaborated in fashioning the semblance of a hull out front. "I reckon this boat oughta be called *The Forgotten Ones*." She announced it in a mock-official style, and at sufficient volume for everyone to hear.

"*Slow but Steady* would be my choice," Eartha countered. "Come on Motte, your turn." She gave Motte an encouraging smile, fully aware that she needed cheering up the most.

"Eh bien…err…*L'esprit d'espoir*," she managed a weak smile. "It's a mouthful, I know, and doesn't roll off the tongue easily, but we're still in French waters I guess, and someone should try to keep that language alive."

"*Wanblee Galeshka*," Lhotse whispered, and was promptly sick.

Once the prow and stern had been fashioned, in a somewhat rudimentary way, and two oars made from one, they at last carved a steady passage through the water. Fin was the constant rower, while Bernina, Motte and Eartha did a rota of short shifts on the other oar, Murchadh focused on direction, and Lhotse on counting their provisions. Gradually their confidence grew that no missile was about to penetrate the cloud barrier to obliterate them.

"So," Murchadh broke the silence that was beginning to becalm their minds, "what about our prisoner? I'll not find Monte Rosa on my own, I'm afraid."

"Who cares? That mountain's gonna be the last place we wanna go. It'll be a trap, is my guess, just like his fake show of buddyin' up. It could be mined, poisoned, or not even exist. The rat's a traitor through an' through."

"Well, he did kinda save your life honey, carryin' you down like he did. Maybe, well, maybe we'd all be dead if he hadn't known every little thing about eruptions."

"But *that* was jus' butterin' us up so we trusted him, so's he could lead us off that mountain of Motte's into this dead-end sea! You heard the guy - '*evacuation over*', next up '*watery grave*'. You an' Motte was jus' taken in by his slick talk, you was listenin' with your vaginas, not yer brains…"

"Honey! No smutty stuff in fronta kids!"

"I knows about a vagina," Lhotse suddenly perked up, "it's down there, next to where I do peepee. But it don't ever do no listening, daddy. You musta meant *ears*."

Murchadh felt fairly confident they were now on course directionwise, but his doubts about the seaworthiness of their craft mounted with each passing minute. Just as the man had foretold, pumice was only impermeable short-term. They still had a fleeting stretch of time to make maximum progress, but once the pumice was saturated the raft would lose all buoyancy. Then they would have to swim or launch his balloon - and for that he would certainly need the man. Plus a wing and a prayer - and he didn't even know *how* to pray (unless he could count occasional vague attempts to commune with the Watan Tanka).

As if tuned to his thoughts the man groaned and stirred. But he was trussed up too tightly to move any muscles beyond facial ones. His eyes at first registered bewilderment, then pain, then alarm, and finally anger.

"What's happened? What've you done? What the *hell*…why'm I trussed up like a chicken ready for the chop, for God's sake? I surely wasn't about to kill myself - or anyone else - was I? Motte, *please* untie me, my whole body's turned numb."

"Sorry, I can't. You're a danger to us all and that's why you're tied - we can't risk you being free to use your hands."

He strained against the bonds until his eyes bulged. "You must've all gone stark staring mad! Is this some kind of sick joke?"

"You was only messagin' your Kratos buddies, ya yella-bellied, two-faced I dunno what!" Fin retorted. "Tellin' 'em as how goddam clever you'd been to get the *evacuation complete,* and how us *seven survivors* were all headin' for a *watery grave*! So, well, you've been took prisoner. You're headin' for yer own *watery grave,* goddammit!"

His eyes swivelled upwards, expressive once again of bewilderment, but this time tinged with sadness. Then he closed them as if engaging in meditation, before they snapped open once more.

"I can't remember anything," he muttered, "I must've been seriously stressed out."

"Oh yeah! Such a goddam' obvious excuse it's pathetic! Listen man, you took some gadget-thing from a Kratos corpse you found, and you talked into it. It was a remote control typa thing, I don't know what 'cos I'm not technical minded. You was communicatin' with the enemy, see, and that's a war crime meritin' death. You should count yourself goddam lucky you're still breathin'".

His eyes searched out Motte. Silently he pleaded with her, reminding her (wordlessly, telepathically) of their special bond, their private relationship that was stronger than any other he had, had ever had - apart from his close rapport with Murchadh which was of course very different. She understood him better than anyone. Surely, then, she could not stand idly by, watching while a jealous man of lesser intelligence, with a hefty axe to grind because he had lost a foot and much of his mobility (equivalent to manhood, for a man of action like himself) venomously held the floor as his judge, jury and prosecutor. Surely, given these circumstances of bias, hysteria and blatant injustice, she would intervene to help him...? Surely, surely she trusted him more than *Fin*?

Her eyes stared back though, coldly, only the faintest embers of former warmth glimmering in their depths. No, they answered him. I won't help you, because although I grew to trust you nearly fully I never trusted you implacably, implicitly - oh what *is* the stupid English word? I'll give you an example why. Yes, you saved my life after I was burned and drugged and for that I am eternally grateful, even though it was no more than I had already done for you. But I never could be sure who attacked me in the first place. It *could* have been you… And that little seed of doubt symptomizes what's been there, troubling me, from the very beginning.

So…yes you were stressed, even out of your mind with exhaustion, but *why* use those words, *why* simulate communicating with Kratos? I'm sorry but it's just incomprehensible, inexcusable. And for that you must remain under a dark cloud of suspicion, like an ash cloud. You must be tied up so you cannot communicate (unless you do it by other means none of us are aware of, like a hiccough, your stupid chip, or the blink of an eye) until we're out of danger. And we might never be safe.

It's the price you've got to pay for your stupid - yes, unforgiveably stupid - outburst.

He closed his eyes in bitter disappointment. Oh, let them get on with it without his help - fools, they'd never manage on their own. But there again he was caught between a rock and a hard place, since if he let them flounder and fail he would inevitably die with them. *If at first you don't succeed, try and try again,* he reminded himself.

"Ahm," he murmured, seemingly apologetically and after a decent interval had elapsed, "it's coming back, my memory of those high mountains east of the Black Sea. The Caucasus, of course! Plenty of peaks there well over four - even five - thousand feet. It's actually a considerably higher range than the Alps."

"Shut the F up! Who gives a rat's fart what the hell's east of this black sea?"

"Honey - *language!* Ain't no way to talk in fronta…"

"It's OK, Bernina. I already…"

"Stage by stage," Murchadh broke in. "We don't need to worry about overshooting Monte Rosa - we're well short of it. I doubt we've progressed more than ten miles, so there's forty to go and we're gradually sinking. How to stay afloat's first on *my* to-do list."

"Is there no more pumice available?" the man asked.

Murchadh shook his head sorrowfully. "We've left it behind long since."

"Can't we jettison any ballast?"

Another mournful shake of the head. "Eartha's done it already. I wouldn't be talking to you, frankly, if it wasn't last-chance-saloon-time. I'd give us two more hours max. Then it's balloon or bust."

"You shouldna be consultin' with the proven enemy, Murchadh. We're sittin' ducks out here."

"I can't help you prepare or launch the balloon Murchadh," the man pointed out. "Not without full use of my hands."

"*See?* Crafty bastard's already wrapped you round his finger all over again! Don't you free them hands nobody, 'cos I've a sharp knife here I ain't afeared to use!"

True to his word he whipped out the knife Motte had used as an amputation saw (previously the property of an avalanche victim). He held it menacingly to the man's throat. Eartha was the only one calm enough and close enough to intervene.

"That won't help, Fin. We've got to keep our brains cool. Oh, I know I'm not one to talk, having been so feeble with my fears before… But we're all in this immediate fix together - the crimes and wrongs can be sorted later. Let's pool our talents, eh?"

"Eartha, the guy's our enemy through an' through. He's tried to get us all killed…," and to show he meant serious business he carved a neat, superficial gash across the man's throat, drawing a line of bright red blood droplets where it pierced the skin.

"Perhaps Fin needs…more…convincing," the man whispered, flinching at the contact with cold, sharp metal and the warm trickling of his own blood. "Bernina, it could be this is your time…to come clean about Holgathon."

It had the desired effect on Fin. Immediately he spun round to look askance at Bernina who quailed under this sudden, in-the-spotlight glare, for all eyes were fixed on her.

"Well, don't stare like it's *my* doin'… Holg, well - he never let on much. He only told me we was goin' to this mountain, Motte's mountain as it turned out, an' that he had a mission there. He'd got talkin' to these stranger guys, see, what came on Mont Blanc sayin' they'd got antidotes to radiation poisonin', like what Holg was sufferin' from. Said they'd fix his health and in return he must do *them* a favour. He was to go off to Motte's mountain, firstly to help fully rehabilitate his health an', secondly, sniff out any traces of a guy that just might've showed up there. Someone who'd done a runner, double-crossed them or whatever an' stolen somethin' valuable that belonged to them." She nodded cursorily in the man's direction. "Holg never knew about him bein' holed up in Motte's burrow so he only told 'em about Motte being there. An' about the water. An' that's all I know."

Fin held his head tilted to one side like a parrot, as if straining to listen back to various past conversations with Holg, searching for corroborating hints that might confirm or rebuff her version of their shared past. He was not about to condemn Holg on any old flimsy, unsubstantiated evidence. But evidently a couple of details resonated awkwardly.

"The rotten scumbag! Why in hell didn't he tell me anythin'? I was his closest ever friend… He shoulda told me - else he was riskin' all our lives, linkin' up with gangsta types and chasin' after some dangerous thief or renegade from their goddam shady outfit." Then he seemed to spot a flaw in her tale. "But Holg hardly went anywhere without me, 'cept to fetch water, so he can't have been seriously lookin' for anyone."

"No, you know Holg. He used Zin as scout, and Zin went everywhere except down Motte's actual burrow where their target was really hidin' - which he never did manage to find. And once Holg got real sick he stopped botherin' altogether, 'cos he knew he'd been cheated and they'd not cured him at all, in the first place."

"Huh, well how was he 'sposed to inform them?" Fin brightened again - as another flaw revealed itself. "By *eaglemail* or somethin'?"

"They gave him a little gadget-thing, of course. I didn't like the look of it, not one bit, and I'd never wanted no part in the whole deal anyways. So I made sure it got buried along with him, to get rid of it," she ended more sparkily, intent on proving she had never been his alibi, either in deed or spirit, on this particular assignment.

The others continued to look stunned, until Fin finally had the good grace to whistle his amazement and admit his hasty judgment (of the man that is, since his judgment of Holg was tardy in the extreme). He frowned in concentration as he wiped the knife clean of blood, then clapped the man on his trussed-up shoulders.

"OK buddy, I'll admit I got kinda carried away there. I'll allow you the use of your hands, maybe untie you right down as far as your waist so's you and I are pretty much even-stevens, both legless, if you get me. That way you can help out Murchadh. But no dirty business, no treacherous messages flappin' off to no-one. Gottit? Else I'll shove you under water quick as a flash, no questions asked…"

While Lhotse was given the task of monitoring the rate at which they were sinking, Murchadh and the man bent conspiratorily over the apparatus built to power their flight, Bernina inspected their rucksack-basket for possible weaknesses, Eartha perused the metres of balloon material for snags, holes or imperfections, and Motte rowed alongside Fin - leaning out to compensate for the fact that her arms were half the length of his.

"I ain't so seasick now," Lhotse reported cheerfully, "is that 'cos we're sinkin' deeper in, Murchadh?"

"Sssh, he can't talk - has to concentrate on that balloon engine typa thing. It could be 'cos you're gettin' used to the sea now."

"Does flyin' make you sick? Oh, I hope it don't…"

When no-one answered she tried again. "Can you even *be* sick when you've had nothin' to eat?"

"Eartha *had* to throw the food out, sweetie. Else we'd have sunk by now, before the balloon was ready to fly." For the first time, Bernina's voice was not entirely steady.

27

The dark, charcoal hued ash plume burst through the horizontal plane of grey cloud forming the so-called 'cloud barrier', then continued rising, still pulsating as it rose, higher, higher, and higher. The barrier had formerly operated like a lid, sealing off the polluted earth underneath it so the upper regions could remain pristine and relatively pollution free - although of course subjected to plenty of other nasties, increased solar radiation being but one.

The piercing of it might now endanger the purity of these upper regions, but presumably it was a worthwhile risk. Or, surely, it would never have been taken...

Streaks of lightning zipped and sparkled at the base of the plume. Not its literal base, which was the conical spout of the volcano underneath the cloud barrier, but its visible base from Albatross's point of view, where it reared up from the cloud bed. This lightning formed zigzag patterns similar to those of a jerky, handheld sparkler, creating kinetic pictures that lasted a millisecond and were all sharp angles, bent elbows, a quickfire series that never once repeated itself. Probably they emitted crackling sounds too, being electrical discharges caused by clashing particles inside the ash plume, but such sounds failed to penetrate the super-reinforced structure of the flying craft. Or else Albatross's attributor was not powerful enough to pick them up.

The most impressive aspect to this massive column of ash was not the tumbling, spewing, frothing segment at its base, but its apex several thousand metres higher, where it switched direction abruptly from vertical to horizontal and swirled away eastwards like a raging river of smoke. Amazing! It was the *exact* phenomenon his shushuist bosses were yearning to hear about. Because it showed unequivocally that the giant turbo that powered the winds and tides had at last been tickled back to life! The phoenix was finally stirring!

"Albatross to Alpha Omega," if he felt mounting excitement, none was transmitted via his voice, "Albatross to Alpha Omega, can you hear me?"

Evidently they could, because he continued.

"Sure, shmure. Yes, yes, I've a sababa view of it all, especially the outflow of ash caught in the jet stream at altitude approx 50,000 feet. Magnivation! OK, I'll descend gradually, para para - I'm not taking any risks like that shmuck Kestrel did."

He warned Skua and Petrel about their enforced descent, then guided the craft down, careful to maintain position at a minimum of five miles from the ash plume and its wild display of pyrotechnics. Even from that distance, he still felt nervous over the possibility a lightning bolt might somehow detach itself from the plume to strike out in their direction. He had never seen lightning before and had no idea of its voltage power. Nor had he ever experienced a volcanic eruption; hardly surprising since none had occurred in the last one hundred and fifty years!

"Come in, Alpha Omega," he had noticed the palpitating light of his receiver despite all the distracting winks and flashes of the not-so-faraway electrical storm. "Nah, no probs Sir. I'll be heading back soon as you give the say-so. From what I'm seeing here, I can only guess at the kappora it must have caused under the cloud barrier. No chance anyone'll've survived, Sir. I'm sure that that nudnik Mister-historyman is deader than a dodo. Yes. Yes, elef ahuz. Lightning strikes are illuminating the ash plume and the winds are mounting, but no rain yet. Sure, shmure. Salamat. Over and Out."

He was about to tell the crew to prepare to re-ascend when he heard a gasp of surprise. Petrel was staring in stunned astonishment at the display screen of his receiver.

"Incoming communic.!" he blanched, as if a ghost were summoning him, and his hand shook wildly, "Struth, they *can't* have all been killed then…!"

Motte sensed the seascape darkening; signifying the onset of night maybe, or else the ash cloud thickening. Darkness would at least hide them better in the event of pursuit (yet none seemed likely now), but it would certainly complicate their balloon flight. She shivered, her tongue probing the sour, metallic taste of fear. As soon as her rowing stint was over she joined the man and Murchadh at the prow.

"How can the balloon fly without any wind?"

"Well," the man raised a tentative smile, "the power's been cleverly built into Murchadh's design. His power-booster (his eyes flicked onto some unrecognisable shape or shapes next to Murchadh, possibly containers or canisters of something or other, and his voice strained to convey optimism) provides both wind propulsion and lift off, if all goes to plan. One or two 'wee' snags need unsnagging before we're fully ready, but he'll have them sorted before the deadline." His smile became almost whole-hearted.

"But how will you recognise Monte Rosa in the dark?"

"I think," he paused tellingly, "that'll be for the Wakan Tanka to decide," and she felt a welcome pressure as he reached out for her hand and squeezed it gently.

Well, she *had* wanted to know. Eh bien. Now that she conclusively understood that they were doomed, that she would never have a child nor live to full adulthood, at least she could find comfort in the idea that Lhotse was the daughter of her heart and her spirit. What did the body matter, really? Even in a healthy world, it had never lasted long. Not in the grand scheme of things. No wonder people had formerly consoled themselves by believing in life after death, and what right had she ever had to be contemptuous of them?

They forged onwards at a steady pace. There was no discernible tide, mere ripples for waves, no sign of tsunamis, and faced with such favourable conditions Fin was able to ponder Bernina's revelations.

"Hey, my mind's been tossin'… What exactly *was* it you stole from Kratos that got 'em so desperate as to hook up with Holg of all people, to get it back?"

"Well, my *brain*. I was the only *intelligence plus* candidate whose territory was the past, the others being specialists solely for the present and the future. I've a gargantuan memory, it so happens… But after I'd wilfully erased all their hard drives and all their back-up then scarpered, they'd have suddenly found themselves in the disastrous position of having no background knowledge whatsoever! They must be seriously floundering now, without access to the past - even though they constantly sought to rewrite it, so's to boost their profile, gain more credit and blacken their enemy's name and deeds - because the past's where all knowledge originates.

If they'd only known how destructive upventing ashclouds are to any forms of rotating instrument, for instance, then they'd never have flown so foolishly close to a central venting volcano come eruption time, and got themselves killed. I confess I was entirely wrong to have celebrated the deaths of those poor scouts, since they're mere cogs in the wheel, slaves to the powerhungry powermen."

"Wow!" Fin whistled. "So, good grief, if I *hadda* killed you back there, all the goddam knowledge of the past would've gone, 'sfar as we know? Wow!!"

The man nodded, but not without a flicker of hesitation. Because that premise assumed they were now the sole survivors - with the rest of the world dead and destroyed, and without *present* and *future* knowledge no-one could claim that.

Motte could not help admiring the skilful way in which he had placed a super-high price on his own head. Somehow, he seemed to detect her thought.

"At least if *I* die and you others survive, Motte can be your prime informational source. I've passed to her as much as I possibly could - she's now your all-time volcano authority, with data, dates, facts and figures at her finger tips!"

"An' she can pass 'em to me," Lhotse declared eagerly, "'cos I'm youngest so I *ought* to live longest." The sudden quaver in her voice showed she had a reasonable grasp of the gravity of their predicament.

Murchadh had been stooped over his contraption so long he had difficulty straightening his back, but he finished simultaneously with Lhotse withdrawing her measuring stick from the water.

"We've sunk deep as deep. We're nearly goin' under," she reported.

Without wasting words Murchadh uncoiled the climbing rope so everyone could be tied to the balloon 'basket'. Unlike a proper safety harness it was not exactly secure, but it would - or should - prevent them falling out at the first unpredictable lurch. He looked gaunt and haggard from the weight of responsibility, knowing he had bitten off way more than he could chew - equivalent to a bull buffalo T-bone steak matched against a scrawny frog leg. If only a benign animikii would swoop down to purvey them safely to their destination... You silly old fool, Murchadh, close your mind to such nonsense. You're dealing with proper science, set in a real world. Get your head straight. Right, here we go...

"Counting down to lift off," he announced, all traces of Glaswegian accent suddenly banished by the clipped tones of efficiency. "Ten, nine, eight...

Everyone instinctively inhaled a deep breath. Then worried that they should have done the opposite - emptied their lungs in order to weigh less, thus aiding the counter-gravity effort of take-off. On the count of *four* Fin threw out the two oars and Eartha frantically baled out everything that weighed anything, leaving virtually nothing.

Three...Bernina's eyes swelled with terror. Her basket, so laboriously sewn from numerous tough canvas rucksacks, using yards and yards of ibex gut, reinforced with all available buckles and straps, then subsequently interwoven with a yet tougher framework of ibex hide to obviate any remaining weaknesses, was about to be tested to the utmost. She suffered a momentary horror vision of failure. It would take only *one* wrong stitch. Or a knot she had not tied tightly enough - despite her effort to tie them to withstand the weight of a hundred stampeding elephants - for the thing to rip apart and plunge them into the sea.

Two...the tension rippled through them as if they were a single sentient being, transforming thoughts into simple, electric impulses that were not translatable into words, even though the man's analytical brain flickered briefly into action, informing him this was a classic example of rear lobe cerebral activity. The animal brain kicking in, fight or flight - and flight was of course the option they were after.

One...No-one heard the *Blast Off* because Murchadh's trembling finger fractionally anticipated it, but they did hear the whoosh of air as the enormous balloon inflated. With eyes fearfully closed they heard a secondary sound, a snakelike hiss, perhaps of pressurised gas, or perhaps unpressurised (only Murchadh and the man would know). Shortly afterwards they were plunged into motion. Their bodies clashed against each other, as if old fashioned washerwomen were thrashing the dirt out of them on a bed of river pebbles, and from the corner of her eye Motte spotted a spurt of liquid flame.

The next discernible sensation was their heads dropping into their stomachs, and their stomachs conveniently vacating that space by sinking into their feet. Motte could smell something unpleasant; presumably a gas (or gases) but she could not pinch her nose to avoid inhaling it when she needed both hands for clinging on. And clinging on required such strength her knuckles gleamed white in the blackness. Suddenly she feared for Lhotse with her small, slender arms, then realised she had a small, slender body to match them, so her main problem would not be strength but stamina.

Now it was Eartha's turn for the horrors. This vertiginous climb was subjecting her balloon fabric and its intricate stitchwork to the most rigorous of examinations. Whereas Bernina's basket merely had to bear their weight, the billowing balloon had to both pull and lift against the forces of gravity, forging a pathway through the gaseous regions which might have their own turbulent currents - and were more likely to once they rose above the cloud barrier and sailed through unknown territory beyond.

It was made of nylon, too, supposedly a dangerously flammable material - yet Murchadh's burner sat perilously close to it, and being two hundred years old it was scarcely in mint condition. She could also, only too clearly, imagine an enormous Kratos army fanning out across the cloud-plateau like a battalion of olden day, medieval infantrymen, all with spears aloft, pointed straight at the flimsy balloon. A single stab would pop it, sending them tumbling to their deaths. She squeezed her eyes shut against the whole ghastly scenario and clung like a limpet to the basket frame.

Above the competing noises of swirling air, flapping, thumping material, the whoosh of gas and gasping of throats struggling to breathe, Motte could hear voices. The screeching must be Fin, who without the support-cage for his leg was forced to take immense pressure on his broken, swollen, toeless foot; the other was the man addressing Murchadh.

"Time to reduce thrust," he said, choking on each word, "down from twenty eight to seven."

Then he warned them to brace for a sharpish braking manoeuvre. This enabled their stomachs to resettle into the correct belly zone, and their brains to reinhabit their skulls - except for Lhotse, who failed to cling on tightly enough. She continued shooting upwards until Motte frantically snatched at her vanishing feet and hauled her back, at which she screamed hysterically, mistaking Motte's grasp for the rapacious beak of Wanblee Galeshka.

"Down from seven to four," the man urged, "conserving gas is..." but the flapping balloon drowned the remainder.

If only Murchadh would contemplate applying formulae outside the narrow perametres of the Sioux magic numbers, the man would have suggested two, even one, as the ideal rate of burn, since the explosivity of the gas was as much a danger as the need to preserve it. But no, he was an obstinate old codger over certain things, so four it had to be.

Prior to take-off they had made these optimistic plans of timing their flight, plotting their direction, even monitoring their speed so as to calculate the requisite minutes afloat before reaching Monte Rosa. But that was out the window now. Murchadh's childhood compass and the avalanche victim's wristwatch were both missing - flung away in Eartha's bailout or during one of the subsequent eratic lurches. They were now floating in the dark - in all senses of the term.

It was a weirdly calming sensation, after a while, blindly levitating above the earth to the gentle, soporific *fffff* of a slow gas burner. It transported Motte back to certain vivid dream experiences. In particular the windswept hillside where she had first experienced physical love; and the forgotten garden of poplar trees where she had lain in the grass and finally summoned the strength to resist it. Yet the instant her mind attempted to resurrect the beach where she had been a helpless, bloated jelly fish, she managed to regain control and forcibly switch it off. In the context of the present, that scene came uncomfortably close to an uncanny premonition of a bursting balloon.

She felt mildly nauseous yet strangely euphoric, increasingly lethargic and ever more readily prepared to die. In this complex frame of mind she wormed her way closer to the man.

> "We *must* lose altitude," he addressed Murchadh urgently. "It's getting too darned cold and I can't think straight. Motte here's already semi-comatose from lack of oxygen, while the others all have similar, if not worse, symptoms of hypoxia."

Murchadh was of course a novice pilot, his controls were rudimentary and his fingers, owing to this hypoxia problem, behaved like thumbs. Consequently they lost altitude too fast in a reckless plunge, and for panicky moments after it they feared both Lhotse and Bernina had fallen out. It was only when Fin overbalanced backwards and found his fall cushioned by a human body, that they discovered them under a flap of rucksack, a sort of lost pocket in Bernina's basket design.

> "Youz OK?" Fin enquired solicitously when Lhotse groaned.

> "I think my arm's got broke," she whimpered. "You weighs a ton."

> "Motte'll soon fix it," he reassured her gently.

With what? Motte wondered, there being nothing left that could act as either bandage or sling.

> "It's my fault," Lhotse conceded in a small, pitiful voice. "I should never've kept Zin, I shoulda throwed 'im out when everythin' else got throwed."

"Zin?" Bernina was aghast.

Lhotse opened her bunched fist to reveal a tiny ball of wool-fluff, so tightly compressed it was no bigger than an apple pip. She hesitated for several seconds before reluctantly blowing it off her palm into the emptiness of space.

"I needed *someone* for a friend, what I could talk to 'bout kids' stuff," she sniffled miserably. "But now he's broke my arm he's gotta go."

"But sweetie, *I* broke your arm."

"No. No more'n I shot your foot. It was the gun what really did it," Lhotse insisted. And they thought it best in the circumstances not to argue the matter.

Motte's thoughts became more coherent at this lower altitude. More reflective too. Maybe she still was that former selfish, blinkered person, but her old scorn had gone and somehow she knew the others more intimately than she had ever expected - to the point where she could sometimes catch the very substance of their private thoughts. But the more she empathised with them, the more she lost touch with herself. A dangerous mental state - inexorably leading towards the Kratos-style climate of group-think and mind control.

This brief, pensive interlude was rapidly brushed aside by the miraculous change from night into day - something she had never, ever witnessed. Colours began to emerge gradually and subtly from the darkness; blackness changed to a deep space of mysterious ultramarine which in turn gradually faded via cobalt to pale pastel blue, bleaching as the light intensified.

The sun was still an invisible presence at this point, a diffused, lemony glow. Then its rim of gold suddenly crested the carpeting cloud, flecking the wave-tips of those clouds similarly to the way ripples on the reservoir had once reflected phosphorescence. It deceived her into believing the unbroken cloud-bank below them was actually the sea, until she remembered liquid reflected light with greater clarity and less haziness.

As the sun climbed higher these golden highlights vanished and the clouds returned to grey, but a paler, softer grey than the underbelly view she was used to. If only they could die now, drifting into sleep in the vault of what people once believed was heaven... *Mais comme tu es stupide, Motte.* It could not end peacefully. Gravity would of course determine that they fall to earth (well, sea) and to a violent, painful death.

Despite the icy coldness of the air, the sun burned increasingly hotter. It reddened and blistered their skin until they tried to hide from it - but dare not overly tip the basket to seek the meagre patch of shade this created. The gut threads attaching the basket to the balloon soon developed beads of sweat and began to elongate alarmingly, so that they dangled progressively further from the balloon with each passing moment. The peace and beauty had been but a fleeting experience; now everything felt precarious. Even the overlay of ibex hide intended to reinforce the nylon parachute fabric of the balloon was thinning and stretching, like the skin of a pregnant woman's burgeoning belly.

The man turned abruptly from his close-study of the flame and fuel that powered them.

"OK. Decision time - and I know you'll want to reach it democratically..." The ghost of a smile played on his lips. "Right now we've sufficient power to stay afloat for roughly two more hours. So, choice Number One: we lose height now, then spend the remaining time below the cloud barrier where, it being daytime, we should be able to see what lies beneath - assuming we're far enough from the volcano to enjoy visibility. It's probably sea and more sea, but with a huge slice of luck we might find a mountain island to land on within the time limit.

Choice Number Two: we carry on in the sunshine. It's beautiful up here, why not? Then, just before burnout time for the fuel, we go into descend mode, gracefully float down and *hope* there's a convenient island sitting there, placidly waiting for us. That's relying on fate, wholly trusting to chance. Using the excellent logic that we're nice people, have shown courage and initiative so hey, our destiny must be to survive. - And that's assuming the ravages of the sun allow us to continue for that long. If you fancy that option, don't look up and notice the heat wrecking the gut; in fact don't look up anyway or the sun might blind you.

Number Three is a halfway house between One and Two: we float for another hour, then descend with a further hour in which to find our island. Sort of hedging our bets, this one. I know we can't calculate our position, having lost all means to do so, but we've a rough idea. Or I have. For instance, we must still be in Europe or thereabouts because the balloon's not travelling at supersonic speeds - it's merely *floating*, isn't it?

We can assume from sunrise position that we're travelling east, and judging by the sun's height above the horizon it should be, now, about two hours after sunrise, so we've probably travelled for five, maybe six hours in all. I can't dillydally explaining how I know this because time ticks on and we can't waste any of it.

I…let's say I *calculate*…, therefore, that we overshot Monte Rosa about three hours ago…!" (Wails and groans interrupted him at this juncture. He waited for them to abate before resuming). "Sorry folks, but that's where it's at and we're powerless to correct it! So, if my map memory serves me well, the Caucasus range rears up East South East of Motte's mountain, but, a touch disappointingly, marginally more than two and a half thousand kilometres in that direction! (Groans and gasps again). It could even be three thousand, I'm really none too sure. Still, the good news is there's not just the one mountain there - but loads! And not only that, another massive range called The Lesser Caucasus just to the south, in what used to be Georgia. Mountains galore I tell you!

So, how about it? Three choices, seven people…let's get voting!"

In the silence that followed everyone busily weighed disadvantages against advantages, struggling the while to maintain their objectivity.

"You seem to kinda favour number three," Fin remarked, "So, well, I don't really care either way. My vote's gonna go to…number THREE!"

"I'm not deliberately being awkward, rocking the boat - balloon I mean, but I'll choose Number Two. I've a foolish trust in fate." Eartha proposed, cool as a snowflake now she had finally mastered her fears.

"Number One's for me," Bernina confessed. "I'm not one bit keen on this balloon flyin' an' I reckon this sun'll fry us any minute. Plus Lhotse needs her arm seein' to, soon as. Plus again, you said beforehand Austria's east of Monte Rosa, so let's go Austria if it's still around!"

"I'll vote with my daddy an' Bernina," Lhotse murmured, deeply subdued.

"Sweetie you can't - we didn't vote the same. You gotta' choose between us. I'm One an' he's Three."

"Well…like my daddy then."

"You gotta go by your mind Lhotse, not mine. That's what democracy's all about."

"Well 'n that case I'll vote what Motte's gonna vote. 'Cos I want my arm fixed."

"Murchadh?"

Murchadh looked haggard and exhausted, his skin drooping in sympathy with the balloon's. "Och ay," he seemed to say, but possibly merely cleared his throat. "Two - or Eartha might sneak a bug into my soup when I least expect it."

"So," the man summarised, "Two and Three share the lead with two votes apiece - Fin rightly pegging my vote on Three. One has a single vote (I'm sure you can all do the Maths). Motte - it totally depends on you now, and remember you carry two votes."

His eyes burned with an intensity similar to the smoldering sun. But Motte avoided being mesmerised by closing her own in an attitude of prayer, although she was not praying. Or not to a Godly force, merely to the silent dictates of her survival instinct, which she still must faintly retain because she could hear again the distant voice of her mother, 'Il ne faut jamais renoncer la vie!'.

"Three," she said at last, "The Caucasus - *allons-y!*"

His expression was exultant. For a fleeting second she feared he was about to reach for another mini-gadget to inform Kratos of their foolish decision, and then they would be forced to overpower him all over again.

Their discomfort fortunately lessened as the sun rose higher. It no longer shone in their eyes and the balloon canopy cast a welcome pool of shade. But the dome of the balloon was at risk due to being fully exposed to the sun's rays, and the fact they could not monitor the damage this caused somehow made it more alarming. Motte, from her forward perch beside the man, felt suddenly certain they must have overrun the agreed hour. And when she whispered as much, he shamelessly corroborated it.

"We'll make faster progress *above* the clouds where the air's thinner and offers less resistence. We're far too far short of the Caucasus to risk descending yet."

"So, by how much are you…what's the word? *fiddling*? the terms on which we voted. Is Number Three now Number Two?"

He grinned impishly, "I've compromised a perfect half between them. One and a half hours' flying, half an hour to descend and search. Yes, yes, I know - it's conniving, deceitful, just like all those pre-GD politicians I've previously maligned… But *please* don't tell the others. If I'm tied up again, we'll die. I'm our only chance…"

The words were barely out of his mouth when a lateral force slammed into them. The balloon shuddered, then tipped alarmingly until it reinflated to the bidding of this new, almost horizontal gale-force wind that forced them eastwards at furious speed. The balloon cords elongated yet more perilously until the basket trailed the balloon by some forty metres - and growing. It hung at such an angle it was impossible to avoid squashing or trampling whoever had the misfortune to be stuck underneath. And, to judge by the pitch of the screaming, it was Bernina or poor Lhotse yet again.

Only the man had the capacity for speech in such a moment.

"The jet stream!" he gasped. "*Could* be a blessing…Eartha spot on …east … fast," but the wind had no respect for his utterances. It whipped up the majority of his words and hurled them contemptuously into their slipstream.

28

Albatross stared unblinkingly ahead, relying on his tried and tested 'refridgeration' mode to maintain his composure. The absolute last thing he wished to do was venture below the cloud barrier into that noxious, subnubean hell-hole, which had thus far dealt the black hand of death to every single one of his precursors. But, if ordered to, he was condemned either way since mutiny was an uncontestable death sentence.

Descending further would anyway serve no purpose that he could see because that jedah Skua had already fulfilled their main objective - to predict the recovery timescale, post-eruption. She reckoned it needed as long as another forty to fifty years before this region of earth would be habitable again. By then, the climate would have normalised and the mountain islands of the Alps should be prettily fecund and fertile again. But unfortunately this was not the 'imminent repopulation' prospects his bosses craved.

So, when he noticed his receiver vibrating and twinkling, he pulsed it with a sickening feeling of dread.

> "Nah, that incoming signal went kaput, sir, it only lasted a millisec. Must've been an aberration caused by the electrical storm around the volc. Permission to now return to base, sir? I'm no shmendrik like Kestrel, and can't see anything's to be gained by diving below the barrier. No-one can've survived after breathing the poisonous black soup still being belched out. Plus, the lightning flare-ups keep defecting the controls, and - surely shmurely - I'm more useful to you alive than dead, eh sir?"

But his rhetoric counted for nothing. Orders were orders. Going through the barrier was their unwelcome destiny, so down they unwillingly had to go…

The clouds enfolded them, a vaporous curtain of fog licked unhygenically at their visibility screen - and the pod trembled in disgust at such intimate contact with an unclean tongue. Vibrations grew clamorous, ousting the smooth purr of normal progress and making the array of panel instruments judder ominously. In the grim, grey light their faces, viewed through the visors of their security helmets, looked an ever sicklier shade of green.

Below the barrier the atmosphere was not discernibly clearer - and only minutely improved by turning their light intensifiers up to super-max. Albatross kept the pod in 'park and hover' mode; not even an Uber-Sir's orders would persuade him to creep any closer to the volcano than his current (self-imposed) five mile exclusion zone.

After extensive scanning of the newly created volcanic plain, the three of them group-watched the attributor readouts, along with each recommended interpretation. One thing was for sure - volcanoes were killers. The quicker they fired off their report, the less likely they would supplement the death toll.

"Albatross to Alpha-Omega, come in, Alpha-Omega. Yah, quick as poss sir, and we'd sure like some credaise for this riskfest. Skeletons and mummified corpses scattered all over. Some ours and recent, some others killed shnat tarapapu - even up to two, three, four hundred years ago. Dead animals aplenty as well, some kinda mountain rat or beaver creatures - plenty of them; plus a lesser number of huge-horned goats. The latter lot are scattered on the shoreline, perhaps drowned and washed up after trying to swimmit. Nothing alive - and no bloody wonder. This place is ipish - and we want outta here! *If* you'll sanction it, sir. Sir? Please, shmlease? Magniv! Salamat. Over and Out."

But he was wrong. His communic. might be ended, but his mission was not 'over' after all. At the very last moment, his finger already gratefully poised over the 'ascend' function, his damnable attributor recorded an unexpected find: a small khaki satchel, apparently abandoned on the shoreline but unscathed - not burnt at all! How *could* it have escaped the raging fires of the volcano, which had incinerated every other thing in their path? Only one answer to that… It must have been put there *after* the eruption. And that proved someone had survived the blast - but of course, they could still have died subsequently. What in hell should he do?

Again he was faced with death down whichever path he chose. The info. on his attributor was non-deletable, it would be detail-checked on his return, so lying about the find was not an option. Or rather, it *was* an option - but one leading straight to court martial and instant elimination. Whereas to investigate meant physically collecting the satchel, probably by overflying it and winching it up into the pod, and going that close to the volcano would also mean inevitable death.

"Benzona!" he cursed. "Son-ov-a…!"

Their eyes streamed, their ears congested - then were pierced by agonizing drill-holes of pain; their lungs burned and their hands gripped, pincerlike, to the canvas while the jet wind pummelled and punched them onwards. Until for no apparent reason, and just as suddenly as they had been caught up in it - suddenly they were free of it! But this gave no cause for celebration, because immediately they were then free falling and at a disconcerting speed. Murchadh's flame had been abruptly extinguished, snuffed by the ferocity of the hurricane-force wind, so gravity was inexorably pulling them down.

It was now Motte's turn to have her contribution to the parachute-balloon put to the test. The intricate, slip-knot arrangements that she had patiently designed to convert their craft from balloon to parachute *must* operate successfully - otherwise there was nothing to act as a brake, and they would plummet too fast and be killed on impact.

Looking up, she could see immediately she must climb the rigging to effect repairs, for the traumas of the jet wind had wrought havoc. Slip-knots were snared and ropes that should hang free were twisted in a corkscrew fashion. Such an entanglement would be easy to resolve with the benefit of a large flat area on the ground and no time pressure; but whilst breathless and falling was a whole different matter...

Although she was a skilled and experienced rock climber, she was no trapeze artist. Balance was probably their only common attribute - apart from a foolhardy courage. Think of it as buildering, she encouraged herself; remember Alain Robert, your old hero. Or see it as a daredevil act, like the story her mother once told of a young boy who had clung upside down to the undercarriage of an olden day jet plane, to escape a country for some reason or other (fleeing Kratos, most probably), and survived a five hour flight in sub-zero temperatures. Some olden day people even used to deliberately jump out of airplanes, only inflating their parachute at the very last possible moment. For *kicks!*

Her hands were numb, thus clumsy, and the motion of constantly falling was alarming - partly from being such an oft-repeated sensation of her dreams, which always ended calamitously. Eventually, watched closely by the man throughout, she managed to unsnare the snares and disentangle the knots, but not without several heart-in-mouth moments when the folded panels of the balloon were freed with too violent a jerk that nearly dislodged her.

Whilst skinning down the cord towards the basket, she overheard him demand:

"Switch from balloon to parachute - pull on the relevant cords Murchadh." Then again, more urgently, *"Come on* Murchadh, balloon to parachute!"

From her obliquely aerial view she noticed Murchadh had slumped sideways. They were descending through the upper layers of the cloud barrier now, so the radiant light and colours of the space-world above had already faded, yet despite the returning murkiness she saw his face only too clearly. His skin was grey-tinged and waxen, his eyes glassy and unseeing. Mon Dieu, c'est comme ma pauvre mère… His failure to respond was neither from exhaustion nor slothfulness, but because he was dead.

Eartha understood it too. She managed, shakily, to remove his stiffening hands from their firm grip on the flame control lever, then pull on the cords of Motte's design. With a few shudders of resistance the fragile balloon opened out from puffball shape to more classic mushroom-like canopy, and their speed immediately slackened. Then they entered the full density of the cloud barrier and could see absolutely nothing.

The world they had re-entered was densely black, seemingly darker than the ash cloud they had fled, and yet they knew from the trajectory of the sun above that it could not be later than noon. Motte recalled these symptoms from previous experience with the light missile; their eyes had been subjected to several hours of blazing sunlight and needed time to readjust. Hopefully, only a fleeting amount of it.

The vision of her inner eye also returned with a sudden jolt: it struck her, suddenly, that the man had always intended on reaching The Caucasus. That Monte Rosa had never been his chosen destination, not even from the very inception of their escape plans. Perhaps Kratos Headquarters were located there, and he equipped with some ineradicable homing device hard wired (whatever that might mean) into his brain…

And perhaps she was his trump card, to be used as trade-off to cancel out his treachery in vandalising vital equipment, stealing their recorded history and escaping - should he in future be found, arrested, and need such a bargaining tool. He had, after all, explained to her that her remarkable health, her seeming immunity to the radiation and diseases that readily killed others, plus her ability to transform into an apparent animal and evade their surveillance, would be an absolute golden goose for them. They could use her as a prototype. Extract her health to benefit future earth dwellers…

"Motte, for God's sake snap out of it! Focus on the *here and now*… I need your help - you've the sharpest eyes of anyone. We're looking for land and its shoreline. This Caucasus range is 160 kilometres wide and over a thousand long, so it's not a mere blip of an atoll."

"What you want is a water runway for a soft landing, where we can glide towards the shore and not have too far to swim, is that it?" In his excited state he failed to note her heavy sarcasm.

"Ideally, yes. Keep keeping your eyes peeled."

When he had admitted to his compromise between choices Two and Three he had confidently stated they would have half an hour to descend and search for an island. *'Searching'* made it sound as if they had an element of control, could steer east, west - that kind of deliberate manoeuvring, so she had been easily misled into believing him at that point, being ignorant of parachutes. Now, she knew better. All they could do was drop, and at whatever speed the laws of physics dictated.

"Oof, I can see sea!" Motte gasped almost in disbelief, only a few minutes later.

"You *sure?* How far below?"

"About the distance from my mountain peak to the old shoreline."

"Ten or twelve minutes left then. Keep watching like a hawk for land, Motte."

"When you wan' us to lean, gi' us a shout," Fin advised the man, before turning to Lhotse, "That way we'll jus' skate along the surface of the water, though we might bounce a li'l at first."

"I thought we was 'sposed to do somersaults. Ain't that why we practiced 'em?"

"They're only for if we land on *land,* sweetie, not water. So's to soak up the shock of impact."

"*Soak?* Ain't that water? You've gotten mixed up, I'd say!"

Motte's eagle eyes recognised the sea solely from its motion, its wrinkling waves surging slowly forward on a diagonal path below them, their occasional crests tipped with foam. She tried to describe them to the man to prove they were not mere wishful illusion, and she not dreaming them.

"White crests?" his excitement flared. "Which way're they heading? It's vital we know, because when close to land they head in its

257

direction, mirroring the shape of the shoreline - something to do with refraction I think, or decreasing depth, or the pull of the moon or…who bloody cares, so long as they truly are nearing-the-shore waves! Now look for a beach, Motte!"

But land continued to elude her, perhaps because it was not moving, or because leaning to one side of the rucksack-basket gave too limited a field of vision. Out of the corner of one eye she noticed Eartha clinging firmly to Murchadh's body, having anchored them both to a rope end, so that when they struck the surface of the water she would not lose him.

"About the distance from upper to lower burrow entrance now," Motte's voice trembled. "Very close."

"OK. Get ready to lean left everyone, feet stretched to the right - as straight as you can - but take care of your broken foot Fin! Then…" a tremble unsteadied his voice for the very first time, "swim for your lives *with* the waves, not against them, and fingers crossed we'll meet on the shore. Oh but don't swim with fingers crossed - sorry if I muddled you there! Counting down: eight, seven, six, five…."

He had tried to squeeze a surfeit of words into too brief a timespace. During the fractional interval between five and four they struck water - although it felt like solid rock.

Albatross was merely the pilot, not the man in command of this particular assignment, despite the fact he was rumoured to enjoy suspiciously close upper-circle affiliations (meaning sexual ones, of course, and perversely deviant, naturally). Petrel was the man formally in charge, and he had never been one to bend the letter of the law, not even fractionally. Much as Albatross stared at the satchel, willing it to disappear or de-fragment, he could only bemoan his impotence.

"We can land closeish to the suspo. package, then scan in sharper detail," Petrel proposed. "It might be a decoy, a bomb masquerading as a kiddie's kitbag, so caution's the name o' the game."

With heavy reluctance Albatross manoeuvred the pod closer and closer to the volcano. The air grew soupier but at least the unnerving flashes of lightning were a phenomenon affecting only the cloud column much higher up, above the cloud barrier, and not even visible from underneath it. Not fully *out of sight, out of mind,* but nearly so. Ash lay like a deep grey snowfall, draping itself over every surface, smoothing all the jagged edges and rounding the contours so that it looked as if it would cushion their landing like a plush, goosedown pillow. But Albatross trawled for hidden ridges and jutting pinnacles with his attributor - any puncturing or buckling which might damage the pod's undercarriage would be desperately bad news.

They landed on a flat shelf of shoreline some two hundred metres away from their target, zipped themselves air-tightly into their safety suits, pulled on their protective head masks, then cautiously ventured out. The ash was a silent, slippery surface for walking on, and they stopped frequently to consult their attributors. Was it a bomb? No, the readout seemed to suggest, its contents might have been dangerous once, when alive, but they were definitely now dead and of animal origin.

Close-up they could see the contents in full colour X-ray mode. It looked like a crumpled up animal skin, complete with head, snarling and half-open mouth, its sharp fangs still intact. Unbuckling the satchel confirmed it was indeed a wolfskin outfit, made from the pelts of several silvery wolverine-type animals. When pressed to give greater detail, Albatross's attributor suggested these wolves were not local to this Vanoise area. When prodded to suggest where they *did* originate (as opposed to where they didn't) it dithered, went opaque and unreadable, until it finally, hesitantly suggested Piedmont, located some distance away in Northern Italy. But the attributor screen lacked all clarity of definition - a sure sign the info. was unreliable. What a shame the wolf was not alive to speak; and what a coup it would be if it told them news of the traitorthief himself, the maven who had dared to steal their history! If only they had brought a DNA tester with them…

They carried it in muted triumph back to the pod.

> "Albatross to Alpha Omega, Alba…," his voice faltered and the colour drained from his face. He turned to the others, "Sorry to bring bad news. No signal, in fact radio's totally kaput - I know it without another try. And it'll be no surprise if the klutzy pod's kaput too. Pfui!"

As calmly and collectedly as he could, he went through all the necessary stages to power up the pod - without any response. Unlike with the radio, he tried and retried, many, many, many times over, but it remained utterly lifeless. All three exchanged a long, probing look of fatalism. They were to be forever marooned, it seemed, on this diseased and deadly earth, this perishing place of pestilence.

They were silenced, too. No radio communic. - which would never have brought them rescue in any event, they knew that. It also meant that they couldn't even impart the news of their potentially momentous find, the possible proof the traitorthief *had* indeed survived, or had until very recently, at least. Albatross morosely placed said wolfskin on the seat beside him, until he noticed that its gaping mouth seemed actually to be smiling - if not openly laughing - at them! For this impertinence he struck it furiously on the nose, until it slithered off to lie supine on the ground, like a dog should at his master's feet.

"That'll teach ya, ya klutzy shmuck," he muttered bitterly to himself.

There was no bouncing along the surface of the sea as Fin had optimistically projected. Following the crunching collision that created tall, shooting plumes of displaced water and seething, spattering bubbles, they promptly sank like a stone.

Once underwater, they were jam-packed together so forcibly that bony knees jabbed at throats and foreheads, sharp elbows slashed against eyes and mouths, while hands clutched onto anything and everything in an effort to become separate from this flailing conglomerate of frantic limbs trying desperately not to drown.

If only they had known it would be like this in advance they might have planned for an orderly evacuation, perhaps in size or age order; Lhotse first, then Motte - that way they wouldn't have fought each other and made a disastrous situation worse.

Down in the dark, swirling water several metres below the surface, Motte at last wrenched herself free from the basket and its agitating octopus of entangled limbs. The sharp physical pain in her chest duplicated her experience in the chemical attack; the same fierce constriction pressing her breast bone forcibly back onto her spine. It made her mistakenly believe she must be inflating with the same jelly substance too. So, instead of struggling she conserved energy, fully expecting her swollen body to effortlessly float to the surface, be washed ashore onto the same sandy cove, and again be punctured by a vicious beak.

She did indeed get washed onto something. It was no beach though, but a bruisingly hard, rocky promontory. The waves continued to attack it with thumping, gurgling sounds. And every so often one of them leapt higher to submerge her dangling feet and calves, half-heartedly trying to recapture her exhausted body and drag it back into the water. In all the confusion of bubbles and salt and somersaulting waves she had temporarily forgotten what had happened, where she ought to be, and who else should be with her. It was not until the bloated body of Murchadh, heaving up and down as the swell lifted it nearly onto the rocks and then teasingly, cruelly pulled it away again, for her memory to flood back.

It was a grim, sad omen that a dead body was first to reach shore. Motte tried not to be overwhelmed by her misery, but after she had, with difficulty, summoned enough energy in her bruised and battered frame to feebly pull the rope end wound around his swollen waist, even worse confronted her. Eartha's body was attached to his by this same rope, and it was probably her fierce knotting and desperation to keep him close that had made it impossible for her to swim free and save herself.

A remorseless wave of desolation swept over Motte. All that super-human effort they both had made to escape the fire of the volcano…for what? To die anyway, having added nothing beyond a few more hours of pain onto their already long life of brave and bitter struggle. If there *was* a God she hated him in that moment. How could such a being be so relentlessly cruel?

And…if the only ones to reach shore were both dead, what chance was there that any others had survived?

Much as she tried to listen to her recall of Eartha's voice reminding her to keep going, to never let down her great great greats, her head sank forward and her tears flowed. Instinctively she reached for Eartha's comforting hand, and shuddered to find it already turning cold - when surely it could not be more than ten to fifteen minutes since it was warm and living? She would have tried the *kiss of life* on her if she had felt there was any hope, but, without going into gruesome detail, it was crystal clear there was none.

"I promise, promise 'n cross my heart, we're honest-to-goodness nearly there. Can't you see Motte, on that rock, waitin' for us?"

"I guess," Lhotse whispered wearily, unless it was a breath of wind faintly stirring the foaming swell.

Motte stiffened, disbelief taunting her over this startling surge of optimism - since the two she could *apparently* hear were the two least likely to have survived such an ordeal by water. Despite fearing that her overloaded imagination had simply invented their voices, she stared intently out to sea, willing the fanciful sight of Bernina and Lhotse chatting on the crest of a wave to realise itself. Logic dicated that if they could see her, she must see them. For several seconds she failed to pick them out because sounds were warped and they were not where their voices suggested, but at last she saw them clinging to an air inflated section of the parachute, drifting slowly in towards her shelf of rock.

"Here!" she yelled, throwing caution to the windless air. "Watch out for that sharp rock!"

She guided them in, happiness dancing in her throat, pushing down on the lump of sorrow underneath. Sorrow for Eartha and Murchadh and - she should admit it - possibly most of all, the man. Fin as well - but less, she should also admit that, even though he had grown on her considerably.

Bernina, enfeebled by extreme fatigue, weakly embraced her. Then they both helped Lhotse off the balloon bubble, very gingerly because her broken arm had worsened considerably in the crash and her face was grey with pain.

Motte had not yet glanced even once in the landward direction; the sea held her unflinching attention, her eyes restlessly scanning the waves for the two still missing. Her responsibility to care for the dead and Lhotse's arm hung over her - but the chance to save someone from drowning could come and go in a split second, so she dare not turn her back on the sea.

"Murchadh tol' me he wanted to lie facing the sky when he died, with nothin' on top of him. He said so, promise - I'm Wakanisha, so I oughta know."

"Let's wait 'till Motte's ready, then we'll do it," Bernina's voice sounded so drained it at last galvanised Motte into tearing her eyes from the sea.

They found a rock ledge where they settled his body, facing skyward so that his spirit would be free to rejoin the Watan Tanka, and with enough space for Eartha to lie beside him, even though she did not share the same spiritual beliefs. Motte felt uneasy about predators, but Lhotse seemed so determined there seemed little purpose attempting to dissuade her. Especially since in her debilitated state Motte had no spare energy to talk. And no desire to either.

In silence she set Lhotse's arm, a silence so consuming Lhotse only uttered a single cry of pain. Like the shrill hunting call of a night bird.

29

They sank into deepest sleep from utter exhaustion, thus darkness had already fallen and the air turned sharply colder when Motte regained consciousness of their external world. The sensation of cold was undoubtedly compounded by an inner chill - her body's subconscious response to intense feelings of emotional loss, added to its literal, physical immersion in the cold waters of the sea.

They had reached the Caucasus, yes, but the victory was glaringly Pyrrhic. Two dead; two missing, feared dead; the sole survivors ostensibly the weakest ones: two barely adult girls and a small child. As if to underline the close presence of death Motte's nostrils involuntarily twitched in distaste, for the air was now disturbingly tainted by its sweet but foetid smell. If she could detect it, then so could other animals. And the man had already told her the Caucasus had once been home to plenty of carnivores - brown bears, wolves and leopards amongst them. Such animals normally ate what they had killed, not secondhand carrion, but no animal survivor these days could afford to be so pickily selective. And anyway, the three of them were edible, living prey…

"Bernina!" she whispered, "wake up!"

"I already am awake," she whispered back.

"There's a cove to the left judging by the sound of the waves - they don't slap, they fizzle. I need round stones for my catapult in case hunting animals come. If one does while I'm gone, throw this at it. OK?"

"Sure."

Although her legs were bruised to the bone and every muscle ached, she crept, marmotlike, across the expanse of rock to a thinly soiled slope, where stunted bushes and thorny shrubs clung on with half-exposed roots and a shale covered gulley led her down onto a shingle beach. She squatted there at the water's edge, feeling for the roundest, smoothest, smallest stones, her antennae on high alert for danger. Even if her human senses were dulled by grief, lethargy and a creeping despair, her animal alertness had returned, tense as a bow string. The potpourri of odours sharpened by the night air showed her the atmosphere here was far cleaner than her own mountain had been; she could even identify ripening berries, aromatic leaves, and...*could* it be?

She squatted high onto her haunches. Distrustful due to those drugs, she still doubted most messages to and from her brain, suspected delusion and trickery permeated every thought and muddied every perception. But this was *so* familiar... Human sweat! *Male* human sweat!

She found him lying on his stomach, his face pressed against the pebbles, foolishly careless of the need to predator-watch. But not asleep, mumbling to himself, on and on repetitively, endlessly in time with the rhythm of the lapping waves. But he still heard the light touch of her hurrying feet.

> "*Motte?* " he seemed to disbelieve his ears - despite the fact her footsteps must be indelibly engraved on whatever lobe of his brain stored his plethora of memories. "Tell me I've not lost my sanity...! *Can* you be real?"

> "I'm the last person to recognise what's real," she answered, her spirits dancing.

> "I swear I said go *with* the waves, they always head for shore! You must've gone off at an angle - but...you're here now." He closed his eyes and shuddered, "Thank you, Watan Tanka."

> "I was so afraid you were drowned... Are you injured? Can you move? And what...what about Fin?"

> "He's over there, as sunk to the gills in misery as I was to think we were stuck with only each other, our loved ones all dead. He can't move any better than before - worse if anything. It wasn't exactly a cushioned landing."

> "Can we move him? We might need his aim, though we've got no bow and arrow yet..."

> "Yes, if we both support him. This broken wrist of mine stops me doing it alone."

He glanced ruefully at his shockingly distorted left wrist which would be a nightmare to realign, and must be agony. It was the same arm that had suffered a shoulder dislocation when she first found him, so he never used it for anything precise or demanding - that at least was fortunate.

> "Who goes there?" Bernina's voice quavered. "Hands up!" she hissed, valiantly trying to sound threatening.

"We've got no hands to spare - they're too busy helpin' me hopalong, else they're injured real bad. Boy, am I glad you guys pulled through. 'Cept for poor ol' Murchadh, that is."

"*And* Eartha, daddy. I don't reckon she wanted to stay alive without him. Wanna see how Motte fixed my arm?"

"Not now, poppet. We gotta be quiet as mice or no predator'll come."

"Do we *want* a predator?" Lhotse was dumbfounded.

"We wanna kill one, else we'll starve to death ourselves. Plus we don't want Murchadh or Eartha eaten, do we now?"

Motte crouched in the darkness. It was a long time since she had killed - apart from dying ibex to cut short their suffering, but she was very capable of it. She had used her skill before to kill eagles in flight when there was good reason, and *this* killing was essential. They needed hide, meat and bones for tools, and even though Lhotse assured her Murchadh cared only that his spirit was free and not one jot what happened to his body, she would hate for it to be mauled or devoured. Eartha's too - illogical, nonsensical, sentimental though this surely was in the current climate of a violent world.

Primarily she listened... The snap of a twig, the rustle of a brushed leaf; night predators moved on velvet paws but never without some audible hint of it. She should also catch scent of their body odour once they were within close enough range.

She had deployed her troups strategically. The man, Bernina and Lhotse were hidden to the seaward side, from where their respective smells should disperse into the damp sea air undetected. Fin was to her right and on higher ground, from where he could shoot his rudimentary, improvised arrows to protect her, and she no more than five metres from Eartha, the 'bait', to put it crudely. The intention was for the predator to attack herself, Eartha or Fin, and for herself and Fin to keep eachother covered. Simple. Except *if* the predator were a pack of wolves, her plan would backfire disastrously. Fin and the man must realise that, but they had discreetly kept their counsel.

Time elapsed, seconds and minutes elongated into what might be hours. And just as time unravelled, so did her ailing concentration. No animal intent on survival would ever let its mind drift from the present emergency, but hers meandered far and wide.

Yet not without relevance and purpose, because it sought to conjure indistinct images for her undoubted benefit - images of the probable predators, prowling out there in the tangled underbrush. Whereas eagles had played an integral role in her childhood, these four-legged carnivores the man had described were totally unknown. She had no mental picture of a bear or leopard (apart from a silken coat of spots), and her only firsthand experience of a wolf was a dead one - the man's wolfskin. She hurriedly bypassed that memory lest it rebirth all her suspicions that he had been in these Caucasus mountains before, that his wolfskin originated here, and that his homing device had somehow impelled him back. Now was not the time to be sidetracked by his possible insidiousness. It was time to fight...

First she imagined a bear. Lhotse loved bears, but in her mind they were innocent, soft, cuddly creatures who lived in cosy forest cottages and breakfasted on honey-sweetened porridge; whereas the man warned her they could kill a human with a single paw-blow, might look lumberingly slow but had such torque and speed they could grab a slippery fish from a gushing waterfall and swallow it whole! Surely such a huge creature would be incapable of gliding silently down a mountain slope, and being an omnivore would not even be desperate for meat.

She had always idealised the leopard... Supposedly it padded silently, a shadow gliding in an undulating way - like a snake, but less rippling owing to the slight jolt of shoulder and hip flexion, a swaying grace that could suddenly translate into a terrifying burst of speed. Its weapons: speed, teeth, claws. She trembled merely thinking of it. Where should she aim? Would she even have sufficient time to aim? She fancied she already felt its hot, ravenous breath burning the side of her face so that all her downy hairs flicked upright. She was a fool to believe she could outwit a leopard and stun it with a puny pebble!

Lastly, a snarling pack of wolves, creeping, cringing, surrounding them in a wide arc before attacking from all sides at once, an impossible jumble of bared teeth, suffocating fur and scratching claws. The glaring difference between all these animals and an eagle was the protecting skull. An eagle in flight was easy to kill if you had good aim; no skull bone, no defensive armoury and its outspread wings opening up a whole vulnerable body to target.

Concentrate, Motte! Her one advantage was anticipation. Knowing a predator would come because instinct had warned her. Just concentrate...

She fingered her round stones for comfort. Perhaps that was their primary function - a placebo to distract from the danger she was in. She thought longingly of the power of a bullet - even better, several bullets; with a gun she would almost have the advantage over whichever predator came, although a pack of wolves might need one of those repeater rifles, machine guns or whatever they were called. They had each brought one vital belonging with them. She had chosen her catapult - if only someone had had the forethought to bring a gun…

Her plan was ill conceived. Why hadn't she devised a trap so the animal was already immobilised and easy to kill? Why not shown patience, waited an extra day…? Because this is the first night, when Eartha's body's still fresh and the predator will come, that's why. Stifle the questions. Concentrate!

She heard, then, the faintest clink from a dislodged stone and at last her errant senses focused fully on the here and now. Hunter, hunted. Electrical currents tingled along her veins, her eyes stretched wider to see beyond the limitations of sight, and doubtless both protagonists' nerves quivered in anticipation of the ultimate kill. With her right hand she swiftly pulled the gut thread back to maximum tension, checking that the stone was centrally aligned. And waited…and waited…until numbness began to settle like a helmet blurring her brain, and like a glove restricting her fingers…and she repeatedly reminded herself to *concentrate*.

A crouching, then springing-to-outstretched shape hurled itself swiftly airborne as if overleaping a six foot high doorway to get to her. She distinctly heard its faint grunt on take-off, then a brief in-breath of extra exertion. Just before the shape loomed almost directly over her, she strained the gut backwards, tauter still - then released its tiny cannonball stone with whiplash speed at what she knew to be the creature's most vulnerable place.

It leapt over her unchecked to land powerfully on the other side, almost alongside Eartha's body. Hurriedly she slotted her second stone into place, deftly lining up her next shot. The animal was seemingly undecided whom to attack first. Its head jerked one way, then the other…until suddenly, quite unexpectedly, its entire body sagged, its front legs buckled and it rolled slowly and heavily onto its side.

The man was first to reach it. He prodded its hind flank gingerly with his foot and it swished its tail in fading, faltering anger, but was so weak it could not even raise its head to snarl at him.

"Straight through the jugular, Motte!" he exclaimed in awe.

She continued to sit there, stunned. As a child she had often dreamed yearningly of a leopard creature. The snow leopard had been her magical, mythical beast like the unicorn to many others; something rare, fictional and mysteriously beautiful. Then, when the man told her leopards were real creatures and truly had existed once, maybe still even did in high, wild regions like the Caucasus, she had longed to see one. Well - now she could. A dead one. A female one, possibly pregnant. It might even have been the very last leopard in existence, ever. And she of all people had killed it...

The man tried to console her. But via a strange, indirect method - by unequivocally blaming himself for Murchadh's death. He should have realised, he confessed, that someone with lungs in such a chronic condition ought never to have crouched for so long with his nose scant centimetres from a toxic, dangerous flame. He even hinted that he *had* known it - but taken the risk regardless, because it was their only means of escape, Murchadh the only person able to operate the flame, who had himself insisted on this role in full knowledge that the Caucasus was the ultimate intended destination.

But...and here his eyes questioned hers, full of warmth and troubled, conspiratorial tragedy: do the means ever justify the end? He had gambled with Murchadh's life, and now Murchadh was dead. The leopard was a similar situation, its death an unfortunate means to a more fortunate end. Surely she must understand this...?

She nodded obligingly, but her mind flickered uneasily. *Why* the Caucasus and not Monte Rosa? Was it all just a means to an end that only he desired? Because, possibly, he was a 'leopard' too... If killing him preempted them walking straight into a Kratos trap he had purposefully sprung for them, then certainly he was. Plus, there was no denying the irrefutable fact he had not lied just the once, but many - arguably *too* many - times. Unlike with the real leopard, however, with him she could afford to bide her time...

Meanwhile his distorted, mangled wrist, which he could not move at all - let alone use to add gesture, flavour and expression to his speech like he normally did - needed urgent attention. But, being an extreme case of dislocation, it was already too late for a mere rudimentary type of manipulation to succeed in realigning it, and the wrist itself too swollen to be manipulated right now. Just to augment the problems, there was also no anaesthetic to dull the pain.

"You're going to amputate?" he asked, fearfully shrinking away from her as she suddenly grasped his forearm with both hands.

Huh, she thought, so we're *both* mistrustful of the other. Or perhaps it's his ploy, an attempt at reverse psychology, using Eartha's theory to unsettle me…unless he's delirious with pain of course, and mistakes me for some Kratos bitch from his past…

"Mais non - tu es vraiment fou!" she protested, waving a withering bunch of leaves in front of his eyes, "unless these help to make the swelling go down, I can do nothing at all."

Before he could respond she swiftly encased his wrist in a poultice of the leaves marinated in an oozy, greenish yellow sauce, the recipe for which he preferred not to enquire about.

"Without the use of both my hands I'm a spent force," he whispered, wincing and grimacing, "and here, being virgin territory, we'll have to build everything from scratch. I *must* be able to sew us new pelts. Is it alright with you, if I'm…the leopard?"

She nodded, secretly relieved because she favoured a bearskin - and the consequent two-footed mobility it would afford, "Even if your hand's worse off, at least you still have your *intelligence plus* to think us out of trouble."

At this he shook his head despondently and closed his eyes, his face a ghostly hue seemingly bled of life, hope and colour. He then lay still for what resembled hours, far paler than the soft underbelly of the leopard where the coat had strangely had no spots at all, silent and exhausted.

"Let's give him a name while he's asleep," Lhotse suggested eagerly. "We never did end up namin' that pumice-boat prop'ly, so I'm voting' Galeshka again. But no 'Wanblee'."

"Okee-dokee. I'll go for a mountain one, like most of us. Makalu'd suit him - it was fifth highest in the world, jus' a titchy bit shorter than your Lhotse mountain, so he can't go pullin' rank on you!"

"Caucasus?" Bernina proposed, but without conviction.

"He should choose his own name," was Motte's vote.

Without anaesthetic or any other means to dull the pain, once the swelling had subsided she would have to act fast, unexpectedly, and whilst his defenses were still at their lowest ebb. That moment came after a long vigil cradling his leaf-bandaged wrist, and the suddenness of her manipulation, along with the iron strength in her wrists and climber's fingers wrenched such a roar of pain from his throat that, had there been spies in the vicinity, they would surely have mistaken it for the leopard male come to avenge its slaughtered mate.

As quickly as a pyro. surges she strapped his wrist to maintain its new position, then slowly, gently, massaged his contorting, convulsing body until it began to settle. And once the lulling sounds of lapping waves had soothed his gradually receding pain, he whispered this confession...

He had bungled hugely, he ruefully admitted. Instead of 'intelligence plus' he had been afflicted with a severe - a disastrous - case of 'intelligence minus'. What's more, he had been resoundingly punished for lying, because his lie had become a horrendous, self-fulfilling truth! And this was how:

When he had declared on the pumice boat that he had destroyed all records of the past stored on Kratos' computer networks, via deletes, worms, viruses, Trojans and every other known enemy to soft and hardware (not to forget the fact their whole system was crumbling anyway - too old, unable to be repaired, retuned or replaced due to a lack of component materials, non-existent these dearthsome days) - that part *was* the honest truth.

But his claim that the *only* memory bank of information concerning the past (relating to science; geography; political, social and cultural history; etc. etc. etc.) was inside his own brain was, well, a...lie. Although, in his defence, he did have a knife tickling his throat at the time he uttered it, which surely partly exonerated him? To cut a long, rambling apologia short, he *had* had in his possession at around that time a miniaturised, back-up info. storage gadget. 'At around that time' being the key words...

Then, at some stage in their traumatic peregrination to the Caucasus, he and it had parted company. He had no idea where or how. Perhaps it had only recently been swallowed by the sea; perhaps the jet stream had snatched it away a little earlier; or maybe it went missing earlier - when he was overpowered on the pumice boat, just before the knife tickled his throat. Or, he might even have already left it, unwittingly, on the shores of Motte's mountain, when he abandoned his knapsack and wolfskin just prior to boarding the pumice boat, because his frame of mind at that time was close to demented. If it *was* left there, it posed something of a worry, because of the risk of it falling into the wrong hands. Kratos' hands. Even though that risk must, fingers crossed, be almost negligeable...

Still, despite *when* it vanished being a mystery, the fact that it *had* vanished was an undisputed fact. So now his lie was true! That vast well of information collectively known as 'the past' now resided exclusively inside his brain - an unreliable place, as had recently been proved.

Thus the only way to preserve it for possible future generations was to now share it with her, well, better still - all of them. That was, after all, the oldenday method from the very earliest of times, the so-called 'oral tradition'.

One that Murchadh had strongly believed in because it was the way of the native American peoples - all illiterate peoples in fact, from the very beginnings of time.

So, he would have to start recounting his story very, very soon - it being somewhat on the longish side. And they must all understand that this 'history' would be edited according to his subjective interpretation, *his* slant on what might have happened, or who did what to whom, or who invented this or that. But this shouldn't pose a problem because all information had always, always been tempered this way. It was all of it biased, sometimes changed entirely, even completely reversed!

He would, of course, in the quest for a better balance and a greater truth, try his very best to provide possibilities for alternative or multiple interpretations, time allowing. And he could assure her, or rather them all, of one definite thing. *His* propaganda would pale to purest, blinding white in comparison to the Kratos' tissues of lies he'd been fed by the murderous bastards. Because Kratos' rationale had always followed this maxim: tell a lie a thousand times and it turns into truth. Tell it a million, six…ten…twenty million times, and then you can denounce all doubters as deranged!

"*I'll* remember it for you," Lhotse, who had crept close to listen in, hurriedly reassured him. "I gotta young mind with space ter spare. I'm already rememberin' lotsa stuff for Murchadh, so don't you worry."

"Your gadget won't be found," Motte was adamant, "because the mountain's erupted again, I know it, how d'you say - *catégoriquement*. When the catapult stone embedded itself in the leopard's throat, and all that blood gushed out, I saw it…differently. I saw instead of blood the magma turning to lava flowing out from the cone again. It swamped the slope, the beach, everywhere - there's little left of my mountain now, and *nothing* left of your rucksack, or of the skymen who took it. I swear it was no hallucination from the drugs. It was a vision. Murchadh would've believed me."

"I don't disbelieve you. I just hope you're right, that's all."

"Hey, you've *gotta* have a name, you know, for a new place," Lhotse interjected, "Fancy Galeshka?"

He gave it some thought. "Do and don't, and on balance don't - sorry Lhotse. That bird came on too strong with the beautiful girl he saved and I wouldn't want that hanging over me." He gave Motte a sly wink.

"Caucasus then, or Makalu," she persisted, "though Motte says you oughta choose yourself," her voice tailed off in disappointment.

"I'll go for Metheus then. There were two brothers, you see, Prometheus and Epimetheus, their names meaning foresight and hindsight. They were half-human, half-God," he at least had the wit to look shamefaced at this. "Prometheus placed himself in danger by helping the human race - and was duly punished by being horrifically tortured somewhere very near to here - on Mt. Elbrus in fact."

"Oh...OK, Metheus'll sort of do, I guess." Lhotse sighed long sufferingly. "But Galeshka'd do *much* better."

Once dawn had shed its clearer, almost limpid light on their new landscape, it confirmed that this new mountain island was larger and far healthier than the sick environment they had fled. Admittedly though, their final memory of Motte's mountain island was of noxious black ash cloud and poisonous air - so almost anywhere would seem an improvement. Motte felt the first surge of eagerness to explore, especially for sources of clean, fresh water and the ripe berries she had already smelt.

"Keep a sharp eye for other predators," he warned her. "And there might be a surprise - have a guess."

"Marmots!"

"No. I'm afraid they were unique to la Vanoise, sadly. But...close."

"Chamoix?"

"Well, there might be marals - they're beautiful red deer, but I doubt they survived the GD. *Something* kept that leopard's appetite satisfied though - try again." He sat up, gingerly cradling his strapped wrist, on nervy tenterhooks.

"Err...ibex?" she asked, her voice trembling.

"Bezoar ibex! *Now* d'you understand why I was so dead-set on reaching here? Monte Rosa was an empty wasteland..."

"That's *not* the reason you chose the Caucasus," she frowned, "don't even try..."

"No." He lay back with a long-drawn sigh, his face still etched by pain. "You're right, Motte, right to be suspicious - but wrong about my motives. Kratos do have an observation post here, on the highest mountain in the Caucasus, Mt. Elbrus, which could be somewhere near, or not - I don't precisely know our current whereabouts.

I'm on a mission now, you'll see. I aim to undermine their pernicious hold on power whatever way I can. Their observation post is - well, *was* - extremely thinly manned, almost a sitting duck for us to successfully attack. But it can wait - there's no immediate hurry yet. First off, I ought to start you on my story. Are you ready?"

"Steady, go!" Lhotse lent forward eagerly. "I do so love beginnings - endings suck!"

"Sssh," Motte warned her, "Let him talk and we'll do the listening. Then, if we don't believe him at any point, we can just act like everyone else always did in the past. We can reinvent it as we wish!"

From the mischievous yet underlyingly serious expression in her dark brown eyes she left him in little doubt that, strong though her love might well grow to be, it would never be foolishly blind.

Perfect trust in someone else is an unachievable ideal, he responded tacitly through look alone, for not a word was exchanged between them. In fact, sometimes we can't even trust *ourselves*! As I've always said, us humans are a fundamentally flawed species, and me especially, owing to my atrociously amoral background. But at least love can provide us with a way to more or less paper over the cracks of our failures and foibles, so please Motte, *please* don't place unrealistic conditions on it.

You've always known what my condition *was*, her slow smile seemed to suggest, right from the very beginning. But perhaps I've grown up since then, because, well, I don't place such an obsessive importance on it anymore.

I would still love to have a child with you, but it's not a condition. Just a - how do you say it? - *pipe-dream* hope I think it is, that's all.

www.ingramcontent.com/pod-product-compliance
Lightning Source LLC
Chambersburg PA
CBHW031116030726
47496CB00002BA/571